The Catcher of Halensee

DAVID J OLDMAN

Published in 2019
First paperback edition

First published as an e-book by Endeavour Media Ltd in 2020.

For the NHS staff who kept me alive long enough to finish this book

Other books by David J Oldman

Looking For Ginger

A Voice from the Congo

On Wings Of Death

A Weapon Of The Bourgeoisie

Dusk at Dawn

The Unquiet Grave

Requiem for a Patriot

The Catcher of Halensee

Contents

Die Einleitung

1

Tuesday 29th July 1947

By mid-afternoon the thermometer outside the hut at the Templehof airfield was registering 33 degrees in the shade. It may not have been the hottest day of the year although of the many reasons I remember this particular day it is the heat which still remains the most vivid.

I was at Templehof because my business partner, Kurt Becker, was meeting his American Air Force contact, a master sergeant named Rafferty. Rafferty was the man who supplied Kurt with the black market cigarettes he traded, courtesy of the USAF PX.

As I was only along for the ride, while they discussed inside how many cartons of cigarettes they could move and how rich they were going to get, I stayed outside, looking at the rising mercury and sucking on a single fag, getting nothing more than a smoker's cough.

Having gleaned all I could from the thermometer, I looked out across the airfield and watched a C-47, a Dakota Skytrain, coming in to land.

It was then that another reason I remember this July day drove by.

This one was sitting in the front of a Jeep and was a man I had not seen for more than a year; a man I had never expected to see again.

Given the dust the Jeep was kicking up I didn't think he saw me. Or if he had, that he would care to acknowledge the fact. So I let the Jeep pass, following its progress as it drove down the track towards the rows of Quonset huts in the compound that was the Templehof Displaced Persons camp.

For a minute or two the dust hung in the air like a gritty mist before it slowly settled back onto the road. As it cleared, I thought about the man and, given longer, might have come up with some tortuous analogy about letting the metaphorical dust of the past settle. But just then Kurt came out of the hut lugging a holdall bulging with cigarette cartons. He tossed a pack of Lucky Strikes at me and I ground out the cheap German brand I was smoking and lit up a Lucky.

'You smoke too much,' Kurt said.

Which I thought was a bit rich since he was the one with a bag full of cigarettes.

'And where would you be if me and all the other addicts gave up?' I asked.

'Ten dollars better off,' he shot back. 'Unless you want to pay me for the pack I just gave you.'

I didn't so decided I'd best drop the subject. I just blew smoke at him instead.

~

It had been hotter the previous month when I arrived back in Berlin. I hadn't noticed the weather then. I was too busy reacquainting myself with the city, comparing what I found with the memories I had formed two years earlier.

It didn't take me long to discover that the one didn't accord with the other; that memories one believes are set in stone don't measure up to the reality one finds.

Although I found plenty of both in the Berlin of 1947. Stone and reality. But if most of the stone was now piled high in rubble mountains, the realities remained everywhere you looked, as hard as they had ever been.

Yet, as I said, it wasn't just the oppressive heat of that particular July Tuesday that now comes to mind. The day seemed full of portents, as if the heavy weather presaged the breaking of something more significant than a mere electrical storm.

Hindsight perhaps, although it seemed real enough at the time.

As it was, thirty-two degrees was as hot as it got that day even if, later that evening pressed up against my fellow travellers in a U-Bahn carriage, it felt at least ten degrees hotter.

Trapped in a corner, there was no escaping the odours of sweating bodies or the stench of the filthy clothes that covered them. I tried lighting another of Kurt's cigarettes, hoping the smoke might mask the sour reek. As a stratagem, though, that didn't work. All I got for my trouble were stares thrown enviously in the direction of my Lucky Strike. Being an American brand I suppose I should have known better than flaunt it.

So I tried thinking of other things to forget the stench. Like attempting to convert the Centigrade temperature of the thermometer at Templehof into Fahrenheit in my head. But I was never able to remember which way round the formula worked and always ended up with a number that wouldn't have kept an Eskimo warm.

Mostly though, I thought about the house in Halensee I had recently moved into and how the rear garden backed onto a lake; how, once home and away from the crush of the U-Bahn, I was going to bathe in its cool water.

Cool water if not very clean water.

It still wasn't uncommon to come across the odd corpse floating in the lake. By then, though, along with everyone else in Berlin I'd learned that beggars can't be choosers.

Or whatever the German equivalent of that particular English phrase is.

But if the lake water was not very clean at least there was plenty of it and in Berlin that summer water was a commodity not always easy to come by. The city's supply was still intermittent and it sometimes seemed that acquiring sufficient to wash in with enough left over to launder one's clothes was as difficult as finding a Berliner ready to admit they'd once been a Nazi.

At the Zoo Bahnhof I got off the subway to switch onto the S-Bahn. Having pushed my way onto the platform, I found I'd merely exchanged the stench of the carriage for the pervasive stink of the tunnels.

That was something else that hadn't changed much in the two years since April 1945. With the Red Army closing in on the city, the *Wehrmacht* had dynamited the railway tunnel beneath the Landwehrkanal, flooding the underground system to delay the Russian advance. After two years, the reek of stagnant water still hung in the subway like a foul cloud.

And as a stratagem that one hadn't worked either, achieving little beyond mirroring below ground the devastation already wreaked above.

Once on the surface and waiting at the Zoo Bahnhof for my S-Bahn, I began to think about Arthur Peston again— something I could rarely help doing whenever anywhere near the Zoo Flak Tower.

The previous day British sappers had demolished the L-Tower, the smaller of the two and the one that had housed the Nazi's communication equipment. The G-Tower, the big one that had supported the anti-aircraft guns, still remained. It was from the top of the G-Tower that Arthur Peston had fallen. He had broken his neck, which wasn't really much of a surprise since the G-Tower was as high as a thirteen-storey building and he broke just about everything else he had as well.

Since Peston was the reason I was back in Berlin his death was never far from my thoughts. Exactly what he had been doing at the top of the tower, or how he had come to fall, had never been satisfactorily established.

The cursory police investigation had put it down to an accident, happy to come to the decision that the death hadn't been suicide or murder.

Nothing suspicious, London had assured me. Nothing to worry about.

But I did, of course. Not because I had known Peston but because Peston's shoes were the ones I had stepped into.

When my S-Bahn arrived it proved almost as stifling as the tunnels, which at least took my mind off Peston. I began to think about the lake again which is why, when the train finally reached the Halensee station, I decided to walk and take the Kurfürstendamm down to Koenigsallee, rather than wait for the inevitably crowded tram.

The apartment I had recently moved into consisted of three rooms on the second floor of a large house at the end of a gravel road off Margaretenstraße. It was looking the worse for wear now but must have been quite a place in its day. At the top of the curving drive that led up to the main entrance two imposing stone pillars stood. At any rate, I imagined they would have looked imposing had they not suffered in the air raids like all the other properties around the lake. Now the pillars were little more than a pair of truncated stumps, the wrought-iron gates they had supported gone along with the iron railings which presumably had once enclosed the entire property.

Berlin, like London, had had its patriotic metal drives, the salvage going to make bombers and artillery pieces or something equally useful. Anything made of iron or aluminium or tin had been swept up, deemed better suited transformed into machines for killing people than left as militarily useless items like saucepans and decorative garden railings.

Unfortunately beating railings into anti-aircraft guns had not turned out to be a guarantee of immunity. Judging by the scale of Berlin's destruction the guns had proved as useful as ploughshares. Even quiet suburbs like Halensee had not escaped the bombing. One or two of the houses skirting the lake did remain more or less intact, but most were now little more than ruins. Not that the area looked as bad as the centre of the city. The two years that had passed since the end of the war had at least allowed the surrounding shrubbery of Lake Halensee to begin softening the appearance of the shattered buildings; what once must have once been an area full of well-tended gardens had now run wild.

The rear of the house in which I lived had become so choked with undergrowth that the path leading down to the lake had become obscured. Any fence once separating the property from the water had, like the railings, also disappeared. Timber for firewood, no doubt, given the shortage the previous winter. Or perhaps for boarding up glassless windows or those holes blown through walls by high explosive.

No doubt all very different from before the war and I often imagined the swimming parties there would have been with boating on the lake. Many of the houses once had their own jetties and boathouses. Not that there was much sign of the jetties now beyond a few stumps showing above the water like rows of rotten teeth. A couple of the boathouses along the strand had manage to survive, courtesy of Berlin's homeless who had moved in seeking shelter and warmth.

And the warmth was why, walking towards the house up the road from Margaretenstraße still daydreaming about my dip in the lake, I found myself almost on top of another of that day's portents before I realized it.

2

Whenever I think of her now, it is always as a girl. At the time though, with dusk falling and having little more than a momentary sight of her, it wasn't easy to say just how old she was. Gaunt, with her head shorn and dressed in clothes little better than rags, my first impression was she could have been anywhere between fifteen and fifty.

Anticipating my swim, I was as surprised to see her as she must have been to see me because she jumped like a startled animal. I believe I saw her eyes widen and certainly heard her give a little cry before she turned and disappeared into the shrubbery. Perhaps it was her agility and her thin body that gave an impression girlishness. The fact was, as I discovered later, she was in her late twenties.

I had seen no shortage of emaciated figures wandering the streets of Berlin since my return. Yet there was something about this one that seemed to set her apart. Perhaps it had been my imagination but I thought in that brief moment I had caught in the expression on her face something of the fear I fancied those poor haunted creatures abandoned in the Tiergarten's Zoological Gardens must have worn during the air raids.

I stood there at the top of the drive for a while, thinking she might reappear. I even peered into the bushes along the road near the neighbouring houses. The light was fading, though, and in the gloom I could see very little. After a minute or so I shrugged it off and turned towards the house.

Passing into the large entrance hall, I noticed the door to Frau Ernst's apartment was shut. Usually she was in the habit of leaving it open, particularly in warm weather so she might catch whatever breeze was blowing off the lake. Having it open also gave her the opportunity to see just who was coming and going in the house.

I walked past her door and up the wide staircase to the apartment, grabbed a towel and skipped back down again. By the time I reached the hall once more, I found Frau Ernst standing at her door waiting for me.

She was a striking woman. Perhaps in her forties, like many Berlin women she appeared older than she might have been with the past few years written plain on her face. Her hair had turned prematurely grey yet she still wore it in a German braid, the style once de rigueur for those among the nation's womanhood who had embraced Hitler's Aryan mythos. I had never found it difficult to picture a younger version of Frau Ernst standing among the adoring crowds at a passing Nazi parade, hair plaited and dressed in a dirndl and tossing flowers and cheering. She might well have been present at the fiftieth birthday bash Hitler had given himself just before the start of the war. A five-hour extravaganza of Nazi might, the parade had passed through the Tiergarten along the east-west axis of what was to be the Fürhrer's new Germania.

But fate's wheel had turned a long way since those halcyon days. I imagined the men and machines parading for the Führer that day would now be little more than a mangled pile of crippled bodies and scrap metal.

And there weren't many flowers to toss these days, either.

Frau Ernst wasn't exactly the house *portiersfrau* although she did have some arrangement with the owner of the house, a man named Neumann for whom she collected the rent when it was due.

I had been told that Frau Ernst once used to live with a man although, if true, he had gone by the time I arrived. Now she lived in the ground-floor apartment with her crippled son, Werner, from where she made it her business to see that the other tenants in the house behaved themselves in the correct German manner. She could often be seen skulking around, keeping an eye on the place. Making sure, I suppose, that no one took any liberties with the property.

As far as I could see that particular horse had bolted some time before I moved in. Damaged in the raids, the house now leaked badly when it rained despite being in better condition than most of the other properties around the lake. Even so, anything of use or value had been stripped out long ago.

I often wondered why Neumann, the absentee owner who apparently lived in Hamburg, didn't rent out more of the rooms, at least those that didn't get too wet when it rained. Apart from Frau Ernst and Werner on the ground floor, there was only an elderly couple occupying the room above me. While it was true that many of the other vacant rooms were barely habitable, with accommodation at a premium in Berlin, I doubted Neumann would have had any trouble finding tenants. No one complained these days about a little water on rainy days or some dust blowing through the shell holes on drier ones.

But apparently Neumann wasn't interested. Which was fine as far as I was concerned as I found the isolation of Halensee a pleasant change from the crowded streets of the city centre and its unending spectacle of destruction. And the house had other compensations. The pervading silence of Lake Halensee and the sense of seclusion permeating the house suited me very well. The lake offered a water supply that couldn't be arbitrarily cut or was likely to dry up any time soon. All this providing, of course, one wasn't too fussy about the occasional corpse.

But corpses had been Berlin's stock in trade for some years even if at Halensee they only turned up occasionally when some poor soul finally came to the decision that the dark waters of the lake were preferable to the drier miseries of the land.

They were certainly preferable to me that evening. Wanting to get in the water and cool off and not stop to talk to Frau Ernst, I merely bade her, 'guten Abend', in my improving if somewhat still formal German.

Formal or not, Frau Ernst reached out a hand and caught my sleeve as I passed.

'The water pressure is down, Herr Tennant,' she declared in her surprisingly good English as if she was announcing the arrival of a train. 'The heat makes the demand.'

'That's all right,' I told her. 'I'm going to take a swim to cool off.'

'Will Frau Meier late again this evening?'

I thought I detected a momentarily malicious smirk curl around her lips, but as the hall was gloomy it might have been a trick of the light.

Even so, since Frau Meier was late every evening—as Frau Ernst well knew—I assumed her asking must have been some sort of jibe. She had addressed me as Herr *Tennant,* after all, so I could only suppose she was trying to make a point about Frau *Meier.*

Not that that worried me. I didn't need any lessons in morality, and certainly not from a German.

If one had to be charitable, though, I didn't suppose there was much joy left in Frau Ernst's life. Not since the Nazi parade had passed by at any rate. Most things must have turned sour on her since those golden days. But she was hardly alone in that. Nor in being a widow with a crippled son to care for.

She stepped out into the hall, pulling the door close to behind her so I couldn't see into the apartment to where Werner usually sat. He was confined to a wheelchair—which again was not something out of the ordinary in the new Germany. Or wouldn't have been if there had been a ready supply of wheelchairs available.

I wasn't sure how Werner had got his injuries. As the result of an air raid, perhaps, or during the battle for Berlin... It was always possible he had served in the army even though, to look at him, one would not have thought him old enough. But the Nazis hadn't been fussy about age towards the end, particularly as the Russians had closed in on the capital. The *Volkssturm,* a National Militia, had been raised to defend the city and had conscripted anyone between sixteen and sixty who was not already enlisted. And I doubt if they were any too fussy about either end of that spectrum providing the conscript was able to lift a rifle.

It was entirely possible that Werner had come out of the Hitler Youth and had already served in the SS. Some of them were more familiar handling a gun than they were a razor. If that was the case he would probably have been keener to serve his Führer than many of the old Wehrmacht sweats who had managed to retreat as far as the capital.

But that was all supposition on my part, a pastime in which I regularly engaged. It was equally likely that Werner had injured himself riding the trains into the surrounding countryside. Every day hundreds did it, to barter with farmers for food or to simply steal it. *Hamstering* it was called and to avoid paying for the ride *Hamsterers* would cling to the side of the trains, jumping on and off as best they could. The result was that many fell on to the rails, those that weren't killed ending up crippled like Werner for their trouble.

The boy still suffered pain as according to his mother the drugs he needed were rarely available. From what I knew of him he suffered in stoic silence. Unlike his mother, although the expression Frau Ernst habitually wore on his behalf was eloquent enough for the two of them.

'Werner used to like to swim in the lake,' she confided, her hand still on my arm.

'You lived here before the war, did you?'

But her confidence apparently had limits for she didn't add anything to her statement.

'If he ever needs help getting into the water...' I offered, assuming that was what she was angling for.

But Frau Ernst shook her head.

'His legs, Herr Tennant. He would sink.'

And perhaps be glad of it, I couldn't help thinking.

With that the conversation seemed to be at an end so I said goodnight and turned down the corridor that led to the rear of the house and to the garden.

Outside the night was dark. It felt close and stifling as I picked my way down the old garden path beneath the growing canopy of vegetation towards the lake. The shrubs and borders had run amok. Even those spindly trees that had escaped the winter demand for fuel seemed to tower over me into the night.

14

At the property's boundary, a path led down to a small beach. A gibbous moon hung heavily in the sky above the black water, its silver light reflecting a shimmering disc on the glassy surface.

Some yards along the shore the remains of a dilapidated jetty ran a few feet into the water, rotting wood now green and mossy in the moonlight. I stripped, hung my clothes on a stump and stepped into the water. It felt colder than I expected but I didn't mind that. Lake mud oozed between my toes and after wading out a couple of yards I pushed off, swimming a few strokes before turning onto my back and floating in the luxury of cool water.

Onshore, I could see the house looming out of the overgrown garden under the moon's silvery light, looking lopsided in silhouette where the roof and some of the timber trusses had collapsed.

As my eyes grew accustomed to the dark and while I was still looking towards the house, I caught a movement in the bushes. I saw a figure emerge by the shore. Too far to be able to see clearly, I couldn't be certain although I thought it was the girl I had seen by the front drive.

She moved towards the remains of the jetty where I had left my clothes and it occurred to me that, in my haste to get down to the lake, I had left my wallet and papers in my jacket instead of in the apartment.

I called out and began swimming for the shore, scrambling until my feet touched bottom. By the time I waded out of the water, naked and dripping weed like some aquatic golem, she had run off again, slipping back into the undergrowth like a wraith.

I picked up my jacket and felt for my wallet. It had gone.

Muttering in the darkness, I cursed her and then myself for being so stupid. I ran up the beach for a few yards but she had already gone. I went back to my clothes, towelled myself off and began to dress. It was as I reached for my trousers that I discovered my wallet lying on top of them.

I assumed I had scared her into dropping it and, feeling a little happier, walked back to the house peering into the bushes as I went.

In the apartment I lit the lamp and found I hadn't scared her at all.

She had taken some Reichsmarks from my wallet but strangely not all of them. And she had left the more valuable American dollars I was carrying. My papers were still there but showed signs of having been examined before carelessly stuffed back into the pocket.

I put it all on the table and poured myself a glass of schnapps. Then I went through everything again.

I had been robbed.

But by a curious kind of thief.

3

I was still awake when Mitzi got home.

She came straight to the bedroom and began undressing. The windows were thrown wide and with no curtains her tall and slender figure was silhouetted against the moonlight. She must have thought I was asleep because she didn't speak, just folded her clothes neatly over a chair and, naked, walked into the hall.

Even if there was no water, we at least had a bathroom down the corridor to ourselves. Which was fortunate as Mitzi had a habit of walking there naked. I heard the faucet squeak as she turned it on then I heard her mutter and the sound of her hitting the taps with the heel of her hand. Having been on the receiving end of that hand on occasion, I knew how the faucets must feel. A moment later she came back into the bedroom.

'There's no water,' I said.

'Did I wake you, Harry?'

'No.'

'Then tell me something I do not know.'

'Do you want a swim in the lake?' I asked. 'I'll come with you if you like.'

'I am too tired.'

'Then come to bed.'

'I am sweaty and I smell.'

'I like the way you smell,' I said. 'It's the first thing I noticed about you.'

She muttered again and in the darkness stood by the open window, catching what breeze was blowing in.

Actually, the first thing I had noticed about Mitzi Meier had been her legs. But then, I had been lying on the floor at the time.

Kurt Becker had told me about the Zoo Club and the first time I went there I had only been in the place ten minutes when some American soldiers started a fight. Even as a kid I'd never possessed much in the way of ball skills although strangely rarely fail when it comes to catching a punch. This one caught me on the jaw and the next thing I knew I was on the floor looking up at Mitzi's legs. The Yanks had gone, along with most everyone else in the club apart from an unconcerned few who were busy picking up the furniture.

Mitzi bent over me and started dabbing at my mouth with a grubby bar cloth. Then she got me on my feet and gave me a drink to see me home. Always a slow learner, I went back to the place a couple of nights later. Mitzi recognized me, perhaps not too difficult given my split lip and bruised face although they at least served as an introduction.

The Zoo Club was on the Kurfürstendamm which before the Nazis brought high explosive raining down on Berlin had been one of the smartest streets in Europe. The club was owned by a man named Karl Bauer, one of the few fat Germans I'd come across and one of Kurt's outlets for the black market cigarettes he traded. Bauer had named the club The Zoo not, as I assumed after my first visit, because of the conduct of its clientele but because it was situated in the basement of a wrecked building a few hundred yards from Berlin's former zoological gardens.

What remained of the gardens lay in the shadow of the *Flakturm Tiergarten,* the tower from which Arthur Peston had fallen.

Not that it could be described as a garden these days. Precious few of the animals it had once housed were left and those that had managed to survive the bombing and the hungry designs of a ravenous populace did little except mooch up and down in their pens.

Karl Bauer, demonstrating that now-scarce German trait of hubris, had originally wanted to call his club The Tower after the *Flakturm*. The authorities had turned that name down since the *Flakturm* had been built to house Berlin's anti-aircraft guns and, as such, was regarded by the Occupying Powers as a Nazi landmark. Those who now ruled over Germany's defeated carcass were intent on destroying anything they saw as a legacy of the Third Reich.

The Russians had tried to demolish the *Flakturm* with howitzers a couple of years earlier without success. After them, the British engineers had also tried their luck, packing both the L and G towers with dynamite. They had only succeeded in partially destroying the smaller L-Tower. The larger of the two that had housed the anti-aircraft guns and served as an air raid shelter still stood, a Nazi monolith astride the south-west corner of the Tiergarten.

Mitzi turned away from the window at last and lay down on the bed beside me. It was too hot for nightclothes, even for a bed sheet, and lying beside her I could almost hear her sizzle.

'I can smell the lake,' she complained.

'Of course you can smell the lake,' I told her. 'The window is open.'

'On *you*. I can smell the lake on you.'

'I went for a swim. There's no water.'

'Do not keep telling me what I know, Harry.' Then she had a change of heart. 'Oh I am sorry, *Liebling*. I do not mind. It is not so bad as sweat.'

I assured her I was doing that as well.

She sighed volubly. 'Do you want to make love, Harry?'

'Aren't you too tired?'

'You know it helps me sleep.'

Which isn't the sort of thing most men care to hear: that their sexual proficiency comes in useful as a sedative. But I'm easygoing about such things and only too happy to oblige if I can.

I turned towards her and she reached for me with those rough hands of hers, Mitzi's equivalent of the Finns beating

18

each other with birch branches, I often thought.

She could be inventive but in this case it wasn't any deviance on her part. For a spell she had been a *Trümmerfrau*, "women of the rubble", who spent their days clearing and cleaning bricks from the city's rubble mountains for eventual re-use. It was heavy work and with the shortage of German men something that was necessarily done by women. Mitzi had done a stint at the airfield the French were building in their sector in Tegel, taking the job because the arduous nature of the work put the *Trümmerfrau* in a higher ration category. That meant more food even if the bricks and the dust did play havoc with the women's hands and complexions.

I was reminded of what Mitzi had done before working at the club every time she touched me. The palms of her hands felt as soft as a plumber's rasp and it was something she was sensitive about. So I tried not to wince too often and, if we were in bed, would pin her hands down out of harm's way at the first opportunity.

She was forever trying to soften her skin and the bottles of unguents and creams cluttering up the bathroom were the first things I had discovered the day I moved in with her. To judge from the amount she had collected, one might have thought she was attempting to corner the Berlin market in skin ointments. I suspected she spent almost as much on the creams as she did on food.

It was debatable, though, whether she could have amassed the number and variety of creams to be found in our bathroom cabinet by simply buying them. I regarded the fact as one of those telltale signs that my predecessor there had been a Yank. Mitzi had done her best to cleanse the place of any evidence of previous occupancy before I arrived although she hadn't been able to bring herself to throw out all that precious cream. Much of it, to judge by those labels she hadn't quite managed to obliterate, had originated in the American PX.

Not that this was something I objected to. After all we all carried a past with us and I daresay mine was as irregular as Mitzi Meier's. Just how irregular hers might have been was something I was curious to know, but it was a subject she never mentioned. Her previous life remained a closed book to me.

On occasion Mitzi liked to tussle although tonight she was too tired. I didn't miss the exercise; she might have been thin but she was all muscle from shifting those bricks and as strong as I was. So we made love tenderly this time, even managing to take some enjoyment from the sweat and stickiness of our bodies.

Once done, though, we soon became uncomfortable and parted, lying side by side panting and steaming gently as we shared a cigarette.

'Someone came to the club asking for you,' she said after a while.

'This evening? Who was that?'

'A woman.'

'What woman?'

'The one with the brown curls.'

I knew whom she meant but didn't care to admit as much immediately.

'There's a lot of women with brown curls,' I suggested.

'You remember, Harry. She came in with Kurt and another man.'

'Just before I moved in with you, you mean?'

'They are friends of yours?'

'Kurt's friends,' I said. 'Their name is Prochnow and the man is her husband. Wasn't he with her tonight?'

'She is attractive, do you not think so, Harry?'

'I'm not one for brown curls,' I said. 'I like them blonde like yours.'

'I think you like them all,' said Mitzi.

'She asked for me? By name?'

'She asked one of the other girls. She sent her to me. She wanted to know how often you came to the club.'

'And she was alone?'

Mitzi shifted on the bed and handed back the cigarette.

'What is her name?'

I drew in some smoke. 'Prochnow, I told you.'

'Her first name, Harry.'

'Gretchen. Are you sure her husband wasn't with her?'

'I am sure.'

'She didn't mention him?'

'No.'

'What did you tell her?'

'I said you might be in tomorrow.'

'It's probably something to do with Kurt's business, Mitzi. That's all.'

'Business, Harry?'

She danced around the subject a little longer then asked:

'You would tell me if there was somebody else, wouldn't you, Harry?'

I put my hand lightly on her stomach, stroking the skin above her pubic hair with my fingers.

'There's no one else, Mitzi.'

'I mean it, Harry.'

'That sword cuts both ways,' I said.

'What sword? What do you mean?'

I patted her stomach. 'I mean if things were the other way round. Would you tell me if there was someone else?'

She leaned towards me and nuzzled her face against my neck, giving a small dismissive grunt deep in her throat.

'But I am happy with you, Harry.'

Which wasn't an answer.

'So this Gretchen is nothing to you?' she persisted.

'Not to me,' I said. 'Although I'd like to know why she came to the club on her own looking for me. I'll talk to Kurt. If she comes again tomorrow and I'm not there, tell her to wait, will you?'

'Sure, Harry,' she said, apparently unconcerned.

Lying on my back, staring up at the dark ceiling somewhere beyond the glow of our shared cigarette, I wondered if there was something up. If Prochnow's wife had slipped her leash, I thought she was more likely to go for Kurt. But it was probably about money. After all, it was Gretchen and money that had brought Prochnow to us in the first place.

Then, thinking about money, I remembered the girl in the garden and how she had stolen some Reichmarks from my wallet.

I told Mitzi about her, leaving out the fact she had stolen my money.

Mitzi took the cigarette from my hand.

'What did she look like?'

I described her as best I could, painting a picture of a half-starved waif.

'Have you seen her before?'

Mitzi's shoulder twitched with an indifferent shrug.

'Sometimes I have seen a girl waiting outside the house,' she said. 'Maybe it is the same girl but I have not seen her for a few weeks.'

'Have you ever spoken to her? What does she want here?'

'Why do you want to know, Harry? She is just a ghost.'

'What do you mean, a ghost?'

'Berlin is full of ghosts,' Mitzi said. 'They are looking for the way things were.'

'Their families, you mean? They are looking for people they knew?'

'Who knows?' said Mitzi. 'Whatever she looks for she will not find.'

She leaned towards the table beside the bed and stubbed the cigarette out into an already overflowing ashtray. Then she turned her back to me, ready for sleep. A few moments later her breathing became deep and regular.

Lying beside her feeling like a used sedative, I was now no longer able to sleep myself.

I thought about Gretchen Prochnow again.

With hindsight, I would recognize that she was one more portent that day, like the weather, the man in the Jeep and the girl who stole my money.

Just then, though, lying next to Mitzi on that hot July night, I couldn't even guess what they foretold.

Der Hintergrund

4

Oddly, whenever I ever think of Berlin now it is the sound of aircraft I mostly remember. I say oddly because I had been in the city almost a year before the airlift began and, strictly speaking, the operation was really no more than a coda to my time there. Like one of an unmatched pair of bookends, the airlift marked an end.

After it began one was always aware of the noise of aircraft engines. Before long we all became inured to the sound, accepting it as the backdrop to city life. It grew to be a constant, even as it waxed and waned in one's consciousness, although exactly how much one was aware of it did depend upon the time of day and what one was doing.

The fact was, by then, I wasn't doing much at all. Mostly I was lying on my back in a hospital bed with little else to do but listen to the drone of aircraft overhead and, given my surroundings, it is perhaps not surprising that for a while I came to think of the sound as a disorder of my own head. Like a severe case of tinnitus I could never escape.

During the day, with the bustle of the hospital around me, the sound would recede into the background becoming little more than a droning accompaniment to daily life. But at night ... at night its resonance filled the air, a reverberation that pushed everything else out of existence.

It was then, in the darkness, I would imagine the planes passing low over my bed, their bomb bays opening to shower the city with butter, eggs and bread, and everything else the waiting Berliners below didn't have.

But it wasn't like that at all, of course. A ride out to Tempelhof would have cured anyone of that illusion. At Tempelhof one could watch the aircraft land, one plane after another in a ceaseless flow that could almost make one believe that somewhere up there in the clouds they were being manufactured in an never-ending line and propelled down to us like children's paper planes.

If the airlift was the end, pinning down the beginning, that other bookend of the unmatched pair, is not quite so easy. One reason is a consequence of getting shot. The slug in the lung left only physical effects behind; the shot to the head bequeathed a side effect beyond the physical, leaving a confusion in its wake about how I remembered events.

For a long time actions no longer ordered themselves in a logical and linear sequence. They came to me in a sporadic jumble. Like a deck of cards, my memory had been shuffled: an eight no longer followed a seven, a queen the knave. And though I undeniably remembered both—queens and knaves— just where they fit in the pack was, for some while, quite indeterminate.

~

In London during the early summer of 1947 I was at one of my periodic loose ends. I had finished working for Jack Hibbert who had been my corporal the previous year while I was running a small war crimes unit for Army Intelligence. After being demobbed, Jack had set himself up in a questionable business dealing in army surplus. When MI5 closed his business down, I was left wondering what to do next. Then, out of the blue, I received a letter inviting me for an interview at an address in Acton.

The letter purported to be from an organization called Parkway Overseas Consultants and didn't give much away. Written on cheap paper with a faulty typewriter key that smudged every letter "e", the note gave the appearance of having been trailed over by the wet paws of a very small cat.

Even at a loose end it hardly filled me with enthusiasm.

I had never heard of Parkway and the invitation offered little in the way of information as to the nature of their business. However, the inclusion of the word "overseas" in their name caught my eye as did their acknowledgment of my former military experience. It indicated they knew something about me and was just enough to pique my interest.

They also alluded to my "previous employment" and although the phrase hadn't been typed in quotation marks, the manner of its inclusion suggested I would comprehend the inference.

I assumed at first they were referring to the weeks I had spent employed by Jack Hibbert. Over the previous winter before joining Jack's business, I had spent a few brief months working for the Security Service. But that was an engagement that had not ended well nor been known to anyone beyond a small circle of Security Service employees.

Come to that, my arrangement with Jack Hibbert hadn't ended well either. While it might have been argued that Special Branch had closed his business down due to the questionable legality of some of the merchandise he handled and the questionable people with whom he handled it, it could equally have been argued that he was shut down because of my prior involvement with the Security Service.

I didn't doubt Jack would get back on his feet sooner or later and although he had known something of my work for MI5 he wasn't the sort of man to hold a grudge. Despite this, it was undeniable that the incident left a cloud over our friendship, a cloud which, as he had made clear at the time, would preclude any future offers of employment.

All this aside, I still assumed that whoever Parkway Overseas Consultants were they had got my name through Jack. Along, perhaps, with the impression that I was the kind of man who wasn't too fussy about the sort of work he did.

The premises in Acton turned out to be located near the church above a hardware store on South Parade. A brass plate by the street door gave Parkway's name along with two or three other business concerns, one of which I noticed—and only because it sounded German—was called Schuyler Imports.

Notwithstanding this, at the top of the stairs I found there was no more than a single door with no further indication as to who might lay behind it. I was obviously at the right place, however, and as I was on time I knocked loudly, opened the door and was greeted by the clacking of a typewriter.

The middle-aged, bespectacled woman who was sitting behind the machine looked up at me. Her hair was grey, coloured possibly by the thin ribbon of smoke issuing from the cigarette protruding from between her lips. It matched the shade perfectly.

She peered at me through the thick lenses of her glasses, took the cigarette out of her mouth and placed it in an ashtray.

'Mr Tennant, is it?'

I said it was.

'Mr Harrington is expecting you,' she said. 'Take a seat and I'll let him know you're here.'

She gathered a few of sheets of paper off the desk and disappeared through a door into an adjoining room.

Apart from her chair, the only other available seat was an upright, severely utilitarian example of the breed which might have been better employed tucked under a kitchen table. I took it anyway, but not before I'd glanced at the paper rolled in the typewriter and saw that she was typing something about electrical equipment and that the text was generously spattered with smudged letter "e"s.

The woman returned almost immediately, stood by the open door and indicated I should go through.

I edged past her into a larger office where a tall, heavily-built man was standing behind a desk. With circular-rimmed glasses and a beaked nose, his was the kind of face a caricaturist would have turned into an owl. His eyes narrowed as he stretched out his hand.

'Mr Tennant? Good of you to come. My name is Bill Harrington. This is Mr Philby, of course.'

He was looking past my shoulder so I turned and saw a second man standing by a window who, until then, had been hidden by the open door. Next to him was a hat stand that held a trilby and a worn grey raincoat.

Philby regarded me in a rather insouciant manner. A hank of untidy hair fell across his forehead and a diffident smile was playing over his lips.

Why he was Philby-of-course, I didn't know but I said, 'How-do-you-do,' and we shook hands all round.

I took the chair Harrington indicated in front of the desk

and he sat down opposite me. Philby remained at the window and out of my sight.

Harrington cleared his throat. 'I hope you'll forgive the unconventional manner of our approach, Mr Tennant, but that's the nature of our business.'

I smiled, just to let him know I wasn't fazed by the unconventional.

'I have to admit,' I ventured, 'that I'm not familiar with the name of your company. Exactly what is the nature of Parkway Overseas Consultants' business?'

'Information,' Harrington said succinctly. 'Our business is information.'

For a second his eyes flicked towards Philby and I had to resist an urge to glance over my shoulder to see if the diffident smile was still on the other man's face.

On the point of asking what the kind of information he was alluding to might be, Harrington forestalled me by pulling one of the files lying on the desk towards him.

'You have spent some time in Berlin, I understand.'

'While I was in the army...'

I began to explain but apparently had no need. Bill Harrington, while only occasionally consulting the file, proceeded to run through my career, such as it was, from the day I had left Berlin.

Listening to it all second-hand, it didn't sound a particularly impressive employment record. Nevertheless, I sat quietly while he ran through the details of the débâcle that had been my last case at the war crimes unit, to my subsequent employment with the Security Service where I was supposed to be looking into the terrorist threat posed by Jewish extremist organizations.

On reflection that had turned into something of a débâcle, too, as I had been caught in bed initially with one of the Jewish extremists and shortly after, and rather more painfully, with a work colleague.

I didn't attempt to offer Harrington any evidence in mitigation. Firstly because there really wasn't much to offer, and what little I might have scraped together would probably have been deemed irrelevant and inadmissible, and secondly because Harrington already seemed to have access to all the information held on me anyway.

Perhaps naïvely, until then I had assumed that this was classified information and safely tucked away beyond reach in the Service's Registry in Leconfield House. Somehow, though, Harrington had managed to get his hands on it and, as the man at the window wasn't asking him to repeat anything, I presumed Philby was au fait with it all as well.

I was still mulling over this turn of events as Harrington concluded by briefly summarizing the few weeks I had spent glad-handing clients for Jack Hibbert. That at least scotched my suspicions that Parkway Overseas Consultants was some shady, hole-in-the-wall black market outfit who had been given my name by Jack as a back-handed favour for ruining his own business.

After all, having access to my file meant that I could be dealing with one of only two organizations.

I discounted the Security Service itself almost immediately. I couldn't imagine that they could have any further interest in me. Even if I was wrong and they did have an interest that lay beyond the scope of my imagination, I was pretty sure they wouldn't have bothered with an approach by letter, no matter how "unconventional".

If MI5 wanted to talk to me, they would have sent Henry Gifford and a couple of his goons from Special Branch round and rousted me out of bed.

That just left the other lot, the Service's sister organization. The one that dealt with matters foreign.

SIS.

If it was them it at least meant the overseas part of their name was accurate. Although from everything I had heard about them while working for the Service, when it came to the matter of consulting they had a reputation for being extraordinarily tight-lipped.

So, as Jack would have been in no position to pass on my name, who had?

Given the manner of our parting when I left the Service, I doubted if either Gifford or Abel Bryce would have given me any sort of reference.

Still less Magdalena Marshall.

Thinking about Magdalena remained a painful exercise and one I usually tried to avoid. Even so, if Magdalena hadn't given Harrington my name, could it have been her friend, Jane Archer?

Jane Archer, or Sissmore—or whatever name she was currently going under—had worked with SIS before returning to the Service where she had spent most of her career. But was Jane Archer likely to leave my name with SIS before she left? Given my involvement with Magdalena and how that had ended, I rather doubted it. Although, as on the one occasion we had actually met I had concluded Jane Archer was an enigma, I couldn't say with any certainty just what she might or might not do.

'We have spoken to Mr Hibbert,' Harrington was saying, waking me from my reverie and muddying the waters again, 'and he assured us you were very quick to grasp the intricacies of his business.'

'He said that, did he?'

Which was good of him, I thought. Particularly as the intricacy of the business wasn't the only thing of Jack's I'd grasped while I'd been working for him.

Harrington closed my file.

'We're hoping that sort of aptitude might prove useful to us.'

I asked in what way.

A furrow developed between Harrington's owl eyes. I heard Philby strike a match and a moment later a wisp of cigarette smoke drifted my way.

'Tell me, Mr Tennant,' Harrington said, placing his elbows on the desk and clasping hands together, 'what do you know about electrical components?'

5

In the two years since I had last been in Berlin, I found that while in many respects life for the inhabitants had improved in many others it had deteriorated.

When I first arrived, in the early summer of 1945 and barely more than ten weeks after the war ended, the awfulness of the battle for Berlin had been clear to see. It was as though the Red Army, coming upon the destruction already wreaked by the Allied air raids and finding there was still some life of sorts crawling though the ruins, had used their artillery to administer the *coup de grâce*.

But perhaps that's a detached view of what, in reality, had been murderous street fighting. In some suburbs Hitler's diehards had only relinquished Berlin block by block, building by building, making the final conquest far harder than the Russians had anticipated. Yet, if anything, that had merely honed their desire for revenge: a revenge for the crimes perpetrated by Germany during its invasion of Russia and a desire they had nursed all the way from the steppes.

The resulting vista, I discovered when I arrived, was a scarred city that outstripped any medieval imaginings of how the apocalypse would look.

What wasn't immediately visible, though, were the psychological scars left by those two months of Russian occupation in April and May of 1945. Their commanders had given the Red Army free rein in the city. Afterwards, even the most insensitive of souls would have felt some sort of pity for Berliners when faced with the social disfigurement left behind by wholesale rape and killing. That, and the looting and the theft and the systematic dismantlement and shipping east to Russia of what remained of Berlin's infrastructure.

The city had become a yawning pit of despair.

And all this, I recall thinking at the time, after twelve years of Nazi bullying, browbeating and murder.

~

Following the interview in Acton, Bill Harrington arranged for me to spend a week at a country house in Cambridgeshire. A nice break, I thought, until I found I was expected to attend morning lectures on the current political situation in Berlin and then, with the help of a linguist, attempt to recall what German I had managed to absorb while I had been posted there.

Afternoons were devoted to physical exercise, refresher courses on weaponry and a beginner's introduction to the mysteries of coding and one-time pads. Any spare time beyond these activities was filled with instruction on how to locate and use dead-letter drops. There were half-a-dozen of us on the course although I was the only one singled out to be the recipient of a stack of technical manuals devoted to electrical components, all of which I was expected to read in the apparent hope that some familiarity with the intricacies of such apparatus might serve to get me out of some sticky but unspecified situation should I be careless enough to fall into one.

The evenings were our own, as was the freedom of the nearest town—if we didn't mind the five-mile walk to get there.

Of those present, I appeared to be the only person bound for Berlin. The others were apparently taking up postings in all manner of exotic locations (all men now that the war was over and women were expected to content themselves concentrating their talents on domestic affairs once again).

I also noticed that my colleagues seemed to be enjoying a training schedule less intensive than my own. This fact suggested two possibilities to me: either that what was expected of them was not going to be particularly rigorous, or alternatively what was expected of me was so pressing I was being stuffed into a breach ready or not.

Rarely fancying the five-mile hike after several hours of P.E., I usually spent my evenings exploring the old house. Although rundown, the place had once been quite grand. I was aware that at the end of the war SIS had absorbed the personnel and assets of the Special Operations Executive and it made me wonder if the Cambridgeshire house had not formerly been a training centre for SOE recruits. On this assumption I took to examining the initials that could be found carved into the oak panelling of various rooms. All in the hope, I suppose, of finding a double "M" that might indicate Magdalena Marshall had passed through its doors during the war. But if in idle moments she had been in the habit of defacing other people's property she hadn't done so at this house.

The week passed quickly. I never saw Bill Harrington or Philby there and at the end of my time I was given two days' leave. That over, I was flown out to Gatow in an old Dakota, sitting on a hard bench that ran the length of the fuselage, chilled to the bone in the unpressurized cabin and deafened by the noise of the engines.

I tried to imagine SOE recruits lined along that bench, flying over occupied Europe and awaiting their turn to jump. I even tried to picture Magdalena there, even though I knew she had failed the recruitment course. But she would no longer come into focus in my head and remained only a fuzzy memory that would taunt me for forgetfulness and inconsistency. So I went back to picturing a line of agents I had never known and so had no reason to remember. Even so, the only conclusion I came to on the journey was that despite any fear they may have felt they were probably only too happy to jump when their turn came, if only to get out of that deafening aircraft.

~

Bill Harington met me off the plane.

He wasn't difficult to spot among those few people waiting at the airfield as I disembarked. He was wearing the old raincoat I had seen hanging on the coat stand at my interview in Acton and on his head was the trilby.

The Watchers' uniform, I couldn't help remembering from my time in the Intelligence Service. All right for a wet street in London, but the sun was shining in Berlin and the day was warm. I didn't suppose anyone would spot him for a Watcher in Berlin but he couldn't have been more English if he had "made in England" stamped on his forehead.

Bill was fully accredited, I discovered. That is, he was a paid-up member of the diplomatic corps and if we'd still had an embassy in the country he would, no doubt, have been the man behind the door marked, *Passport Officer*.

It had always been a thin fiction that covered the activities of the men who ran British agents in foreign capitals. I doubt anyone fell for it anymore but if there was ever to be a change of designation I daresay Whitehall would need to constitute a sub-committee to produce a consultative document for study and debate before anything would have got authorized.

Given the circumstances it was as well that this didn't apply in Berlin. According to Harrington, the old embassy at Wilhelmstraße 70 had never been popular with the staff, being too draughty and uncomfortable for cosseted diplomats. The building had once been known as the Palais Strousberg, an ornate confection built by some German railway king in the last century. The British had purchased it before the Great War when they'd probably got it on the cheap. But over the years it had become increasingly hemmed in by the ever-expanding Adlon Hotel next door and was so heavily damaged during the air raids that it was now awaiting demolition. The ambassador and his staff had moved out upon the declaration of war in September 1939, of course, although to hear Bill Harrington speak, it wouldn't have surprised me if before they packed their bags someone hadn't nipped up to the roof and left a light burning in the hope of guiding our bombers and finally getting rid of the place.

Now, in the absence of a proper embassy, our consular duties in Berlin were conducted in Nissen huts where, no doubt to the chagrin of some, classical baroque and rococo embellishments would have looked out of place on corrugated iron.

The huts of the British Staff Occupying HQ were out at Charlottenburg on what had been the old Reich Sporting Field. The stadium had been used for the 1936 Olympics where Hitler had hoped to demonstrate the physical superiority of German athletes and where Leni Riefenstahl's camera had captured each bronzed triceps and pectoral muscle for cinematic posterity.

British Tommies bashed the stadium square now, for the most part scrawny individuals in comparison to Riefenstahl's Aryan specimens and no doubt falling some way short of the filmmaker's ideal of perfection. But the British had made themselves comfortable, taking over the athletes' accommodation building to the north of the stadium and having the impertinence to erect their barracks on Hitler's hallowed grounds.

It was here that Bill Harrington handed me my necessary papers, ration cards and the permits and licences required to enable me to operate the business that was supposed to be my cover.

'You've taken over the Berlin end from Arthur Peston, should you be asked,' he said. 'Sent out by the London office.'

Peston's name had been in the briefing file I'd been given before leaving.

'It mentioned in the file he had an accident,' I said.

Harrington nodded soberly. 'Fell from the *Flakturm*. You know the place I mean?'

'The Zoo flak tower? I thought they demolished that. At least, that was the talk when I was here last.'

'Yes. It's regarded as a Nazi monument. Scheduled for demolition.'

'But it's still there if Peston fell off it.'

Bill Harrington's expression was almost apologetic.

'There have been several attempts to knock it down but so far no one's managed it.'

'Was it an accident? Peston, I mean.'

'You're meeting Kurt Becker later,' Bill said, which was no answer. 'He runs the office here and will show you the ropes.'

'Becker is German, I suppose.'

'His mother was Dutch. His father was a German communist. Kurt was born in Berlin but when Hitler purged the communists the family moved to the Netherlands. Being a neutral country they thought they'd be safe.'

He smiled. At the irony, I assumed, although there was nothing remotely amusing about it.

'I suppose Hitler caught a lot of people out like that.'

The purging hadn't stopped with the communists. He had purged all the socialists, too, those whose party name wasn't prefixed by the word "national", that is. Like the communists, a lot of them had tried to get out of Germany only to find later that their refuge was overrun by the Nazis as well.

Harrington nodded.

'After Hitler invaded the Low Countries Kurt's father was sent to a camp. He died there as far as anyone knows. Kurt was conscripted into the foreign labour force and shipped back to Germany for factory work. His mother died a year or two later.

I said I'd heard the Nazis had been pretty rough on the foreign labourers.

'Kurt was lucky. There was an accident and he lost some fingers off his right hand. He couldn't work so they sent him home.'

'But he came back to Berlin?'

'After the war. You know how things were with the Dutch. Kurt decided he might as well starve in Berlin as in Holland. He'd made some contacts here working in the factories and thought he might be able to make a living if he came back.'

'Black market?'

'Yes. It seems he'd already been doing a bit of dealing during the war.'

'I thought the Gestapo shot black marketeers if they caught them.'

Bill raised an eyebrow. 'The Gestapo were in the habit of shooting people for all sorts of things.'

As there didn't seem to be much to add to that, I asked him if Arthur Peston had recruited Becker.

'Yes. Arthur thought Kurt's contacts might prove useful.'

'Is Becker's help based on ideological grounds, or is it purely commercial?'

'Well,' Bill said, 'he's always been grateful to the British for liberating the Dutch.'

It was my turn to raise an eyebrow.

'Hardly a personal favour.'

'Are you're thinking of the father?'

'You said he was a communist.'

'True,' Bill agreed. 'But Arthur knew all about that and was happy to vouch for Kurt.'

Which under any other circumstance I would have considered good enough. But the man had contrived to fall off the Zoo tower, which at least suggested that somewhere along the line Peston's judgement left something to be desired.

'One thing, though,' Bill added. 'As far as Kurt's sidelines go, I advise you not to get involved. In a way they provide his cover, but it wouldn't do to risk drawing attention to yourself.

35

From the German authorities, I mean. Kurt is regarded as German. You're not.'

'Are you saying that the civil authorities here won't be aware I have Intelligence connections?'

'No they won't. And officially neither will you as far as we're concerned. You're what we term an "illegal".'

'*Illegal*? In what way?'

'In the sense that the diplomatic corps here and SIS back home will deny any responsibility for you. If you're caught doing anything regarded as against the law. It also means you can't expect much in the way of assistance from the military authorities in the British sector, either.'

'So I'm on my own.'

'Naturally I'll give you what assistance I can when necessary,' said Bill, 'but it can't be seen to be in any official capacity.'

'That sounds a precarious position to be in,' I said.

Although, upon reflection, hardly a new one as far as I was concerned. Ever since Harrington read out my *curriculum vitae* in the office in Acton I had come to realize that I had been walking a tightrope from the moment I had been demobbed from the army.

Don't look down is the advice generally offered under those circumstances and so far I never had. Yet it wasn't until that moment in Berlin that I became aware how little solid ground actually lay beneath my feet.

But as I soon found, everyone in Berlin was trying not to look down. We were all insecure; all collectively wobbling on a high wire and doing our best not to fall off.

6

'Don't make a habit of coming out to HQ,' Bill warned me. 'If it's legitimate Schuyler business and you need to straighten out the paperwork, okay. But don't come looking for me.'

We were in the Grunwald, the forest east of the River Havel that bordered the south-western suburbs. Before the war Germans had a reputation for enjoying outdoor activities and the area had been a popular destination for picnickers. It still was, perhaps, although I didn't suppose picnics were as much fun these days as there was so little to put in the hamper. Even so, given the weather and the time, I daresay the odd hiker looking for respite from the devastated city could still be found. Here in the Grunwald or at Müggelsee, the lake in the Russian sector. Or by any of the many lakes and rivers Berlin was able to boast.

Walking through the silent pines with Bill, anyone with a vivid imagination could have been excused for thinking that the events of the past few years had never happened. But I didn't think Bill Harrington's imagination was that vivid or that he was in the Grunwald to forget the war.

Still in his raincoat and trilby, he had spirited me away from the British HQ just as soon as he could. As if, being an "illegal", I had already become *persona non grata* at HQ.

'The important thing,' he advised, repeating much of what I had already been told on my course, 'is not to get complacent. It's easy to fall into bad habits. Remember, they're watching us as closely as we're watching them.'

He gave me the impression he needed to cover a lot of ground quickly and he swiftly went back through the best places for dead-letter drops and the best strategy to adopt if I thought I was being followed.

'Use the S-Bahn and U-Bahn. The stations often coincide and it's easy to give someone the slip between the two. Make a habit of travelling into the suburbs regularly. Places like this, then don't do much when you get here. Most people are lazy. They get bored and if you go somewhere several times without meeting anyone they're just as likely to assume you're never going to.'

He paused to draw breath and promptly contradicted himself.

'You'll have a routine as far your Schuyler work goes. Then you'll have preferred places to eat and maybe a favourite bar... But if you are meeting anyone, vary it. Always assume you are being watched.' He turned to me expectantly. 'Or maybe I'm teaching my grandmother to suck eggs.'

'Not at all,' I said. 'This isn't exactly the kind of Intelligence work I'm familiar with.'

Even though while in Cambridgeshire the tradecraft they were attempting to cram into me seemed adequate at the time, I was beginning to realize that in the field it might be a different matter.

'Clubs and bars are best for arranging chance meetings,' he went on before I was able to dwell upon the matter. 'Working men's haunts. Or where servicemen drink. And don't purposely avoid the Russian sector. All the same, watch your step there. Several German nationals that the Russians have a grievance against have been kidnapped. So far they haven't tried snatching a British or American national, but if they get suspicious about you don't go making it easy for them.'

'No,' I said, wondering what I was getting into.

'There may not be much we could do for you in that sort of situation. You understand,' he added once more, 'you'll be pretty much on your own.'

'Yes,' I said. 'You've made that clear.'

My tone either didn't register with him or he was practised enough to ignore it.

'Oh, and one other thing,' he said.

'What?'

'Girls.'

'What about them?'

'I mean working girls. Stay out of the brothels, Harry. They're just the sort of honey-traps freelancers like to use.'

'Freelancers?'

'There's a market in Berlin for compromised agents.'

'Blackmail, you mean?'

Bill nodded.

'Right,' I said. 'No brothels.'

'There's no shortage of available women, Berlin being what it is. Not professionals, you understand, but open to offers. Kurt can put you right as far as that goes. You'll soon learn which places are popular with the Occupation Forces. Officers and enlisted men usually favour different bars... Well, you were in the army, you know the ropes. I advise you to use both to get the feel of things. And you'll check the rear entrances as a matter of course.'

'Of course.'

We came to a café by the river and stopped for a beer. A few small sailing dinghy's were pulled up on the narrow shore and some skinny kids were splashing in the shallows, limbs like brittle twigs and ribs sticking visibly through their white skin.

Bill Harrington lit a cigarette and we sipped our beer as we watched the children. I was reminded of some of the street urchins I'd seen in London before the war, just as skinny but with rickets, their legs bowed like parenthesis. These looked reasonably healthy but I couldn't help thinking about how the poor devils had spent the last few years.

Harrington's mind was still on the job.

'Right, Harry,' he began busily. 'First things first. As you know your job primarily is to act as a go-between. Kurt Becker is our spotter. He has the contacts and a good cover that allows him to mingle in all strata of society here. Well, almost all. Counts and barons aren't that thick on the ground anymore. When Kurt finds a decent prospect he leads them to you. You vet them—find out if they are in any position either to gather general information for us or, better still, hard copy.'

'Hard copy?'

'Documents, photographs ... anything that might give us an insight into Soviet thinking and doing.'

'Right,' I said. 'Kurt Becker identifies the prospect and once I'm satisfied he's a runner I try and persuade him to work for us.'

'That's it. But you have to move cautiously. Approaching everyone willy-nilly will soon blow whatever cover you have out of the water. You'll be of little use to us if that's the case.'

'I assume before Becker brings anyone to me he's already decided he's a good prospect.'

'Kurt knows what he's doing,' said Bill.

Which naturally made me wonder if he thought I might not.

'We already have a couple of agents that Arthur was running. Kurt has been handling them since Arthur's death, using dead-letter drops for anything they're passing. But it isn't satisfactory. That's not Kurt's job and it only cuts the odds of his being blown. He's too useful a man to lose.'

'Understood,' I said.

'Our main concern at present, though, is a chap named Prochnow. Arthur said he was pretty well-placed and looked promising. Arthur had high hopes he might bring us something important. After he died, though, Prochnow got cold feet and pulled his horns in. Things have rather stalled since then. Kurt has kept in touch and thinks Prochnow might be ready to get back into the game. That's why we need you to pick up the reins as quickly as you can. It's one reason we haven't been able to give you as much time as we might have liked.'

'Who is Prochnow exactly?'

'Gerhard Prochnow,' Bill said. 'He's a Party worker for the SED. That's the Socialist Unity Party.'

I had sat through enough lectures on the intricacies of German politics while on my course in Cambridgeshire to know that the most notable thing about the Berlin political parties was their ability to induce sleep. They were almost as effective as a bottle of Seconal. But I must have managed to stay awake long enough for at least the basics to sink in as I recalled that the previous year the SED had merged with the KPD—the German Communist Party.

'So Prochnow is a Communist,' I said.

Bill shook his head. 'No. It was a merger of the parties, not a takeover. The SED is still a separate entity in Germany. They had been hoping to do well in the elections for the Berlin Municipal Assembly last October. There was talk at the time about the SPD joining the communists as well.'

'The Social Democrats. They're the other German socialist party.'

'Yes. But more moderate than the SED. They decided to wait until after the election before making their decision. In the event it was the SPD who won a majority of seats in the Assembly.'

'And what makes this Gerhard Prochnow so special?'

We had finished our beer and were walking along a track through the trees. Bill dropped his voice as if eavesdroppers might be hiding in the woods.

'Prochnow works on Liepzigerstraße.'

I said that as far as I remembered Liepzigerstraße was a

long street.

He gave me one of those smug, irritatingly superior smiles that those in the know are fond of employing with those who are not.

'In the Air Ministry building?'

Which was something else I remembered. One of the first things that almost everyone who arrived in Berlin at the end of the war did was to take a tour of Nazi landmarks. Or what was left of them. And as it turned out, there had been quite a bit left of the Air Ministry.

'It used to be Hermann Goering's HQ,' Bill said before I was able to demonstrate that I did know the odd fact or two. 'Now it's the central administration offices for the Russian Zone of Occupation.'

'And that's good?'

'Arthur thought it was very good.'

'What does Prochnow do there?'

'Propaganda mainly ... statistical planning and assessment... Low grade stuff but he intimated to Arthur that he had access to SED files. We assumed that since the merger, that would mean KPD files as well.'

'But you say he's not a Communist.'

'No. He's SED, and that's the point.'

'In what way?'

'Because now the SPD is in the ascendancy, in the future there will be only so many jobs to go round for SED men.

'At the moment, despite the election results the SED still have their people in the top jobs in the administration. They run the police, for example, although it won't always be that way.'

I said I thought Berlin was policed by the Occupation Forces.

'So it is,' he replied and pulling a face. 'In a way. I'm speaking of the civilian authority. The old Orpo and Kripo that the SS ran out of the Berlin police headquarters at Alexanderplatz have gone. But so has the Alex. The building is so badly damaged that Berlin's new police chief, Johannes Stumm, decided to relocate to Friesenstraße in the American sector. That provoked a bit of a row on the Russian side with their police chief, Paul Markgraf. So now the Russians have pulled out of the policing agreement and established their own HQ in their own sector at Keibelstraße. That's just a few hundred yards from the old Alex. That means each sector now recruits their own men. It's all still under military control, of course, although I'm afraid there is very little liaison between them. A bit of a dog's breakfast, really.'

'Sounds it,' I said.

'There's also another fact to consider. As I said, top jobs in the administration are still run by SED members. And while the different police forces don't liaise much, the Administration still has effective control. The point is, the Occupation Forces can't be bothered with run of the mill police work and, consequently, organized crime is rife. So there is a thriving black market as you'd expect. What you always have to remember, Harry, is that the SED have fingers in every pie. Housing ... rationing ... all the utility services... And for SED you can now read KPD. That means, ultimately, NKVD. That's why no one can ever be sure that their phone line isn't tapped, regardless of which sector they're calling from.'

'So why,' I asked, 'if this fellow Prochnow is an SED Party member and they're the ones running the show, is he willing to help us?'

'Because Prochnow was expecting the SED to win the election. And he expected to get a better job on the back of it.'

'It's one thing to be disappointed when you don't get a promotion,' I suggested, 'quite another to betray your own side because of it.'

Bill stared at me as if he thought I was a slow learner.

'It's not a question of betrayal, Harry. And as far as Prochnow goes it's a little more than just disappointment.'

'How?'

'Climbing the Party ladder doesn't only mean more prestige. It means more money and better rations.'

'From what I gather,' I said, 'Party men don't do too badly as it is.'

'It's true Party members get more perks than other people. But the higher you go, the bigger the perks.'

'So it's just venality?'

'In a way,' said Bill. 'Prochnow was spending money on the strength of advancement.'

'Money he didn't have? That's a neat trick.'

'Until you have to pay the bill, it is. The problem is Prochnow's wife, Gretchen, likes a good time. And he likes to keep her happy, take her out and buy her nice things.'

'And where in Berlin can he do that?'

'On the black market mostly. That's how Kurt Becker got on to him. But it takes a lot of Reichmarks, or better still American dollars. If you can get them. Prochnow was banking on advancement after the SED won the election and spent money before he earned it. Now they've lost the election there's no new job and no extra money for him. Unfortunately for Prochnow, Gretchen has got used to a higher standard of living.'

'So he is in debt. Who on earth did he manage to borrow money from on the strength of an election and promotion?

Bill smiled. 'Kurt Becker.'

'Ah,' I said.

'And that's how you hooked him?'

'Gretchen likes to dance and eat in restaurants. Prochnow's share of Soviet *pajoks* isn't enough anymore.'

'*Pajoks?* They're the extra rations the Russians hand out to Party members, aren't they?'

'That's right. The communist version of the CARE packages the Americans distribute in the western sectors. The Soviets didn't want to look bad in front of the Party so they came up with *pajoks*. They're nothing special but it's something the ordinary people don't get and in Berlin these days people are grateful for anything.'

'But not Gretchen?'

'It seems not.'

I had only been back in the city for a few hours before I discovered that the end of the war hadn't meant the end of inequality. The rationing system was harsher than it was back home although, if you knew the right people or managed to get the right job, there were always perks to be had. Perks that ordinary Berliners didn't get, perks like the American CARE packages and the Soviet *pajoks*; like the hot meals provided everyday for anyone who worked for the Administration and which didn't count against rations.

Something for the stomach, they called it.

But most people weren't eligible for that little luxury and couldn't afford to supplement their rations through the black market. It seemed to me that as a Party member Prochnow must have got more than most although it seemed that still wasn't enough for his wife, Gretchen.

'So either Prochnow cooperated or Kurt called in his debt? Is that how it worked?'

Bill affected a wounded expression. 'Despite appearances, Harry, we're not quite as crude as that. Prochnow is in a position to get Kurt off his back if he needs to. He's a Party man, after all. A word in the right ear and Kurt would be picked up by the police for black market trading. Or simply disappear. As I told you, the Russians aren't above the odd kidnapping if it suits their purpose. But doing that doesn't solve Prochnow's problem. He would still need money and if he did have Kurt arrested he could never be sure of what Kurt would tell his masters.'

'So how did we play it?'

Bill ground out the butt of the cigarette he had been smoking on the gravel path.

'Once Kurt manoeuvred Prochnow into his corner, Arthur Peston persuaded him that we were willing to pay for certain information. Nothing of importance or what might be seen as sensitive, Arthur made clear. Just routine information.'

'At first, you mean?'

'Well,' Bill admitted with a knowing smile, 'once Prochnow has put his foot in the water there's no going back of course. The Party doesn't take kindly to those who are seen to collude with the Allies, no matter how innocuous the material he might have been passing. Whoever they are, they're still regarded as traitors.'

'So what's been happening since Peston's death?'

'Not a lot,' Bill admitted. 'The kind of merchandise Prochnow was giving us up till then was nothing special. It mainly consisted of statistical information collected by their social analysis department.'

'Sounds dry.'

'Wait till you read some of it. Mostly it's computations and appraisals of the information they gather through the questionnaires they distribute among the population in the Soviet sector. Much the same as the surveys the SS's Intelligence Service, the *Sicherdienheist*, did during the war. *Stimmungsberichte* they called it then—mood reports on the moral and attitude of the German civilian population.'

'So much for de-Nazification,' I said.

'No, you're wrong there, Harry. Using ex-Nazis is something the Russians are dead against. Using the old methods is a different matter. But the point is, the results are hardly state secrets.'

'And that's not what you expected from him?'

'We did expect more meat. Prochnow had access to SED files and after the merger we thought there was a prospect of his getting into the KPD files as well. If that was to be the case, according to Arthur there was a possibility Prochnow could be in a position to identify those German communists who have been infiltrated into the Allied Zones.'

'Agents?'

'Yes.'

'So what happened?'

'Arthur died before he was able to take it further.'

'Couldn't Kurt Becker handle it?'

'No. Prochnow got cold feet. Arthur's death may have been an accident but it was enough to scare him off. Prochnow told Kurt he couldn't bring us anything more.'

'But you were holding his debts over him,' I said. 'And the fact he had worked for us.'

'As far as the money goes, somehow he managed to pay Kurt back. And us ratting him out to the NKVD would just bring them down on Kurt, too. We could have pulled Kurt out and gone ahead, of course, but that would just have been sour grapes on our part. It seemed more sensible to wait. What with Prochnow and his wife's spending habits we didn't think it would be too long before he came back to us, ready to deal again.'

'And he has?'

'Yes. Now the dust has settled over poor Arthur, Prochnow has been borrowing off Kurt once more. We've had some of the same kind of merchandise he passed Arthur but what we would like is sight of that list of agents he hinted to Arthur he could get us. It was Kim's idea to put a little more pressure on Gerhard Prochnow.'

'Kim?'

'Kim Philby.'

'The other man at interview in Acton,' I said.

'At the time I assumed you two knew each other. But Kim tells me you have never actually met.'

'What made you think we might have?'

'Because it was Kim who put your name forward.'

'*Philby* asked for me?'

'He said the recommendation came from a mutual acquaintance in the Security Service.'

Which narrowed the field down but still left me none the wiser. To the best of my recollection I had never heard mention of Kim Philby while I was working at the Prince's Gate office. The only possible acquaintance I could think we might have had in common was the late Brian Ogilvy. Although the chances of Ogilvy recommending me to SIS before his death were so vanishingly small as to be hardly worth considering.

Bill had explained why they needed to get somebody out to Berlin as quickly as possible, but he had shed no light on why they had settled on me.

'Surely there was someone else in SIS who could have stepped into the breach under the circumstances,' I said. 'Someone who knows the set-up here.'

'Kim felt we needed a fresh face. Berlin being what it is,' he added.

'And what is that exactly?'

'Being this far in the Soviet camp, so to speak. Deep in the Soviet Zone of Occupation. We're virtually isolated here. It makes it very difficult to operate undercover with any measure of security. Arthur's credentials were sound as a bell. He was actually in electronics before the war and anyone looking would have found his and Schuyler's background solid as a rock. That's why we didn't have any qualms about bringing you out under Schuyler's umbrella.'

Remembering those shabby offices above a hardware store in Acton, I hoped no one from the other side had thought to take a look at Schuyler's head office. Peston may have been in electronics before the war, but from what I had seen of the supposed electrical components exporter's set-up, it wasn't enough to establish the bona fides of a church mouse.

'No qualms as long as you brought me out as an illegal, that is' I said. 'Someone deniable.'

'Exactly, Harry.'

'So how much do we actually know about Prochnow? Is it likely he can produce what he says he can? Or is it just so much hot air hoping he can keep himself buoyant?'

Bill sounded upbeat. 'Everything we've found out about him suggests he's the genuine article. Whether or not he can actually lay his hands on a list of KPD agents is another matter. Kurt says he is willing to deal again but he's still nervous. We asked Kurt to try and get something out of him on account but Prochnow is wary of involving Becker in this.'

'What, Kurt is good enough to borrow money from but not good enough to trust?'

'Something like that,' said Bill. 'That's why we didn't want to waste any more time in getting you out here.'

'And you say there isn't any doubt about Peston's death being an accident? Under the circumstances, I mean.'

Following the track, we had come out of the trees and on to the Havel again. Bill gazed across the river.

'No, I don't think so, Harry. The police were satisfied it was an accident. Arthur had been seen drinking in a bar earlier that evening and they decided he was drunk, slipped and lost his balance. The autopsy showed he did have a lot of alcohol in his system. We looked into it ourselves, naturally, but Kim is of the opinion it was just an unfortunate mishap.

'We'll all miss Arthur, of course,' he added. 'But as Kim said, this does at least give us the opportunity of sending in someone new. Someone they can't possibly know.'

I followed his gaze across the river. Even if I understood the logic, it still seemed a little odd to me that they didn't have anyone to hand who was familiar with the work.

'We are assuming you made no waves while you were here in '45,' Bill said. He was smiling although there was no doubt that what he said was meant in earnest. 'Kim had your background examined thoroughly, of course. But you had better tell me now if you remember anything that might have brought you to the attention of the Soviets at the time. They won't know you, will they Harry?'

Just to give him something to worry about I said:

'That depends on how good their record-keeping is.'

The smile faded.

'What do you mean?'

'If you remember,' I said, 'patrols back then had to consist of one member from each sector. The Russians were sticklers for it. And everyone had to keep duty rosters for serving personnel. You know, name, rank and number. The usual ID. That way everyone knew that no one was trying to pull the wool over anyone else's eyes.'

He relaxed. 'That's not a problem,' he said. 'You're a civilian now. Any paperwork they might still have shows that back then you were nothing more than an ordinary conscript.'

'A volunteer,' I corrected him, just so *his* paperwork was all in order. 'I was in the police. I didn't have to join up.'

'No, of course not, Harry,' he amended quickly. 'You were a lieutenant while you were here, that's right isn't it?'

'I received my captaincy just before they called me home.'

'To set up that war crimes unit? Interesting work, I imagine,' he said.

'It had its moments.'

Although in truth it had been anything but interesting. The one case of significance that I did turn up was the investigation that got me sacked.

'Then you're clean as far as they're concerned,' he said.

'Whiter than white.'

'You have to be, given that you'll be operating on something of a limb. You do understand that, don't you Harry?'

I understood. I had only arrived that morning but he had still managed to tell me several times already.

'That you need to maintain deniability, you mean.'

'Yes.'

'And if I do run into trouble?'

He smiled, but sympathetically.

'You'll find that not doing so is the trick of it, old chap.'

'Well,' I said, 'I didn't suppose it was going to be a holiday.'

7

Arthur Peston had kept an apartment in Moabit, the industrial suburb that lay to the north of the Tiergarten between the River Spree and the Hohenzollernkanal.

'That's the address,' Bill said, slipping a piece of paper across the table towards me. 'Kurt will be waiting for you there. It'll be as well if you go on your own. The less we're seen together the better.'

We were drinking what passed for coffee having eaten dinner in a restaurant off Savingy Platz, not far from the Zoo Bahnhof where I had left my suitcase.

His caution prompted me to look around, half-expecting to catch people at the other tables looking our way. But the place was almost empty, which came as no great surprise now I'd eaten there. I had been thinking that parting with some of my precious ration cards for the meal we were served a poor exchange. A good portion of mine still lay on my plate, a conspicuous heap of soggy sauerkraut, abandoned when I found it tasted even more sour than it was supposed to.

'The flat is rented through Schuyler Imports,' Bill went on. 'Since Arthur set up the Berlin end, he found it convenient to live near the warehouse. That's on Stromstraße. It's only a short walk from there to the apartment. Take a day or two to reacquaint yourself with the place, Harry. When you're ready, Kurt will set up a meeting with Prochnow.'

'I thought time was of the essence. That's why you got me out here.'

Bill shook his head. 'Another day or two won't hurt. I'd rather you got to know the lie of the land first. Before you get involved.'

It seemed to me a little late in the day for voicing that sentiment. But if Harrington thought it all right I was happy to take a couple of days adjusting to Berlin again.

He leaned back in his chair. 'I don't suppose BRIXMIS means much to you, does it Harry?'

'What is it, some new breakfast cereal?'

He smiled indulgently.

'It's an acronym, sort of. It stands for the British Commanders'-in-Chief Mission to the Soviet Forces in Germany. It was set up last September, after your first tour here. Mostly we call it the Military Mission.'

'As a matter of fact,' I said, 'Last time I was here I did hear talk about a Military Mission. Liaison, isn't it?'

'That's right. It's supposed to cover several areas of mutual interest we have with the Soviets. Repatriation of POWs, graves registration ... co-ordinating anti-black market operations, that sort of thing. Also liaison concerning the tracking down of war criminals. That's why I asked, given your involvement.'

'No,' I said. 'My unit had no dealings with them. Am I likely to run into them?'

'The agreement grants us and the Soviets access to mutually approved areas of each other's occupied territory. That's here in the British sector and in the British Occupied Zone. We have access to some areas on the Russian side. The Americans and the French both have similar agreements although on a smaller scale.'

'"Mutually approved"? Sounds like anywhere they don't mind us seeing,' I said.

Bill nodded. 'To a degree, yes. But it does allow some latitude.'

'To gather information?'

'That thought wasn't lost on us,' he admitted.

'How much do I need to know about it?'

'Only that we have a man on the inside. The BRIXMIS HQ is in Potsdam. Or at least would be if the property the Soviets have allocated us was habitable. While it's being refurbished BRIXMIS are working out of the HQ at the Reich Sporting Field.'

He passed me a card.

'They also keep a small office here in the city. That's the address and telephone number. It's on Hohenstaufenstraße, to the south of Viktoria-Luise-Platz. If you ever need to contact me urgently or need to get anything to me at short notice, go through them. Sergeant Andy Thurston is the man to talk to. He knows who you are.'

I slipped the card into my pocket.

'The office is supposed to be under the radar,' Bill said, 'although, needless to say, if you need to telephone them, be circumspect. The line could be tapped.'

'Understood,' I said.

'The same goes for the warehouse and Arthur's apartment. We swept both locations after Arthur died, just as a precaution. They're clean but we have no control over the telephone system. If you have to, use public telephones for our business.

'BRIXMIS apart,' he added, leaning across the table once more, 'we'll draw up a schedule of where and when you and I meet. We'll vary location and time and operate a rota system. Rather like a one-time pad, you might say. Here, let me show you...'

We spent the next fifteen minutes organizing a rota until he was certain I had memorised each location and understood the rotating sequence of the place and time of each meet. Then he pulled a few Reichmarks from his wallet and dropped them on the table to cover the bill.

'As I said, if you have to get in touch between meetings—'

'Go through the Military Mission on Hohenstaufenstraße,' I finished for him.

'Good,' he said. He gathered up his cigarettes and lighter. 'Finish your coffee and have another cigarette. Take your time. There's no hurry.'

Perhaps there wasn't, but it had been a long day and one that was beginning to catch up with me. As suggested, I had another cigarette after he left but passed on the coffee. Then I headed for the Zoo Bahnhof to retrieve my suitcase from the station locker.

Walking north through the Tiergarten past the flak tower

looming above me in the fading evening light, I noticed the place had been cordoned off. A couple of British soldiers stood sentry duty on the Nazi landmark to stop the curious like me from getting too close. I didn't suppose too many Germans were curious about the place, having lived with the hulking building for several years already. Many of them would have crammed behind its reinforced concrete walls every time the sirens wailed and the bombs began to fall. Designed also to be a *Hochbunker*, they must have packed themselves inside as tight as panicking sardines. When last here I had heard some had died in the crush, kept upright by those around them until the all clear sounded. If that was true, I didn't suppose the tower prompted much nostalgia as far as the general populace was concerned. I couldn't help thinking, though, that Arthur Peston had found some reason for going there. A fact I still found curious.

Crossing the river and passing Stromstraße, I considered taking a look at the warehouse. But it was starting to get dark and I supposed there would be plenty of time for that. The apartment was just south of Alt Moabit on Calvin Straße.

Seeing the destruction all around it struck me as having been aptly named—the annihilation probably resembled Calvin's idea of hell. The only difference here was that the fires were now out.

Given the widespread damage, I was surprised to find Peston's apartment block relatively unscathed. Once you discounted the cracked masonry and broken glass. In fact the place put me in mind of my old Cowcross Street flat back in Clerkenwell in London. But then most buildings look alike once you've dropped several tons of high explosive on them.

Peston's flat stood on the top floor. The building had a lift but a scrawled sign hanging on the grill informed the optimistic that it wasn't working. So I climbed the stairs in the gloom, found number ten and knocked on the door.

In the stillness that followed I wondered if Becker had tired of waiting and gone home. After a moment, though, I heard the lock turn.

The door opened a few inches and a sallow-skinned individual peered at me through the gap.

'Kurt Becker?' I asked. 'My name is Harry Tennant. From the London office.'

He opened the door wider to reveal a crop of wiry hair and a body oddly bent like a used pipe cleaner. From what Bill Harrington had already told me of him, I didn't suppose Becker could be much more than thirty yet, like most people who had been on the wrong end of a war, he seemed older. I stepped into the apartment. He closed the door behind me without speaking and led me down the hall to a sitting room where the air tasted stale and thick with dust.

'I have been expecting you, Herr Tenant,' he said in good English.

We shook hands, his grip reminding me that he had lost some fingers in a factory accident. He turned and scooped up a pile of papers that were lying on a table and handed them to me.

'These are this month's dispatch manifests, Herr Tennant. They are all in order and you will see that Herr Peston countersigned some before his death. You will need to sign the others before we can take delivery of the remainder.'

Since Becker seemed to be restricting himself to discussing only Schuyler business, I played along despite the fact Bill Harrington maintained they'd swept the flat for bugs.

'Thanks,' I said. 'Did Herr Peston keep the account books here or at the warehouse? I'd like to go through them as soon as possible.'

Becker bowed slightly. 'Of course, Herr Tennant. They are at the warehouse. You will find all the paperwork is in order. Herr Peston was a most correct man.'

'I am sure he was.'

'We will examine them tomorrow if that is convenient. Or would you prefer to start this evening?'

'Tomorrow,' I said. 'It's been a long day.'

'As you wish, Herr Tennant. You have eaten? I am afraid Herr Peston always preferred to eat out. It has been several weeks since his...' he left the sentence hanging in the air. 'There is nothing here,' he finally added.

'I've had dinner,' I said. 'I'll manage.'

He executed another short bow. 'In that case, Herr Tennant,

I will leave you to rest. Will you make your own way to the office tomorrow or would you like me to call for you?'

'I'll see you there,' I said.

Alone in the flat I became aware of the pervading silence. No sound came from the street or from any of the other apartments. I sat at the table glancing through the manifests but with my mind on other things. The stilted conversation Becker and I had still hung in the stale air, as if our exchange had been conducted for the benefit of a third party. Despite Bill Harrington's insistence that the place had been swept through, I would have started looking for microphones myself had I not been so tired.

During my brief employment with SIS's sister organization, MI5, I had learned first-hand of the deficiencies of the Security Service. I had found they operated in the main through a combination of the class system and tradition—a mixture that left little room for the application of logic. SIS sending out a novice like me to fill an unexpected gap in Berlin seemed to smack of a similar lack of logic. Nothing that had happened since my arrival had instilled me with confidence that working for SIS was going to be any different.

But there I was, sitting at Peston's table with my suitcase at my feet. I was going to have to make the best of it.

I looked around the room. The curtains had been drawn and the weak light of the overhead bulb cast a pallid sheen over the floral design of the stained wallpaper. The heavy, old-fashioned furniture looked shabby and the rug on the floor was worn to its thread in places. Next to a half-filled bookcase against one wall, a standard lamp stood poised over a battered armchair as if it was awaiting a reader. I picked up my suitcase and carried it into the bedroom. There was nothing much there either to suggest that Arthur Peston had been anything other than a practical man, from his sagging bed to the utilitarian side table and wardrobe. A man apparently unbothered by concepts such as comfort and style.

In the wardrobe I found his trousers and jackets still drooping lifelessly from their hangers. Opening the wardrobe drawers, I discovered his shirts alongside his socks and his underwear. An old suitcase stood at the back of the cupboard, presumably having made its last journey.

I unpacked and, as I made room for my clothes beside his, it struck me that not only was I about to fill Peston's shoes but that I had also assumed possession of his vacated life.

I wandered idly through the rest of the apartment looking for a clue as to the kind of man I was replacing. Yet ten minutes later I was none the wiser. Peston appeared to have left little of himself behind. I found no personal papers, no letters from family or friends from England; nor did I find any photographs. Someone might have gone through the apartment after his death, packed up his personal belongings and sent them home, of course. But if that was the case, why leave his clothes?

It seemed to me to be equally possible that Peston had not possessed any of the personal trappings that most people collect over the years. If that was so, I suppose it had made him the perfect man for his job: an Intelligence officer with no ties or associations. Nothing of substance that might offer a lever for those who might wish to manipulate him.

I couldn't help wondering if that was a description of myself; if that was what had drawn me to the attention of Philby and Harrington.

It was a depressing thought so I didn't dwell on it.

In a cupboard I found a set of clean sheets and I stripped the bed and remade it. Then, finding there was no hot water I contented myself with cleaning my teeth and having a quick wash down in cold.

By the time I finished it was after midnight. I got into the bed and listened to the silence around me, wondering how often Arthur Peston had done the same thing.

8

The Schuyler Imports warehouse on Stromstraße had been a flourmill until an air raid had put it out of business. Industrial Moabit would have been a prime target for the bombers although, to look at the destruction wreaked on the rest of the city, one would be forgiven for thinking that everywhere in Berlin had been a prime target.

The mill backed onto the Spree close to the Lessing Bridge with the grain, I assumed, arriving by barge along the river. Bread being a staple of the Berliners' diet, baking had been one of the few services to keep operating right to the end of the war. Back in London everyone had complained about the bread flour being adulterated to make up the weight and I didn't suppose Berlin was any different. Nor did I suppose that the German miller who had run this particular operation would have needed to go far to make up his weight; the daily air raids probably supplied all the sand and grit he'd ever want.

I had no idea when milling had ceased in this particular mill although, looking around that first morning, it appeared to have been out of business for some while. Part of the roof had caved in and a gaping hole in the west wall gave unorthodox access to Stromstraße. An attempt to block the hole had been made using baulks of the timber that had fallen from the roof and most of the rubble cleared away. But the old millstones and hoists that had come through the ceiling from the floors above still lay where they had landed. A tangled mess of frayed rope and rusting iron, they resembled outsize doughnuts resting on a giant bird's nest.

Despite all this there still remained sufficient space on the ground floor for a variety of tables on which were spread an assortment of electrical bits and pieces. A large sideboard with an array of cupboards like the kind that could have once be found in apothecary shops stood against one wall. There, I suppose, the multitude of small drawers would have held things like mandrake roots, slivers of willow bark and an assortment of herbs and the like; here, the drawers contained an equally esoteric collection of electrical components, the use for most of which I couldn't guess.

What space was left was occupied by a stack of wooden crates, the kind I'd been told arrived periodically for Schuyler Imports.

I was early yet Kurt Becker was already at work. That wasn't a problem for him as apparently he lived in a room on an upper floor. When I walked in he was busy opening a crate marked *Schuyler* with a crowbar, displaying a surprising dexterity considering his lack of fingers.

The wood splintered as he prised the lid off and I sauntered over and peered inside. The crate held a number of boxes containing various electrical components, some of which I recognized from my course in the house in Cambridgeshire and all second-hand as far as I was able to tell.

'What do we do with these?' I asked Becker.

He continued rummaging through the crate.

'*We* don't do anything with them,' he said, accentuating the pronoun in a tone markedly different from the one he had used with me the previous evening. '*I* dispose of them.'

'What, throw them away? That's a waste of resources. They've only just shipped them over to us. Why don't they send us something useful? Like food.'

Kurt Becker adopted an expression of exaggerated patience.

'I do not throw these away, Herr Tennant. I know people who are willing to pay money for these parts.'

Bill Harrington had told me about Becker's sidelines and I assumed it must be some sort of black market fiddle.

'Who buys this rubbish?'

He picked through a jumble of capacitors.

'It may look like rubbish to you, Herr Tennant, but some people pay money for it. The parts are bought here but maybe they go somewhere else? Do you understand?'

'Where?'

'To the east maybe?'

'The *east*?'

I did begin to understand. The Russians had shipped anything of an industrial nature and remotely portable they had found in Berlin back east. I assumed from Kurt Becker's insinuations, that that's where Schuyler's electrical components would end up, too.

Bill Harrington had warned me not to get mixed up in Becker's black market dealings, but it seemed to me that supplying the Soviets with British commercial material was decidedly unpatriotic. Not to mention completely defeating the object of our being there. I may not have been the kind of man who stands to attention every time the national anthem is played, or salutes whenever a Union flag is run up, but treating with the enemy was a step too far, even for me.

I told Becker as much.

He scowled at me. 'These are *used* goods, Herr Tennant.'

'Even so...' I said, 'I assume they still work.'

'*Used*,' he repeated, belabouring the point. 'As in maybe not reliable?'

'Oh,' I said, the penny dropping. 'You mean they're liable to fail? So what's the idea? Sabotage? Surely it won't take the Russians long to twig to that. Why would they buy faulty second-hand goods? Why don't they make their own?'

'*Twig?*' he repeated, looking puzzled.

'Realize,' I explained. 'Learn their lesson.'

He shrugged and went back to sorting through the crate.

'Perhaps. But Russian stuff is not so reliable either. And maybe their method of manufacture is not suited to machinery stolen from Germany. You must remember, Herr Tennant, much of what the Nazis used was originally shipped here from France and Belgium and Holland. The Russians acquired it third-hand.'

'I see,' I said and decided to take Bill's advice and not get involved.

Exploring the mill, I found a kitchen at the rear. It didn't have much but there was a sink and a kettle and it was equipped with a teapot and caddy. I didn't find any food but there were a few old tealeaves dusting the bottom of the caddy so I put a pot on to brew. I went back to where Becker was still delving into the crate and lining up the components he retrieved on a table.

'I found some tea back there,' I said. 'Yours?'

'Herr Peston's.'

'I've put a pot on. Any cups?'

Becker squinted at a bulky component I didn't recognize, turning it over in his hand.

'Herr Peston kept them in the top drawer of the filing cabinet.'

'Right. Do you want a cup?'

'If there is sufficient, Herr Tennant.'

'Call me Harry,' I suggested.

As Arthur Peston's name had come up, I took the opportunity when I returned with tea to ask Becker about my predecessor.

'Bill Harrington didn't tell me much about Arthur Peston,' I said. 'His clothes are still in the flat but not much else. Were his personal belongings sent back to England?'

Becker looked sideways at me. 'This is something I think you should ask Herr Harrington.'

'Did Peston keep anything of his here, do you know?'

'His tea,' he said.

'How did you get into his apartment yesterday? Do you have a key?'

He stopped his rummaging and took a key from his trouser pocket.

'I must apologise, Herr Tennant. I meant to give it to you yesterday. There was another key in the apartment, I think?'

'Harry,' I said again. 'And yes, I found it. Who gave you this one?'

'The police. They said it was in Herr Peston's pocket when he fell.'

'Was there anything else? Papers, perhaps? Money? I assume he carried a wallet.'

Becker shrugged his thin shoulders. 'If there was anything else, it would have been given to Herr Harrington at the British headquarters, Herr Peston being English.'

'But not the key to the apartment,' I said. 'They gave that to you.'

He shrugged again. 'Business. The apartment is rented through the company.'

'They came here did they? I suppose they looked the place over. Did they ask you anything about Peston? Why he was up the tower, for instance?'

Seemingly satisfied there was nothing else of interest in the crate Kurt Becker picked it up and stacked it alongside the others against the far wall.

'They asked the usual questions,' he said, coming back to the table and his electrical odds and sods. 'You know the police.'

I didn't seem to be getting far. Becker was just as tight-lipped as Bill Harrington on the subject.

'What kind of man was he?' I persisted. 'Did you get on well together?'

He gave me a blank look as if he hadn't understood the question. Like many of the Dutch I'd met, though, Kurt Becker had a better grasp of English than my still uncertain one of German. His lack of understanding wasn't based upon linguistic interpretation.

'I do not know what to tell you,' he finally said.

'What was he doing up the Zoo Tower?' I asked, getting straight to the point.

'I do not know. Herr Peston did not tell me what he was doing.'

'That day or every day?'

'I cannot tell you, Herr Tennant. Perhaps this is also something you should ask Herr Harrington.'

'Call me Harry, for Chrissakes,' I said, beginning to get irritated. 'It *was* Peston who recruited you, wasn't it?'

'Ah, this, I think, is what Herr Harrington has told you.'

He stood a little straighter, the pipe cleaner un-kinking. I appeared to have hit a nerve.

'I think "recruited" is not the right word to use, Herr Tennant. You think that perhaps I am a spy. This is not so. I am a businessman.'

'Call me Harry,' I said again, trying not to grit my teeth.

'If this is what you prefer,' he replied evenly.

'Businessman?' I repeated, gesturing at the ragbag collection of electrical components on the table. 'You mean this business?'

'Yes. Among other things.'

'But Schuyler is just a front,' I said bluntly.

'Perhaps for you and for Herr Harrington. But it is how I earn my money.'

I found it hard to believe he would make much out of the rubbish in this particular crate.

'But this isn't what you did for Arthur Peston,' I said. 'Harrington told me Peston recruited you because of your contacts. Because you know people and you hear things. Isn't that right?'

'It is true I was able to put Herr Peston in touch with certain people. People he might have found it difficult to approach himself. I am what you would call a...' he faltered. '...I am not sure of the word in English.'

'Try it in German,' I suggested.

'*Ermöglichen*,' he said.

That didn't help either.

He tried again. 'I make things easy between people. Do you understand?'

'You're a go-between,' I said. 'A facilitator. I hear you also deal in cigarettes.'

'Something else Herr Harrington has told you? Do you need some perhaps?'

I laughed. I always needed cigarettes.

'I'll know where to come when I do,' I told him.

'I have many brands...' Kurt said as if about to launch into his sales patter.

'But you've no idea what Peston was doing up the Zoo Tower? Would he have been meeting someone? Maybe he was depressed,' I suggested. 'Tired of this city? Tired of trying to squeeze information out of tight-lipped Berliners?'

His eyes narrowed, indicating that English sarcasm was not entirely lost on him.

'Herr Peston told me very little of what he did,' he said once more.

'That must have made things difficult. Do you think he jumped?'

He almost smiled. I didn't know the German for sardonic but I suppose it looks the same in any language.

'Are you asking me if he was pushed?'

'Was there anyone who wanted him dead?'

'You ask a lot of questions, Harry.'

'Isn't that what I'm here for?'

'Then maybe it is better if you ask *why* someone would want Herr Peston dead.'

I considered that. It was still an evasion but at least this one had a bit of meat on it.

'Did he have friends?'

'German friends?' He pursed his lips. 'It is possible. Our connection was not what you would call a social arrangement.'

'What about women?'

'The kind you pay for, perhaps. Herr Peston was not...' he looked past me as if the term he needed might be found framed and hanging on the wall. '...how do the French say ... a roué?'

I laughed again. For the first time Kurt returned a shy smile.

'So I can rule out some Mata Hari.'

'You think his death was suspicious?' he asked.

'Don't you?'

'I think it better I keep my opinions to myself.'

'Then you're a wise man, Kurt.'

He grinned and relaxed visibly.

'I think maybe we will get on together, Harry.'

'I hope we do,' I told him. 'And just so you know in advance, I've no plans for jumping off the Zoo Tower.'

'That is good to know.'

'In fact,' I confided, 'I have very few plans at all.'

He shrugged. 'No one in Berlin has plans these days.'

'Except the Russians perhaps?'

'Do not worry about the Russians, Harry,' he replied, almost voluble now. 'You do what I do and we will do all right.'

~

Having arranged for me to acquire the necessary paperwork I would need to live and work in occupied Berlin, Bill Harrington had left me in the hands of a helpful Welsh corporal named Dai Edwards at the British HQ. I would need ID papers and the various licences and permits that allowed me to operate a business in the city. Also I needed a ration card—the *Bezugkarte*.

I was accustomed to rationing, of course, having had to get used to it at home like everyone else once I left the army. The German system was similar, if confusing to an outsider. Once mastered, though, as one might have expected of the Germans, it proved orderly and precise.

Kurt walked me through it, explaining (with a Marxian echo that would have had Hitler turning in his unmarked grave) how everyone was placed in a group according to the number of calories the authorities had decided was sufficient for their needs. These groups were in turn subdivided into narrower categories depending upon the applicants age, whether they had children and if so their ages. Or if the applicant was a pregnant women or nursing mother.

'You are not pregnant or a nursing mother,' said Kurt.

'I'm the type who takes precautions,' I told him.

He said none of the other categories were likely to trouble me either.

'You are Group III.' He pointed at my *Bezugkarte*. 'An *Angestellte*. What is called a white-collar worker.'

'At least they haven't taken me for a labourer.'

'No, no, it is good to be a labourer, Harry,' he insisted. 'Heavy work means you get a bigger ration. This is how it works. Maybe you sit in an office all day so you need only two thousand calories.'

'Two thousand? A day? How do they expect anyone to live on that?' Even in austere Britain the subsistence level was more generous than that. I gave him my coupons. 'What can I buy with these?'

'*Bezugsbeschränkle Waren*,' he said. 'Normal food. But only what you find in the shops.'

'Normal?'

'Special goods are *beschlagnahmte Waren*. These you cannot buy with your coupons.'

'What kind of things are *beschlagnahmte Waren*?'

'Luxury goods. Like coffee.'

'Coffee is a luxury?'

'In Berlin, yes. It is not so in London?'

'Real coffee is, yes. But you can still buy it if you can afford the price.'

'It is the same here,' said Kurt. 'But you will need even more money. And a permit. This is called *Bezugsschein*. It allows you a single purchase of one luxury item.'

'And how many *Bezugsschein* are you allowed?'

'Not many. And they are issued for ten day periods only. If they are not used they are worthless. It is the same with *Bezugsbeschränkle Waren*, like these.'

He gave me back my coupons.

'So when do these expire?'

'Tomorrow.' He sighed. 'It is a pity.'

I lit a cigarette. 'I need to go shopping.'

'You will need to register at shops. Come, I will take you.' He paused, nodding at my cigarette. 'Also tobacco is rationed. But you do not have to worry about this. Cigarettes I can always get. If you want to kill yourself smoking, it will not be a problem.'

'Thanks a lot,' I said, picking up my ration card and following him.

On the street, turning one way then the next between the rubble mountains, Kurt said, 'You are sometimes entitled to extra rations.'

'How?'

'If you can prove you are *Offer des Fachimus*. Then you are entitled to a higher level than your group.'

'And what does *Offer des Fachimus mean?*'

'A victim of fascism.'

'That's me,' I said. 'I was in the army six years because of the Nazis.'

He smiled regretfully. 'I think this is not good enough, Harry.'

'Oh? Then what does it take?'

He shrugged. 'Who knows? Look around. Who in Berlin is not a victim of fascism?'

I registered in the nearby shops and exchanged my ration coupons and Reichmarks for what little was on offer. I carried everything back to Arthur Peston's apartment and with time on my hands decided as an exercise in German and to familiarize myself with the rationing system, to attempt translating the small print on the back of the coupons.

Half an hour of consulting a dictionary, though, was sufficient to discover that the small print consisted mostly of warnings about lost or stolen cards. They would not be replaced. Nor were they transferrable. And if that wasn't enough, it put in writing the reality I had found on the street: that although the coupon stated the amount or the weight of goods allowed, the holder was by no means guaranteed that they would receive those amounts in practice.

The universal disclaimer writ in German.

To enshrine this caveat the meat and fish coupons were stamped F/A for *Fleisch/Austauschwaren,* which meant that in the place of meat one might get an alternative.

Just what the alternative might be was not specified and what small pleasure I derived in learning a new German phrase was immediately undercut. Memory brought on a feeling of queasiness.

As a schoolboy I had read a book about famous murderers, one of whom was a German named Fritz Haarmann. Known as the Butcher of Hanover, Haarmann had been guillotined a few years after the Great War for preying upon the young homeless youths who were washing through Hanover at the time. Tried and found guilty of murder, it had been revealed that he had disposed of the bodies of his victims by selling their flesh as meat in his butcher's shop.

~

After six years of war it was no secret that the Nazis hadn't been particular about those they enslaved. Kurt was half Dutch and although the other half of him was German it hadn't bothered them recruiting him as a foreign worker. Brought back to Berlin, the city of his birth, he had become another conscript in the army that Hitler had termed, *Auslälandische Arbeitskräfte.*

To everyone else they were simply *Zwangarbeiter.* Slave labourers.

I discovered Kurt to be remarkably phlegmatic about the experience.

Until the foreign workers had been forced to pick up the reins, it had been Jewish slave labour that had kept the factories running. Once the Nazis had squeezed all the work they could out of the Jews, it was found to be quicker to ship them straight to the death camps rather than exploit the diminishing returns of working them to death.

As more and more German men were conscripted into the army, the Reich resorted to scouring the conquered territories for fresh labour. At first a guest worker scheme had supplied their needs although as the war economy began to demand even greater productivity, Albert Speer, the Minister for Labour, discovered it easier to raise the numbers required at the point of a rifle, coercion being a more effective stratagem than relying on Joseph Goebbels' mendacious propaganda to entice workers to the Fatherland.

'It wasn't so bad,' Kurt said. 'My father was German so they could have put me in the army. Or the Waffen SS. I was lucky to end up in a factory.'

'I thought the Waffen SS were all volunteers,' I said.

'Maybe they were. But they were not all Nazis. Some joined for the food.'

I remarked it was surprising the ideology hadn't stuck in their throats.

Kurt shrugged philosophically.

'A man will swallow most things if he is hungry enough.'

I didn't recall Napoleon specifying the precise contents of the stomachs his Grand Armée had marched upon although I doubted it was ideology. Bread had always been the soldier's staple, which seemed fitting as our building had once been a flourmill.

Not that it looked much like one now. The semi-industrialized suburb of Moabit had been hit hard by the Allied bombing and at first glance one might have been forgiven for thinking that the whole area had been destroyed. Yet amid the ruins many habitable buildings could still be found. Places like the mill where, with a little imagination and salvaged timber, buildings that had once been working-class apartments could be turned into tolerable hovels.

Damaged as it was, the mill served not only Kurt Becker's needs but those of Schuyler Imports as well. That first morning after he had finished ferreting around in the crate and sorting through the saleable material, he gave me a run-down on Schuyler's operation.

Despite being set up as a front for intelligence gathering, Kurt had managed to turn it into a going concern. It helped, of course, that he did not have to pay for the electrical goods SIS sent us, but his entrepreneurial skills gave a credibility to the operation that, with luck, might fool anything other than a determined examination.

Most of what Schuyler handled came in by rail through the checkpoints at Oebisfelde and Griebnitzsee. Anything from the British Zone by road used one of Hitler's showpiece autobahns. Now and again an occasional crate was air-freighted through Gatow, the airfield in the Spandau district that served the British sector. This allowed Schuyler to keep a small office on the airfield, ostensibly to service imported air freight but mainly to enable us to send London anything that proved too awkward for Bill Harrington to handle. Since Schuyler's few goods were a drop in the immense ocean of material ceaselessly being ferried into the city to supply the Occupying Forces, it was thought anything coming or going our way would pass unnoticed.

As Arthur Peston had been in the habit of spending at least one day a week at Gatow, as well as making an occasional visit to the American airfield at Tempelhof, I assumed I was expected to carry on in the same fashion.

That was one reason why I was out at Templehof that particular morning in July when Kurt had business with his American black market connection.

The routine, alternating between Gatow and the mill on Stromstraße, was far from onerous. When not scouting out prospective dead-letter drops, or observing the possible candidates flagged up by Kurt and through whom we might possibly glean useful information, I busied myself with the paperwork. This, in reality, was little more than acknowledging and receipting the shipping manifests. I left Kurt to supervise the logistics of moving anything that turned up for Schuyler, arranging to have it collected and driven over by lorry to the mill. In return for this apparent commercial activity on our part, once a month the Schuyler Imports' account was credited with our operating expenses.

After looking through that one crate at the mill I didn't

trouble myself too much with the actual contents of what arrived. I left it to Kurt to handle. I suppose if I'd possessed any business acumen I might have started something on my own account. Importing genuine goods for sale, for instance. God knows Berlin was short of everything anyone could ever want. But the snag was most Berliners were also short of money, something that tends to put a crimp in any entrepreneurs' business plan. Not that there wasn't enough variety in the currency in circulation—westmarks, ostermarks, Nazi Reichsmarks ... even some of the notes printed long before the war by the old Weimar government.

Not to mention the almighty dollar, of course.

If I had ever thought of branching out on my own, however, electrical goods wouldn't have figured very high on the list of items to import. The city's electrical current was AC, the acronym universally used for alternate current. In Berlin, though, alternate current had now come to mean: now it worked, now it didn't.

Strompeere the Germans called it. A word which, unlike many of those harsh German compounded words, I thought sounded rather innocuous. The English translation was power cuts and the truth was, in Berlin, these could be lethal. The previous winter several thousand Berliners had died, those who hadn't succumbed to starvation simply freezing to death.

I had had a taste of that winter myself in England even if now, like everyone else in the city, I was complaining about the heat. So when I wasn't riding the malodorous U-Bahns or catching up on the tedious paperwork that even a front for a non-existent business apparently requires, I used to enjoy spending my time at the mill on Stromstraße.

It was a pleasant spot and if I didn't have much else to do I would clamber over the rubble of the ruined millstones, push the doors to the embankment open and smoke cigarettes while watching the barge traffic chug slowly up and down the river.

It was an agreeable means of idling away a summer morning while reflecting on what the hell I was doing there.

Die Fall

9

I had been in Berlin around ten days when Kurt announced he had persuaded Gerhard Prochnow to meet me. Kurt would bring Prochnow and his wife to the Zoo Club, one of the outlets for his the black market cigarettes.

The Zoo Club was where Mitzi Meier worked and the first time I went there I got socked on the jaw. That was a few days after my arrival and shortly after I had grown bored of staring at the wallpaper in Arthur Peston's apartment.

Back before the war I had read Christopher Isherwood's account of his stay in Berlin although if I had been expecting a post-war version of the Kit-Kat club I was disappointed.

At the foot of a flight of stone steps in an alley off the Kurfürstendamm, my first impression of the gloomy basement was of a castle dungeon the chatelaine had neglected to sweep through. The ceiling was low and some cardboard cut-outs of animals had been hung on the walls. Not that I had much opportunity to admire the decor that particular evening; no sooner had I bought a drink than I was laid out by a heavy-fisted Yank.

It was all over by the time I came round and in those moments before my head cleared, for some reason I imagined I was back in a tent in North Africa. I felt hot and dizzy and vaguely wondered if I hadn't picked up one of those bugs that were always doing the rounds in the desert. Then I became aware of the smell of beer and that a woman was dabbing my face with a damp cloth. I knew it was a woman because I could see her legs so something had to be wrong.

We had occasionally managed to get the odd bottle of beer in Africa but I couldn't remember ever having the opportunity to entertain women in our tents. When she spoke in German, since I knew I wasn't a POW, I jettisoned the whole notion of Africa.

I opened my mouth to reply but my still incomplete grasp of the language seemed to have been knocked out of my head. Not managing German, I said something in English.

'You are British?' she asked in English through a heavy German accent.

I tried to get up.

'Be still,' she insisted, 'You have not been awake.'

She went back to wiping my face with the cloth. I asked what had happened.

'It was nothing,' she said. 'A small fight. No one was hurt.'

The remark sounded a little callous from where I was lying but as I'd already come off second best in one argument I didn't feel up to starting a second.

When the bar cloth allowed, I took a peek at her. Her blonde hair framed an attractive face even if her hard blue eyes gave her—in a stern, Germanic sort of way—a somewhat unsympathetic appearance. But she was cradling me in her arms so I supposed there had to be a streak of compassion in her somewhere. I managed to push myself upright and saw the rest of her seemed in pretty good shape, too.

She helped me to my feet as one of the few fat Germans I'd seen since my return came waddling up. His pudgy cheeks wobbled as he apologised and brushed my clothes down with his pudgy hands.

'A drink, Mitzi, quickly,' he said, turning to the girl. '*Quickly*. On the house.'

Mitzi went around the bar, poured a glass of schnapps and placed it in front of me.

I drank the spirit, wincing as it stung a cut in my lip.

'It is split,' she said. In case I was wondering, I supposed. She filled the glass again.

'Look after him, Mitzi,' the fat German said as he hurried off in the wake of a couple who were heading towards the door.

'How do you feel?' the girl asked.

I took another sip of schnapps.

'Do you want to lie down?'

I wondered if that would be on the house as well. To judge by her expression, though, it hadn't been a business proposition.

'I'm okay,' I told her. 'Does this sort of thing happen often in here?'

'Fights? No. The military police come every night. The soldiers behave themselves.' She shrugged. 'The Russians are loud but Karl knows an officer. A *political* officer, if you know this...? Karl tells them this man's name, the Russians are all meek like *kinder*.'

'Good for Karl,' I said. 'Which one is he?'

'The fat one who gives you the drink. He is Karl Bauer. The owner.'

'And your name is Mitzi?'

'Yes. Mitzi Meier.'

'I'm Harry,' I said.

I offered her my hand but she didn't take it. Instead she jerked her chin at my mouth.

'Go home and clean up, Harry. Do you live far from here? You are not army, I think.'

'Not anymore,' I said. 'I live in Moabit.'

'You have a nice apartment? Is it in a good area?'

Given that most of Moabit had been flattened, I thought it an odd line in small talk. But perhaps Mitzi had an interest in real estate.

'Not bad,' I said. 'It's near the prison. You'll have to come up and see it sometime.'

Mitzi shook her head.

Mae West had always had better luck with that line than I ever did although I thought it might have been the proximity to the prison that hadn't impressed her.

I finished my schnapps and thanked her for wiping me down. As I started to leave she laid a hand on my arm.

'You will come back and buy me a drink sometime, Harry?'

With the German accent the suggestion sounded somewhere between an order and a proposition. It made me grin but that just opened the split in my lip again.

'I might do that,' I said, wiping away the blood.

I had satisfied one appetite that evening by eating bread and *wurst* in a bar I found down an alley off Klausewitzstraße before going to the Zoo Club. Meeting Mitzi Meier stirred another that had been lying dormant since my abortive affair in London with Magdalena Marshall.

I found Mitzi attractive. She had that somewhat dour appearance to which I have always been drawn. There had been a sadness about Magdalena which I had found appealing and I tried to recall if there had been a similar quality about my ex-wife, Penny. I didn't think so. At least, not when we first met. After we had been married it had been a different matter. I supposed it was possible that was the effect I had on women.

The idea it might be me that turned women sullen wasn't the sort of thing I cared to contemplate so I went back to thinking about Mitzi and her long legs.

She was tall and blonde in the way many German women were and also slim, again in the way many Germans in Berlin were. That, though, wasn't a voluntary condition. The club's owner, Karl Bauer, appeared to be an exception. He didn't look to have been constrained by rationing and was fatter than most. Fatter even than some of the Berlin politicians whose photos I'd seen in the newspapers.

You could usually spot anyone who worked in the higher echelons of the Administration by their silhouette. Neither did they wear that look of continual hunger which was to be found in the faces of ordinary Berliners. They had an inside track to better rations, a complaint as continual among those who didn't benefit as their hunger.

When I came to think about it, none of the Occupation Forces went hungry either. Or the black-market profiteers like Kurt, although for some reason he didn't seem to put on any weight. Then there were those in the Russian Sector where all the Party men got something on the side ... and their camp followers, the informers, the spies...

Looking at it from that perspective, the list of those doing better than the ordinary Berliners was even longer than Mitzi's legs.

And nowhere near as attractive.

10

Kurt's suggestion that my first meeting with Gerhard Prochnow at the Zoo Club should look like an accidental encounter struck me as a bit clumsy although I assumed he knew what he was doing.

So on the appointed evening I sat at a corner table nursing a beer trying not to look like a man waiting for someone to turn up.

As Bill Harrington had intimated, Arthur Peston's death had made Prochnow nervous and unwilling to continue the arrangement he had with us. In a way I could almost sympathize with him, stuck as he was between a rock and a hard place.

Like me Prochnow was classified as a group 3 *Angestellte* which entitled him to a bare two thousand calories a day, even though he also received the Russian *pajoks*. Gretchen, as a housewife, could expect even less.

Though the system had improved since the previous March when what was known as the "Hunger Card" had been in force—a Group 5 which had lumped housewives in with former Nazis and allowed only one thousand calories a day—it was still an iniquitous arrangement. One that people had learned how to circumvent by using the black market; a little extra food and clothing could always be bought if you had the money. But Kurt told me that now Gretchen wanted a better apartment and she wasn't going to buy that on the black market. Even if she could have, her husband didn't have the money.

It all suggested that if Prochnow wanted to provide Gretchen with what she wanted, he was going to have to run just to stand still.

In the event Kurt and the Prochnows were an hour late. By then my beer had gone flat and the subterfuge of an accidental meeting starting to wear thin.

'Harry,' he said, leading the others through the crowd and playing the scene as if he was auditioning for a film out at the old UFA studios. 'What are you doing here?'

Prochnow, trailing behind seemed less at ease with his part, acting more like a man in the grip of stage fright. His wife, a vivacious, oval-faced brunette didn't appear enthusiastic about the surroundings either.

As Kurt made the introductions, Prochnow's eyes darted from table to table. He had thin, sharp features and a nose with the kind of hook that on a fatter face one may not have noticed. In hungry Berlin it was as prominent as a meat cleaver.

I still hadn't broken the habit of fitting every German I met with a uniform and Gerhard Prochnow was no exception. I didn't think he was the kind of man who'd be comfortable in the field grey of the Wehrmacht but I had seen similar, arrogantly flared noses under the rakish angle of an SS cap. In a black uniform and sporting those lightning flashes and the death's head emblem, I thought he might have looked quite the part.

There had been no shortage of women who had found that combination attractive and I wondered if Gretchen Prochnow had been one of them. There must have been something about Prochnow that had snared his wife. With her dark curls and bright eyes Gretchen Prochnow would have stood out in a blackout.

I imagined that before war she would have been a conversation-stopper. Even to my uncritical eye, the war didn't look to have taken too much of a toll on her. Unlike Mitzi, I couldn't picture Gretchen Prochnow as a *Trümmerfrau* and wondered if she had perhaps spent the last few years sequestered down in Bavaria. Or in one of the old spa towns away from Berlin's rubble and the privations of war. And the lustful Russians who had followed it.

Skilfully made up, she wore a little blue jacket above one of those tight, tapering skirts that had been all the rage in the 1930s. Her auburn hair was tucked under a small cocked hat that had a touch of the German alps about it. Appropriate, as the glint in her eyes when they met mine shone bright enough to melt a glacier.

She smiled and I smiled back, beginning to understand why Prochnow was spending money to keep her happy.

'Harry's from London,' Kurt said, managing to make it sound like one of Thomas Cook's more exotic destinations.

The smile I was giving Gretchen was still pasted on my face as Mitzi walked up, saw it and threw me the kind of glare that could chill beer. Kurt dropped a pack of Lucky Strikes on the table and Gretchen's hand darted out like a striking cobra. She extracted one and held it expectantly towards Kurt's Zippo. Having recently bought the lighter off a Yank, it was now permanently glued to his hand.

'You are English?' Gretchen enquired through the smoke with exaggerated politeness, as if we hadn't spent the last years trying to bomb the hell out of each other. 'You must tell me all about London, Mr Tennant.'

'Harry,' I said.

'Drinks?' Mitzi barked curtly.

Kurt lit the rest of us up and I asked what everyone was drinking. In a moment we were raising enough smog to ground aircraft.

'You are with the Occupying Forces, Mr Tennant?' Prochnow asked, sustaining Kurt's fiction.

We were speaking German and I gave him the story about how a friend from the army had needed a man in his Berlin office.

'This is how Harry and I met,' Kurt put in. 'He handles the permits and licences.'

'Paperwork,' I added vaguely.

'We import electrical equipment. Everything has to come through the British or the Americans.'

'Or the French,' I added to shore up allied solidarity.

Mitzi brought our drinks and I dropped some Reichsmarks on her tray.

'Do you live in Berlin, Harry,' Gretchen asked as if it was possible I flew in everyday.

'Moabit,' I said. 'And you?'

'Pankow,' she replied, not sounding too happy about it. 'I would like to move.'

'I heard Halensee is nice,' I said, glancing at Mitzi who was still hovering over the table. 'Do you know it?'

Mitzi muttered under her breath and walked away.

'But of course,' said Gretchen. 'Before the war Gerhard used to take me boating there.' She turned to her husband and laid a hand on his. 'Good days,' she added.

Prochnow's mouth twitched beneath the hatchet nose, as if nostalgia for pre-war Germany was an unfit topic for polite conversation.

Gretchen prattled on regardless. 'Wouldn't it be nice if we could find a new apartment, Gerhard? Charlottenburg, perhaps. Pankow is so dirty.'

'Rooms are not so easy to find,' Kurt offered unhelpfully. 'It is expensive.'

Prochnow face soured and he shifted in his chair.

'We have a good apartment,' he said to his wife.

She pouted. 'The rooms are nice but I do not like Pankow, Gerhard.'

She held the pout a little longer but it must have been a touchy subject because she didn't pursue it and instead told her husband she would like to dance.

Being a Saturday night when troops had weekend passes, Karl Bauer had hired a band and cleared a space for dancing. The band was no great shakes, then perhaps the line-up were more accustomed to handling standard issue Gewehr rifles than musical instruments. Like good tailors, though, musicians were hard to come by in Berlin and we had all learned to cut our cloth accordingly.

Gretchen took a turn on the floor with her husband and then with Kurt. Dancing being my Achilles heel so to speak, when my turn came I made my usual excuses. But Gretchen wouldn't take no for an answer, grabbed my hand and pulled me onto the floor.

As I was English she might have been expecting a Buchanan. But I'm more of an Edgar than a Jack and after kicking her shin and stepping on her toes an American sergeant took the opportunity to cut in.

I saw Mitzi watching from across the room and executed a tactical withdrawal.

Back at the table I saw Prochnow had his jealous eye fixed on the American sergeant, still glued to his wife. He got up, excused himself and walked across the dance floor.

Kurt leaned towards me. 'He will meet you tomorrow morning. He says it will have to be early.'

I had told him I wanted to meet Prochnow alone as soon as feasible.

'Where?'

'He has suggested the Swiss embassy in the Tiergarten.'

'Where's that?'

'On Fürst-Bismarkstraße. You cannot miss it. It is the only building left standing.'

I remembered it then. The Russians had used it as a command centre for their final attack on the Reichstag. Every other building around it had been demolished, either in the fighting or earlier by the Nazis themselves in preparation for their "Great Hall", the building that was to be the showpiece of Hitler's new Germania.

'I know it,' I said, watching Prochnow cut in on the sergeant. 'What time?'

'Eight.'

The Yank reluctantly released his hold on Gretchen and the pair rejoined us.

Prochnow glanced at me and I nodded. Then Gretchen announced she was hungry, so they finished their drinks and we all shook hands again.

Mitzi wandered over to clear the table once they had left.

'You do not go with your friends?'

'Kurt's friends,' I said. 'I only just met them. They're going to eat.'

'And you are not hungry?'

'I can eat tomorrow.'

She frowned as if that made no sense.

'You should never refuse a meal,' she said.

'In that case, I'll buy you lunch tomorrow.'

'All right, Harry. Where?'

'Anywhere where the food is decent.'

'Anywhere that has food is decent,' she replied.

'Shall I come to your apartment in the morning? You could show me round Hallensee.'

'I like to sleep in on Sundays,' she said.

'So do I,' I said.

She didn't take the bait.

'Tomorrow afternoon. I can meet you here at three.'

'Isn't that a bit late for lunch?'

'Then we will call it something else.'

'Okay. Three it is.'

She brought me another beer and I lit a cigarette. I had to smoke my own since I had noticed Gretchen slip Kurt's pack into her bag as they were leaving.

11

The Swiss embassy on Fürst-Bismarkstraße lay a couple of hundred yards within the northern boundary of the Tiergarten. In the morning I took Alt Moabit east and crossed the Spree by the Moltke Bridge. A little further south near Konigs Platz were the remains of the Reichstag. When the building burned down in 1933 Hitler took over the Kroll opera house for use as the German parliament. It was at the Kroll from then on where the elected members sat waiting for the Führer to tell them how to vote.

I was tempted to take a stroll down there and pick through the rubble myself, to see if there were any souvenirs the Russians had missed. But the Red Army was known for its thoroughness and a Johnny-come-lately like me would have been wasting his time.

The Tiergarten had once been popular with Berliners out for a stroll. But it wasn't the park it used to be. Now its acres were unkempt, strewn with rubble and overgrown by scrub and weeds. And eight on a Sunday morning was too early for anyone except the odd dog-walker. One reason why, when I reached the embassy, it wasn't difficult to spot Prochnow. He was standing outside the building apparently admiring the architecture. Not that there was much to admire, not unless he was a connoisseur of scarred brick and pockmarked stone.

'Herr Tennant,' he said, trying to inject a measure of surprise into his voice, in the hope I suppose that anyone within earshot would take our meeting as chance.

'Herr Prochnow,' I retorted in a tone that wouldn't have

passed muster in a seaside pantomime. 'Did you enjoy your meal last night?'

'Yes. But of course it was very expensive.'

'Kurt is a generous man,' I said, assuming it had been Kurt who had picked up the bill and that I'd find the sum added to that month's expenses.

Prochnow answered judiciously, 'Yes, but more I think like your Shakespeare's Shylock.'

'You're saying Kurt's a Jew?'

Prochnow appeared concerned, as if I was accusing him of anti-Semitism. 'No, no, Herr Tennant, you misunderstand. I mean he will need to be repaid ... he will want his pound of flesh.'

That remark brought the Butcher of Hanover to mind again and I wondered where Kurt had taken them to eat.

'Kurt isn't the only one who will be wanting his pound of flesh,' I said. 'So will the people I work for. I am in Berlin to take over from Arthur Peston.'

'Herr Peston, yes,' Prochnow replied solemnly, the sorrowful note in his voice as artificial as our greeting had been.

We turned away from the embassy. In the early morning light his narrow face and sharp nose suddenly resembled an axe.

'His death was a shock, Herr Tennant. Even in this city where there have been so many deaths. Kurt tells me he fell from the *Flakturm*. It is not so easy to fall from the top, I am told. So how did Herr Peston fall, do you think?'

'I was going to ask you the same question.'

He looked shocked. We were back with pantomime again, Prochnow playing Babes in the Wood.

'I know only what Kurt tells me, Herr Tennant. This has caused me a problem, you understand.'

'Not just you,' I said. 'London regrets the delay. They are anxious to resume our exchange.'

'Exchange?'

'Of information.'

'Ah, I see. But this is not what I mean.'

'What do you mean?'

'You must know what I have been able to offer Herr Peston.'

'I know,' I said, 'and I have to tell you that London has not been impressed with the quality. We understood from Arthur Peston that you might be able to supply us with something a little more interesting.'

'Yes, yes, I am aware of this.' He faltered. 'Herr Peston, before he died ... he was impatient that I bring him more important material. I told him that regretfully this was not possible. That I have only restricted access, you understand. I work with SED statistics. Herr Peston was always asking for particular information.'

'Names? I understood you told him you would be able to supply us with names that would interest us.'

Prochnow's expression suggested the previous evening's meal was giving him indigestion.

'In a general manner this is true, Herr Tennant. The names of the SPD members who are sympathetic to a merger between our parties...'

'We don't need you to tell us that sort of information,' I assured him.

'No, of course. You mean that Herr Peston asked for names of KPD members working in the American and British sectors, I think. Unhappily for such information I do not have access.'

'I understood you were going to be even a little more specific than that, Gerhard.'

He looked surprised. 'In what way, Herr Tennant?'

'Not just names of those working in the Allied Zones. I mean names of those who are actively engaged as agents.'

His features set grimly.

'To this I have no access.'

'That is not the impression Arthur Peston received.'

'Perhaps Herr Peston believed I am a more important man than I am.'

'Now where could he have got that idea?'

We were walking along Alsenstraße towards the river. Beyond us a coal barge was making heavy way upstream. Its engine was coughing like a consumptive, trailing a sooty cloud of smoke in its wake.

'Perhaps Kurt...' Prochnow began before trailing off like the smoke.

We stopped by the embankment.

'Then we have a problem,' I said. 'I cannot persuade London to finance the purchase of information we could gather in a cheaper way. This will mean you will not find Kurt as generous as he has been. As for his pound of flesh ... well, he is a businessman as you know. But perhaps your employers will take a sympathetic view if you are in financial difficulties.'

'Herr Tennant—'

I turned to him. 'Unless you can think of an alternative solution?'

Prochnow looked at me earnestly, his brows knotting like corrugated iron.

'Before his death...' he began, 'I may have suggested to Herr Peston that there might be a way...'

'A way where, Gerhard?'

'There are those I know who are granted this sort of access. Members of the KPD who have a higher clearance than I. They are staunch comrades, naturally. Although I believe not all are happy with the way our Soviet colleagues treat us Germans.

'In what way are they unhappy?'

'Nothing is said openly, you understand.'

'Of course.'

'It is unspoken yet the atmosphere leads me to believe it is possible there are those who are not entirely content.'

'Not content? Do you mean by that they would be open to an approach?'

'You must not take me literally, Herr Tennant...'

Tired of listening to him dance all around the houses, I said:

'Do they have wives who like to spend money?'

When he began muttering reproachfully I interrupted.

'Tell you what, Gerhard, why don't you do a little scouting? Do you follow? You have friends who have access to what we want and you have friends who are unhappy. Why don't you see if you can't put two and two together and come up with a name?'

'This is not so easy,' he said hesitantly. 'By giving you a name I could be putting myself in danger. If the man does not think as I believe he might.'

'It sounds to me,' I said, 'as if you already have someone in mind.'

He started to wriggle, a worm on a hook.

'Does he have a name?'

'There is one man,' he finally allowed. 'A very cautious man, you understand.'

'He is KPD? Of good standing in the Party?'

'Oh, yes. During the war this man was in Moscow with Walter Ulbricht and Wilhelm Pieck. And with many of the other good communists who escaped the Nazis.' He inched a little closer and lowered his voice. 'But Comrade Stalin decreed that many of these Germans were not good Party men at all. And not only Germans, you understand. Also Hungarians and Czechs and many from the Baltic States... They were purged from the Party and sent to the Russian labour camps. Sometimes worse.'

'And your friend?'

'A colleague,' Prochnow amended. 'He is a colleague only. But he knows Pieck well and perhaps this is why he was not on any of Comrade Stalin's lists. When he returned to Germany he was given a good job. He knew many of those who were purged, however, and knew them to be innocent of the crimes with which they were charged.' He looked across the Spree. 'Those that *were* charged and who were not just taken away in the night. I have heard this colleague say that this is not the communism he fought for. He says he fought for a socialist Germany, not for a Russian puppet.'

'He says a lot for a cautious man, this colleague of yours. What do you say?'

Prochnow shrugged his shoulders apologetically.

'I am just a clerk, Herr Tennant. A small man trying to get by.'

Such self-effacing humility was a little hard to swallow that early on a Sunday morning. But I gulped it down and asked what kind of information this colleague of his had access to.

'He is well-placed and trusted,' Prochnow insisted. 'Through his work he mixes with the Russians, you understand. He makes contacts. He has access not only to the German KPD but to some Russian files, too. These are security files that are passed to the German security police. Translations, naturally, as we do not all speak Russian but too sensitive for our ordinary translators. This is why I think it is possible my colleague may have seen what you are looking for.'

'NKVD files?'

'They are now called the KGB,' said Prochnow.

Same fist, different glove, I might have pointed out.

'So, do you think your colleague would be prepared to meet me?'

Prochnow shook his head emphatically.

'As I have told you, he is a cautious man. I am telling you what I believe he may think. But it is not wise, Herr Tennant, to trust anyone on belief only. I would have to be certain of his discontent before I approach him.'

'Does he trust you?'

'Yes, he trusts me.'

'Is he married?'

'No.'

'Take him out for a drink,' I suggested. 'Take Gretchen along. Men like Gretchen. Perhaps your friend might like Gretchen.'

Prochnow stiffened, his hatchet nose wrinkling as if smelling something it didn't like.

'What is it you imply?'

'Relax, Gerhard. I only mean that he may be willing to talk more openly in an informal atmosphere. Away from the Party offices.'

He didn't reply immediately, pausing to light a cigarette.

'It might be possible,' he admitted. 'But to take him out for a drink or perhaps a meal would cost money, of course. And it could not be in the company of Kurt Becker. Or you either, Herr Tennant. I could not take him anywhere like that Zoo Club, you understand.'

'One of your straight-laced Party men, is he? You can take him to the Karl Marx Club as far as I'm concerned. I don't care where you go.'

'There is somewhere I know,' Prochnow said. 'In the French sector. I believe my colleague would like the atmosphere there. It is very relaxing.' He shrugged again. 'But such a place takes money...'

I took out my wallet and handed him a fistful of notes. He glanced around and quickly slipped them into his pocket.

'When you have news for me,' I said, 'you know how to get in touch.'

I walked away then looked back after a few yards to see him hurrying towards the Konprinzen bridge. He stopped to gaze down into the murky waters of the Spree for a few seconds before looking back in my direction. He saw me watching, straightened and headed off again, towards the Russian sector.

12

When Bill and I had arranged the place and time for our rotating meetings, one of the locations I suggested was the bar I had come across the first evening I had visited the Zoo Club. In the alley off Klausewitzstraße, it was quiet and out of the way yet only a few yards from the Kurfürstendamm.

I was seeing Bill there at noon. After that I was meeting Mitzi Meier outside the club at 3.00pm. Since I was early with time to kill, I decided to take another look at the Zoo Tower. After talking with Prochnow I had been thinking about Arthur Peston again and how he had fallen from the top.

Despite what Bill said, I was not convinced that Peston's death had been an accident. I had been up the tower when I'd been in Berlin in '45 and unless the layout had changed since then it wouldn't have been at all easy for anyone to fall from the top. Not unless they meant to. It was true that I didn't know much about Peston but from what I did know I had no reason to believe he would commit suicide.

Bill nor Kurt nor Prochnow had admitted to being aware that Peston was planning to meet anyone at the tower, yet he went there for some reason. Prochnow had also denied telling Peston he could supply us with the names of Soviet agents in the Allied sectors. Bill had told me Peston had intimated to him that he could. They couldn't both be right.

Conflicting statements weren't much to go one but if Peston's death wasn't suicide or, given what I knew of the tower, likely to have been an accident, it only left the conclusion that, if he had fallen he must have had some help.

I was new to Berlin in '45 and knew little about the city. One place I had heard of was the Tiergarten and its zoological gardens so when I was able it was one of the first places I visited. What I found there had proved a surprise.

The *Flakturm Tiergarten* was one of two gigantic platforms built in Berlin as anti-aircraft gun emplacements. The first time I saw it I was reminded of a drawing I'd seen of the storming of the Bastille during the French Revolution. In the picture the Paris mob were tiny, ant-size figures swarming beneath this huge *ancien régime* prison. Whoever the painter was, he'd taken some artistic licence. In reality the Bastille hadn't been that big.

The Zoo Tower was.

It had been one of the last places in Berlin to fall to the Red Army. Of the two towers in the Zoo complex the G-Tower was the main anti-aircraft platform. It also functioned as an air raid shelter and storehouse for safeguarding Berlin's art treasures.

Initially the Red Army had tried to destroy the towers with howitzers. When that didn't work the German officer commanding was offered the chance to evacuate the fortress. He used the opportunity to get his men away, leaving behind to the mercy of the Russians the thousands of petrified Berliners who had been taking shelter inside the fortress. When the Red Amy finally took the tower they found crammed alongside the civilians the contents of Berlin's museums and art galleries.

The civilians were turned out and the artworks shipped back to Moscow.

A few months later, the British tried their hand at bringing the towers down. Their efforts were no more successful than those of the Russians.

When I got there after leaving Prochnow that morning I saw the area had been cordoned off and a detachment of sappers packing the place with explosives ready for another try. It meant I couldn't get up the tower to test my hypothesis about how easy it might be to fall off and instead I spent an hour walking around the thing, thinking of how, if you wanted to meet someone, it would be so much easier to do so on the ground.

Having come to no definite conclusion, I did what the Paris mob outside the Bastille probably did and knocked off for something to eat. It would have been nice to eat some decent food and drink some good coffee sitting in the sun on a café terrace. Like most Berliners, though, I didn't have the money or the ration coupons to stretch to that sort of luxury so headed for the bar where I was to meet Bill and see what they had to offer.

A lump of solid German bread and *wurst* as it turned out, although washed down with a glass of beer it didn't prove too bad. Good enough for a prole like me, anyway. And probably far better than most of the malnourished indigents presently roaming Berlin's streets could expect for breakfast. Or lunch, or dinner too, come to that.

Bill was late.

'This is a hell of a place to find,' he complained, flicking open his old raincoat and dropping into the chair opposite me. 'I've been traipsing up and down the Kurfürstendamm for half an hour.'

'It's out of the way,' I agreed. 'That's why I suggested it.'

'Well, I'm here now.' He lit a cigarette and grumbled through the smoke. 'How are things going?'

I signalled the waiter to bring two beers.

'I met Prochnow last night.'

He perked up at that.

'I saw him again this morning, too.'

'Are we back in business?'

'He insists he hasn't got the access to what we want.'

'Being sorry butters no parsnips,' Bill said.

'I didn't say he was sorry. He says Arthur Peston must have misunderstood what he could deliver.'

'Arthur wasn't in the habit of misunderstanding that sort of thing.'

'Prochnow say he doesn't have the clearance.'

Bill's expression hardened. 'Then we'll cut the bastard off at the knees. See how he likes trying to raise the money to keep that wife of his somewhere else.'

The waiter brought our beers. Bill clammed up and went back to sucking on his cigarette.

'That's more or less what I suggested,' I said once the waiter had gone.

'And what did he have to say to that?'

'That he might know someone who could give us what we want.'

'I thought as much. Does he have a name for us?'

'Not yet. Did Arthur Peston say anything to you about a colleague of Prochnow's? Someone with Russian connections who spent the war in Moscow with Wilhelm Pieck?'

Bill sipped his beer. 'No, nothing that specific. Is that what Prochnow said, "Russian connections"?'

'Apparently this man is a KPD member.'

'And in Moscow with Pieck? If Arthur had told me something like that I'd have remembered. What he did do was hint that he might soon get something of real value. He didn't elaborate although I assumed it would be coming through Prochnow. Arthur always did like to play his cards close to his chest. He would never say much until he was ready. Did Prochnow actually tell you he talked to Arthur about this colleague of his?'

'No. But I think he would have if Arthur Peston was pressing him. Unless Prochnow is stringing us along, of course. Playing for time.'

Bill ground out his cigarette. 'All right. Let's assume he's not for the moment. Did he tell you why this man might be in the market? Is it money, like him?'

'No, nothing as specific as that. He did intimate that this man has become disillusioned with the comrades. The Russian variety, anyway.'

'Oh, how's that?'

'Because of Stalin's purges. Of the foreign communists in particular. According Prochnow, the only reason this colleague of his wasn't purged is because he's close to Pieck.'

'Can he arrange a meeting?'

'Not yet. Prochnow says this man's very cautious and he's

wary of approaching him directly in case he's not as disillusioned as Prochnow thinks he is. I told him to take the man out for a drink. An informal chat. I told him to take his wife along. She could butter Beria up.'

Bill grunted. 'Maybe, although I'm not sure how much she knows about where her husband's been getting his money. Kurt has always been careful not to say too much in her presence.'

'That's another thing,' I said. 'Prochnow wants to keep Kurt out of this.'

'That might be for the best. At least at first.'

'Would Peston have told Kurt if Prochnow had another source?'

'Anything's possible, Harry, but I doubt it. Arthur never gave much away until he was sure of his ground. It seems he died before he could take it any further.'

I glanced at my watch as Bill lit another cigarette.

'You got an appointment?'

'As a matter of fact I have. Three o'clock.'

'Anyone I know?'

'Just a girl,' I said.

'Is she clean?'

'I don't know her that well yet, Bill.'

'You know what I mean.'

'She didn't come looking for me, if that's what you mean.'

He let my reply hang in the air for a moment then reverted to business.

'Let's see how it develops shall we? Assuming it's not a fairy story and this colleague of Prochnow's is as good as he maintains, it'll be worth letting him have a little more rope. Not too long. If he thinks he can keep us dangling on a line he'll have to think again. Give him a week, Harry. Then he'll either have to put up or shut up.'

He finished his beer and dropped some coins on the table.

'Good work, Harry. Let me know as soon as you've got something.'

~

I stayed at the bar for a while after Bill left, thinking over what he'd said about Mitzi.

I may have been a novice in the game but I wasn't stupid. Since Mitzi and I had met there had been no explicit overtures made. I really couldn't see any way in which I was being set up. It had been my decision to visit the Zoo Club that first evening, and to go back there after having been knocked cold in the brief fight. That could hardly have been staged to ensnare me.

It was still possible, of course, and that there was more to Mitzi Meier than met the eye. From what I knew of the Russians, though—or the Germans for that matter—they were rarely that subtle. If they did know why I was in Berlin, there were far easier ways to pick me up than through the route Mitzi had taken.

But she *had* picked me up, of course. Literally and off the floor. Since then, though, I had been the one making the running.

Trying to get to know her better and using English rather than my less than fluent German, I had asked the usual questions: where was she from and what had she done before the war? Apart from telling me she was a Berliner, though, she had given very little away.

Anywhere else I might perhaps have taken such reticence as a lack of interest. But I had found most Germans reticent when it came to talking about the recent past. Those who didn't think too deeply about these things might have put that down to a sense of guilt. Or one of shame. There were plenty, of course, who did have something to hide but for most it was no more than a wish to avoid remembering the horrors of the last few years.

So if Mitzi Meier had been married, had a family, and what she had done before working in the club I didn't know. Apart from the fact she had been a *Trümmerfrau*. But that wasn't something easily hidden given those rough hands of hers.

I couldn't really blame her for a reluctance to speak about the past. Now the war was over, like many Berliners Mitzi seemed unwilling to talk about anything except the present. It was a demonstration of a detachment from reality, I recalled being told in one of the lectures I'd sat through back in

Cambridgeshire before coming out. Mostly tedious exercises in supplying information for which I could see I would have little use, this particular address had been given by a psychologist who was attempting to forewarn those bound for post-war Germany of the situation we would find in a defeated country. The talk had concerned the psychological state of the populace; how they regarded the Occupying Forces and the question of guilt.

It was one thing, I found, to sit in rural Cambridgeshire discussing the guilt a population might feel for what had happened in the war, and quite another to walk through the destruction that was Berlin and not feel some culpability oneself. In that situation it hardly mattered whether those one was passing on the street had supported the Nazis or not.

But one thing did stick in my mind. It was a term the psychologist used to describe the reaction many Germans suffered. He called it, *Emotionslämung,* an obscure German word that translated as "emotional paralysis".

It described a state of mind, the psychologist had explained, where normal feelings no longer applied, an emotional state of suspension where nothing penetrates deep enough to reach the soul.

Sometimes while talking with Mitzi, I couldn't help wondering if perhaps she was suffering from *Emotionslämung.* If she was, then I was doing little more than scratching at the facade she would present to people like me, those who were part of the machine that had destroyed her city and her country. And perhaps had destroyed her life.

I was not unaware that there was an argument to be had there. It was one that could often be overheard in cafés and bars and usually involved members of the Occupying Forces.

An argument which invariably ended in the statement: *You deserved what you got.*

I didn't know if Mitzi Meier had got what she deserved, but I was coming to realize that it was a pointless exercise attempting to engage her in discussing it.

~

She was waiting outside the club when I arrived. She took my arm as we walked towards the Tiergarten.

The afternoon was warm and there were more people in the park than earlier that morning when I'd met Prochnow. The sappers were still at work by the Zoo Tower and a crowd stood watching them.

'They're going to try to blow up the towers,' I told her.

She regarded the scene phlegmatically. 'Why go to this trouble?'

'Becuase they decided the *Flakturms* are monuments to National Socialism. A reminder of the Hitler years.'

She laughed humourlessly. 'Do they think we will forget when the towers are gone?'

'I think we're the ones trying to forget,' I said.

'We?'

'Well, I can't speak for the Russians but I'm sure the British and the Americans would like to forget. And the French, too. Certainly the French, under the circumstances. I wouldn't mind forgetting myself, come to that.'

'Why you, Harry?'

'Because these last few years everything has changed. We're different people now.'

She gave my arm a tug and we turned away from the towers.

'How are you different?

'Would you believe that before the war I was a policeman?'

She looked at me sideways. 'What kind? *Kripo?*'

'No. Just an ordinary copper.'

'*Copper?*'

'A policeman in uniform. Bottom of the ladder.'

'And now? You are still a policeman?'

'No, not now. I told you. I'm a businessman.'

'Export and import?' she said, phrasing the words the way people usually did when they didn't believe it.

'Only import,' I said. 'You want a capacitor or a radio valve, I'm the man who can get you one.'

'What is a capacitor?'

'Much like a condenser.'

'And this is what you import?'

'Yes.'

'Why don't you bring us something useful. Like food.'

'That's exactly what I said,' I told her. 'But if we tried, the Russians would steal it at the border.'

'And they don't steal your capacitors?'

'No. For some reason they don't.'

'Then they have no value,' said Mitzi.

I wasn't sure she wasn't right and changed the subject.

'What is it you want to do, Mitzi? Not work in a club for the rest of your life.'

She looked at me in amazement. '*Do*? I want to eat. Don't you?'

We found a restaurant where I was profligate with my money and ration coupons in the hope of impressing her.

I don't know if it worked but she seemed happy enough in my company. Conversation didn't prove difficult although despite remaining unforthcoming about her own past, she displayed no reticence in asking me what I had done in the war. Perhaps she was checking if I had been in a position to shoot one of her relatives, I don't know. I was pleased to oblige her and gave her a rundown of my time in North Africa and Italy. If I'd been hoping my reminiscences would draw some from her, I was disappointed. By the time we left the restaurant I'd learned no more about her than I already knew.

And there wasn't much of that.

She didn't have to work that evening and at nine announced she was going home. She liked to sleep in on Sundays, she said, and preferred to go to bed early too if she could. The way she put it didn't sound like an invitation to join her so I bit back the sort of rejoinder that usually springs to my lips under those circumstances and walked her to the nearest S-Bahn. I gave her a chaste peck on the cheek and told her I had enjoyed the day. Then I reluctantly bade her goodnight.

13

The next morning at the mill Kurt asked how it had gone with Prochnow. I told him the SED man had been full of excuses. How he had suggested that Arthur Peston had misunderstood the level of access Prochnow had at Liepzigerstraße 35.

'Herr Peston was not a man to misunderstand something like that,' said Kurt.

'That's what Bill said.'

He was boxing up components for selling on, casting around for packing material. He picked up some old newspaper and a length of string.

I asked if Arthur Peston had ever mention a possible new source to him. Someone Prochnow worked with at Liepzigerstraße.

Kurt closed the flaps on his cardboard box and wrapped string around it. He stopped halfway through tying the knot.

'I do not think so, Harry. If there was a new source he would have told me. Herr Peston arranged everything through me. This is the way we worked.'

'That's what I thought,' I said.

'Why do you ask? Has Prochnow said there might be a new source?'

'It was probably just another excuse,' I said.

He put his parcel aside and began filling another box.

'Bill told me to give Prochnow a week,' I said. 'If he hasn't come up with anything by then he wants to cut him loose.'

Kurt looked up sharply. 'He wants to drop Prochnow?'

'If he's not bringing us anything.'

'What about my money?'

'That's the point,' I said. 'We're not going to keep paying for worthless information. Bill told me Prochnow had settled your debt.'

'Yes but now he owes me again. I paid for everything on Saturday. The dinner, the drinks... He asked for another loan also. Gretchen has seen a new dress. It is very expensive, he told me.'

'He wants you to buy it?'

'No, Harry. *He* wants to buy it. I am only supposed to give him the money.'

'Gretchen is a demanding woman.'

Kurt shrugged. 'He likes to keep her happy.'

'Maybe he does, but he'll need to keep us happy if he's going to keep her happy. How much did you give him?'

'Enough for the dress. I thought you would want to keep him happy.'

'Don't give him any more,' I said. 'The next thing will be Gretchen wanting gloves and a hat to go with the dress. As it was I gave him some Reichmarks yesterday to take this colleague of his out.'

Kurt's ears pricked up. 'What colleague? Who is this?'

'Oh, one of the people he works with,' I replied as casually as I could, annoyed for mentioning the man when I hadn't meant to. 'That's why I asked if Arthur Peston had said anything.'

Kurt was looking at me reproachfully. 'Prochnow should come to me first if there is another source. That is the way it works, Harry.'

'It's just as likely,' I told him, wishing I'd kept my mouth shut, as neither Prochnow nor Bill had wanted Kurt involved, 'he made this colleague up because I was putting pressure on him. He may not exist at all.'

'But you still give him money,' Kurt grumbled. 'I think maybe I should talk with Herr Prochnow.'

'No, don't do that,' I said. 'Bill said to give him a week. So let's see what happens. The last thing we want to do is scare him off again.'

Kurt muttered, far from mollified. 'A week then. But we make sure I get my money back before we drop him, okay?'

'Sure,' I replied. 'Keep a note of what you've spent and gave him and I'll add it to next month's expenses.' Then, before he could complain any more, I said, 'I think I'll go out to Gatow this morning. There's that delivery coming in. I'd better chase it up in case it's important.'

We had been advised to expect something by air freight in the next week and, although as far as I knew no delivery we ever received was important, I didn't want to discuss Prochnow and his colleague any further.

I stopped to pick up the papers on my way to the StadtBahn Bahnhof. One of the suggestions I'd been given during my Cambridgeshire course was to study the local press, not just as a way to keep abreast of the political currents running through the city but also to improve my German.

There was only just so much news to be had in Berlin, though, news that was fit to print anyway. I skimmed what there was while I rode out to Gatow.

Despite the fact there were several different newspapers in the city they inevitably all covered the same stories. Each paper had its own slant depending upon which side of the political divide they stood. The SED ran *Neues Deutchland* and *Täliche Rundschau,* both of which toed the Party line and parroted whatever view the Soviet sector rag, *Berlin am Mittag,* printed. The American sector put out *Der Tagesspiegel* while the British had *Telegraf,* both much of a muchness in their respective attitudes. The French had their own paper, *Der Kurier,* although I rarely bothered with that.

Aptly enough, the most entertaining and informative paper was a woman's weekly called *Sie.* I had come across Mitzi reading a copy at the club one slack evening and had taken it back to Peston's apartment with me once she had finished with it.

I say "aptly", because the impression one got in Berlin was that it was the women who had kept the city on its feet. Most of them had managed to keep their spirit up too, despite what the Russians had done when they'd taken the city. Stories of mass rape and murder back in April and May of '45 were rife. It was easy to believe that the only German the Russians had bothered to learn was *'Frau komm,'* an order which generally proved a prelude to rape.

I would have liked to know how Mitzi had fared after the fall of the city, yet it wasn't the sort of question one could come straight out and ask. I was hoping that on better acquaintance I might be able to raise the subject, but we hadn't reached that stage yet.

Once I got to Gatow and established there was nothing waiting for Schuyler Imports, I hung around the airfield until boredom reached a critical level. Then I rode back into the city to find somewhere to eat and kill the time until the Zoo Club opened.

Since my strategy was to demonstrate an interest—but not an unhealthy over-eagerness—in Mitzi, I gave it half-an-hour after the doors opened that evening before I descended the steps into Karl Bauer's club once again.

Being early the place wasn't crowded. A smattering of uniforms were milling around the bar, a group of Russians among them whom everyone, notably the girls, were giving a wide berth. Karl Bauer was trying to push a couple towards the Russians but they didn't look very enthusiastic.

I took a table, noticing that Mitzi was keeping out of the Russians' way, too. Perhaps she sensed me looking at her because she glanced in my direction and walked over.

'Harry,' she said, giving me a weak smile. 'I hoped you would come. I do not feel well. I will tell Karl I want to go home.'

'What's the matter? Can I get you something?'

She looked all right to me although there was always talk of typhus and cholera in Berlin. The intermittent nature of the water supply never did much to instil confidence in its cleanliness.

'I feel faint,' she said. 'I will go home. Would you walk me to the station, please?'

'Of course.'

She went over to speak to Karl who was still trying to chivvy his girls towards the Russians. One said something to Mitzi and I saw them exchange a few short words. The Russian glanced in my direction then turned away. Karl Bauer to judge by the expression on his face he wasn't being sympathetic but after a moment he shooed her away with an impatient hand.

She came back to my table. "Thank you, Harry. Karl said I can go home.'

At the door we stepped aside for a group of noisy Yanks coming in. One of them addressed Mitzi, took her by the arm and tried to turn her around. I was on the point of stepping in despite the sock on the jaw I'd got when she said something to the Yank I didn't catch.

'Sure, honey,' he said, letting her go and continuing down the steps into the club.

'A friend of yours?' I asked as we reached street level.

'No, Harry,' Mitzi said. 'He is only a customer.'

She took my arm as we walked towards the Zoo S-Bahn.

'How are you feeling?' I asked while we waited for the train to Halensee.

'Better,' she said. 'It was hot in the club. But I feel better now. This is very good of you, Harry.'

I hadn't noticed it had been any hotter than usual. Concerned she might be coming down with something, when the train pulled into the station I suggested I'd better ride along with her.

'Just in case,' I said.

'I do not wish to spoil your evening.'

'It's no trouble.'

We managed to find a seat.

'I see you had some Russians in,' I said.

'Did we?' she replied. 'I did not notice.'

At the Halensee Bahnhof she said she would take a tram.

'It is not far but I do not want to walk.'

So we waited until a tram came along, not speaking until we reached Koenigsallee. We got off. Out of the city she seemed to brighten up and as we turned into Margaretenstraße she said:

'Where I live is not far. If you have the time I can give you coffee. *Real* coffee, I mean.'

'Only if you are feeling up to it,' I said.

'I feel much better now. Thank you.'

'So, where did you get real coffee from?' I asked.

'From Karl. He keeps it for his rich friends.'

'And he gives you some?'

'No, Harry, of course not.'

'What, you mean you steal it?'

She turned towards me in the twilight. 'Why not? He steals it, so what is the difference if I steal from him? Or maybe you have scruples for such things?'

'No,' I said.

'Even when you are once a policeman?'

'I wasn't a very good policeman.'

We turned onto a gravel road. She linked her arm through mine.

'Do the English not drink real coffee in London?'

'If they are rich enough,' I said.

'And you are not rich, Harry?'

97

'I wouldn't be in Berlin if I was.'

She fell quiet. At the end of a gravel drive a house loomed out of the dark ahead of us. No lights showed at the windows and remembering the Russian and the Yank in the club, I wondered what I was letting myself in for. Mitzi took a key from her bag and unlocked the front door. I waited in a large and gloomy hall while she flicked the light switch up and down to no effect.

'No electricity,' she said.

'Does that mean no coffee?'

'I can make it on my stove.'

She took my hand and led me towards the dark stairs.

A few steps up I heard a door open in the hall below us. Mitzi took no notice and we climbed on up two more flights. She led me down a corridor to a door.

'This is where I live.'

Inside the apartment, last of the evening light was filtering through an uncurtained window.

She let go of my hand, crossed the room and struck a match, bending over a tile stove. Paper flared and kindling began to crackle. The light from the flames made our shadows dance across the walls. Mitzi filled a pot with water, took a jar down from a cupboard and put the coffee on the stove.

She excused herself.

'The bathroom is down the hall. I will not be long.'

The light shed by the stove cast a sinister shadow across the room and while she was gone I looked around, paying lip service to Bill's concerns. The stove stood beside the sink and some ill-matched furniture was spread around the room: a sofa with ripped upholstery, a heavy table and chairs and an old dresser. The wallpaper was stained by damp and hung in strips in places like peeling skin.

I had been expecting better I suppose. That said, it was no worse than some of the other Berlin apartments I'd seen. A door led into a bedroom. I struck a match and saw a double bed, side table and a dressing table by its light. It looked neater as if this might be where she spent most of her time.

I was back in the sitting room looking out the window when she returned.

She stood next to me.

'There is a garden and a lake.'

'All your own?'

She pulled a face as if my question had been serious.

'Of course not. But no one uses it now. You will not have a lake at your apartment near the prison, Harry. It is better living here, I think.'

As far as the decor and furniture went, I didn't think it was, although I wasn't about to tell her. I didn't have a lake, it was true, but I had the Spree close by. And even if I couldn't quite see it from any of my windows, I could at least smell it.

'Do you live alone?' I asked.

'Do you mean am I with a man?'

'I suppose I do.'

'I live by myself.'

It was fully dark now except for the glow from the stove. But I didn't need a light to know she was standing very close to me.

The window wasn't big and we had already seen all there was see yet she didn't move away. So I put an arm around her and pulled her even closer.

She came willingly and, occupied as we were for the next few minutes, when the coffee finally boiled we didn't even didn't hear it.

14

Kurt was eating sauerkraut on black bread that looked as hard as the millstones piled at the other end of the room. He glanced up, spooning cabbage from a jar big enough to marinade a U-boat and made a comment about the fact I hadn't shaved.

'No time,' I said.

'Too busy?'

'That's right.'

'Maybe you wear the same shirt, too?'

'Maybe I do,' I said.

'Was it a girl from the Zoo Club?'

'A girl?'

'Which one, Harry?'

'Which one do you think?'

'Mitzi,' he said without hesitation.

'How did you know?'

'She is your type.'

I didn't ask what my type was. I wasn't sure I wanted to know.

'She lives in Halensee?' Kurt asked.

'Yes.' I sat at the table and lit a cigarette. 'What do you know about her?'

'Only that she has worked for Karl since I supply him with cigarettes. What is it you want to know? If you can trust her?'

'I suppose so,' I said.

He shrugged. 'Why not? But it is better you do not tell her what we do. She is smarter than the others, I think. Her and that other one.'

'The tall one with the shoulders?'

'Yes.'

'Marthe,' I said.

Marthe and Mitzi had been friends since they had both been *Trümmerfrau* together. I didn't think either were typical bar girls although I supposed it beat cleaning bricks.

'Have you ever seen Mitzi with anyone in particular?' I asked, watching him eat.

'Marthe,' he said.

'I mean a man.'

'There was a Yank who used to go to the Zoo Club.'

'Recently?'

'I have not seen him for maybe three weeks ... a month.'

'What happened to him?'

He shrugged again. 'What happens to all of you in the end. He went home.'

I might have reminded him that Arthur Peston hadn't gone home, but it was hardly relevant.

Kurt went back to his bread and sauerkraut.

If he knew anything else about Mitzi it didn't look as though he was going to tell me. I sat at the desk and started going through the latest shipment manifests.

~

For the rest of that week I spent my evenings at the club and my nights with Mitzi in Halensee. After Kurt's remarks I took the precaution of leaving a razor and a couple of clean shirts there. Not because Kurt's questions embarrassed me but in case I saw Bill. He wouldn't have missed that sort of sign either. Then on Thursday while we were in bed Mitzi mumbled something in my ear about how nice it would be to have me there in Halensee when she came home from work. Given what we were doing at the time, I didn't think she was talking about having a hot meal waiting.

I gave the idea some thought, weighing up the pros and cons for a couple of seconds, then said I could bring my things over the next day.

On Friday morning, though, Kurt announced that Prochnow had been in touch and wanted to meet me again.

'Where?' I asked, relieved that something was happening at last.

'The Swiss embassy.'

'Again? Is that wise? What time?'

'Seven.'

'This evening?'

'Tomorrow morning.'

'Christ, Kurt! Does it have to be so early?'

'It is so he has time to get to work. The Party make the comrades work on Saturday mornings and no one must be late. They have to show they are fully committing themselves. If not it could mean they lose their *pajoks*.'

'The workers' paradise,' I said.

It didn't take long to realize that if I spent the night with Mitzi in Halensee I'd have to get up at some unfeasible hour of the morning to catch a tram and a train to make sure I'd be at the Swiss Embassy for seven. So, in the club that evening I made an excuse about having to get to work early and that I'd sleep over at the apartment in Moabit.

'You work on Saturdays now?' she said sulkily. 'Or are you tired of me already? Have you someone else so soon, Harry?'

'No, of course not,' I said. 'I have to meet someone, that's

101

all. He insists it must be early.'

'Who is this? A woman?'

'A man,' I said. 'No one you know.'

'I thought we would go shopping.'

It was the first I'd heard of it.

'Running short of cream?'

'It is not a joke.'

'I won't be long. I'll see this fellow, pick up my things and bring them back with me. You'll probably still be in bed by the time I get there.'

'Then I will wait for you in bed,' she said, having already found my Achilles Heel.

In the event I was late leaving the club and overslept.

With my razor in Halensee and no time to shave anyway, I dressed hurriedly and crossed the Moltke Bridge into the Tiergarten, worrying that Prochnow might not wait if I wasn't there by seven.

I reached Fürst-Bismarkstraße sweating and as dishevelled as if I'd slept the night under the bridge.

Prochnow didn't appear too fresh either, looking like a man who was losing sleep.

'Have you talked to your colleague?' I asked before he could start on his excuses.

'I spoke to him but this takes time, Herr Tennant. You understand, one cannot come straight out and ask a man if he is willing to compromise his principles.'

I felt like asking if it takes any longer than finding a euphemism for betrayal they were both happy with. I didn't know the German for "euphemism" though, so I asked if we were going to get what we had been promised.

'My colleague made no promises.'

'You're the one who made the promises, Gerhard,' I reminded him. 'If you can't come up with what you said you could, how do I know this friend of yours can?'

'As I have explained, he is not a friend he is—'

'I know, a colleague. What does this *colleague* say?'

He glanced around before moving away from the embassy gate and walking a few paces. I pointedly sighed and followed.

'He is prepared to discuss your offer,' Prochnow whispered.

'But he needs safeguards.'

As I hadn't yet made any offers it wasn't the answer I was looking for. I was about to let him know as much when he took a sheet of paper from his jacket.

'He told me to give you this.'

I unfolded it and saw half-a-dozen typed German names. There was no heading or official stamp on the paper, nothing that might suggest from where it had come.

'Are these the names of KDP agents working in the Allied sectors?'

'My colleague told me you should give it to your people. He said they will appreciate its value.'

'Do you know these people?'

He shook his head. 'No. My colleague did not tell me, only that you will recognize some of the names.'

I folded the list into my pocket. 'Is that it or will there be more?'

Prochnow was looking pleased with himself.

'He told me to tell you it is an initial gesture of good faith. A demonstration that he can get you not only what you want but also more. Something big, he says. He did not tell me what exactly. Just something big. But, as I said, first he needs certain safeguards.'

'Such as?'

'I cannot say. You are to pass the list to your superiors. If when we meet next you are convinced he is able to supply what you want, we will talk again.'

'Will I meet him, to discuss these safeguards?'

'No. I told you, he is a very cautious man. Once you have evaluated the list and he is satisfied the conditions are right, he is prepared to meet you.'

'Okay,' I agreed. 'I'll get these names to my people. Once I hear from them I'll get Kurt to let you know.'

'I trust you have not told Kurt about this, Herr Tennant. As we agreed?'

'Everything is on trust, Gerhard. That's how it works.'

I could see he was working himself up towards some sort of complaint so I quickly reminded him he needed to get to work if he wasn't going to be late.

At the mill I showed Kurt the list, telling him it came from Prochnow.

'I know two of these names,' he said. 'They are men who have jobs in the Administration. Another I know by reputation.'

'Which one?'

'Günther Krause. If it is the same man.'

'What kind of reputation? If it is the same man.'

He passed the sheet back.

'I heard he used to be Gestapo.'

'And what is he now?'

'Now? He could be anything.'

'I understood the Russians won't use ex-Nazis.'

Kurt shrugged. 'But the Allies have no such scruples. They would rather employ an ex-Nazi than a communist. So, if this man was Nazi but is now communist, what is a better cover?'

The Military Mission on Hohenstaufenstraße was a small dusty suite of rooms in what had once been a lawyer's office. The man's shingle was still attached the wall next to the front door even if the rest of the building looked like something Henry VIII had left behind once he'd finished dissolving the monasteries.

I asked for Sergeant Andy Thurston and despite it being a Saturday was lucky enough to find him on duty. He came through from the back office, a bluff, heavy-set man who once out of the army might well be able to make a decent living in films playing bluff, heavy-set NCOs

He looked me up and down as if sizing me for a uniform.

'I'm Harry Tennant,' I said.

He pulled on his fleshy nose with a thumb and forefinger then pointed them at me like a gun.

'Harry Tennant,' he said. 'Of course. Used to run that army unit with Jack Hibbert a year or two ago. Graves Registration, wasn't it?'

'That's right,' I said, playing along. 'Jack told me to look you up when I got to Berlin.'

'How is he?'

'In trouble as usual.'

'That's Jack,' Thurston said. 'I was about to brew up. If you've got time, come on through and we can have a natter.'

He closed the office door behind us and put out his hand.

'Bill Harrington said you'd come by if you had anything for him.'

I took Prochnow's list from my pocket.

'He'll know where I got it. I just need—'

'No details, thanks Harry. That's between you and Bill. Not BRIXMIS business.'

'Right,' I said.

'Sit down and have that tea. Ten minutes will do it, just for form's sake.'

He put his head out the door and called for two mugs of tea then came back and slipped Prochnow's list into an envelope.

'I'll get it couriered out to HQ. Bill can contact you if he needs to?'

'I'm due to see him tomorrow. I thought he might want a look at that first.'

Thurson wrote something on the envelope, walked out the office again and came back a minute later with two mugs of tea.

'He'll have it in half an hour.'

After ten minutes spent drinking Thurston's tea and passing the time of day I went back to Peston's apartment. The water was still on so I drew enough for a decent bath, dressed and packed all my clothes apart from one clean shirt and a change of underwear in my suitcase. That done I locked Peston's door behind me and took the S-Bahn to Halensee.

As I had expected, I caught Mitzi still in bed. What I hadn't expected was for Frau Ernst to catch me, creeping through the hall, suitcase in hand, like a travelling salesman who'd got lucky.

'Herr Tennant, is it?'

Since she had cornered me and Mitzi a couple of days earlier, pointedly waiting until I had been introduced, I didn't think I'd get away denying the fact.

'Frau Ernst,' I said. 'Are you and your son well?'

Which was a stupid question as it gave her the perfect gambit to begin voicing all her grievances.

'He has pain, Herr Tennant. The drugs he needs are expensive and difficult to find. You are a businessman, Frau Meier tells me. You have connections with British doctors, perhaps?'

Her eyes strayed to my case as if hoping I travelled in pharmaceutical supplies and the thing might be stuffed with samples.

'Electrical components,' I said.

'Electrical? Ah, I see ... there is a shortage in Berlin. But Germany is short of everything these days, is she not?'

She glanced at my case again.

'You are thinking of staying with Frau Meier, Herr Tennant?'

'She did not tell you?'

'No, Frau Meier has said nothing to me. Her business is none of mine, of course, and I know only too well how difficult it can be for a widow. But still...'

She left the moral admonition hanging in the air.

'A widow?'

Frau Ernst feigned discomposure, implying she had said something more than she should.

'Excuse me, Herr Tennant. She calls herself *Frau* Meier. I naturally assumed... The war, you understand. So many men killed. But, as I say, Frau Meier's business is not mine.'

I made to leave.

'Of course,' Frau Ernst went on quickly, 'if you are to share the apartment this will regrettably mean an increase in the rent. After all, the water and the electricity... Two people will use more than one. You must appreciate this. And I will have to consult the owner, Herr Neumann, naturally.'

Mitzi hadn't warned me about this but I wasn't going to stand in the hall, suitcase in hand, arguing the toss.

'I am sure we can come to some arrangement, Frau Ernst.'

'And the rent was due yesterday...'

We haggled for a minute or two and came to an agreement on an only marginally outrageous sum. Once the notes were in her grasping hand Frau Ernst let me go and withdrew into her own apartment.

Upstairs Mitzi was asleep. I looked at her enviously, having managed only a few hours myself the previous night, rushing ever since from pillar to post. I put my suitcase down, undressed and climbed in beside her. She turned, opened her eyes briefly to identify the intruder then muttered something in German and fell asleep again.

We got up late that afternoon. Shopping was now off the agenda and instead Mitzi cooked a small meal and made an even smaller space in her cupboards for my meagre wardrobe.

We took a walk by the lake and I told her how Frau Ernst had said the rent would rise if I was staying there.

Mitzi used one of the coarser German words I was familiar with.

'The witch will pocket the money herself. She will not tell Herr Neumann anything. You should not have paid her, Harry. I will talk to her. She knows better than try to argue with me.'

I was hoping to bring up the subject of Frau Ernst believing Mitzi to be a widow. But on reflection and under the circumstances, I decided it would be politic to suppress my curiosity for a little longer.

~

I was to meet Bill in the Grunwald the following afternoon. He was sitting outside the café we'd used the day I arrived, a packet of Gold Flake on the table in front of him beside a coffee cup and an ashtray. The cup was empty; the ashtray was full.

He looked up in that lugubrious manner of his, at odds with both his build and his owlish expression, and signalled to the waiter for two more coffees.

'You look tired,' he said. 'Are you getting enough sleep?'

Being Saturday the club had been busy and Mitzi and I had been late getting home. I had planned to let Bill know I had changed my address but after his remark about sleeping changed my mind.

'It's probably the warm weather,' I said instead, reaching for his Gold Flakes. 'Do you mind? It'll make a change from American smokes.'

'Help yourself,' he said. 'How are you getting on with Kurt?'

'Fine.'

The waiter brought our coffee and left with Bill's money.

'Did you get the list?' I asked once the waiter was out of earshot.

'Yes.'

'Any good?'

'A couple of surprises. The others we knew about.'

'Kurt said one was ex-Gestapo.'

'You showed it to Kurt?'

'I told him it originated with Prochnow.'

'What else did you tell him?'

'Nothing.'

Bill sipped his coffee. 'Günther Krause. He was one of the surprises.'

'The fact they are using a Nazi?'

'In part. More that Krause is willing to work for them.'

'What happens to him now?'

'Not my decision,' Bill said. 'But we'll probably try to turn him. I doubt he'll take much persuading given his past. He knows he won't have much of a future if we throw him back so he doesn't have much choice unless he works for us.'

'What good will he be?'

'Probably as a channel for letting the comrades know things we'd like them to believe. But, as I said, that's up to London.'

'How is it he's working in the Administration? Kurt knew he had been Gestapo. Others must have.'

'You're right there, Harry. Others must have. But that's the reality of life here. There's a lot like Günther Krause still out there. Small fry who have been through de-Nazification and taken back. If Krause had been big enough I daresay he would have been prosecuted. He wasn't, so...'

I pulled on Bill's Gold Flake, hoping to take away the taste, and not only of the coffee.

'What do you want me to tell Prochnow?'

'Tell him that as an indication of his colleague's good faith it's a start. Anything more will depend on what else he's got to offer.'

'Something big, according to Prochnow.'

'They all promise something big, Harry. That's another of the realities of life here.'

'Do you want me to find out what his terms are?'

'Yes. Prochnow needs to tell us precisely what this fellow is offering and what he wants in return. Arrange a meeting if possible. Tell Prochnow we're happy to go through him for the moment but make it clear that we will need to know exactly who we are dealing with if anything significant is in the offing. That you will have to meet this colleague of his at that point.'

'Have you considered the possibility that what they are offering might be what they would like *us* to believe?'

Bill smiled. 'That's the trick of it, old son. Being able to tell the difference. You're the first hurdle he has to jump. Once he's over you, he's got to clear me. That's why, just now, the substance of what he's offering doesn't concern you. What concerns you is the man himself. Is he right, or is he wrong?'

~

Over the next few days I had time to consider what had given Bill the idea I was capable of evaluating whether a man was dependable or not. I still had no idea who had recommended me to Kim Philby and, while I may have come to them with a reputation, I didn't think it would have been for being a good judge of character.

On Monday I told Kurt to get a message to Prochnow to the effect that we were pleased with what he had brought us and that I would like to meet him again him as soon as possible.

That done, there was little for me to do except to wait.

I assumed the new source, Prochnow's colleague, would have his own ideas as to how he wanted to proceed as regards communication. In the interim though, in case they were needed, I spent a couple of days scouting for likely dead-letter drops, haunting the ruins of the Tiergarten like a landscape gardener bereft of ideas.

Towards the end of the week Prochnow sent a message through Kurt that he was ready to meet me again. I was to be at the Swiss Embassy once more at seven o'clock on Friday morning. That irritated me because, despite the caution of the unnamed colleague, Prochnow seemed oblivious to the risk he was running reusing the same venue simply because the embassy was conveniently close to his place of work. It also meant I would have to spend the night at Peston's apartment again instead of at Halensee.

Thursday evening, having left Mitzi at the club, I unlocked the door to the flat in Moabit aware of there being something oddly alien about the place.

I had been vaguely conscious of its peculiar atmosphere while living there. The place called to mind memories of my grandparents houses, oppressive and gloomy shrines to the Victorian conception of middleclass virtue. Amid the heavy-furniture and clutter, admonitions to silence were rarely necessary, the atmosphere of itself enough to strike any child dumb. More like joyless waiting rooms for the hereafter than homes, it seemed to be this feeling that Peston's apartment evoked. Despite lacking that Victorian clutter, the flat spoke silently but eloquently of something even more missing.

The man himself, I presumed.

Friday morning I walked down Alt-Moabit towards the Swiss Embassy for the third time, passing men on their way to work. Near the embassy, a couple of street urchins passed me pulling a small hand cart loaded with an assortment of useless rubbish they had scavenged from the ruins.

I was a minute or two late and Prochnow wasn't there. I waited until eight o'clock, compulsively looking at my watch every few minutes and trying not to appear like a man who had been stood up. I couldn't believe that despite the apparent strictures on his being on time for work Prochnow wouldn't have waited at least five minutes. I gave him another quarter of an hour then, once that had expired, extended my deadline until eight-thirty, my sense of frustration beginning to build.

When eight-thirty went by without him showing I finally gave up and retraced my steps back along Alt-Moabit to the mill.

'He wasn't there,' I said to Kurt who was already at his table, breaking cigarette packs into single smokes and drinking a cup of the brown concoction he called coffee.

'There is enough if you would like some,' he said, seemingly unconcerned that Prochnow had missed the meeting he had asked for.

'No,' I said. 'What do you think could have happened to him?'

'Maybe he stayed in bed with Gretchen.'

Obviously deriving some vicarious enjoyment at the thought he added, 'This would be better than meeting you, I think.'

Having spent the night at Peston's apartment, passing up Mitzi's bed to be at the Swiss Embassy, the idea of Gretchen and Prochnow in bed didn't give me any vicarious enjoyment at all.

'You told me he couldn't afford to be late for work.'

'This is what he said,' Kurt replied.

He sounded off-hand, not bothering to pause from his cigarette sorting.

'You're certain he meant seven this morning?'

'I am certain.'

'Not this evening?'

Kurt shrugged.

With little else to do, I idled the day away and was back at the embassy at seven that evening. In the meantime Kurt assured me he would make some enquiries.

An hour later nothing had changed. With no sign of Prochnow, I had to accept that neither he nor Kurt had made a mistake about the time. Something else had prevented his meeting me and, short of banging on the door of the Air Ministry on Liepzigerstraße and asking, I didn't know how I was going to find out what.

I spent the evening at the club in the faint hope that Kurt might find him and bring him in although, if Prochnow and Gretchen were out on the town, the Zoo Club wouldn't be on their usual itinerary.

The weekend passed without news and my weekly meeting with Bill threw up no explanation other than that Prochnow had got cold feet again. Or worse, had been arrested.

Unable to do anything except wait and sick of kicking my heels, on Tuesday I rode out to Templehof with Kurt to pick up his latest consignment of cigarettes courtesy of Joe Rafferty.

Hanging around outside the hut, the temperature hitting 33C, I was beginning to feel like a cog in a machine that was turning over only very occasionally. The rest of the time I felt like a redundant appendage, killing days and getting bored.

The truth was I had come to the conclusion that the spying game wasn't what I had expected. I had anticipated more action and less idling; I was beginning to think it was time to reassess my future.

Perhaps that's why, when I saw that old acquaintance of mine riding by in his Jeep and later, when I came across the girl hanging around outside the house at Halensee, I was prepared to look for some other avenue of stimulation.

What I should have done was ignore the portents, bury my curiosity and send Bill Harrington notice to quit. That way I could have left Berlin, none the wiser.

No wiser but a whole lot healthier.

Die Täuschung

15

Wednesday 30th July 1947

I slept badly. The heat and Mitzi's fitful restlessness hadn't helped. I don't know what had filled her dreams but mine had flickered through my head all night like a collage of the day's events. I had been trapped in an airless, overcrowded train carriage, watching through the window as a Jeep carrying a face from my past drove by alongside the girl who'd robbed me by the lake. Then, in the way people sometimes do in dreams, the girl changed into Mitzi. As they passed the carriage window my old acquaintance turned and grinned mockingly at me before speeding away with her. Leaving me trapped in the carriage, smothered by sweating Berliners.

That last scene woke me and as it receded I felt a hollow emptiness settle in the pit of my stomach.

It was light outside so I got up, confirmed my suspicion that there was still no water and dressed. I left a note for Mitzi to say I would see her in the club that evening.

I thought briefly about having another dip in the lake, but since I wouldn't come out any cleaner than I'd go in I decided that if I was going to go to the trouble of dreaming of sweating Berliners I might as well make an early start for the train and get my own back by sweating on them first.

At the mill there was no sign of Kurt and the door to his room was locked. I smoked three cigarettes and drank a pot of tea before he turned up, sauntering in as if he hadn't a care in the world, carrying a bottle of milk and the mail we had delivered *poste restante* to a nearby post office.

Our correspondence only ever consisted of meaningless letters for Schuyler Imports, props designed to maintain our cover. There was never any post for me. Perhaps because I couldn't think of anyone back in England to write to, or

113

anyone who would care to write to me if I did.

I took the bottle of milk to the kitchen and made Kurt a cup of his vile coffee while he sorted through the post. When I came back he had dropped most of it onto the table and was slitting the last envelope open with one of the fingers he still had left on his right hand.

The phone began to ring. He glanced at me but I wasn't answering it. That was his job. He put the letter down and picked up the receiver.

'Schuyler Imports.'

He listened to whoever was on the other end of the line, said, 'Yes,' and 'that's right,' and then something about an electrical generator.

He scribbled a note on the pad beside the telephone and replaced the receiver. A box of jumbled components on the table by the phone caught his eye and he pulled it towards him, frowning like a bomb-maker who needed one last piece to complete his next device.

'Who was that?' I asked. 'You haven't got an order for Schuyler, surely?'

'Yes, an order,' he replied drily. 'But for you, Harry, not for me. You are to be back at the flat for eleven.'

'Was it Bill? Has he heard something about Prochnow?'

'It is possible,' he said, losing interest in the box of components and picking up the half-opened letter again. 'They did not say.'

He finished the job and pulled out a single slip of paper.

'I did not speak to Herr Harrington,' he said absently. 'It was someone who passes messages. It is best not to say too much on the telephone.'

He finished reading and handed the letter to me.

Only it wasn't a letter. It was a German air-freight manifest for cargo dated the previous day. A crate had been shipped out that morning from Johannisthal airfield in Treptow in the Russian sector.

'Shipped to Moscow? The Russians sent it?'

I didn't understand. The description of the cargo had been stamped on the manifest.

Unzuverlässige Waren.

114

I knew *Waren* meant goods, but *Unzuverlässige* was a new one on me.

'Unreliable,' Kurt said. '*Unzuverlässige Waren.* Unreliable goods.'

I gave the manifest back to him.

'Why send this to us?'

'It is a joke, I think,' he said, not looking in the least amused.

'The Russians don't have a sense of humour,' I said. 'Not unless you think shooting a man in the back of the head is funny. Anyway, I thought they weren't supposed to know what we do here.'

'Calling the cargo *Unzuverlässige Waren* is the joke, Harry. And it is most likely that it comes from a German working at Johannisthal. Not from Russians.'

I had never been convinced that Germans had much of a sense of humour either, although I was always ready to be proved wrong.

'Who do we know at Johannisthal?'

'Better ask who at Johannisthal knows us?'

'All right, but why send it here?'

'Think about it, Harry.'

I thought about it and still didn't get anywhere.

'*Unreliable* goods,' Kurt said again with emphasis. 'I think they have put Prochnow in the crate, Harry. I think he has been shipped back to Moscow.'

'Prochnow? Are you serious? What makes you think it was him?'

'He missed the appointment with you on Friday. It has been five days now and still we have heard nothing. Not one of my contacts have seen him either.'

Which brought to mind what Mitzi had said when she got home the previous evening.

'Gretchen was in the Zoo Club asking for me last night.'

'For you? What did she want?'

'I didn't see her. Mitzi told me she had been in.'

Kurt frowned. 'Is that why you are here so early? You have seen Mitzi this morning? Or maybe you have spent the night together?'

I wasn't prepared to go into that again so I just said:

'Gretchen was on her own.'

'Because Gerhard is in Moscow,' he declared flatly.

'Bill isn't going to like this,' I said.

'Why did Gretchen ask for you?'

'You mean why didn't she get in touch with you? I don't know.'

He smirked at me.

'Maybe you have you made another conquest, Harry. What do you think?'

I was thinking that if Gretchen wanted to get in touch with me she would have contacted Kurt first. But if it was Prochnow's colleague trying to get in touch, being the cautious man Prochnow insisted he was, he would not have wanted to go through Kurt.

'What did you tell Mitzi?' Kurt asked.

'I said it was business. Something about your American cigarettes. I told her that if Gretchen came back again tonight to tell her to wait. That I'll be in later.'

I finished my tea and pocketed the freight manifest.

'Was Bill in the habit of telephoning messages here if he needed to see Arthur Peston?'

'No. I told you, it was only a message. Herr Harrington does not call. We do not speak of important things.'

'Perhaps Bill has heard something. It's as well I came in early.'

Kurt shook his head. 'They would call the flat before telephoning here.'

And found I wasn't there of course.

At Peston's flat I opened the windows to air the place. I'd only been there the previous Friday but in the hot weather the apartment had reverted to exuding that same smell of stale emptiness I had found when I first moved in. My brief presence hadn't changed anything much and the apartment stubbornly retained its aura of vacancy.

Thankfully I had left some tea in the caddy so I put the kettle on and brewed a pot, assuming Bill would appreciate a cup.

He was prompt but wasn't in the mood for anything as mundane as a cup of tea.

I showed him the freight manifest. He glanced at it and said:

'*Unzuverlässige Waren?*'

'Unreliable goods,' I said.

'I know that,' Bill answered testily.

'Kurt thinks it means Prochnow. He also thought it might be a joke. But not a Russian joke.'

'Then whose?'

'I don't know. He didn't think the Russians sent it, that's all.'

'Well, he's right. It is Prochnow.'

'How do you know?'

He pinched the bridge of his beaky nose between his finger and thumb.

'We've got a man at Johannisthal airfield. He's there to keep an eye on what the comrades are freighting in and out. Most of their stuff comes in by rail but they occasionally send something important in by air. Or out. This must have been important.'

'Perhaps it was your man who sent us the manifest,' I suggested.

'No. He doesn't know about you. Or Kurt and Schuyler.'

'Well if you're right and it was Prochnow in the crate, where does it leave us?'

'Up shit creek,' Bill said bluntly.

I said, 'That might explain why his wife was looking for me last night.'

'Gretchen?'

'She went to the Zoo Club. That's where Kurt arranged for me to meet Prochnow that first time.'

'I remember. But she asked for you, not Kurt?'

'That's what Kurt said.'

'Is she likely to have gone there of her own accord?'

I wondered how I was supposed to know that. I hardly knew the woman. If her husband had left some sort of instruction in the event anything happened to him, I'd have thought he'd have told her to go to Kurt. If she needed money, Kurt was the

117

one who had it. But if it was someone else and not Gretchen who wanted to get in touch, that might be a different matter.

'Do you know if this colleague of Prochnow's knows Gretchen, Harry?'

'I don't think he did. Not until I suggested Prochnow take him for a drink to sound him out. I thought if he took Gretchen along it might help soften him up.'

Bill expression was implying I'd told Prochnow to pimp his wife.

'You know how some men are over a pretty face,' I explained.

He still regarded me doubtfully so perhaps he didn't.

'Did he mention anything about it the last time you saw him?'

'No. When I first suggested it he said he knew a place in the French sector this man might appreciate. Then he came up with that list of names so I assumed Prochnow had persuaded the man to cooperate, one way or another.'

'Let's suppose he did meet Gretchen,' Bill said. 'If that's the case and Prochnow's colleague wants to get in touch again, Gretchen would be his only point of contact? Right?'

'If we assume Prochnow didn't tell him about Kurt.'

'You told me Prochnow wanted to cut Kurt out of the loop. That his colleague was cautious and he didn't want Kurt involved. That's what you said, isn't it?'

I said it was, as far as I knew.

'Then this man might ask Gretchen to go back to this club again.'

'I've left a message for her if she does. She's to wait for me.'

Bill picked his hat up off the table.

'All right, Harry. Then that's as much as we can do for now. If Gretchen turns up I want you to find out what she knows about her husband's disappearance and if this colleague of his suggested she talk to you. If so, I want you to arrange a meeting with him. We can't use Gretchen as a go-between. Not if her husband has been arrested. They might decide to pick her up, too. Get back to me as soon as you know anything. I'm afraid this has got a familiar ring to it.'

'How do you mean?'

He didn't reply. Instead, pausing with his hand on the door handle, he looked around the apartment as if he, like me, had noticed the atmosphere.

'How are you getting on here? Arthur always said he found it handy to be close to the centre.'

'I'm fine,' I said.

He seemed on the point of saying more but then must have thought better of it.

'Use the Military Mission if you need to get in touch quickly,' he said.

Once he had gone I went back into the kitchen. The tea was still standing on the table, untouched.

It would be the second pot I would have to drink by myself that morning.

~

Kurt usually ate at the same workingman's café, a place that would fill your empty stomach without emptying your pocket at the same time. It wasn't *haute cuisine* but then neither was anyone required to dress for dinner. Over a plateful of something I couldn't identify I told him Bill had confirmed what we assumed the freight manifest had meant.

Kurt pushed his empty plate aside and took out a cigarette. As was his custom he didn't light it immediately, a habit that gave me the impression he always considered its value before setting fire to the thing.

'So,' he said, 'how does Prochnow repay me from Moscow?'

'If I see Gretchen tonight I'll tell her you're worried about your money. You don't think he'll be coming back, I take it?'

Kurt finally struck a match and lit his cigarette.

'That is not the way they do things.'

'It all seems a bit melodramatic to me,' I said. 'Shipping him to Moscow in a crate. What he passed us was pretty basic stuff, after all. None of it was high grade. He didn't have the access for that. At least, that's what he kept telling me. If they wanted to teach him a lesson, why not do it here in Germany?'

'It is not the importance of the product they consider, Harry.' He squinted against his smoke. 'With the Russians it is the principle.'

From what I had seen of them I wasn't convinced Russians were too strong on principles. I hadn't read the Communist Manifesto's small print, it was true, but I didn't think it contained a code of ethics.

'This way,' Kurt went on, 'it is not only Prochnow they give the lesson to but everyone else.'

'He's a German citizen,' I said. 'How is it they can they just ship him off to Moscow?'

He smiled. At my naiveté, I assume.

'And who will complain? Do not hold your breath waiting for Walter Ulbricht to protest, Harry.'

'What do you think they'll do to him? Sweat him then shoot him?'

He shook his head. 'No, I do not think so. He will tell them what they want to know and then send him to one of the re-education camps.'

'What's a re-education camp?'

'It is a more polite name for a concentration camp. They like to make examples. A dead man is only an example once. In a camp he is always an example. It shows the other offenders the error of their ways.'

It occurred to me that the other camp internees would already be aware of the error of their ways. And while a dead man may only be an example once, it is a pretty emphatic example.

'You think he will talk?'

Kurt chuckled.

'I think he will have told them everything they wanted to know before they nailed down the lid of the crate.'

'About you and me?'

'I do not think I will come as much of a surprise to them, Harry. But if we have luck he will not give them your name. I think it will depend on how things are with Gretchen. If he thinks you can help her he might not talk about you.'

'We had better watch our step then and assume he has talked.'

Kurt peered at the end of his cigarette. I felt there was something on his mind.

'You asked,' he began after a moment, 'if Prochnow had ever told Herr Peston of someone else he worked with at Liepzigerstraße? A new source, perhaps?'

'It was just a thought,' I said.

Kurt blew a stream of smoke over my head.

'And if Prochnow approached someone, it was maybe this man who betrayed him?'

'That's a possibility.'

One I hadn't considered, it was true. But if Prochnow had been careless in approaching this supposed colleague of his, he might have ended up hoist by his own petard.

If that was the case, though, where had the list he had given me come from?

~

That evening I was at the Zoo Club by nine and took my usual table, away from the bar and in the shadows. It was a weekday and quiet. The only people in were a handful of servicemen and a smattering of those Germans who still had money to spend. Mitzi was sitting with me when she saw Gretchen come in.

'Here is your friend,' she said. 'The one with the brown curls.'

'Bring her over, will you sweetie?' I asked nicely. 'I'll find out what she wants.'

'What do they usually want?'

'And bring us a couple of beers,' I added, refusing the bait.

I'd found that usually it wasn't always easy to read the expression on Mitzi's face. This time, disdain was clear.

'Big spender,' she said.

She did as I asked, though, and walked over and brought Gretchen back to the table.

'Harry,' Gretchen said as she sat down, brown curls bobbing, 'it is good to see you again.'

She took a cigarette from her handbag, her hand shaking as she held it to my light. Her face was pale and she didn't look to have taken a lot of trouble with her makeup. A small arc of red lipstick had escaped the contours of her lips.

Mitzi stood over us watching until I mouthed "beers" at her. She turned on her heel.

Gretchen breathed in smoke.

'Gerhard is missing,' she said. 'He went to work as usual last Thursday but has not come home. I have asked at the Party offices and they tell me they have not seen him. Then yesterday a man Gerhard knows came to see me and tells me he thinks my husband has been arrested.'

'By the police?'

Gretchen drew on her cigarette again, her hand still shaking.

'The security police.'

'You didn't go to the city police when he didn't come home last Thursday?'

'No. On Thursday I went to Leipzig for the weekend to see my mother. Gerhard was to join us on Saturday but when he didn't come I thought he must have to work. It has happened before.'

'He didn't telephone?'

'My mother has no telephone.' She shrugged. 'I was not worried. Sometimes Gerhard cannot get away. But when I got home on Sunday, Gerhard was not there and there were no signs he had been. Then I start to worry.'

'And why does this man think that it was the security police who arrested him?'

'Because at the Party offices no one will speak of him. This is the way it happens if the Russians are involved.' Her lips began to quiver and I thought she was going to cry. 'No one will tell me anything.'

Mitzi came back with our beer. She banged them down on the table without a word, splashing some over my sleeve.

'But you haven't reported him missing to the city police?' I asked again, ignoring Mitzi.

'If it is the Russians who have him as this friend of Gerhard's thinks, then the city police will do nothing. Besides,' she added, sucking in smoke, 'they might ask awkward questions. You understand, I think.'

'Awkward? In what way?'

'Gerhard's arrangement with Kurt.'

I didn't say anything. Her eyes drilled into mine.

'I did not know what to do, Harry.'

'So you came looking for me.'

'Yes.'

'Not Kurt.'

She hesitated. 'Gerhard told me that if anything happened to him I was to talk to you, not Kurt.'

'But your husband hardly knows me,' I said.

'We met here,' she countered. 'Also Gerhard told me he has seen you again.'

Her eyes dropped to her untouched beer and she ran a finger around the rim of the glass. She raised her pretty head.

'And Gerhard owes Kurt money. He said Kurt would want the loan back if anything happened to him.'

'And so he will,' I said. 'Do you have any money?'

'No. Of course not. Gerhard always handles our money. Now he has gone I have nothing. What am I going to do? Should I go to the police or to the Party?'

She gazed across the empty room.

'This friend of Gerhard's,' I said. 'Is he the one you and Gerhard took out for a drink the other night? To the French sector, wasn't it?'

She turned back sharply. 'How did you know that?'

'I'm afraid I don't think either the city police or the Party will be able to help you.'

'Why not?'

'Because I hear Gerhard is in Moscow.'

Her eyes widened. 'Moscow? Why do the Russians take him to Moscow?'

'I think you know the answer to that one, Gretchen. And the security police will almost certainly want to talk to you at some point. To find out how much you know.'

'But I don't know anything!'

'You knew Gerhard was passing information to Kurt and was receiving money for it.'

She began shaking her head, making those curls bounce.

'No, no... What he gave to Kurt was of no value. Gerhard swore to me he would never give him anything important.'

Which meant either Gerhard had been lying to his wife or

lying to us.

'Important enough to sell,' I pointed out.

'It was only a loan. Until Gerhard's promotion came through.'

'Even if you're right,' I told her, 'the Russians see these things differently.'

'What will I tell them, Harry? I do not want to go to Moscow!'

'If I were you,' I said, 'I'd play the dumb little wife. When they ask how is it you thought you could afford to eat out and how Gerhard could buy those presents he gave you, tell them he told you he had been promoted at work and had been given a raise.'

'But they know he was not.'

'They won't know that you knew that,' I said.

'Will they believe me?'

'Flutter your eyelids at them, Gretchen. Like most men they'll swallow anything if it's fed to them by a pretty face.'

I don't know if she believed me but she appeared to like the compliment. She put a hand over mine just as Mitzi came back collecting empty glasses. I glanced up at her and raised my eyebrows helplessly. But Mitzi wasn't swallowing that and my face had never been that pretty.

'Tell them Kurt is a friend,' I said to Gretchen. 'He supplies Gerhard with cigarettes.' Adding, more for Mitzi's benefit than Gretchen's, 'If they mention my name say you only met me because I'm a business acquaintance of Kurt's.'

'But that is the truth,' Gretchen said.

I smiled at her. 'Of course it is.'

She sipped her beer and grimaced. Mitzi picked up my empty glass without comment.

'This man who told you that it was the security police who arrested Gerhard ... the one you had the drink with. What is his name?'

'Fischer. Albrecht Fischer.'

'And he works at the Liepzigerstraße offices with Gerhard?'

'In the same building although they are in different departments.'

'If he's the one I'm thinking of,' I said, 'he is a member of the KPD? He spent the war in Moscow? Is that Albrecht Fischer?'

'Yes. How did you know this?'

'Gerhard told me about him. Your husband said he trusted him. Do you trust him, Gretchen?'

'Of course. Why should I not?'

She had been pulling hard on her cigarette and worn it down to its butt. She crushed it into the ashtray and managed to wait ten seconds before fishing in her handbag for another.

'Did Albrecht Fischer suggest that you come looking for me?'

'No. Why should he? He doesn't know you, does he?'

'No, but I'd like to meet him. Do you think he would talk to me if you asked him nicely, Gretchen?'

She squeezed my hand. 'Do you mean if I flutter my eyelids at him, Harry?'

'Yes, you do that, Gretchen. Maybe between us we can think of a way to help Gerhard. You still want that don't you?'

'Of course, Harry. Gerhard is my husband.'

16

Things livened up a little later when an argument broke out between a couple of Tommies. Just as it was about to come to blows a squad of MPs arrived and broke things up. They cleared the servicemen out and were scanning the room for any other trouble-makers while the rest of Karl's customers followed the uniforms. Not looking to catch another punch on the jaw, I had been sitting well away from the action although not so far away that one of the redcaps didn't spot me, a burly-looking brute who was clasping his nightstick as if itching to find a head on which to use it.

'You!' he shouted at me in English, not troubling to use the native language while he had the whole of the British army behind him. 'Out. The place is closed.'

'I'm just having a quiet drink,' I told him. 'It's not any concern of mine if a couple of your squaddies want to beat each other's brains out.'

'I said the place is closed,' he repeated and took several steps towards me.

Karl Bauer came bustling over, pushing past Mitzi and some of the other girls.

'We are closed, Harry. No trouble, please. Come back tomorrow. I will give you a drink on the house.'

He must have been concerned if he was willing to give out free drinks so I crushed out my cigarette and told him I'd see him tomorrow. I waited by the door while Mitzi got her bag, the MPs eyes on me and Karl's eyes on him.

Going up the steps to the street I said to Mitzi:

'What's that guy's problem? It wasn't even a fight.'

'*Him*,' she said. 'He is a nasty one. He comes around once a month to shake Karl down. He threatens to have the club closed permanently. Karl has to pay him off.'

'What's his name?'

'Brewer ... Brewster... Something like this. I do not remember. He would have not looked strange in a SA uniform. Like one of Röhm's bullies.'

'Ask Karl his name, will you?'

'Why Harry?'

'I'm just curious.'

I was thinking of letting Bill know that one of the British army's redcaps was running a protection racket although I wasn't sure if it was a sense of moral indignation or my getting shouted at that had irked me more. I suppose if I'd stayed there I could have made more of it. And probably finished on the wrong end of the nightstick for my trouble.

Mitzi was hungry. She possessed the capacity to eat at any hour. We walked down the Kurfürstendamm to a place that stayed open late and while I picked over a gritty sausage she tucked in to a plate of cabbage and potatoes. It wasn't until we finished and were sharing a cigarette over schnapps that she asked about Gretchen.

'She's lost her husband,' I said.

'So she looks for another?'

'No, I think she'd rather have the old one back.'

'The way she was holding your hand I am not so sure.'

'I'm way down the list,' I told her. 'She knows I can't afford her.'

'So where is the old one?'

'I heard he was in Moscow.'

'Is that good or bad?'

'Not so good, I think. At least for him.'

We jumped a tram to Koenigsallee and went the rest of the way on foot. The night was still warm and I wanted to walk off the sausage. Mitzi complained that she had been on her feet all night but complaints were part of who she was, a character trait that came with the rest of her. I didn't mind so much, the rest of her being too good to quibble over trifles.

We had just turned off Margaretenstraße onto the gravel road when I spotted the girl again. She was ahead of us and going towards the house.

'There's your ghost,' I said to Mitzi.

'What?'

'The girl I told you was hanging around the house last night. She's back again.'

'To steal something, I think.'

'You go ahead,' I told her. 'I'll cut through the gardens and see if I can catch her.'

'Why do you want to catch her?' Mitzi protested. 'Are two women making eyes at you in one evening not enough?'

I pulled her to me and kissed her on the lips.

'When do you ever make eyes at me?'

'Pah!' she said, turning her mouth down in that dismissive way she had.

I ducked into the grounds of the property on our left. It was the garden the girl had disappeared into when eluding me previous night. A few feet in I found what would once have been a garden now a wild tangle of overgrown shrubs. The house itself lay beyond a weed-strangled driveway, a ruin and unfit for occupation. I had scouted the neighbouring area a few days after moving in with Mitzi, finding several well-trodden paths between the gardens and through broken fences that were probably scavengers' trails.

The tangled vegetation screened the road from me although I heard Mitzi calling to the girl. I didn't hear her reply and a moment later became aware that someone was moving through the undergrowth ahead of me. I ducked behind a tree and after a few seconds saw the girl pass no more than an arm's length from me. I made a grab for her and she squealed, struggling, kicking and scratching for all she was worth.

There was nothing of her, though, just skin, bone. And teeth. I felt the latter as they sank into my arm. Despite her slightness she was surprisingly strong. She struggled a little longer then abruptly stopped as if what energy she had left had suddenly drained out of her.

'I'm not going to hurt you,' I said in German. 'I'm the man you saw last night. Do you remember?'

She peered at me through the darkness.

'I am not a thief,' she said.

'I know that.'

'Harold Tennant,' she said then, almost whispering. 'You are English.'

'Yes, I'm English. But they call me Harry. You saw my name on my ID papers while I was swimming in the lake. You took some Reichmarks out of my wallet. Why didn't you take all the money?'

'I am not a thief.'

'I'm not saying you are.'

'I took no American dollars,' she said, as if Reichmarks didn't count.

Mitzi called from the road.

'That's Mitzi,' I said to the girl. 'Mitzi Meier. You've seen her before, haven't you? She lives in the house next door.'

'The woman with the sad face?'

'Yes,' I said. 'That's her, I suppose.'

I had my arms around her and loosened my grip, expecting her to start struggling again. She made no attempt to break free though.

'You must be hungry?' I said. 'We have some food in the house. Why don't you come in and eat something?'

She eyed me suspiciously. 'You will send me back,' she said.

'I don't want to send you anywhere. You can eat and then leave if you want. Whatever you want.'

'I can leave?'

Mitzi found the path and me with my arms around the girl.

'You will get a reputation,' she said.

'This is Mitzi.'

I let go of the girl. Mitzi reached out a hand and touched her.

'What is your name?'

'My name? I used to be Shoshannah Lehmann,' she said.

'Used to be?'

I was about to ask what she meant but Mitzi was scowling at me. She put her arm around the girl and led her back to the gravel road and towards our house.

At the door I put my key in the lock. The girl became agitated again.

'The woman,' she said. 'The one with the crippled son. She will call the police if she sees me.'

'That's Frau Ernst,' I said. 'She's harmless. She won't call the police.'

I unlocked the door. Mitzi flicked the light switch and the pale light illuminated the girl's gaunt face. Framed by the rat's tails of her lank hair there appeared something skeletal about her, like those wretched souls freed from the Nazi's camps. Still on the doorstep, she was staring at me out of blue watery eyes that were ringed black.

'Is Walter Frick here?'

'Frick? I don't know who you mean,' I said.

'Walter Frick,' she said again.

'There's no one here called Frick. Did he once live here?'

'I lived here.'

'You? When?'

'Before the war.'

Mitzi had just managed to coax her inside when the door to Frau Ernst's apartment opened.

'Oh, it is you, Herr Tennant,' Frau Ernst said, stepping into the hall. 'And Fraulein Meier, too,' making it sound as if we had possibly run into each other on the doorstep.

I glanced back at Mitzi. The girl had gone.

'Frau Ernst,' I said. 'You are up late.'

'I thought I heard voices. You have company, perhaps?'

'No, Frau Ernst. Just us two.' I gestured towards the light bulb. 'I see we have electricity tonight. Is it too much to hope that we have water as well?'

'No, Herr Tennant,' she said, 'there is water,' before adding, 'but little pressure, of course,' as if one couldn't expect too much at any one time in a city like Berlin.

'Then we can wash tonight,' I said.

'Of course,' Frau Ernst replied evenly. 'Cleanliness is so important. Do you not think so, Herr Tennant?'

She was asking me but looking at Mitzi.

Mitzi walked past her and up the stairs without a word. I followed, pausing on the bottom step.

'Tell me, Frau Ernst, do you know if someone called Walter Frick ever lived here?'

Her eyes flickered so briefly I would have missed it if I'd blinked. Then her features assumed their usual mask.

'No, Herr Tennant. I do not think so. I know no one by that name.'

'Would Herr Neumann know, do you think?'

'Herr Neumann has owned the property for some years, I believe. You would have to ask him yourself.'

Which was something easier said than done as I had never laid eyes on Herr Neumann. Neither had Mitzi as far as I knew. She had already disappeared up the stairs. I lingered on the bottom step.

Frau Ernst was regarding me with that joyless gaze of hers.

'Herr Neumann lives in Hamburg, does he not,' I said to her. 'Do you have an address to which I might write?'

Her expression did not change. 'Why do you wish to write to Herr Neumann?'

'If I am to ask about Walter Frick,' I said.

Her face set grimly. 'I am sorry, Herr Tennant. I do not have his address.'

'But you send our rent to him, don't you?'

'I pay the money into his bank here in Berlin.'

'They would have his address no doubt.'

'No doubt,' she echoed, 'although whether they would give it to you I am not so sure.'

She smiled smugly.

'You have his telephone number perhaps?'

'I am afraid I do not have Herr Neumann's number either.'

'But how,' I asked, 'do you contact him if there is a problem with the house?'

'A problem with the house? I do not understand... Do you have a problem?' When I didn't say anything she went on, 'Was there something else I can do for you, Herr Tennant?'

'I heard a family named Lehmann might once have lived here,' I said, trying a different tack with the name the girl had given us. 'Would you remember them?'

'I cannot help you, Herr Tennant. I came here in 1942. The house was empty then. Who may have lived here before that was no concern of mine.'

'Surely you must communicate with Herr Neumann sometimes, Frau Ernst?' I insisted.

'He does call me on the telephone from time to time,' she finally allowed. 'If you wish, the next time he calls, I will ask from whom he purchased the house. Since you are so interested, Herr Tennant.'

'Thank you,' I said, having no expectation that she would.

'I suppose,' she said suddenly, 'you have been talking to that street girl. Has she been loitering outside the house again?'

I did happen to see a girl yesterday,' I admitted. 'But she wasn't what you would call a street girl.'

'You must telephone the police if you see her again, Herr Tennant. She has claimed the house once belonged to her family. This is nonsense, of course, and she only looks for an opportunity to steal. You will tell me if you see her again. I will contact the authorities. She has already spent time in prison and that is the best place for her. Will you inform me if you see her again?'

'Of course, Frau Ernst,' I said. 'As you wish. I hope we haven't disturbed you and Werner.'

Her dead eyes held mine. 'Werner is in bed sleeping, thank you Herr Tennant.'

'Then I won't keep you from yours,' I said, starting up the stairs.

Mitzi was in the bathroom. I could hear water trickling out the faucet. The pressure was never good and, in hot weather, hardly more than a dribble and barely clean. Always unpleasant to drink.

In the bedroom I stripped off and waited for Mitzi to finish. I knew that Frau Ernst had been living on the ground floor when Mitzi moved in but very little else about the place. I wasn't even sure how long Mitzi had lived there. As with much else about her life, she rarely volunteered information. I rarely asked. I did suspect she would not have been able to afford the apartment on her own, at least not by working at the club. When she was a *Trümmerfrau* she might have earned enough, but I assumed that before me she had been living with someone else.

I was pretty sure she had cleaned the apartment before I first saw it although some small telltale signs of a presence preceding me always remained. If you knew what to look for.

Now and then I came across something Mitzi had missed: hair cream in the bathroom that was anything but feminine; a book on a shelf in English that she wouldn't have read even in a German translation... And once, reaching for a few pfennigs that had rolled under the bed, I had found a man's undershirt lodged behind the bed leg. The vest label was American but not of service issue. It all made me curious but not sufficiently curious to question Mitzi about it.

As Frau Ernst had informed me, I had coincidentally moved in on rent day. Or then again, perhaps not so coincidentally. But these things rub both ways. Mitzi's rooms may not have been as handily located as Peston's apartment but the place had other attractions. And I wasn't only thinking about Mitzi. On fine mornings there was the view of the lake from the bedroom window. Through cracked glass, admittedly, but there was glass nonetheless. And beyond the lake you could see what was left of the trees and the villas on the far shore.

The house was no less convenient for both Gatow airfield in Spandau and Templehof in the American sector as a rail line through Wilmersdorf ran just beyond the ruined street to the north.

As I said, the rent had been due the day I moved in and Frau Ernst had collared me as I carried my case up the stairs. Although Mitzi had introduced us without the least trace of embarrassment before then, if Frau Ernst had any reservations about my arrival, my counting out more

Reichsmarks than she was due into her waiting palm seemed to have dispelled them. It was then, after I had hauled my case up to our rooms and was unpacking, that Mitzi told me about Frau Ernst's understanding with the owner of the house, a Herr Neumann who apparently lived in Hamburg and whom Mitzi had never seen.

Before the war the house must have been quite a prestigious property. Even despite the damage and dilapidation that aura of comfort and affluence still lingered on, like an unquiet ghost. Something Peston's apartment in Moabit lacked.

Until I ran into the girl, I hadn't given any consideration as to who might have actually originally owned the place. So much property had been seized by the Nazis in the years preceding and during the war that any notion of legal ownership was still something of a fluid concept, not only in Berlin but in the whole of Germany. Some sort of system of reparation was beginning to be put in place to right the wrongs of Hitler's regime although I suspected that the best living in the post-war years was going to be made by the lawyers.

Mitzi came back from the bathroom, naked with her clothes folded neatly over her arm. She hung them in the alcove that served as a closet then walked to the dressing table and, in the weak light, peered at her face in the mirror. She only had to move her eyes slightly to see me sitting on the bed directly behind her.

'Perhaps you had better wash some of your clothes while we have water, Harry,' she suggested, smearing cream on her face.

I supposed I had although could find little enthusiasm for the chore. Living with Mitzi didn't come with the comforts and services provided by most hausfraus. We ate out as often as not, I did my own laundry, and the only cleaning undertaken as far as I was aware had been when she had attempted to cleanse the place of any evidence of my predecessor.

'Tomorrow,' I said. 'I've had a long day.'

'Oh? And what have you done today?'

'The owner, Neumann... Didn't you tell me he once lived downstairs?'

Her naked shoulders rose and fell in an indifferent shrug.

'I was told a man used to live with Frau Ernst but I never

133

saw him. It may have been Neumann, I do not know. Someone else, perhaps.'

'How is it you came to live here?'

'A friend rented the apartment. We shared until my friend moved out.'

I couldn't help noticing she kept her friend gender-neutral.

'Who was that?' I asked. 'One of the girls at the club?'

'Why is it you want to know about Neumann, Harry?'

'Because of that girl,' I said.

She hadn't answered my question about who had been living there with her but I didn't feel inclined to pursue it further.

'What did she say her name was?' I asked. 'Shoshannah Lehmann? Did she say she once lived here?'

'She said her name *used* to be Shoshannah Lehmann. That is a difference in English, I think, is it not, Harry?'

'I suppose it is,' I said.

'Tell me your interest.'

'I don't know,' I replied truthfully. 'I suppose I'm just curious, that's all. Frau Ernst told me to call the police if I saw her again.'

'Why does Frau Ernst think the police will be interested in that girl?'

'I don't suppose they would. She seems to have got under Frau Ernst's skin, though.'

It had been a fair question. Having been de-Nazified, the new Berlin police seemed more concerned with not overstepping their authority than keeping the riff-raff off the streets. They had their hands full trying keeping a lid on the rising tide of crime in the city. There were still all those old Nazis lurking under unturned stones who needed to be rooted out. The military police had enough on their plate controlling their own Occupying Forces and—to judge by that evening's evidence—shaking down German businessmen.

They weren't going to be bothered by some waif caught hanging around Lake Halensee.

Whatever Frau Ernst might want.

Mitzi's finished her nightly routine of applying cream to everywhere she could reach, particularly those rough hands of hers. She began replacing tube-tops and lids on jars.

I was still waiting.

'Are you coming to bed?' I asked.

'Are you going to wash?' she countered.

'Of course I'm going to wash.'

'Then I will come to bed when you have finished washing.'

17

Thursday 31st July 1947

In the morning Kurt listened without comment as I told him what Gretchen had said at the club.

'So,' he began once I'd finished, 'Gretchen came looking for you because her husband told her that I would want what I am owed. She was not wrong, Harry. But who will pay me now? Will Gretchen have the money? I do not think so.'

'You're right,' I said, just to irritate him. 'Gretchen doesn't have any money.'

'So will you pay me what I am owed, Harry?'

I sighed heavily and looking anywhere but straight at him, just to let him know I was getting tired of talking about who owed what to whom.

'I told you. We'll put what he owes you on your expense claim. I'll give it to Bill and he'll send it to London.'

He grunted and played with a cigarette before lighting it, mollified but obviously not satisfied. 'It takes so long, Harry.'

'That's bureaucracy for you,' I said. Then to ginger him up, added, 'Of course, they might want to make an allowance for the electrical components Schuyler sends us. The ones you sell on, I mean. And don't forget they are paying you a retainer every month as well.'

'This is all for your cover, Harry. Am I supposed to put myself in danger for nothing?'

'No, Kurt. Just don't overdo it, that's all. Ask for too much and you'll get nothing. I've worked for these people before and generosity isn't one of their faults.'

'I ask only for what I am owed.'

'Then there shouldn't be a problem,' I answered, knowing there would be one way or another.

Before he was able to say any more, I switched the subject.

'Tell me, how would I go about finding out who once owned a house in Berlin?'

He stared at me nonplussed, as if I had suddenly asked him where Captain Kidd had buried his treasure.

'What house?'

'Where Mitzi lives.'

'Why would you want to know this, Harry?'

'There's a girl whose been hanging around the place. She told us she used to live there.'

'Do you know who owns it now?'

'Someone named Neumann according to Frau Ernst. That's the woman who lives downstairs and collects the rent. Neumann lives in Hamburg apparently, and she looks after the place.'

'Why not ask this Frau Ernst?' he said, as if that wouldn't have occurred to me. 'Or maybe ask Neumann.'

I explained that Neumann never seemed to visit the house and that Frau Ernst insists she knows nothing about the place before she moved in.

'Who is this girl?'

'She said her name was Shoshannah Lehmann.'

'Jewish?'

'I suppose so.'

He sucked on the last draw of his cigarette and stubbed out the butt.

'If a Jewish family owned it then I would forget it, Harry. The house was most likely seized by the Nazis. Along with everything in it.'

'Wouldn't there be a record of it somewhere if that happened? I thought the Nazis were meticulous about their bookkeeping. Even when they were robbing you blind.'

'So they were,' Kurt agreed. 'But you have noticed how things are here. Many records were destroyed in the air raids. Much of what survived was either looted when the Russians arrived, burned for fuel if it had no value, or shipped back to

Moscow if it had.'

'Everything can't have got burnt. Property records have no value. Except to the former owners, I suppose.'

'Who would have been sent to the camps if they were Jewish. How did this girl survive?'

I helped myself to a cigarette from Kurt's pack of Chesterfields.

'I don't know,' I said. 'Maybe I'm wrong and she isn't Jewish. Frau Ernst complained about her hanging around the house. She said she had spent time in prison.'

'Prostitution?'

'I doubt it. Not even Berliners are that desperate, looking the way she does. She also asked me if a man named Walter Frick was living there.'

'Maybe he used to own the house and she only worked there. Maybe she was his mistress. Maybe she used to look better before the war. How old is she?'

'Old enough, I suppose.'

'Of course,' Kurt went on, 'if it was owned by a Jew you could always try the Yanks. I hear they are gathering information on what happened to all the Berlin Jews who were deported after 1941. They are putting together lists. If they have names, maybe they have addresses too. Ask Herr Harrington. He will know about this.'

I didn't want to ask Bill. I didn't doubt he would know what the Yanks were up to but I suspected he wouldn't care for me making enquiries about anything other than SIS business. My status as an illegal might mean I fell outside of normal diplomatic convention, but I didn't suppose it gave me the latitude to chase after answers to questions I posed myself. Drawing unwanted attention to myself would be something of which Bill would not approve. And if Bill didn't approve, I suspected I wouldn't remain in the employ of SIS for long.

'I can ask Joe Rafferty,' Kurt suggested. 'I am going out to Templehof again this afternoon.'

Master sergeant Joe Rafferty was the sort of man who could probably find out anything about anyone; he was also the sort of man who wouldn't do something for nothing. I didn't have any money or anything to trade.

Mention of Rafferty, though, brought to mind the fact that I already knew another American who could probably tell me everything I might want to know about what had happened to the Jews in Berlin.

'No,' I said to Kurt, 'don't ask Rafferty about that. What you can ask him though is where I can get in touch with a USAF officer I know. He's here in Berlin but I don't know where. If I can find him, he'll be able to tell me what I want.'

'What is this officer's name?'

'Tuchmann,' I said. 'Ben Tuchmann. He's a colonel. I saw him the day before yesterday when I was out at Templehof with you.'

Kurt shrugged. 'That will be easy enough for Joe. This Colonel Tuchmann, he is a friend of yours?'

'Not exactly,' I said. 'We met last summer in London. I did him a favour. Even if I didn't know I was doing it at the time.'

Kurt frowned.

'I'll explain another time,' I said.

'Okay. You want Joe to give Tuchmann your name?'

'Better not. See if you can get an address for him. An office where I can reach him. Better still, a home address if he's got one. And don't let Rafferty know I'm the one asking. Let him think it's something you want.'

'Me? I do not think Joe will care for me talking to an American colonel.'

'Tell him it's about electrical parts. Schuyler business. I don't want to risk anything getting back to Bill Harrington. That I'm asking questions about some other matter.'

I couldn't see that there was much likelihood of that happening, but I was thinking that if it turned out Rafferty wanted a sweetener for getting Tuchmann's address it would be cheaper if he thought it was coming from Kurt. And I could always add the money to his expense sheet for what Prochnow owed him.

I reckoned SIS owed me that much, if only for getting me out to Berlin under false pretences.

~

There was a note waiting for me at the club that evening. Mitzi pulled it out of her dress pocket and handed it over without comment.

'Who's this from?'

'Why do you not read it and see?' she replied tartly.

It was apparently going to be one of Mitzi's acerbic evenings.

'Was it left here for me?'

'You told me you were a policeman, Harry. Work it out.'

'My speciality was burglary and assault,' I said as I tried to decipher the note, 'not criminally bad handwriting.'

I gave it back to her. I had trouble with printed German; handwritten letters were far and away beyond my linguistic skill.

Mitzi read the note. 'It is from your girlfriend. She wants to meet you.'

'How do you know who it's from? Even I could make out there is no signature.'

'Because it was this woman of yours, Greta, who left the note.'

'*Gretchen*,' I said. 'And she's no woman of mine. Did you see her leave it?'

'She gave it to Marthe.'

I always had the impression that Marthe didn't care much for me. It wasn't something I took personally as I didn't think Marthe cared much for men in general. Mitzi wouldn't hear a word against her, though. They had been *Trümmerfrau* together and that left a bond. It was the kind of friendship between women that always prompted questions. Questions between men, anyway. I took the easy way out and never asked them. Karl Bauer, never one to miss a business opportunity, used the fact that Marthe appeared to prefer the company of women as another string to his bow.

'And Marthe gave it to you,' I said to Mitzi.

'Of course. The note was meant for you and we are together. Or am I wrong about that, Harry?'

I glanced towards the bar and saw Marthe watching us. Or watching Mitzi more likely.

'Of course you're not wrong, sweetie,' I said to her. 'So what

139

does the note say? You still haven't told me.'

'That you are to be at the Austrian café on Pariser Platz at ten tonight.'

'Nothing else?'

'What else do you expect?'

I wanted to say reassurance. Pariser Platz was a favourite black market haunt and was also in the Russian sector. It was an open secret where to connect to the black market in Berlin. Everyone knew the places to go. Everyone also knew that every so often there were crackdowns, both by MPs and by the city police. But in the Russian sector you not only had to worry about the military and the civil police, you had to worry about the NKVD as well.

Travelling in and out of the Russian sector was no problem—often one wouldn't even be asked for papers. In the last few months, though, kidnapping was becoming one.

Politicians, journalists, criminals... People were being picked up off the street in the Russian sector with alarming regularity. Mostly no one was held for long. Even knowing that, I still didn't want to find myself among their number. Or be the contents of the next crate shipped out of Johannisthal airfield, come to that.

'You will meet her?' Mitzi demanded.

'It's business, Mitzi.'

'What business is she in?'

'Not the one you're thinking of. It'll be about her husband again.'

'Then why does she not come here to see you? She came to leave the note.'

As usual Mitzi was asking the pertinent question. And before I had thought to ask it myself. This time I didn't have a ready answer.

It wasn't yet nine and I had the time for another beer. When Mitzi brought it I tried to talk her around and came to the conclusion that the drink was all I was going to get out of her that evening.

I knew she wasn't jealous. Yet for some reason she seemed to think she ought to pretend she was. I had never fooled myself that Mitzi and I were a love match. We liked each other well enough and, as far as I was concerned, were well suited. Her reaction to the note, though, signifying I ought to read more into our relationship than was actually there, seemed to suggest that she assumed I wasn't smart enough to know how things really stood between us.

She soon left me to my beer and my brooding. I didn't know why the matter worried me but it did. And it didn't help when Marthe came over to ask if I had got the note.

'Yes, Marthe,' I said. 'Thank you.'

'She is a pretty one, this other woman.'

'She's not an "other" woman and she's not my type,' I said, insinuating she might be hers.

But I didn't think *pretty* was Marthe's type either. I always assumed someone like Mitzi was. Then I supposed Marthe was looking at Gretchen from my point of view; someone else, like Mitzi, who was trying to double-think me.

Marthe could hardly be described as pretty herself. Her blonde hair was cropped too short and her mouth was a little too wide for any accepted measure of beauty. Despite it she was undeniably attractive. To men, anyway. I couldn't speak for women. Taller than Mitzi—and taller than me, come to that—she was what people called statuesque, with those square shoulders one often finds on swimmers. I didn't think she was anyone's stereotypical idea of a lesbian. As far as that went, in post-war Germany at least, I didn't suppose anyone looked for that stereotype beyond those women who'd been concentration camp guards. We had all seen pictures of them, the ones who had been put on trial for war crimes. They had all been meaty, hard-faced women.

Marthe was quite a different proposition.

There was an unnerving intensity to her gaze. And, like Mitzi, the hard work they had done together had left its physical mark. She was lean and muscled and Leni Riefenstahl would have loved her, either hurling a discus or throwing a javelin. Or maybe even in bed, for all I knew. I have to admit I was attracted to her myself, a fact I had always found rather unsettling. Although, unlike with Mitzi, I wouldn't have cared to tussle with Marthe. I'm a man who has always known his limits.

'But maybe you are *her* type, Harry,' Marthe said, interrupting my speculation and giving me the benefit of her intense stare. 'I wouldn't want you to mess Mitzi around.'

'Mitzi can take care of herself, Marthe,' I said. 'And if she needs help I'm sure you'll always be there when needed.'

'Maybe, Harry, but you can't count on anything these days.'

That sounded vaguely like a threat although I didn't have the time to enquire. My watch was telling me it was time I was at the Austrian café in Pariser Platz.

Marthe gave me a last pointed pat on the hand and walked away, to pick on some other defenceless man I presumed.

The trams were still running and I hopped one going my way. Pariser Platz was on the Russian side of the Brandenburg Gate and, in the dusk, I could feel the monumental arch looming above me. It had been badly damaged in the war but was still standing, something that could not be said of many of the buildings around it. Frozen in time atop the arch, the Quadriga remained, the chariot of Victoria the goddess of Victory, drawn by four horses.

Back around the beginning of the 19th century when the French defeated the Prussians and Napoleon was enjoying a winning streak, he shipped the Quadriga to Paris. It didn't stay long. After Waterloo and the occupation of Paris, it was restored to Berlin. When the Russians' turn came they hadn't bothered claiming the statue. They probably had their the hands full with all their other loot. So the Quadriga and Victoria remained on top of the arch, tarnished and battle-scarred and worse for wear and with only one horse's head left intact.

And still looking east, I couldn't help noticing. Whether that was in remembrance of Hitler's dream of Germanic expansion or whether it was towards a Russian future planned for us all, I wouldn't have wanted to guess.

Most of the rubble around Pariser Platz had been cleared away and some bright entrepreneur had fashioned a café in what was left of the ground floor of one of Berlin's old administrative buildings. One might have been forgiven for supposing that anything as entrepreneurial as owning a café would run counter to the Soviet's ideology of a levelled mediocrity. When I got closer to the Austrian café, though, I saw it fitted right in with its surroundings: dirty, dusty and unattractive.

Why it should be called the Austrian café, I didn't know. As far as I could see there wasn't an alpine hat in sight. Or a mountain, unless it was one of rubble. What there was were some grubby tables and chairs, a concrete floor and makeshift counter, and a smattering of Berlin workers who either didn't have anyone to go home to or, if they did, couldn't face the hausfrau who was waiting. Several glanced up as I walked in but only one man continued to look.

I asked for a beer. The man watching me left his table and sauntered over. Smaller than average, he was dressed like a worker with a soiled jacket and trousers and a cap pulled to one side of his head. When he reached the bar he took the cap off and placed it in front of him. He was in his mid-thirties and already bald, although if he was the man I supposed him to be and he had spent the war in Stalin's Moscow, he'd have had good reason to lose his hair.

'*Entschuldigung*, mein herr,' he said conversationally, 'but do you happen to know the Zoo Club?'

'As a matter of fact,' I said, 'I've just come from there'.

He didn't look surprised. 'I have a friend who knows it very well. Perhaps you know her?'

'A woman? Perhaps I do. What is her name?'

'Gretchen.'

'Yes,' I said, 'I know Gretchen. In fact I was expecting to meet her here.'

'Here?' He glanced over his shoulder at the stained tables and the equally stained clientele. 'You would not find a woman like Gretchen here.'

'No, you are right,' I said. 'But I received a note to meet her here.'

'I wrote the note,' he said. 'My name is Albrecht Fischer.'

We didn't shake hands. Two strangers passing the time of day rarely do. I glanced around the café to see if I could spot the secret policeman but everyone looked like an ordinary workman to me. Then I suppose the NKVD would call what they did work, even if in their line they'd need to wash their hands a little more frequently than most.

The barman put my beer in front of me.

Fischer said, 'Drink it, but please take your time. Then come to the Gate. I will be waiting there.'

He put his cap on again, paused to light a cigarette and said a cheery goodnight to the barman before ambling out the door. No one followed. I stayed at the bar, sipping my beer and wishing for my bladder's sake I hadn't had the last one at the Zoo Club.

To pass the time I lit a cigarette of my own, wondering at Fischer's nerve in contacting me. If Prochnow talked, and I didn't suppose for one moment he wouldn't, he'd surely have given them Fischer's name, assuming Fischer was the colleague he had spoken to me about. There was always a chance they wouldn't arrest Fischer immediately, but I was certain they would watch him. And if that was the case, I thought they would be watching me at that very moment. The thought exacerbated the urge to empty my bladder. I looked around again but, if I was being watched, someone was making a good job of making it look as if I wasn't.

I finished the beer, pushed a few coins towards the barman and went out.

The night was black. Only the great silhouette of the Brandenburg Gate loomed above me. I walked towards it then into rubble of Pariser Platz's buildings. I undid my fly and had just started to urinate when a voice called softly out of the darkness:

'Herr Tennant?'

I finished off, buttoned my fly and turned towards the voice.

'There you are, Herr Tennant,' the small man said, this time speaking English. 'I thought I had missed you.'

'I am here, Herr Fischer. Gretchen spoke of you the other evening. So did her husband the last time I saw him, although he would not tell me your name. He told me you were a very cautious man.'

'And so I am.'

'The last I heard, Gretchen's husband was in Moscow. Is that correct?'

'It is what I hear, also.'

'And are you not concerned he might talk about your friendship?'

'We are not friends,' Fischer explained just as Prochnow had before him, 'merely colleagues.'

'And his wife?' I asked, adopting Fischer's discursive manner in avoiding Prochnow's name.

'We have met only recently.'

'Her husband gave me something the last time we met,' I said.

'Oh?' Fischer responded, as if the fact was news to him.

'A list of names.' I repeated as many as I could remember. 'Our friend led me to believe it came from you.'

'I certainly gave him no list,' Fischer contended. 'I may have mentioned those particular names in conversation with him. If he made any sort of list and then gave it to you, I can only assume he exceeded his authority.'

I tried to make out his face in the darkness, wondering how long he wanted to play this game. I decided to get to the point.

'Prochnow told me quite a bit about you,' I said, using the man's name so there could be no misunderstanding. 'He said he had the impression that you were not happy with the political situation here.'

'Who is?' replied Fischer with equanimity.

'I meant with respect to the Russians. Are you not worried that he will tell them everything he knows?'

'What does he know? They have methods to ensure he will tell them all they wish to hear, of course. But this is not the same thing as everything he knows.'

I assumed he was talking about torture. It was a blunt method of interrogation, as a tortured man will make up any story, give up any name, in order to stop the pain. But then, as an inquisitor, if you are unconcerned about sweeping up the innocent as well as the guilty, it would hardly matter.

'And if he mentions your name, Herr Fischer?'

'I have nothing to fear. I have committed no crime.'

'In Berlin the two are not mutually exclusive,' I said. 'You have risked meeting me. That might be construed as a crime in today's political circles.'

A group of uniformed men crossed the other side of the

145

platz. We edged deeper into the shadows.

'Do you not think that as a colleague of Prochnow's you will be watched?'

'We are all watched, Herr Tennant. Some of us learn how to circumvent these inconveniences.'

'Am I right in thinking that Prochnow approached you about a proposition he thought might interest you?'

'This is precisely why I am meeting you.'

'I was told you could provide certain material our friend could not obtain.'

'He told you this?'

'Also that he thought you regretted the lack of true German leadership in Germany now the Nazi regime has been defeated.'

'Indeed. I would have thought all right-thinking Germans would regret this.'

'And left-thinking Germans?'

'All Germans,' Fischer said.

'Then it might be,' I suggested, 'we could help each other while helping Germany. All of Germany.'

'You may be correct, Herr Tennant. Although you must appreciate that now circumstances have changed. As I have said, I do not believe that I am in any immediate danger. Our friend told you that I spent time in Moscow with Walter Pieck? This is why, if our friend mentions my name, he will not be taken seriously. They will think he is merely supplying names to save himself. But, to be sure, they will make some discreet enquiries. They will not approach me directly at first. All the same, they will want to assure themselves that our friend was indeed lying to save himself. I know how these things work. Sooner or later they may begin to watch me more closely. Such observation breeds suspicion, regardless of what is observed. After all, if a man is being watched there must be a reason for it. And, once under suspicion, my usefulness to the Party comes to an end.'

'That is regrettable but true,' I said, trying to sound sympathetic.

'It is the way they operate in uncertain times. It is what is happening in Germany today.'

'And this worries you?'

'Oh yes, Herr Tennant, It worries me greatly. That is why I cannot do for you the service our friend suggested.'

'Then why are you taking the risk of meeting me at all?' I asked.

'Because, as I have explained, sooner or later, with or without evidence, I will be taken. To be on the safe side, as you English say. Many good German communists were liquidated in Moscow before the end of the war under the same reasoning. To be on the safe side. When that time comes my friendship with Walter Pieck will not help me. He, too, may conclude I am an embarrassment and he will worry that our association could tarnish his reputation. His reputation for ideological orthodoxy, you understand.'

'It seems to me, Herr Fischer, that you are in something of a fix. What will you do?'

'What I obviously cannot do is to promise to be of any continuing service to you. What I may be able to do is to bring you something of such value that, in return, you will think of a way to extricate me from my "fix", as you put it.'

'You are suggesting a one-off trade?'

'In return for a safe haven for myself.'

'You alone?'

'I have no family, Herr Tennant.'

'A haven here in Germany?'

'Oh, no. I do not think I will ever be safe in Germany. My haven, regretfully, will have to be either in England or America.'

'But you haven't approached the Americans.'

'No, because what I am offering has specific relevance for the British.'

'I see,' I said, trying not to bite his hand off but rather convey a sense of reluctance. I peered into the deep shadows again before saying more. I couldn't see anything in there, certainly any good reason that might convince him we wouldn't want to play.

'Whatever you offer,' I suggested, 'would have to be valuable enough to outweigh the consequences.'

'The consequences?'

'Of your "extrication", as *you* put it. After all, a friend of Walter Pieck changing sides? The comrades are not going to like that, are they? Pieck will not like it at all. There will be a fuss. Suggestions of kidnapping, perhaps. There may be diplomatic repercussions.'

Fischer sighed theatrically. 'I am afraid you may be right, Herr Tennant. Which is why, what I am offering will be something your colleagues cannot refuse.'

'You sound very confident of that, Herr Fischer. I can't imagine what the nature of that might be.'

'You have a list of names,' he said. 'Imagine another list, but this time of agents who are currently working undercover in your diplomatic and intelligences services. Do you think that is something you might be able to imagine, Herr Tennant?'

18

Friday 1ˢᵗ August 1947

The temperature had dropped several degrees, still warm although not warm enough to persuade Bill to discard his raincoat. As he approached, I thought he resembled nothing quite so much as one of those statues the comrades favoured come to life: grey, monolithic and unsubtle.

I had sent him a message through Andy Thurston at the Military Mission on Hohenstaufenstraße. Emphasising it was important, I said I'd wait until he arrived. So there I was, sitting by the Havel just above the bridge that separates Großer Wansee from Kleiner Wansee. The café was on the Strandbad Wannsee lido which I'd heard had once been a fashionable nudist beach between the wars. While the Strandbad was still popular with those who had the time and money to spend, from where I was sitting I couldn't see much in the way of skinny-dipping going on.

The lido had been Bill's choice for a rendezvous. Despite this I wasn't expecting to see him shed the raincoat and start splashing around in the water in whatever it was he wore beneath.

He walked up, drew out a chair and sat across the table from me.

'So what brings you out here on this fine and sunny morning?' he asked, making it sound as if I had invited him over on a whim.

'Albrecht Fischer,' I said.

A waiter came up and Bill ordered a beer.

'Tell me more,' he said as soon as the man left.

'Fischer is Prochnow's colleague at the Air Ministry.'

'You've met him?'

'Last night in the Pariser Platz. A dump called the Austrian café.'

'The Russian sector? Watch your step, Harry. Beware of Greeks bearing gifts.'

'I would have if this one hadn't have come through Prochnow's wife.'

The waiter brought Bill's beer. He sipped at it tentatively as though, like Berlin's ersatz coffee, it might not be what it claimed.

'Prochnow was right. Fischer is interested. The only thing is Prochnow's trip to Moscow has changed the rules.'

'In what way?'

'He believes he's safe enough for the time being. Sooner or later, though, he thinks he's going to fall under suspicion as well.'

'What does he suggest?'

'A one-time transaction. He claims he can come over with something we can't refuse.'

'It would have to be good. Very good if it's to keep him in the manner I assume he'd like to become accustomed. Does he have has access to something that good?'

'Prochnow maintained he has. He's got contacts with some of the top names.'

Having approved his beer, Bill lit a cigarette.

'Pieck?' What about Ulbricht and Meikle?'

'Who's Meikle?'

'Erich Meikle. NKVD but German. He was involved in organizing the merger between the SED and the KPD. Before

149

the war he was a well-known communist agitator. He ran off to Moscow after he murdered two Weimar policemen. We're pretty sure he had a hand in purging the ex-patriot German communists. Some say the Russians have earmarked him to be their German security chief.'

'Sounds like an unpleasant character,' I said.

'I agree. A man to avoid if at all possible. If Fischer moves in those circles, though, is there any chance he's more than Prochnow thought he was?'

'You mean German Intelligence?'

'Or Russian,' said Bill.

'Well,' I allowed, 'that would throw a different light on things. But if we can trust him and what he's offering is as good as he says it is, I think he's right in saying it's something we can't afford to turn down.'

'What is it, the Soviet Order of Battle?'

'No, but something that might be almost as useful. Fischer says he can provide us with the names of communist agents currently working within our Foreign Office and Intelligence Services.'

Bill's cigarette stalled halfway to his mouth.

'He said that?'

'Yes.'

The cigarette resumed its journey. 'Interesting.'

'Of course,' I said, 'as you say, he may not be the real thing. If we're careful, though, and don't take him at face value, we can always throw him back if what he gives us isn't up to snuff.'

Bill smiled. 'You're all heart, Harry.'

'After all,' I added, having had time to think it through, 'finding out the names of a few people working in our Foreign Office wouldn't be that difficult. There's always mileage in muddying the water. Have us chase our own tails while we run checks on each other. I don't know how easy it might be to get names of our people in the security services. At the very least, though, any names of our people he does give us that prove correct will demonstrate how much they know about who is working for us. Even if they don't turn out to be Russian agents. The trick will be telling one from the other.'

'And the only way to do that,' Bill said, 'is chase our own tails doing it.'

'So either way, genuine or fake, we get disrupted?'

He didn't reply. Instead he stared out across the Großer Wansee towards an island not far offshore.

'That's Schwanenweder Island,' he said. 'It used to be the place to have a house before the war. You know, the moneyed classes. A lot of industrialists and bankers lived there... If they were rich Jews the state seized their houses and threw them off.'

For a second I thought he might be alluding to my attempt to find out about the Lehmann family and wondered if Kurt had said something about it to him. But Bill was just musing. Something I had discovered he often did. Talking to himself, almost.

'Goebbels and Speer had homes there,' he went on. 'Goebbels bought his from a Jew for a song. Speer, too, probably. Goebbels' place managed to escape the air raids undamaged although the Russians more or less destroyed it when they arrived.'

'Revenge or spite?' I asked.

'Who knows? Both? Perhaps they were just looking for loot.'

He drew on his cigarette, turning back to me again.

Something else was on his mind. Schwanenweder Island had been no more than a hiatus in his contemplation of Albrecht Fischer.

'Do you remember in Arthur's flat I said this business with Prochnow sounded familiar?'

'Yes, I do.'

'Although I don't suppose the name Konstantin Volkov will mean anything to you?'

The Christian name, Konstantin, brought back a few unpleasant memories. But I didn't suppose Bill knew anything about my Konstantin and I didn't know his Volkov.

'There's no reason it should,' Bill went on. 'I was in Istanbul before being posted here. Konstantin Volkov was the Soviet vice-consul there. In August of '45 he approached the British embassy with a story about how he could name three-hundred and fourteen Soviet agents in Turkey and another two-hundred and fifty in Britain.'

'Good God!'

For a moment I couldn't think of what to say.

'That many?' I finally said. 'Surely that was just too much lard to be kosher.'

Bill's lips curled but I didn't think he was really amused.

'What was even more alarming was that he maintained two British diplomats in the Foreign Office were Soviet agents. And that they had a high-ranking man in our own Intelligence Service.'

'SIS?' I said. 'But was it likely a vice-consul would have access to that sort of intelligence?'

'No more likely than a KPD hack working out of Berlin has,' Bill countered.

'I can see why this business with Fischer sounds familiar. What was Volkov after? Money?'

'Money and assurances. Much the same as Albrecht Fischer wants, I imagine.'

'What happened?'

'Naturally our people in Istanbul were as suspicious as we are now. They arranged a meeting. That's when they found out Volkov was NKVD.'

'And in a position to know what he was talking about.'

'Precisely.'

'And you're wondering if Fischer is NKVD as well?'

'We have to consider the possibility.'

'That doesn't invalidate the offer,' I pointed out.

'No, it increases its value.'

'Did Volkov come over?'

'London had to be informed, of course. Volkov insisted we shouldn't use cables. He said the Soviets could read our cipher traffic.'

'He was taking a big risk.'

'Yes, he was. We couriered his offer to London where it was passed to the Soviet section. It was big enough to persuade Kim he'd better come out to Istanbul to handle it personally.'

'Kim Philby?'

'He was head of the Soviet section at the time. Unfortunately for one reason or another Kim was delayed. By the time he arrived Volkov and his wife had disappeared. We heard later a heavily bandaged man had been seen being put aboard a plane to Russia.'

'Someone betrayed him?'

'Not necessarily. It turned out that our embassy in Ankara had discussed Volkov's case over the phone and that they were tapped. Kim was livid about it, needless to say.'

'So Volkov was the real thing?'

'We still can't be one-hundred per cent sure. Some continue to maintain he was a plant and that for some reason they got cold feet over the operation.'

'Why would they get cold feet?'

'No one has come up with a satisfactory answer to that one yet. As it happens, Kim was made Head of Station in Istanbul earlier this year. If he'd been there at the time things might have turned out differently.'

'I assumed he worked in London since he was at Acton.'

Bill shook his head. 'He just happened to be in London. He had an interest so he decided to sit in on your interview.'

'If Volkov wasn't a plant,' I asked, getting back to the main point, 'Is it possible their man in London tipped off the NKVD before we could get him out?'

'If they really do have one,' said Bill. 'That's what we don't know, of course. If Volkov *was* genuine, however, we let a golden chance slip through our fingers.'

'And maybe Fischer's a second bite of the cherry?'

Bill smiled again. 'All things are possible, Harry. But this time, until we're ready, I think it might be best if we keep Albrecht Fischer between ourselves.'

I assumed Bill's remark included Kurt although I didn't think it would be easy keeping him in the dark. When I got back to the Mill that afternoon he wanted to know if I'd seen Gretchen. I could have lied, but since he might get the story from Karl Bauer or Mitzi, or Gretchen herself, to be on the safe side and without going into any details I told him she'd left a note at the club, putting me in touch with a friend of her husband's.

'You met him?'

'Yes.'

'What did he say?'

'He said he heard Prochnow was in Moscow, too.'

'Is this the one Prochnow told you about? He will take Prochnow's place?'

'We haven't come to any agreement,' I said. 'He's worried he'll come under suspicion, too.'

'I meant with Gretchen.'

'Oh.' I shrugged. 'Who knows?'

'Maybe this one already has a wife. Am I to take her round the clubs as with Prochnow? Dance with some fat hausfrau to keep everyone happy?'

'You could hardly call Gretchen fat,' I said.

'No, not Gretchen,' he agreed.

'Consider yourself lucky,' I told him. 'There are whole armies here in Berlin who would give their right arm to get their hands on her.'

'Hand, Harry, if they give their right arm.'

'Better than using a rifle,' I said.

'And this other one?'

'You've nothing to worry about there,' I assured him. 'There's no wife.'

He grunted.

'Have you heard anything from her?'

'Gretchen?' He shook his head. 'Perhaps she has found herself another man already. Do you want me to ask around? Maybe they took her to Moscow, too. Are you sure it was Gretchen who left the note.'

'So Marthe said. She's the one Gretchen gave it to.'

'Marthe? Can you trust her?'

Not wanting to go into all of that, I said:

'Gretchen's not in Moscow. Fischer would have mentioned it if she was.'

'Who's Fischer?'

I could have bitten my tongue but it was a bit late for amateur dramatics. Marthe would have been a safer subject.

'Albrecht Fischer,' I replied, sounding as off-hand as I could. 'This friend of Prochnow's.'

Kurt grunted and went back to sorting through the

paperwork that had been occupying him when I arrived. Then he looked up again.

'I have almost forgotten. Joe Rafferty has an address for you.'

I had almost forgotten Rafferty myself and for a second couldn't think what he was talking about.

'Colonel Tuchmann,' Kurt said.

He handed me a slip of paper.

'That was quick.'

He shrugged. 'It does not seem to be a secret where this man works.'

The address was an office on Bayreuther Straße. Number 39.

Before leaving London I had taken the trouble of buying myself a Baedeker for Berlin. There hadn't been an edition in English published since 1908 but I'd managed to find an old copy of that one in a second-hand bookshop. As the guide hadn't been updated since before the Great War, one had to make allowances for the changes made in street names, first by the Nazi and then by the Russians. That aside, the guide was still good enough to get me around the city.

Bayreuther Straße 39 was listed in the index as *pensionate Clare*, run by a Mrs Bennett. She sounded to me like a Jane Austen character on her uppers and I couldn't imagine that, after all these years, the place would still exist. When I looked on the map, I couldn't even find the street.

'Off Wittenberger Platz,' Kurt said, stabbing one of his remaining fingers at the map when I asked.

Managing to decipher the map's barely legible print, I saw Bayreuther crossed Augsburger Straße south of Wittenberger Platz.

'Did Rafferty say what sort of office it was?'

'No. Why do you want to see this Colonel Tuchmann?'

'This girl, Shoshannah Lehmann. You remember, I'm trying to find out about her family.'

'She is pretty?'

'I told you, quite the contrary. She's half starved. And a little touched, too, I think.'

'Touched?'

'Deranged,' I said.

'And she is connected to Albrecht Fischer?'

He had remembered that name without any trouble.

'No, Kurt. Not at all. The girl told me she used to live at the house in Halensee where Mitzi is now.' Then, as it seemed as good a time as any to let him know about my change of address, I said, 'I'm interested because I've moved in there with her.'

He eyed me slyly. 'You have told Herr Harrington this?'

'Not yet.'

'He will want to know all about her, I think.'

'You mean he'll want to look into her past?'

'Does she have one?'

'Everyone has a past,' I said.

'Yes, Harry. But in Berlin many would prefer if theirs was forgotten.'

~

Before Ben Tuchmann's name occurred to me I had wondered if Dai Edwards might be able to help with who had owned the house in Halensee before the war. Dai was the useful corporal who had arranged my residence and working permits. He seemed to know his way through the maze of forms I'd needed to fill in and steered me through a few useful shortcuts as well. Having had occasion to consult him at the British HQ at the Reich Sporting Field a couple of times since, I stood him a drink when he had a pass one weekend and we spent a boozy evening touring the underbelly of Berlin.

I decided, though, that finding out who had once owned the Halensee house might be a little off the beaten track even for Dai. So when I remembered Ben Tuchmann I took an alternative route.

Now I had the address on Bayreuther Straße, what did occur to me was that Dai would probably be able to tell me which of the many military and civilian organizations in the city were compiling lists of Berlin's missing Jews.

I took the S-Bahn out to the Sporting Field and tracked him down to one of the Nissen huts erected in regimented rows where the old Olympic accommodation had once stood.

Dai was up to his arms in a filing cabinet, neat as ever and pin-bright, and army down to the shiny caps of his regulation boots.

'Harry,' he said cheerfully as I walked in. 'In trouble already? What have they done, rescinded your license?'

'No, they haven't tumbled me yet, Dai. I'm after something else this time.'

'And what'll that be?'

'Missing persons.'

He laughed. 'Missing persons? In Berlin? Are you pulling my leg?'

'No, I'm serious. I thought you might be able to point me in the right direction. I've got a name and an address.'

'All right, I'll bite. Who was he?'

'It's a she not a he and she isn't missing. It's her parents I'm after.'

'Right,' he said, as if he understood.

'I was told the Yanks are drawing up lists of everyone deported by the Nazis from Berlin after 1941.'

'Not everyone,' he said. 'They're trying to trace Jews.'

'I'm pretty sure this family was Jewish.'

'That'll make it easier. No one's bothered much by missing civilians at the moment. If they were Jews, though, they were probably caught up in what the Nazis called the "Resettlement Programme". What that meant was a bullet or a concentration camp. Poor bastards.'

'There's an American air force colonel I think might be able to help me. I'm told he works out of an office at Bayreuther Straße 39. I'd like to know who they are before I go crashing in.'

'Bayreuther?

Dai dragged a large ledger off one of the shelving units lodged up against the curving sides of the hut. He dumped it on his desk and began flipping through the pages.

'We're trying to assemble a street directory,' he explained, 'to keep track of all the organizations working in the city. Only trouble is a new one starts up every time an old one closes. Here ... Bayreuther Straße ... United Nations Office for

157

Dependent Persons Repatriation and Resettlement... That any good to you?'

It sounded more than good. It sounded like just the sort of organization Ben Tuchmann would be working for. The last time I'd seen him he'd been connected to the UN, digging out a Frenchman who'd been complicit in sending French Jews to the extermination camps. As the man had had a connection to my wife's family I had been involved, albeit unwittingly.

Dai Edwards wrote the organization's name down for me.

'Only the office here, Harry. No personnel I'm afraid. If you get no joy, give me a ring and I'll see what else I can dig up for you.'

I told him I owed him a drink.

'You're on, but no more pub crawls. I've still got the headache from the last time I was out with you.'

I left the base and took the S-Bahn back into the city, switching to the U-Bahn at the first interchange. Coming up at Wittenberger Platz I followed my map to Bayreuther Straße.

I could only assume the street was named for Bayreuth, the Bavarian town where Hitler's favourite Wagnerian music festival had been held before the war. It would have predated Hitler, of course, being in my old Baedeker, but even so, walking through the ruins I still didn't find much to sing about. Passing some men working on the gas holder on the corner of Bayreuther and Augsburger Straße, attempting to get Berlin's infrastructure up and running again, I wondered if Wagner, in his imaginative way, might have seen them as a gang of Nibelung dwarves, hammering and welding at Siegfried's bidding. But my grounding in German mythology had always been pretty thin and my imagination almost certainly less vivid than Wagner's.

The building that had once housed Mrs Bennett's *pensionate Clare* had lost much of its nineteenth century facade and all its attraction. The stairs creaked as I climbed to the first floor, an unpleasant odour wafting along the hall ahead of me. Gas from the holder, I thought, although Berlin was full of unpleasant odours. All the old corpses might have been buried but there were always new ones turning up. The stench of shit was ever-present, too, and would be until the day the dwarves got the sewers flowing again.

I found the door of the office was open so I walked in. Several girls were sitting at desks, paper and files piled high in front of them, and one or two glanced up without much interest before looking back at their work again.

I stepped up to the nearest desk. The girl behind it was in her twenties, wasn't wearing any sort of uniform and the civilian clothes she was wearing seemed of a better quality than anything I'd seen in any of Berlin shops.

'Colonel Tuchmann?' I asked her in English. 'USAF. I was told I might find him here?'

She raised a decently plucked eyebrow that turned out to be American.

'Did you have an appointment? I'm afraid Colonel Tuchmann isn't here this afternoon. Can I help?'

'It's the colonel I need to see,' I explained. 'It's rather important.'

'You could try the synagogue on Levetzowstraße. Do you know it?'

'I didn't know there were any synagogues left in Berlin.'

She smiled sadly. 'The Levetzowstraße synagogue only survived because it was used as an assembly camp prior to Jewish deportations.'

'Oh,' I muttered, unable to think of much else to say.

'From the synagogue they were taken to Sachsenhausen in Orianienburg,' she said. 'It's where Colonel Tuchmann conducts his interviews.'

I thanked her and told her I'd try the synagogue.

'Levetzowstraße, you said?'

'In Moabit. Would you like to leave a message for Colonel Tuchmann in case you miss him?'

'No,' I said. 'Thanks anyway. I'm sure I'll catch him sooner or later.'

I left the American girl to what I imagined could only be her deeply distressing work, sitting like the other women in the office behind mounds of Nazi documents. All piled on their desktops like surrogate gravestones.

19

The Levetzowstraße synagogue lay north of the Tiergarten across the River Spree and not a million miles from the mill and Peston's apartment. I wondered at the irony of a synagogue being used as a gathering point for Jews prior to deportation. Had it been deliberately chosen to provide one last point of familiarity for those doomed in an increasingly alien city? Or had the choice been no more than a demonstration of contempt, an appallingly bad joke that had tickled some macabre Nazi sense of humour?

By the time I crossed the bridge over the Spree and walked up Levetzowstraße it had already gone five. More intent on how I would tackle Tuchmann if I found him than where I was going, I found him sooner than I expected. Turning the corner of Solingerstraße, I bumped right into him.

He wasn't in uniform and, not immediately recognising him, I muttered an apology and stepped aside before realizing he was the man I had come to see.

As an accidental meeting it couldn't have been bettered.

I believe he recognized me before I recognized him and for a split second I saw the impulse in his eyes not to acknowledge me. But a heartbeat later he must have known it was too late.

He pasted a grin on his face.

'Harry? Harry Tennant? You're the last man I expected to run into in Berlin.' He held out his hand. 'What are you doing here?'

He hadn't changed. Easy and self-confident, he was east coast American down to the shiny tips of his bespoke shoes.

When I first met him the previous summer he told me he had been a New York lawyer until America had entered the war. By then he had been seconded into what was becoming the United Nations War Crimes Commission. At the time he compared his work with the United Nations to what I was doing at my war crimes unit. To me it seemed likening a tin of SPAM to the sort of meal one could still get at the Savoy Grill.

Inevitably, when one of my investigations had crossed paths with one of his, mine had come off a bad second. At the time he had been squiring my ex-wife's aunt about London which only made things more complicated. They had made a handsome couple for a while although I heard later that my wife's aunt had come off second best in that encounter as well.

I shook Tuchmann's hand and, in an attempt to wrong-foot him, said:

'As a matter of fact, Ben, I was on my way to see you.'

His eyebrows lifted, although you needed to be quick to notice, and that was as much wrong-footing I got out of him.

'You knew I was in Berlin?'

'I saw you out at Templehof a few days ago. You were riding a Jeep and in uniform. A full colonel now?'

'I prefer civvies in the city, Harry. Like you.'

His eyes drifted down to my suit. It was a little creased and a little worn like its owner, and not a match for what he was wearing. I could only assume he hadn't wasted any time finding a good tailor while he'd been in London.

'I'm out of it now,' I said. 'Before we last spoke as a matter of fact. They closed my unit down and demobbed us all.'

Tuchmann smiled sympathetically. 'I heard that, Harry.'

I thought he probably had.

He regarded me with that quizzical amusement I recognized as one of the manifestations of his self-confidence. Like most Americans, the easterners at least, he gave the air of finding Englishmen to be somewhat enjoyable curiosities.

'So, Harry, what are you doing in Berlin?' he asked, seemingly over-keen to demonstrate no curiosity about why I was coming to see him.

I gave him a modest shrug. 'I'm in the import business these days. Electrical components.'

The brow furrowed slightly, as if he didn't know whether he should believe me or not.

'Is that right? How's business?'

'Up and down,' I said.

He smiled. 'Look, there's a café I know near the schloss. Nothing fancy but they do a good strudel. You did say you were coming to see me, right?'

'It's not going to cost me a week's coupons, is it Ben?'

'You won't need *Marken,* Harry. I always take care to carry the almighty dollar.'

'They must blow a fanfare every time you walk through the door.'

He laughed. 'Same old Harry,' he said, as if we'd once been the best of friends.

The café was on the Spree Weg, on the edge of the grounds of what was left of the Schloss Bellevue. The place had an awning, some tables and chairs under a few splintered trees and a proprietor who recognized Tuchmann. He didn't blow a fanfare but I doubted it would have taken much persuasion to get him waving a Star-Spangled Banner.

'Don't drink the coffee, Harry,' Ben warned as we sat down.

Since I had already learned that lesson I sipped a Pilsner while we waited for our strudel.

'I assume you didn't look me up to talk over old times, Harry.' He lit a cigarette and blew the smoke in the direction of the ruined schloss. Further along the road, towering over the Tiergarten's main hub, the *Siegessäule*—the Prussian Victory column—still stood where Speer had moved it from its original location outside the old Reichstag.

Tuchmann saw me looking that way.

'Did you know there used to be some stone busts around that column? Who was it? Bismarck, Moltke and a fellow named Roon? All big Prussian heroes, they say. The column was put up to celebrate a Prussian victory over France. Now the French have helped win one back, they want to dynamite the thing. To rub German noses in it.'

'It's still there,' I said.'

'The column, yes. Not the busts.'

'Did the French smash them?'

Tuchmann shook his head.

'You're not going to tell me the Russians took a fancy to Prussian statuary?'

'Not the commies this time, Harry. It seems some Berliners didn't care for the thought of the Allies smashing up even more of their history than we already had. They arranged for the busts to disappear. The French had to be content with a few reliefs that footed the column. They're back in Paris now, apparently. Rumour has it the busts are buried out there in the park somewhere. Waiting until we leave, I guess. The way things have worked out, though, that could be some time.'

'Do I detect a moral in this story, Ben? What is it? Strike while the iron's hot? Don't put off till tomorrow what you can do today?'

Tuchmann pulled on his cigarette. 'For the French, perhaps. But I see it more as a small lesson in not grinding our boot in their faces again. We made that mistake before.'

'Versailles? Well, as I remember it, that was the French. And us.'

'Luckily the French won't be getting much of a say this time.'

Nor us, I thought, although Tuchmann was diplomatic enough not to say as much.

'What about that,' I asked, tipping my glass across Park Bellevue towards the wrecked palace. 'Did we do that on purpose? Or was that ... what do you Yanks call it ... collateral damage?'

Tuchmann looked at rubble. 'Oh, on purpose, I think. That's where Molotov and his delegation stayed when they came to visit Hitler in 1940. I'm reliably told the Nazis really pushed the boat out for their Russian allies back then.'

'Did we think Molotov was still there when we bombed it?'

Tuchmann chuckled. 'No such luck.'

Our strudel arrived and Tuchmann ground out his cigarette. He forked some of the pastry into his mouth, looking up at me as he did so.

'You didn't answer the question, Harry.'

He was right. I hadn't.

'About old times? That's because I'm not sure they would bear much talking about.'

'Maybe you're right. I hear you're divorced now.'

I wondered where he could have heard that.

'The decree won't come through for another eight or nine months,' I said, 'but it's settled apart from that.'

'I'm sorry,' he said.

'It probably would have happened sooner or later.'

'I mean if I had any part in it.'

'At the time,' I said, 'it felt as if I was the only one who didn't have a part in it.'

'Even though you caught most of the flak?'

'You could put it that way. Water under the bridge now. How did you hear?'

'The divorce? A mutual friend. Of Julia's, I mean. She keeps me up to date.'

'She?'

'It's not Penny. I don't think you know the lady.'

I wondered if I did, although I had never moved in the same circles as Penny's aunt Julia. One of the other bones of contention between me and my wife's family.

'Do you keep in touch?' he asked.

'No. So I'm not expecting an invitation to the wedding.'

He seemed puzzled.

'Penny and my brother,' I explained.

He waved his fork in the air. 'Oh, that's off. Didn't you hear?'

'No. As I said, I don't keep in touch.'

I would have liked to know more although not if it had to come through Ben Tuchmann. To shift the subject I asked if he was still in the same business.

'That depends on what business you're talking about,' he replied.

'I went to your office on Bayreutherstraße. They're the ones who told me I might find you at the synagogue. So it's still the United Nations and war crimes, is it?'

'Is that why you're looking for me? War crimes? I thought you said they closed your unit down.'

'They did. This is a personal enquiry.'

'Into what?'

'A Jewish family.'

'And where do the electrical components fit in?' he remarked acerbically.

'This is something else, Ben. Something I've become curious about.'

Tuchmann went back to his strudel, smiling in that amused way of his once more.

'I remember that curiosity of yours, Harry. It's not going to get you into trouble again, is it?'

'Not this time,' I assured him. 'I've just moved into a house down by Lake Halensee in Wilmersdorf. There's a girl who's been hanging around the place. She says she used to live there and that her name used to be Shoshannah Lehmann.'

'*Used* to be Shoshannah Lehmann? What before she married? Who is she now?'

'She's not married, at least as far as I know. That's the thing. She's a little touched, if you know what I mean. She's obviously been through a lot but she insists she once lived in the house with her parents. I assume they're dead but I suppose there's always a possibility they might have survived.'

'It's happened.'

'She also mentioned a man named Walter Frick.'

I kept my eyes on him but there was no sign he recognized the name.

'I asked the woman who looks after the house. She maintains she doesn't know anything about the previous residents.'

'The girl is Jewish, I assume?'

'With a name like Lehmann, I'm assuming so.'

'And you think the family was sent to the camps and the house appropriated. Is that right?'

'Again,' I said, 'that's what I'm assuming.'

'Who owns the house now?'

'I'm told it's a man named Neumann. He lives in Hamburg. I've never seen him. Nor has Mitzi.'

'Who's Mitzi?'

I drank some beer before answering.

'The girl I live with,' I said.

Tuchmann was grinning at me.

'Mitzi's been living at the house for some while,' I went on, ignoring his amusement. 'She says she's never laid eyes on him.'

'What's the place like?'

'We just rent a couple of rooms. It's been damaged but it would have been quite a grand place before the war. Whoever the Lehmanns were, they must have been pretty well-to-do.'

'Just the sort of place a Nazi would covert by the sound of it,' he said.

'Yes.'

'And you're trying to find out if the Lehmanns survived and who stole their house.'

'That's about the strength of it,' I said. 'But I don't really know where to start. 'I heard that lists are being compiled of Jews who went missing from Berlin during the war and when I saw you down at Templehof near the DP camp I thought it was the sort of project you might be involved with. Or at least know someone who was.'

'Still playing your hunches, Harry? That's what I always liked about you. Well, you're not wrong. You'd like me to find out if there's anything in the files on a family named Lehmann, yes?'

'If possible,' I said.

'Okay. Give me the address of the house and what you know about this family and about the present owner. I'll see what I can turn up for you.'

He finished his strudel and placed his fork carefully on his plate.

'Between you and me, Harry, I wouldn't hold out too much hope, though. As we both know, the Nazis took a great deal of care to preserve the regime's records but unfortunately a lot of the information concerning property ownership and land registry was destroyed in the bombing. If the family were Jewish, unless they had the opportunity to emigrate, they were probably living in the property until at least October 1941. That's when the deportation of Berlin Jews began. How long they managed to stay in the house after that date would depend on their status. Whether they were full-blood Jews, of mixed Jewish blood, or in a mixed marriage. Those the Nazis deemed to be "privileged" Jews also survived longer. A privileged Jew could mean a decorated veteran of the Great War, say, or members of a profession. A doctor, for instance, someone who worked at the Jewish hospital on the Iranische Straße in Wedding.'

'I didn't know the Nazis discriminated,' I said. 'I thought that if you were a Jew you were going to end up in one of the camps regardless.'

'In the end, they did. They all shared the same fate whether they went to Sachenhausen, Ravensbrück, the women's camp north of Berlin, or Theresienstadt. After the first transports, though, most were shipped directly to Auschwitz-Birkenau.'

'Shoshannah Lehmann managed to survive somehow.'

'Perhaps she was liberated from one of the death camps,' he suggested. 'Is that possible? If that's the case, I'm not surprised she's a little touched, as you put it. What they had to go through is beyond most people's imagination. Of course,' he added, 'there are other possibilities.'

'Such as?'

'She may have been what they called a *Taucher*.'

'What's a *Taucher*?'

'Literally a U-Boat. It's the nickname they gave Jews who went underground. Went into hiding rather than be deported. There were several thousand who did. It's surprising how many managed to survive.'

'What, right through to the end of the war?'

'Hard to believe, I know,' said Tuchmann. 'They say the Russian didn't believe it was possible when they first arrived. They'd liberated the death camps in the east, of course, and when Jews started to surface after Berlin was liberated they said no, you can't be a Jew. All the Jews are dead.'

'And they lived here in Berlin?'

Tuchmann nodded. 'In Berlin and other German cities. It was a lot easier to hide in a city than in the countryside. In a city it's not that difficult to be anonymous. If you were lucky enough not to look particularly Jewish, had blond hair and blue eyes, say, like a German Aryan and you managed to get hold of false papers ... with luck you could blend in with the rest of the population.'

'I wouldn't say Shoshannah Lehmann looks particularly Jewish,' I said.

'Then maybe that's how she survived. Leave it with me, Harry, and I'll see what I can find out for you.'

For a moment I thought he was going to add, 'I owe you one,' but he didn't. I tore a page out my notebook and wrote down as much as I could remember about Shoshannah and the house. He read it through and folded the paper into his pocket.

'You don't know anything more about this man Neumann

who supposedly owns the place now?'

'Only what Frau Ernst, the caretaker, told me. She collects the rent and pays the money into Neumann's bank account here in Berlin. She maintains she doesn't have an address in Hamburg for him or even a telephone number.'

'How likely is that?'

'She says Neumann rings her occasionally to make sure everything is okay.'

'What about contents?'

'The house? There's not much. Certainly nothing of value there now.'

'If the house was Jewish property and appropriated,' he said, 'the contents would most likely have been sold at auction. Most deportees were required to provide an inventory when they arrived at one of the collection points. Like the synagogue on Levetzowstraße. When the deportations began, the former owners were often given a small amount in lieu of their property. This was to maintain the fiction it had been sold legally and to sustain the pretence they were all being relocated rather than murdered. If they received anything, it would have been no more than a token amount. The money raised from any sale went straight into Party coffers. That is, after the Gestapo or the SS had reserved for themselves anything that might have taken their fancy. Sometimes someone in the Party might take over the property and contents lock, stock and barrel. To get away with that, though, whoever it was would have to have been a pretty high-ranking functionary. Or at least have some weight.'

'Neumann, perhaps?'

'If that's his real name,' he said. 'The name itself suggests it might not be. Neumann: *new man?* Not much of a joke, perhaps, but I've never been convinced the Nazis had much of a sense of humour. At least, not the kind we'd find funny.'

'That occurred to me,' I said.

He called for the bill.

'Leave it with me, Harry, and I'll see what I can find out. If you see the girl again I'd like to hear her story. It does happen that we get results from less promising leads. Where can I reach you?'

Since I didn't want Tuchmann to know why I was really in Berlin, instead of giving him the address of the mill or the house in Halensee where Frau Ernst might find out I was making other enquiries, I told him he could find me at the Zoo Club most evenings.

'It's on the Kurfürstendamm, just west of the old zoological gardens. If I'm not there ask for Mitzi. She'll take a message.'

We shook hands and I left it with him.

I walked south, not quite knowing where I was going. It was still too early to go to the club and I didn't feel much like drinking beer all evening while waiting for Mitzi to get off.

Passing the *Siegessäule* I wondered if perhaps Tuchmann had been right in that we had deliberately targeted the Schloss Bellevue. It hardly mattered. After all, we had deliberately targeted the suburbs and civilian housing. By all accounts we had burned other cities to a cinder, too. Notably Dresden. So what was another odd palace or two?

Until 1943 raids on the capital had been small-scale affairs. A few sorties were flown in 1940 and 1941 to show we were capable of reaching Berlin, but they had been pretty ineffectual. Apart from some low level bombing by Mosquitoes, by 1942 our air raids on the capital had almost ceased.

It had been 1943 when the RAF had resumed a large-scale offensive from the air. By then we had developed the Avro Lancaster heavy bomber and radar-jamming equipment. So, despite the formidable air defence system the Germans put in place, we had gained an advantage.

In late July of 1943 a series of raids on Hamburg killed forty-thousand civilians and destroyed much of the city. Berlin's turn came in November, despite the Nazi boasts that we would never bomb the capital.

I suppose Berliners must have known it was coming. I'd been told over seven hundred and fifty aircraft had taken part in the November raid. The target had been the west of the city, from the Tiergarten and Charlottenburg out to Spandau. I'd seen myself in '45 that in the diplomatic quarter to the south of the Tiergarten hardly a habitable building had been left standing. We hadn't managed to dent the Flak Tower in the Zoological Gardens, but the zoo itself had been totally destroyed. Thousands of animals were incinerated by the high-explosive and incendiaries we'd rained down from the sky.

I don't know why but somehow I found the death of the animals harder to come to terms with than the civilian deaths. At least Berliners knew what was happening. They could point their accusing fingers at us or at their own political regime—who, in any final analysis, had been responsible for bringing the bombs down on their heads.

What could those wretched animals do? Howl in their cages while deafened and burned, ignorant of the price they had to pay for human folly?

In 1945 it had not only been me who had been shocked by the devastation we had found upon reaching Berlin. They had brought it upon themselves, we told each other. They had either supported, or meekly acquiesced to, Hitler's assumption of power—those who hadn't were no longer in the city, of course. They were either dead or dying in the concentration camps. Hitler had made sure he first rid himself of his enemies before he began liquidating the Jews.

Even so, the fact still left me with a perverse attitude to the destruction of the city.

Our aim, beyond simple revenge and retaliation I recall hearing at the time, had been to demonstrate to the civilian population that Hitler's aggressive policies had brought devastation to their country. But in 1943 they were still not willing or perhaps still unable to do anything about it. So the slaughter continued while we, no doubt, hoped that someone would cry enough before we dragged ourselves down to the Nazis' level of inhumanity. And it was their inhumanity, it seemed to me, that was our only saving grace.

The more I came to hear of their atrocities, the more I gave silent thanks that we had ended the whole foul business. There was nothing I could do about the atrocities—they had been committed long before I came to hear about them—but the very fact they had happened was, for me, a justification for what we had done to Germany in return.

Well, they deserved it, didn't they?

And looking around Berlin, I told myself that, yes, they did.

But the problem now was, I was beginning to think this was a naïve point of view.

Looking at the ruins of the zoo left me with a sensation of despair. A despair made almost physical in a tingling of the tips of my fingers. A despair that bordered upon panic.

And one that couldn't avoid the unspoken question:

Now, what is it we deserve?

20

I couldn't deny that meeting Ben Tuchmann again had thoroughly depressed me. Seeing him had raked up memories of a past to which I thought I had become inured. It made me think about my wife, Penny, and what she might be doing now she was no longer going to marry my brother, George.

I walked in no particular direction but one I hoped would leave the memories of home and my troubles over the ethics of carpet bombing behind me. Yet that was easier said than done. The results of the air raids were all around. Shattered buildings and shattered lives. No matter who deserved what, the harm damages everyone in the same way.

I found myself on Taeuntzien Straße and continued walking southeast through Hollendorf Platz, or what was left of it. I turned up Potsdamer Straße and headed back towards the Brandenburg Gate. Everywhere to the east lay in the Russian sector, just as devastated and barren but now under Stalin's thumb rather than Hitler's.

The thought brought Albrecht Fischer back to mind. Bill had given me the go-ahead and I was to tell Fischer that, as soon as he could supply what he was offering, he could come over. I knew Bill was running a risk. He was prepared to accept Fischer's terms without clearing it first through London, in effect committing financial resources he had no authority to commit. That would not be not my problem, he had assured me, implying without actually saying so that I was just the messenger and could not be held responsible if no one liked the message.

Which was all well and good. But I had already worked for the Intelligence Service in London and discovered that when things go wrong it's the man on the ladder's lowest rung who gets kicked in the face first.

Fischer had told me he'd be in touch yet had given me no way of contacting him. Now Bill had agreed, I was anxious to start the ball rolling. The problem was, having already decided not to involve Kurt, they only person I knew who knew Fischer and could get a message to him was Gretchen.

The first evening I met the Prochnows Gretchen had said they lived in Pankow, complaining how dirty it was and how she would like to move. Pankow was one of the industrial suburbs in the Russian sector north of Prenzlauer Berg. Kurt had given me their address should I ever need it so I took the next tram north into the Russian sector and got off at Alexander Platz.

In Hitler's day and before, Berlin's main police headquarters—the 'Alex'—had dominated the platz. Run by the SS during the war, it hadn't been somewhere anyone went out of choice. The air raids and the subsequent battle for Berlin had so badly damaged the buildings, though, that the police had moved to a new HQ not far away on Keibelstraße. I doubted much had changed now the Russians ruled the roost though and it still wouldn't be anywhere anyone would want to go through choice.

With that in mind I wasted no time sightseeing and took the A1 U-Bahn line north.

The address I had for Prochnow's flat was on Spiekermann Straße, somewhere halfway between stops at Schönhauser Allee and Vinestraße. The A1 line was one of the first reopened in 1945 although not before some tinkering had been done to a few place names. The Russians had taken exception to Horst Wessel Platz, named as it was for the SA thug who died in a skirmish with the communists back in the thirties. They renamed the square Liebknechtplatz and, more recently, Luxemburgplatz, after Rosa.

Coming up from the subway it looked to me as if the name was the only thing new about the place. Once among the most populous areas of Berlin, Pankow and Prenzlauer Berg seemed to have attracted more than their fair share of high explosive. Like an x-ray of a city, skeletal buildings towered seemingly unsupported out of the rubble. Teetering walls enclosed mounds of brick and stone filling the empty interiors like undigested meals.

Making my way to Spiekermann Straße, I could understand why Gretchen had wanted to move. "Dirty" hardly did Pankow justice. Even with the light breeze blowing that afternoon dust swirled in the air like a mist of grit. I suspected if it ever really got windy Pankow's residents first job each morning would be to dig themselves out.

After a couple of false turns due to a dearth of street signs and roads that went nowhere unless one counts a rubble mountain a destination, I finally found Spiekermann Straße in what was left of an industrial quarter. There was still a little business going on to judge by the smell in the air. That suggested Gretchen lived not far from a brewery, a fact that may have enhanced the neighbourhood for some residents but would do little for a girl with pretentions to sophistication like Gretchen.

The apartment building stood a block past the junction with Neumann Straße, a name that, I admit, gave me pause for a moment. But my interest in Neumann and the girl in Halensee was just an indulgence. Fischer was business.

There was no lock on the front door and by the look of the ill-fitting door itself, I'd have said that at one point there had been no front door either. But someone had improvised a stopgap, in the literal sense. I supposed it might keep the rain out but couldn't have been much of a deterrent when the Red Army arrived.

Prochnow's flat was on the second floor. I climbed past the first through a miasma of boiled cabbage to the second and along a grimy corridor to the fourth flat. The door displayed a name card announcing that Gerhard Prochnow lived inside.

Not any more, I said to myself and knocked on wood.

She was certainly surprised to see me. Momentarily flustered, she clung to the half-opened door as if it was the only thing keeping her upright.

'Herr Tennant,' she said awkwardly. 'What are you doing

here?'

'It's Harry,' I said, 'remember?' And I hung my most charming smile on the words. 'I thought I'd come by and see how you were getting along, Gretchen.'

'Getting along?' she repeated, as though she had no idea what I was talking about.

'Managing,' I said. 'Without Gerhard. I missed you at the Zoo Club but I got your message. Perhaps I could come in for a moment?'

She still hadn't opened the door and was blocking my view past her.

'It is a little difficult just now,' she said.

'If you've got company...'

I made it sound as if I knew how things could be with a wife whose husband was not around.

'No ... no,' she said quickly, 'of course not. There is no one here.'

'I'll only stay for a minute,' I assured her, my foot already in the door and giving her the choice of either opening it wider or shutting it on my instep.

'Of course,' she said again, regaining some composure. 'It is nice of you to call, Harry.'

I followed her down the short hallway, noting a chaos of clothing on the bed as we passed the open bedroom door. The living room was no tidier. Possessions lay scattered about. The drawers of a chest hung open like the tongues of panting dogs and a pile of books stood on the floor in a tottering tower.

I might have thought she'd been burgled except this housebreaker seemed to have left more behind than he found there.

'I am moving,' she explained.

'Charlottenburg?'

She patted at her brown curls, wondering belatedly, I supposed, whether or not she looked presentable.

'No. I have been asked if I wish to join my husband.'

'In Moscow?'

'Yes. He wishes me to come.'

'And you are happy to go?'

'Of course.'

I thought I might have misjudged her. Somehow, though, the idea of Gretchen playing the dutiful wife seemed to me a case of bad miscasting. Then again, being "asked" to join her husband by the Soviets was no doubt a euphemism for something that offered few choices.

'It gets cold there,' I said bluntly. 'Best take a warm coat.'

And a decent shovel, I might have added, in case she ended up in one of the Russian labour camps alongside her Gerhard. It would be a cruel end for a girl as attractive as Gretchen although, as I had recently discovered, what you were didn't count half as much with the Soviets as who you were. Or had been.

Perhaps Gretchen had a stoical streak I wasn't aware of because she didn't looked so broken up as I would have imagined. Or maybe it was Gretchen who didn't have the imagination. As had been obvious before the war, it was difficult for some people to believe what Russia could actually be like for those who incurred the displeasure of the Party.

Even so, I would have thought that that was unlikely for anyone who had been in Berlin when the Red Army arrived.

'I will have to leave so much behind,' she was saying. 'Many nice things that Gerhard worked so hard for.'

'Well, there's always the black market if you've surplus to sell,' I suggested cheerfully. 'I'm sure Kurt would make you an offer. Good clothes and kitchenware are always in demand. Would you like me to mention it to him?'

'Oh no,' she said quickly. 'Please, do not bother Kurt. I have friends who will buy anything I cannot take with me.'

'Speaking of friends,' I said, seeing another opening I could stick a metaphorical foot in, 'I got the message from Albrecht Fischer you left for me at the Zoo Club—'

'I didn't read it,' she said hurriedly.

'It wasn't private. We met and have come to an agreement.'

Gretchen held up a hand. 'I do not want to know this ... this intrigue... It is why I must leave Berlin.'

'There is no need for you to know. But you did carry the note for Herr Fischer.'

If the remark sounded like a threat, Gretchen chose to ignore it.

'Herr Fischer was very good to me when Gerhard was missing. It was the least I could do.'

'Of course it was,' I agreed. 'Now, just one more thing. For Herr Fischer, you understand. I don't know where he lives. I would like you to let him know that I am happy to do as he wishes. No more than that, Gretchen. You will see him soon, I am sure. Then it will be over for you.'

She was still hesitant. I thought a few dollars might be sufficient to persuade her and reached for my wallet. She put a hand on my arm.

'No, Harry, that is not necessary.'

She was full of surprises.

'I will give Herr Fischer your message. But how will he contact you when he needs to?'

'Ask him to leave another note at the Zoo Club. Tell him to give it to the girl named Marthe. She will make sure I get it.'

I didn't want to involve Mitzi and there was some satisfaction to be had in using Marthe as a go-between. She would do it, I was certain. Passing me a note from another woman would be more than Marthe would be able to resist. Besides, refusing to do it and annoying me would also displease Mitzi and I suspected displeasing Mitzi was the last thing Marthe would want to do.

'Very well,' said Gretchen.

We looked at each other without speaking, as if we'd forgotten our lines. She held out her hand and I shook it awkwardly.

I followed her back down the hall and she saw me out the door. Going down the stairs past the still boiling cabbage, I felt the final exchange had been oddly disquieting.

I wasn't sure what I'd expected. A peck on the cheek in farewell, perhaps. Or even more. Not a tumble on the bed among her unsorted clothes exactly, but more of a connection. She had acted differently when I had first met her. There she had flirted, had even made a few coded suggestions. And again, when she came to tell me that her husband was missing, she remained in character; the distressed wife but still someone who could not resist a flirtation.

Something about her behaviour that afternoon struck me as

off-key.

I took the U-Bahn back to the Alex and, still thinking about Gretchen, rode the first available train out of the Russian sector. I trusted she would do as I asked and pass Fischer my message although there was absolutely no reason she should. It occurred to me she might get the idea she could try to bargain with the Russians, betray both me and Fischer to them. They would listen. The fact her husband had probably have already done as much would be seen by them as corroboration. There wasn't much I could do about that, though, so I tried not to worry about it.

Seeing Gretchen had done nothing to dispel the sombre mood I had fallen into since meeting Ben Tuchmann. If anything, her telling me she had been "invited" to join her husband in Moscow had only deepened my feeling of despondency.

The thought of Tuchmann and his strudel reminded me I hadn't eaten and looking at my watch I saw it was already 8.00pm. I recalled a restaurant I had passed a few days earlier on Bellevue Straße, off Potsdamer Platz. The place looked a little more up-market than the sort of eatery I generally frequented, boasting pressed white linen tablecloths and printed menu cards. Had I had any spare, I would have laid money the chairs weren't even scarred by cigarette burns. It was the sort of *Gaststätte* that wouldn't sully your evening by haggling over ration coupons; the kind of place that party hacks and Administration bureaucrats would frequent.

After all, they were among the minority in the city who were in a position to pay over the odds for their dinner.

Once there, I counted how much money I did have. There were a few dollars and some Reichmarks, most of it money I had been keeping aside for taking Mitzi somewhere decent. But she was working, I was hungry and I had already opened the restaurant door: a *fait accompli* in any language.

A maitre d' decked out like the conductor of the Berlin Philharmonic escorted me to a table. He did a little fawning on account and put a light to the end of my cigarette almost before I had the thing out of the pack. Then he snapped his fingers at a waiter loitering nearby who held out the *carte* for my inspection.

Luckily I hadn't started eating or I might have choked on the prices. But I knew when aplomb was in order so asked for a glass of schnapps to be going on with.

All the old favourites were present. It was a bill of fare that might have taxed even fat Hermann's reputation for gluttony. There were dishes which, until then, I had only heard tales of, usually recounted by undernourished Germans who maintained such food was plentiful before that Austrian corporal had turned up and spoiled everything.

Maultaschen, Leberkäse, Spätzle, Königsberger Klopse...

I ordered *Sauerbraten,* a pot roast generally only served during the colder months. But since the very thought of it sent a shiver down my spine I decided it must be close enough to winter to count. For added ballast I asked for a side helping of *Spätzle,* a dumpling made of eggs and flour. Between that and the *Sauerbraten,* I estimated I probably wouldn't need to eat again until the autumn.

My glass of schnapps didn't last long so I had a second, following that with a *schwarztsbier* to drink with dinner.

Maybe it was the alcohol. Perhaps I had a guilty conscience for sitting down to a good dinner without Mitzi. Somewhere between perusing the menu and the arrival of my dinner, though, I lost my appetite. Even the smell and the look of the food when it finally arrived didn't help.

Trying to do it justice and generate some enthusiasm for the meal, I attempted to identify a piece of meat from the *Sauerbraten* I was chewing on. I didn't think it was pork or mutton and it didn't taste much like beef. The more I chewed, the chewier it got. Since I had no idea where the restaurant sourced their ingredients, I was beginning to suspect it might be horse. I called the waiter.

'*Beef,* mein Herr,' he replied when I asked, his air of arrogance suggesting he thought I might not be used to eating good food.

I should have known better but found myself suddenly needing someone on whom to take out my ill humour. At that moment an arrogant German fitted the bill perfectly.

'It doesn't taste like beef,' I argued. 'Where'd you get it? In the Russian Zone? It's got that tang of state-issue meat about it.'

'No, mien Herr!' he insisted. 'Not the Russians. We do not deal with the Russians here. We have our own supplier in the Allied Zones.'

'Sure you have,' I said sarcastically. 'So exactly where does this so-called "beef" come from?'

'From Hanover, mien Herr. Reared especially for us.'

My plate swam before my eyes. I lost interest in baiting the waiter. Looking down at what now seemed a suspiciously greasy *Sauerbraten,* my eyes centred with nauseating deliberateness on a sinewy lump of floating meat. I thought of Fritz Haarmann once more, of the Beast of Hanover and those vagrant boys...

Ill humour always has a tendency to rebound on the out-of-sorts. Like the grey waters of Biscay, the *schwarztsbier* I'd drunk began to chop and churn in my stomach.

I belched uncontrollably.

The waiter didn't attempt to hide his disgust.

'The bill,' I said.

'The meal is not satisfactory, mein Herr? *Sauerbraten* is the house speciality...?'

'The bill, please. I've lost my appetite.'

I saw the waiter exchange a few words with the maitre d' as he passed and they both stared at me with a mixture of disdain and mystification. The bill arrived. I paid without quibble.

On the street I lurched a few yards then hung over the gutter, ready to vomit. But I'd not eaten enough and whatever was in my stomach stubbornly stayed there.

I walked on slowly towards the Kurfürstendamm, stopping in a bar on the way for a schnapps and a cigarette to settle the stomach. After a while I stopped sweating and once assured it would stay where I put it drank a glass of brandy. Back outside I continued on to the Zoo Club, breathing deeply of Berlin's tainted air with every step and feeling like a fool.

'You don't look well, *Liebling*,' Mitzi said.

She never called me darling, rarely using the word at all unless she was talking to Marthe. But she was offering me sympathy so I didn't think it was the best time to tell her how much money I'd just wasted.

'I felt a little sick,' I confessed.

'Something you ate?'

'It might be.'

'Some places do not care what they sell. You have to be careful. Do you want a drink?'

'Just a glass of water,' I said.

Aware of a sour reek of sweat coming off my shirt, I decided to clean myself up. I locked myself in the staff toilet, the one reserved for the girls. The men's toilet was like the Alex and not a place to go out of choice.

I splashed a handful of the discoloured dribble that passed for water over my face. I started to rinse my mouth out with the same stuff before deciding beer would be more sanitary.

I ran into Marthe on my way back to my table.

'You look awful,' she said.

'So would you,' I told her, 'if you'd eaten what I thought I just ate.'

She winced at my mangled German. 'I do not understand.'

'Fritz Haarmann,' I said. 'Remember him?'

'Haarmann? I do not know anyone named Haarmann.'

'From Hanover?'

'You are not making sense, Harry.' She shook her head. 'I do not see what it is Mitzi finds in you.'

'Maybe it's the fact I'm a man,' I said.

She said, 'Pah!' in the way Mitzi often did, which left me considering who copied whom.

She moved away and I caught her by the wrist, leaning close.

'While you are here, Marthe, I want you to do me a favour.'

She must have caught a whiff of my shirt, twisted her arm free and stepped back.

Her eyes narrowed. 'What do you want?'

'Not what you think,' I said.

'That is as well. I would have to tell Mitzi.'

'That's what I like about you, Marthe,' I said. 'You're straightforward. After a fashion.'

She batted that away without comment.

'Why should I do you a favour, Harry?'

'Because I don't want to involve Mitzi.'

'In what?'

'I'm expecting a man to leave a message here at the club for me. I asked for it to be left with you.'

'So you do not want to involve Mitzi but you will involve me?'

'That's about the size of it.'

'Who is this man?'

'No one you know. He's to let you know where I'm to meet him. That's all.'

She raised an eyebrow with mock suggestiveness. 'And what will you do for me in return, Harry?'

'Anything you want,' I said. 'Within reason.'

Mitzi came up and said to Marthe, 'Harry has eaten something that disagreed with him.'

'I think there is much disagreeable about Harry,' she replied. 'Take him home, Mitzi. He smells and we are not so busy. I will make it good with Karl.' She glanced at me. 'I will think of something reasonable, Harry.'

'As soon as you hear anything,' I said.

Mitzi pulled me towards the door. She collected her handbag and stared at me as one might at a troublesome pet as she put her jacket on.

'What did Marthe mean when she said she would think of something reasonable?'

'I asked her to do me a favour, that's all.'

'What favour?'

'To take a message.'

'From this Gretchen woman?'

'No. From a man. Gretchen is to join her husband in Russia.'

Mitzi looked incredulous.

'Of her own free will?'

'I doubt it,' I said.

On the street she began casting around.

'Do you want to eat? You should have proper food.'

'I'm okay, but we'll stop if you want to,' I said.

'Coffee?'

'Not Berlin coffee.'

'Home then,' she said. 'I will make you real coffee.'

'The purloined kind.'

'What does purloined mean?'

'Stolen,' I said, 'although what it has to do with loins is beyond me. Then again, you making purloined coffee for me is how we got together, remember?'

'You getting punched in the face is how we got together,' she said.

I took her hand. 'I don't deserve you Mitzi.'

'And you have just realized this?'

'I'm a slow learner.'

It was late but the trams were still running. We walked west along Kurfürstendamm towards the next stop.

'You should have seen this street before the war,' Mitzi suddenly said, looking at the ruins around us.

'You should have seen me before the war,' I said.

'I am serious, Harry. Berlin was a good city.'

'Run by people that weren't so good, I've heard.'

'That was politics. What did that achieve?'

'Nothing. But it was more than politics,' I replied, getting a little philosophical now my stomach had settled down. 'They were trying to fashion the world in their image, twisted as it was.' I gestured at the ruins. 'They brought it all on themselves.'

'That's what you and the Americans always say.'

'Is it us you blame?'

'I blame everybody.'

Which was a valid view, I suppose. If not one that was going to advance the argument. From my point of view the argument was a pointless one anyway. We were where we were and there wasn't much to be gained in doing anything other than getting on with it.

That was what Mitzi usually did. I saw her as the arch-pragmatist so it wasn't often I got a glimpse through the cracks to see what lay beneath.

We rode the tram down the Kurfürstendamm to the junction with Koenigsallee. The destruction this far south of the city centre not been quite as severe although to look at the

182

crumbling walls and windowless houses one wouldn't have been blamed for thinking that Bomber Command had had plenty of explosive to spare.

There hadn't been much industry in Halensee but I suppose the prevailing opinion at the time was that any German would do.

21

The street was dark. A house on the corner of the gravel road leading down to the lake had taken a direct hit and the darkness seemed somehow deeper for the building's absence.

As we turned off Margaretenstraße, the beam of Mitzi's torch swung across the brick-filled crater where the villa had stood.

Anything useful had been robbed out of the ruins long ago. Here and there, where a wall had collapsed, a few rooms remained now oddly open to the elements. Truncated pipework lay exposed like severed intestines; wallpaper stripped by the passing seasons hung in tatters.

One evening a few days after I had moved in with Mitzi, I had poked around some of these ruins myself. Having lived in London and now in Berlin, shattered buildings soon become so much brick and rubble. Until one comes upon a child's broken toy or the sodden remains of a photograph album. Then one is reminded that these were once people's homes and anything left was once part of the fabric of their lives. Looking through the few items I found, I discovered that curiosity was one thing and intrusion quite another. I had let their ghosts lie. I had felt too much like a survivor picking over the dead remains of those who had not been so lucky.

Still in my philosophic mood, I was thinking about this again until I suddenly found I was walking in darkness. Behind me Mitzi had stopped and was playing her torch across the tangle of shrubbery beside the driveway of the house next to our own.

'What's the matter?'

'I heard something,' Mitzi said.

I listened. There was nothing to hear except the usual night sounds. An owl hooted.

'Birds,' I said.

'A big bird,' she replied sarcastically.

We turned onto our drive. There were no lights on in the house but that wasn't unusual. Even when the electricity was on Frau Ernst didn't waste money on luxuries such as light. If someone tripped over and broke their leg they should have learned to see in the dark.

Frau Ernst would be in bed anyway. Werner might still be awake. I wondered what went through his head, imprisoned in his chair and staring into the night day after identical day. Did he blame someone for the way he was? The Allies or the Russians? I doubted it would be Hitler. Not with a Nazi cheerleader like his mother constantly in his ear.

'There!' Mitzi cried, making me jump. She shone her torch towards the trees.

'Where—'

Then Shoshannah Lehmann stepped onto the drive. She held up a hand, shielding her eyes from Mitzi's torch.

Mitzi lowered the beam.

'What are you doing?' I asked.

'I thought you were Walter Frick.'

I stepped towards her. 'I told you, there's no one here named Frick.'

'Yes,' she insisted. 'I have seen him. Here. They will have to believe me if you tell them he was here.'

'Tell who?'

She stared back dumbly in the pale light of the torch.

'Where did you see him?'

'Coming out of the Schneiders' house.'

'Who are the Schneiders?'

'They lived next door. Our neighbours.'

'The house next door is a ruin,' I said. 'No one lives there now.'

'Walter Frick was there.'

'Who is he?' Mitzi asked her.

'He is the devil.'

'Come inside,' Mitzi said. 'Have you eaten anything today?'

I glanced at Mitzi sideways. It wasn't like her to give food away.

'That woman will call the police,' Shoshannah Lehmann said.

'Frau Ernst will be in bed,' I told her. 'Don't worry about her.'

She hung back. Mitzi put her arm around her shoulder.

'Do not worry. You can come inside. Just for a moment.'

Hesitantly, the girl allowed Mitzi to lead her down the drive to the house. I rummaged in my pocket for the key. Inside, I switched on the hall light. Frau Ernst's door was shut, the house silent.

Shoshannah Lehmann peered into the hall. Then she bolted past Frau Ernst's door and up the stairs. By the time Mitzi and I followed she was pressed into the shadows on the half-landing. We took her up to the second floor and I unlocked the door to our apartment. Mitzi put the kettle on the stove, took what was left of our bread and began slicing it. I wasn't minded to give her any of Mitzi's good coffee but we still had some tea left, not good but still better than the coffee.

I put the cups out while Mitzi spread some lard on the bread. The girl ignored us and walked around the room, touching the furniture.

'This was not here,' she said, standing by the table.

'When do you mean?' I asked.

'When I lived here.'

'Before the war? With your family? Where are they now?'

'Harry...' Mitzi began but the girl answered readily enough.

'Dead,' she said.

'Your family were Jewish?'

Shoshannah Lehmann didn't reply. She went to the door, opened it a crack and peered into the hall. She closed it again and gazed around her.

'This was Asher's room,' she said.

'Who was Asher?'

'My brother.'

Mitzi held a slice of bread out. 'Would you like tea?'

The girl took the bread and ate it quickly while Mitzi poured the tea. She took the cup and swallowed, still looking around.

'There were pictures on the walls,' she said.

'What kind of pictures?'

'Animals. Walter Frick stole them.'

'I don't know who Walter Frick is,' I said. 'Frau Ernst says a man named Neumann owns the house. Perhaps he has the paintings.'

'Who is Neumann? He cannot own this house. It belongs to me. I am the only one left.'

'What happened to your brother Asher?'

'Dead,' she said again. 'Walter Frick took him. He lied when he said he wouldn't. He took all of them.'

'Walter Frick took them? Was Frick Gestapo?'

'First he was a policeman. Then he was Gestapo.'

'And he took your whole family?'

'Harry, please...' Mitzi said again.

'All dead,' Shoshannah Lehmann went on. 'They were sent away. Because of Walter Frick.'

'Why didn't he take you as well?'

Her eyes flared. She lunged for the remaining slice of bread, grabbed it and ran to the door. By the time I followed she had flown down the stairs.

I went after her. The front door was wide open. I looked around outside then came back in, locked the door and went back upstairs. Mitzi was still standing at the table with one of those 'I-told-you-so' looks on her face.

'What?' I said.

'You frightened her with all your questions.'

'She was already frightened. Beside, how else am I going to find out anything?'

'What business is it of yours, Harry? What does it matter now? She is what she is. Why do you not help her instead of scaring her?'

'You're very solicitous all of a sudden,' I replied. 'A couple of days ago you said she was probably a thief. One of Berlin's ghosts, you said.'

'And so she is. Berlin is full of girls like this. After the Nazis it is the Russians. And now it is you.'

I was taken aback, her lumping me in with the Nazis and the Russians. There was no point in arguing, though, so I poured myself a cup of tea. There was no bread left and I made do with the crumbs on the table. Having forgotten all about Fritz Haarmann, predictably I felt hungry again.

'Aren't you curious about her?' I asked. 'About her brother Asher and this man Frick? How it was she managed to survive?'

'No, Harry' Mitzi said. 'I am not curious. I am going to bed.' She jerked her chin at me. 'And you should wash, I think. Before you come.'

22

Saturday 2nd August 1947

Being a Saturday Mitzi was going to have to be at the club early although that still wouldn't be until seven that evening. I didn't have to be anywhere. On weekends Kurt was occupied with his cigarettes and anything else Rafferty thought might turn them a buck. They had been talking of going into nylons. The way things were, though, nylons remained a luxury for most women in Berlin, one they couldn't afford.

Despite having nothing to do I woke early and lay in bed listening to Mitzi's breathing. I was wondering about the future. Unlike the way I had felt during the war, I was now pretty confident I had one. That knowledge might have been enough for most people although for me all it did was bring worries about what I'd do with it. There would always be a need for spies, that was pretty obvious, but I wasn't sure I was cut out for the life.

Most of the time I wasn't spying at all, merely waiting: waiting for someone to contact me ... waiting for something to happen ... waiting to be told what to do next... Meanwhile life went on all around me. Other people were improving their lot. Kurt was making money. I was marking time.

I speculated on the possibility of Kurt cutting me in on one of his rackets. There were several ways I could be useful and the black market was a growth industry just then. But something was holding me back from asking him. My reluctance could have been rooted in the fact I'd once been a policeman. Black market dealing was a crime, after all, and maybe I was still carrying the values of those who championed law and order. Not that that had stopped several policeman I'd known from profiting from their position before the war. A little bribery and a little graft went a long way then. Now peace had come I could only see it going further.

Sometimes I fantasized about offering myself for private investigations. There was always scope for those with an inquisitive turn of mind although, a few months before I came out to Berlin, I had found myself on the receiving end of the quotidian aspect of the business. I witnessed first-hand what a grubby trade it could be. I was also realistic enough to realize that the glamour of the American detective films was only fiction. Reality would inevitably be bread and butter divorce work, shabby hotels and shabbier clients.

All a long way from Humphrey Bogart and Dick Powell and the rest of the private eye gang.

'What are you thinking?' Mitzi asked having woken without my noticing.

Some eye, I thought, one that didn't know what the person lying next to them was doing.

'About the future,' I said after a moment.

'Which future?'

'Do we get a choice?'

She stretched languorously and draped an arm across my chest.

'Is that not up to us, Harry?'

'Do you mean you and me?' I asked.

'Perhaps. If you would like.'

I considered whether or not I did. It would be one way of applying a full stop to my past. Start afresh with Mitzi. But where would we go? What would we do?

She ran her hand down my chest and onto my abdomen.

'Where would we go?' I said, voicing my concern.

'I do not understand,' she said, moving her hand lower.

'Oh, I think you know where you're going,' I replied.

For once I wasn't to be distracted. Even so, I did bail out of the bigger question.

'What I meant was, why don't we do something? Go somewhere. You're not working tomorrow, are you?'

'No. Where do you want to go?'

'What about Potsdam?' I suggested. I was beginning to get distracted despite my best intentions. 'That's supposed to be nice.'

Potsdam wasn't far south of Berlin and had been the city where the old Kaiser had had his palace, the town from which the Prussians had ruled the rest of Germany.

She edged closer to me.

'It is like Berlin,' she murmured. 'And it is in the Russian Zone.'

'That's okay,' I said, giving in and rolling on top of her. 'They won't mind us having a peek.'

'Potsdam is just more rubble, Harry.'

'Yes, but surely it's a classier kind of rubble.'

~

Mitzi went back to sleep. I was now too restless to stay in bed and so got up and went down the hall to the bathroom, only to find the water was off again.

It was Saturday. Everyone wanted a wash on a Saturday.

There wasn't any food, either, since we had given Shoshannah Lehmann the last of our bread. There was nowhere close to buy anything either so, since Mitzi would happily sleep in till noon, I scribbled a note to say if I wasn't back before she left I'd see her later in the club.

I would to have to spend my evening waiting to hear from Albrecht Fischer, that was assuming Gretchen would deliver my message. Until then, though, there were one or two things I could be getting on with.

If I got to the mill early enough there was a chance I might catch Kurt before he went out hawking his black market goods. After talking to Shoshannah Lehmann, it had occurred to me that if I wanted to find out anything about Walter Frick, Kurt would be as good a place to start as anywhere else.

Going downstairs I saw Frau Ernst's door was open again.

She must have heard me coming because she was there, waiting in her doorway like a spider in her web, ready to trap any morsel that passed by.

I didn't suppose I was particularly nutritious but she snared me anyway.

'Have you seen that girl again, Herr Tennant? The one we spoke about?'

'No, Frau Ernst. Have you?'

'You will be sure to call the police if you do. She is trouble, that one.'

'She looks harmless enough to me,' I said. 'You have not heard from Herr Neumann, I suppose?'

'Herr Neumann? No. Why should I hear from Herr Neumann?'

Conversing with Frau Ernst was like communicating with a brick wall. Or a more apt analogy might be one of Albert Speer's Brutalist creations. Either way, she wasn't designed to give anything away.

I left her to get on with whatever it was she found to fill her days. When not waylaying Herr Neumann's tenants that is. I walked down Margaretenstraße to Koenigsallee and took a tram into the city.

Kurt was busy with a carton of Luckies when I reached the mill, breaking the packs into single smokes for those who could only afford to ruin their health one cigarette at a time. I noticed he had a few bars of PX chocolate as well.

He looked up as I walked in. 'Can you smell it, Harry?'

'No, but I can almost taste it,' I said.

It had been a long time since I'd eaten a chocolate bar, even one as second rate as the stuff the Americans made. Sweet and gritty, it was all right in a pinch if only to serve as a negative reminder of what good chocolate should taste like.

He eyed me eyeing the chocolate. Then, looking more reluctant than Abraham must have while holding the knife over his son Isaac's throat, broke one of the bars in two and handed me half.

'I don't want to eat into your profits,' I said, through a mouthful of the stuff.

'Do not worry, Harry. I will think of some way you can make

it up to me. Why are you here this morning?'

'Hoping I'd catch you,' I said.

'Why, what is the trouble?'

'No trouble. Do you remember that girl I told you about?The one who mentioned a man named Walter Frick? I don't suppose you've heard the name before, have you?'

He gave it some thought.

'The only Frick I ever heard of was the Reich Minister. But he was not a Walter, I think.'

'This Frick used to be a policeman. Gestapo, too.'

'I kept out of their way if I could,' Kurt said, packing some loose Luckies in a box.

'I'd like to talk to someone who might remember him. But I'm not sure where to start.'

'You are looking for a policeman in Berlin?' He laughed. 'There were a lot of policemen here in the Hitler days, Harry. Anyone will tell you that.'

'I know. That's why I want to find one who might remember him.'

'I made sure I did not know many policemen.'

'Yes, but what about the other side?'

'What other side?'

'Criminals. There were plenty of those, too, weren't there? Did you meet any of them?'

'Maybe,' he said cautiously. 'Is this business?'

'No, not our usual business. Not the kind that anyone with a past needs to worry about, anyway.'

'Except maybe this Walter Frick?'

'Maybe.'

Kurt stopped packing cigarettes and briefly stared across the room to where the doors onto the Spree had been opened. The unsavoury smell of the river hung in the air.

'There is maybe a man I know,' he finally said. 'And he might know someone else. But no promises. And it may be he does not want to talk.'

'He wasn't a policeman?'

'No. The other side, as you say. He was a thief. But he got to meet a lot of cops that way. I cannot say if he ever knew this Walter Frick, but it is possible he knows someone who did.'

191

'What's his name?'

'Heinrich Möser.'

'How do you know him?'

'Now and then the Nazis would crackdown on petty thieves. Before the war Heinie had been in prison. After it started he spent time in one of the Nazi camps. When he came out they put him to work in my factory. Heinie was there when I lost my fingers.'

'And he's still around?'

Kurt nodded. 'I see him from time to time,'

'So where can I find him?'

'On a Saturday he is usually in a bar on Munchener Straße. That is off Viktoria-Luise-Platz. Tell Franz the barman I sent you and if Heinie is there he will point him out.'

'What's the name of the bar?'

'The Köln.'

'Okay.' I picked up two packs of Luckies. 'What are you charging for these?'

'You going to smoke them?'

'They'll be introductory gifts,' I said.

'In that case for what I paid Rafferty. Plus only fifty percent. But please do not make a habit of this, Harry. I am trying to make a living.'

I took out what money I had left after having wasted most of it the previous evening and paid Kurt for the cigarettes. I pocketed them and said I'd see him Monday.

At the Bellevue I took the S-Bahn to the Zoo Banoff then switched to the U-Bahn. The flak tower still loomed over the park, reminding me of Arthur Peston again. It was a Saturday and a few children were watching the British sappers at work. In better times they might have been at the zoo, staring at the animals. Now there wasn't much to stare at there except empty pens and memories.

I took the A11 line to Nollendorfplatz. The station had been badly hit in the raids and Nollendorfplatz closed until the previous April. A shuttle service had taken those riding south around the blocked B1 line but things had changed in the few months I had been back. Now Nollendorfplatz and the B1 was open as far as Bayerischer Platz. I only wanted to go as far as

Viktoria-Luise-Platz and from there walked south along Munchener Straße, picking my way round rubble that had slid into the side-streets like stone avalanches.

The Köln was a seedy looking joint full of seedy looking customers. But I didn't suppose it looked any worse than the real Cologne did now we had finished bombing it. Kurt hadn't said what kind of business Heinie Möser had been in before the war, or if now it was over he was still keeping his hand in. If he ever needed a peter man for a job, though, the Köln seemed a likely place to find one. Most of the drinkers stopped slurping their beer and gave me the once-over as I walked in before going back to what they did best, staring into their glasses.

It had always been my experience that most old lags could sniff out a copper quicker than a pig could find a truffle. It had been a long time since I'd been a policeman but I did wonder if some residue of my past still remained. Then again, they showed so little interest in me after a second or two, I thought it possible I was getting to look as seedy as everyone else in Berlin.

I ordered a beer and asked the barman if he was Franz.

'That's right,' he said. 'I haven't seen you in here before.'

'No. I'm a friend of Kurt Becker's. Kurt said if I asked you nicely you might point out Heinie Möser to me if he was in.'

Franz looked sceptical. 'Kurt? How's he doing these days?'

'Better now he's got a regular supply,' I said and slipped a pack of Luckies across the bar to him. 'He asked me to give you these.'

'Good of him,' he said, his mitt snapping shut over the cigarettes as quick as a trap. 'He must be doing well.'

'Is Heinie in?'

'The table by the back door. The guy on his own.'

'Thanks,' I said. 'Why don't you bring over a glass of whatever he's drinking?'

I peeled a note off my diminishing roll then sauntered towards the back of the bar and the man sitting at a table by the rear door.

Möser was in his fifties with a thin pockmarked face and suspicious eyes that had started watching me several tables out. He was nursing a beer, his mouth hanging open as if I'd interrupted his drinking. As I got near he made to get up which explained why he sat by the back door.

'Relax, Heinie,' I said. 'Kurt Becker told me I'd find you here.' I pulled out a chair. 'You remember Kurt don't you?'

'Becker?' he said, his voice a rasp you could have filed metal with. 'Do I know a Becker?'

'He told me you were in the factory when he lost his fingers.'

He relaxed a little. 'Oh, that Kurt Becker. I thought you were a bull.'

'I used to be before the war,' I said.

'England?'

'Yeah.'

'You've got a bad accent,' Heinie said. 'You with the army?'

'No. I'm in business with Kurt. My name's Harry.'

I tossed the second pack of Luckies on the table.

'He said to say hello.'

Franz had been quick but Möser had the edge, his hand darting out with the speed of a praying mantis' tongue. He scooped up the cigarettes and slipped them into his pocket.

'How's Kurt doing?'

'Not bad,' I said. 'He told me you might be able to help me with something.'

'That depends. What is it you want?'

Franz arrived with another beer for Möser. I waited a moment then said:

'I'm looking for anyone who might have known a man named Walter Frick.'

Möser freshened up his drink. He pursed his thin lips and shook his head.

'Don't know the name. What was his line?'

'Frick really was a bull,' I said. 'Or so I'm told. I don't know much else about him except that he picked up Jews to be sent to the camps. He may have joined the Gestapo.'

'*Jüdischer Fahndungsdienst?*' Möser asked.

'I don't know. What's that?'

'What they called the Gestapo scouting service. Looking for Jews.'

'Right. That's probably what Frick was then.'

194

'I was in a camp,' he said. 'Did Kurt tell you? A year. I was lucky. I walked out.'

'Frick picked up a family who lived by Lake Halensee. Name of Lehmann. The daughter was lucky like you. She survived. She said she saw Frick just the other day.'

'Who's looking for him? The British or the Yanks?'

'Neither as far as I know. The daughter is a little unstable, if you know what I mean. Maybe she saw him, maybe it was her imagination.'

'What is it to you? You're not a bull.'

'I told her I'd ask around, that's all.'

Möser shook his head again. 'I met my share of bulls before the war but I don't remember any Frick. What did he look like?'

'I don't know.'

'Halensee, you say? When was this?'

'1940 ... '41.'

'And picking up Jews? That had been taken over at the Alex by then. I did know a bull who worked out of the Kaiser Allee station in Wilmersdorf before the war. That wasn't far from Halensee. Maybe this Frick worked there, too. He might have known him.'

'Do you know if he's still around?'

'Yeah,' said Möser. 'Still a bull, too.'

He dropped his voice and leaned across the table.

'Supposed to have gone through de-nazification, for all that's worth. As far as I'm concerned, once one of those bastards, always one of those bastards. You know what I mean?'

Since he was keeping his voice down and his opinion between the two of us, I had to wonder how many of those bastards were in the habit of drinking in the Köln.

'What was this bull's name?'

'Kittel. Klaus Kittel. They used to call him Killer Kittel.'

'Was he? A killer?'

Möser shrugged. 'He liked to bust heads, for sure. Maybe he hit some too hard. I don't know. This was back during Weimar, of course. Before the Nazis. He was originally from Pankow, or maybe Prenzlauer Berg. One of those communist strongholds, anyway. Back then it was NASPD heads he liked to bust.'

'And when the Nazis took over?'

'Switched horses like everyone else. Anyone who saw which way the wind was blowing did.'

'Where could I find this Kittel now?'

'Not in the American sector, that's for sure. He hates those bastards like poison. He had a wife who was killed in one of their raids. Last I heard he was working in the Russian sector somewhere. Gone back to his roots. Probably cracking old Nazi heads again.'

'Can you remember what he looked like?'

'Yeah,' said Möser. 'Like a bull.'

'What, you mean he looked like a policeman?'

'No. I mean he looked like a *bull*. You know, the animal. Big head and shoulders. Kittel didn't have a neck.'

I dropped a few of my remaining Reichmarks on the table next to his bottle and got up.

'Thanks, Heinie,' I said. 'Have another on me.'

He grinned through rotten teeth and squirrelled away the notes with his pack of Luckies.

Out on the street, I considered whether it was worth crossing into the Russian sector and asking around after Klaus Kittel. I could pick up a tram going east in Bayerischer Platz easily enough. If I had any idea where I was going.

I didn't, though, and didn't think questioning policemen under the noses of the Russians was a very good idea, either. Bill had told me to watch my step in the Russian sector and I didn't think he'd be pleased if he heard I'd drawn attention to myself by asking questions.

There was always a chance Ben Tuchmann could help. It wouldn't have surprised me to find he had contacts in the Russian sector, given his search for Berlin's missing Jews. But Tuchmann was already looking into the Lehmann family for me as well as making enquiries in Hamburg about Frau Ernst's Herr Neumann. Another request for help would me mean getting deeper into hock with him. That was something I wanted to avoid until I knew exactly what I was doing.

I hadn't eaten yet but didn't have enough money for much.

So I stopped off at a beer hall that did a decent line in bread and saukraut then, not wanting to hang the around the city for the rest of the day until the Zoo Club opened, rode the tram back to Halensee.

23

Mitzi had already left. I looked for a note in reply to the one I had left her but found only mine, screwed up and dumped in the waste paper basket. The water was running so I wallowed in the tub for an hour before dressing and pouring myself a schnapps. Glass in hand, I put my feet up in the living room. I didn't suppose Mitzi had got up much before noon; I felt as though I had put in a full day.

Maybe if we'd hadn't taken so much exercise first thing I would have felt fresher. Despite my intention when I'd left that morning, the thought of traipsing back into town and killing time at the club until Mitzi got off didn't seem as attractive as an early night.

There was always the chance that Gretchen wouldn't deliver my message. And even if she did and Fischer was quicker responding than I expected, he would leave a message with Marthe and Mitzi would tell me when she got home. If worse came to worst and he wanted to meet straight away, I'd just have to stir myself and get up early.

I poured myself a second glass of schnapps, lit one of Kurt's cigarettes and mulled over what Heinie Möser had told me. If he was right and Kittel now worked in the Russian sector despite having been a policeman for the Nazis, I guessed he had gone back to his communist sympathies and that the comrades were overlooking the time he had spent working under the Nazis. Not that any of it helped me much. Like the Allied sectors, there was no shortage of suburban police stations in the Russian sector, or in the Soviet Zone come to that if he no longer worked out of a Berlin station. The new Russian sector HQ was on Keibelstraße and the logical thing to do was walk in and ask for Kittel by name. But logic often served up more than the answer you wanted.

I finished my schnapps and decided to take a walk along the lake shore before turning in. Not so much for the exercise but rather to take a look at the back of the house, specifically at Frau Ernst's apartment.

According to Mitzi, our *portiersfrau* had once lived with a man. Although I'd never seen evidence of one, Frau Ernst seemed so evasive whenever I asked about the owner, Neumann, that I couldn't discount the possibility that he was the man she had lived with and that he was still around, keeping out of sight. It wasn't only the Allies but the Russians as well who hadn't stopped looking for those Nazis on the wanted list who had gone missing. It was entirely possible that many of them were still hiding in Berlin.

After all, from what Tuchmann had told me, many Jews had managed to survive in plain sight, those *Tauchers* or U-boats as he called them. So why not Nazi war criminals?

The windows to Frau Ernst apartment were closed, as were the drapes. It was unusual in warm weather although not particularly surprising. Not if she thought Shoshannah Lehmann might still be hanging around, waiting for an opportunity to steal whatever it was Frau Ernst imagined she had worth stealing.

The girl was the other reason I had for walking round the lake. I was hoping I might run into her again myself. Despite what Mitzi said, I didn't think she had run off the previous evening because I'd scared her with my questioning. I suspected what Shoshannah Lehmann really wanted was someone to whom to tell her story. And, if I gained her confidence, why shouldn't that someone be me?

I had no idea where she went between visits to her old house or how she spent her time. So, until she turned up again, short of putting her on my list of missing persons along with Kittel, I had little option to wait until she came back.

I sat by the rotten jetty where she'd stolen my Reichmarks and smoked another cigarette. I listened to the rustling in the shrubbery, but it was probably foxes or even one of the feral cats or dogs that had somehow managed to survive the hungry years.

Apart from that, some other snuffling animal and an

occasional owl, the lakeshore was silent. I couldn't hear anything much beyond the gentle lapping of Halensee's waters as they broke on the muddy strand.

I gave her half an hour then went back inside. In bed, I began thinking of Mitzi as I was wont to do. Saturday was the club's busiest night and Karl wouldn't close until he had squeezed the last Reichmark possible out of his last customer.

I was feeling a little guilty. The U-Bahn and the trams would have stopped running by the time she got off and although Mitzi wasn't adverse to walking home if I was with her, it was a fair stretch alone. Particularly after a long evening on her feet. There wouldn't be any cabs available as the Occupying Forces generally monopolised them on weekends. The only thing there would be no shortage of on a Saturday night was drunken soldiers.

Not that I was particularly worried for her. She had managed before I came along and sometimes on weekends—or any other night for that matter when I wasn't there and Marthe could persuade her—Mitzi would often stay at Marthe's flat. That was only a block from the club on the corner of Meineke and Lietzenburger Straße.

It was a situation I didn't care too much for, in my chauvinistic way, but still one preferable to thinking of her walking home by herself. What they might both get up to was something else I preferred not to think about—not unless I'd had a few drinks, anyway. The truth was, Mitzi and Marthe had been friends a long time and I was just a newcomer.

As it was I didn't have to avoid thinking about it for too long. I fell asleep and, when I woke, found Mitzi's side of the bed empty. It was still early and being a Sunday she wouldn't be in any hurry to get up and come home. That probably meant our trip to Potsdam would have to wait, something else I wasn't too worried about as I didn't have the money for a day out. What might be worse though was if Karl asked her to work that evening. If that was the case she might not bother coming home at all.

I got up and dressed and looked for something for breakfast. That didn't take long as there was no food in the apartment. But it gave me the idea of surprising them both at

Marthe's place.

Even on a Sunday there was usually some shop or other open where food could be bought. As long as one had money and the *Marken* in the pocket. I didn't have the money and being a Sunday the banks weren't open either, so I raided the box where Mitzi kept a few dollars for emergencies. I was still in credit in the account my salary was paid into and, once I could get to the bank, I could pay Mitzi back before she noticed the cash had gone.

I would stop off at a shop on my way in. I didn't suppose either of them would be too pleased to see me first thing on a Sunday morning although in Berlin these days any visitor, unexpected or otherwise, was welcome provided he came bearing gifts.

And in Berlin these days a cabbage or a piece of sausage was as good a gift as anyone could think of.

Die Folgen

24

Sunday August 3rd 1947

Marthe lived off the Kurfürstendamm in a district once favoured by the well-to-do. Until the war not only thinned out the well-to-do but reduced the area to a wasteland as well. Not a stone's throw from her apartment, to the north-east and bordering the southern edge of the Tiergarten, lay the old diplomatic quarter that had been the fashionable site for embassies and foreign missions. They had gone the way of the well-to-do now and any building still habitable had been taken over by the less august survivors.

That was true of Meineke Straße where Marthe had her flat. The house had never been as grand as the embassies once were, but bombing is a great leveller and embassies, apartment buildings and rooming-houses all looked much the same once the American B52s and the RAF's Lancasters had finished with them.

Like Mitzi, though, Marthe had been a *Trümmerfrau* so she was an old hand at clearing up a bombsite. She had scrounged some furniture, a few tattered drapes, and much else of what she needed while breaking her back for the Administration. I had picked Mitzi up there once before and while to my mind the flat looked a bit austere and lacking in what we men like to call feminine touches, the same could have been said of Marthe herself.

I had managed to lay my hands on three inches of sausage that hadn't cost me more than one arm and a foot, but cabbage was off the breakfast menu. What I had found was a fistful of limp spinach which, while a bit dusty, I'd made presentable by wrapping in newspaper. I thought the combination might put enough iron in our blood for us to face the rest of the day. Something of which I'm sure Adolf himself would have approved.

Marthe opened the door. Her hair, short as it was, was mussed and she had wrapped herself in a thin robe, making a poor job of it as it was obvious she was naked beneath. She saw who was calling and pulled the fabric a bit tighter which, if anything, accentuated her attractions.

'Harry,' she said, her expression making it clear she wasn't about to rush off and kill the fatted calf, 'what do you want?'

'Mitzi. If she's here.'

I unwrapped the sausage and spinach to show I hadn't come empty-handed.

'What's that, a bribe?'

'I thought it looked like breakfast.'

Her wide mouth didn't exactly break into a smile but she took the offering nevertheless, turned on her heel and left me to close the door.

I followed her down the hall towards her small kitchen. Passing the bedroom door I saw Mitzi was still in bed. She was naked, too, my guess being that Marthe didn't have any spare pyjamas. And since there was only the one bed it would have made for a jolly night.

'You didn't come to the club,' Mitzi said as I loitered in the doorway.

'Something came up. We were supposed to be going to Potsdam today.'

'It is too late now,' she said, although it was still only nine o'clock. 'Next Sunday, Harry, okay?'

'Sure,' I said.

'How did you know I would be here?'

'I used to be a policeman, remember?'

That didn't amuse her much. She might have thought I'd supposed she'd gone home with a customer from the club.

She raised her chin and asked, 'What are you now, Harry?'

'What's that supposed to mean?'

'Someone left a message with Marthe for you at the club last night.'

'Who?'

She climbed out of bed and reached for a robe. Marthe may not have kept spare pyjamas but she obviously provided robes for special occasions.

'It was not that Gretchen woman this time,' Mitzi said, slipping on the robe.

I was about to remark that she had managed to remember Gretchen's name this time, but that would have provoked an argument, Marthe would have joined in and sided with Mitzi and I was in no condition to handle both of them. Iron in the blood or not.

I went into the kitchen. Marthe had washed the spinach and had water on the boil.

'Mitzi said someone left me a message last night?'

Her square shoulders rose and fell under the thin robe.

'A man. He did not give me his name. He said he would be at the *Siegessäule* at ten.'

'What did he look like?'

'Forty. Balding. Not my type, Harry.'

I bit back the obvious retort and looked at my watch. I had just under an hour. The Victory Column wasn't much more than a twenty-minute walk but I didn't want to leave it to the last minute.

Given it was sheer chance I had decided to come into the city that morning to find that Albrecht Fischer would be waiting for me, I cursed myself for my previous evening's laziness. I resolved not to let it happen again.

'I'll have to go,' I said to Marthe, more sorry to leave my inch of sausage than the two women.

Mitzi was in the bathroom. The robe was off again and she was washing. I leaned against the doorframe admiring her slender arms and legs and her tight stomach. Then I became aware that Marthe was behind me doing the same.

'What is this, a peepshow?' Mitzi asked, seeing us both.

'I've got to meet someone,' I said. 'It shouldn't take long. I'll come back here after I've seen this fellow and we can go home together.'

'No, Harry,' Mitzi said with a sigh. 'One of the girls is sick and I told Karl I would cover for her. I cannot bother to go home if I have to work tonight. I will stay here. Marthe and I can find something to do this afternoon, can't we, Marthe?'

'Of course we can, *Liebling*,' said Marthe. 'After we have

eaten Harry's sausage.'

The remark made me glance over my shoulder at her but Marthe was looking as innocent as a newborn.

'Don't tease him,' said Mitzi.

'You only bully me because I'm not as tough as you two,' I said. 'I'll come by the club tonight. I promise.'

~

By the time I reached the Victory Column I still had half an hour to spare. I climbed up to the colonnaded tier below the column itself but there was only so much pleasure to get out of staring at the thing. Although the entrance was locked now, I had once been right up to the top platform where you could stand just under the statue of Victory itself.

Or "Golden Lizzie" as she was known in Berlin.

From the top one had fine views along the thoroughfares that radiated through the Tiergarten. The time I saw it, the avenues looked more like neglected roads driven through a neglected farm.

Even from where I stood below in the colonnade I could still see along Charlottenburger Chausee towards Pariser Platz. I couldn't see as far as the Brandenburg Gate and the Unter den Linden. The street had been cleared of all the broken armour, the shattered trucks and the other detritus of war, but it had lost the Linden trees that had given the wide boulevard its name.

It wasn't easy for me to get any sense of how it would have looked to my imagined Frau Ernst and the rest of the adoring crowd that had lined the road when the Nazis put on their flag-bedecked parades along the Chausee. As part of the plans for *Germania*, Speer had widened the avenue to the Brandenburg Gate and built a ring road around the *Siegessäule,* incorporating four tunnels beneath the road leading to the column for those who didn't want to dodge between the traffic.

The crowds had gone now and there wasn't much traffic to dodge either. The last time I'd used one of the tunnels it had been more redolent of a French *pissoire* spiced with human ordure than anything Albert Speer had in mind. The once-thick woods of the Tiergarten had been thinned and weeds were growing in the cracks of the Chausee.

It was a hot and sunny morning but I could see only a handful of pedestrians, mostly solitary. There was something about the desolation of the park that people chose to avoid, seeming to prefer the streets despite the rubble and the ruins. Perhaps, unlike the Tiergarten, the wrecked city looked more human.

I was still watching those lonely pedestrians when I caught sight of Albrecht Fischer. He was approaching the column like a Prussian Junker out for a stroll round his estate. He saw me waiting between the columns, crossed the road and joined me on the upper tier.

'We walk, Herr Tennant,' he announced as he sauntered up. 'Like two friends taking the morning exercise.'

We took the steps back to street level but instead of crossing the road he led me down one of the tunnels.

It stank as badly as I remembered although Fischer barely seemed to notice. Halfway along he stopped, looked ahead and then back the way we had come.

'Here,' he said, pointing to the brickwork a foot or so above the concrete walkway. He squatted on his haunches and worked at a loose brick. 'When you need to contact me, leave a message here. Remember, Herr Tennant, halfway along the north tunnel.'

He pushed the brick home with his shoe and we continued down the tunnel to the outer edge of the ring road. Walking back to the east-west axis we headed along the broad Chausee towards Pariser Platz.

I remarked that he was behaving very openly.

'Should I skulk like a man guilty of something?'

'Aren't you?'

I reminded him he had told me they would be watching him after they took Prochnow.

'Yes,' he agreed, 'but not on a Sunday morning. You must remember, our German agents are very lazy. Besides, I am a creature of habit and all my colleagues know this. I take a walk in the Tiergarten each day and it is in no way suspicious behaviour.'

'Not even to a Russian agent? Or are they lazy, too?'

'They are busy training us to police our own country. Unfortunately, now we are at last rid of the Nazi police and SS, we find we have no one left who has the necessary experience. But that is a consequence of political idealism.'

As opposed to pragmatism, I assumed. He was taking a dig at the Allies' less idealistic policy of employing ex-Nazis to fill their vacancies if there was no one better to hand.

He must have known what I was thinking.

'But of course who else is there left in Germany now? In your western zones, I mean. Those old communists who survived naturally prefer to live in the Soviet Zone. But I am sure that once all the foreign armies have left our country and Germany has a new generation, all the old Nazis will finally be purged.'

'Are you so sure you will ever be rid of the Red Army?'

'One day,' Fischer said optimistically. 'Although they will not leave until the Americans do.'

'You sound like a man having second thoughts,' I said.

'Not at all. I have always been a German first and a Communist second. I went to Russia simply because I would not have survived if I had remained in Germany. Do not think, Herr Tennant, that now I am considering abandoning communism in favour of a capitalist society that I have lost my idealism. The reason I am offering my services to you is that having seen the Russian version of communism at first hand, I do not believe it offers humankind the freedoms I believe in.'

'And you don't think by staying in Germany you can influence German communism?'

He smiled regretfully. 'Not while it is led by Germans like Walter Ulbricht and Erich Meikle. They have enthusiastically adopted the Russian version of Marxism. Of tight Party control. That is the sort of communism that inevitably leads to men like Joseph Stalin. Had Karl Liebknecht and Rosa Luxemburg lived things might have been different. But now I fear if I remain in Germany I will not survive a Marxist-Leninism regime any more than I would have survived Adolf Hitler's.'

'Are you so sure there is no room for different views in the new Germany?'

Fischer regarded me oddly.

'Are you trying to dissuade me from leaving, Herr Tennant? Why would you do that?'

'Not at all,' I assured him. 'Moscow to Washington seems a large step to take, that's all.'

'But I'm not going to Washington, am I? That is why I have come to you, the British. I think you have a more tolerant society. In England I may remain a communist without fear of the knock on the door in the early hours. I am not sure that is now the case in America. Besides, the information I bring has a British significance. That strengthens my case, does it not?'

'Yes, I am sure it will. Although you must realize you will still be of interest to the Americans.'

'Am I to be sold to the highest bidder, Herr Tennant?'

'Not at all. Although your value to us will have a bearing upon the matter.'

He smiled again. 'And I thought that the English still championed fair play.'

'We do,' I assured him, 'although we too have to be pragmatic at times. As do even you Germans.'

'Do you have a point in that regard, Herr Tennant?'

'Yes. You said the Russian sector does not employ ex-Nazis in their new police force. Yet I know of one who is still working as a policeman.'

'Oh?'

'His name is Klaus Kittel.'

That Albrecht Fischer might be able to help me find Kittel was an idea that had germinated in my head overnight. If he had access to the sort of material he claimed to have, the personnel files of those working in Paul Markgraf's People's Police shouldn't have been beyond his reach.

'I am not familiar with the name,' Fischer said.

'There is no reason you should be. He was a policeman during the Weimar republic. A communist, too, back then. When the Nazis took power Kittel was pragmatic enough to change his allegiance. He didn't go to Moscow, he stayed in Berlin. These days I assume his sympathies are communist once again or I don't suppose you would employ him.'

'Does this man Kittel have any bearing on our arrangement?'

'No. It just happens that I'm looking for him.'

'Because of his past activities?'

'No, because he may be able to tell me about another policeman I am interested in. His name was Walter Frick.'

Albrecht Fischer shook his head.

'I do not know this name, either. I do not understand, Herr Tennant.'

'I am hoping you may be able to find out where in the Russian sector I might locate Klaus Kittel.'

'I see. And does my success or failure in this have a bearing on our business together?'

'No, no bearing.'

'Then what is your interest in Kittel and Walter Frick?'

'Frick became a Gestapo officer. He hunted Jews for the deportations. He took the family of a girl who used to live in the house where I now live. They were Jews and so were sent to the camps. The daughter survived and has returned.'

'A Jew?' Fischer said. 'And still causing trouble? What is it she wants?'

I said I didn't think it was the Jews who had caused the trouble.

'No?' Fischer asked. 'Would Germany be where it is today if Hitler had not had his obsession with the Jews?'

'You can't lay Hitler's obsession at the door of the Jews,' I said. 'And I doubt, even without the obsession, that Germany would have survived Hitler's desire for rebuilding the German empire. The Jews were just scapegoats.'

'And you believe he could have united the country behind him without using the Jews as scapegoats? This is how he managed to defeat the Communists.'

'People like you, you mean?'

'Indeed. We had nothing against the Jews. Many of the old Bolsheviks were Jews.'

'So they were,' I said. 'Remind me where they are now, Herr Fischer.'

He smiled once more.

'Purged. Like the old German communists. It is the reason I

am here, is it not?'

'Of course,' I agreed. 'And you have brought something with you?'

'Something, yes. But I am not so careless, Herr Tennant, as to be caught carrying a compromising document. Our German secret police may be lazy but show them evidence and they will be reminded of their duty.'

'So, what are we talking about this morning?' I asked.

'The time and place that I come over to you. That is when I will bring the names. And I must insist that this will only happen if I meet with *two* of your senior MI6 agents here in Berlin. You will excuse me, Herr Tennant, but I will only hand myself over to someone with the appropriate authority and there must be two men present.'

'Why two?'

'That is non-negotiable. It is my insurance.'

'Then that is understood,' I said.

'And as a gesture of goodwill I will try to find out what I can about this policeman of yours. You say his name was Kittel?'

'Klaus Kittel.'

He reached into his jacket pocket and withdrew an envelope.

'You will give this to your people. They will understand the contents.'

'And you tell me you do not carry incriminating documents?'

'There is nothing here that is incriminating,' he said. 'Nothing I cannot explain if I need to. But I have one more thing for you. Or rather for your American allies if you care to share it with them.' He leaned a little closer. 'Harry Dexter White.'

'Who?'

'*Harry Dexter White.*'

'And who is he?'

'It should not be too difficult for you to find out who he is. What you do with the name is up to your people.' He nodded to me. 'And, if I am able, I will see what I can find out about Klaus Kittel. Should I have anything for you I will send a message as I did yesterday.'

'Not the dead letter drop in the tunnel?'

'No. That is for you to contact me. Use it when you have a response to this.'

We had reached the Bellevue Schloss and he handed me the envelope.

'Auf wiedersehen, Herr Tennant,' he said with a wave of the arm and turning sharply away. 'No doubt we will meet again.'

I watched him leave, gave him a couple of minutes then walked back through the Tiergarten to the old zoological gardens where the Zoo Tower was still casting its gloomy shadow. I headed towards Viktoria-Luise-Platz and the Military Mission on Hohenstaufenstraße.

It was Sunday and I didn't expect to find Andy Thurston on duty so I stopped at a café on the way, wrote a short note outlining Fischer's requirements and put it in a new envelope along with the one Fischer had given me. I addressed the envelope to Thurston.

In the note I asked Thurston to have the enclosed letter couriered to Bill as soon as he was able. That wouldn't be until the following morning at the earliest but I didn't think the matter was any more urgent than that.

I left my envelope with the clerk at the Military Mission.

'For Sergeant Thurston as soon as he gets in,' I told him.

I crossed Viktoria-Luise-Platz wondering how to spend the rest of my Sunday. There was some paperwork at the mill I'd been putting off but there wasn't much of it and what there was hardly seemed worth the walk. I could go back to Halensee and amuse myself for a few hours although, if I did that, I would only have to come back into town if I was going to keep my promise and meet Mitzi at the club that evening. I could always take the tram in, I supposed, although if I went back to the apartment there was the danger I might feel like I had the night before and not want to come back into town again.

And a promise is a promise.

I considered looking for Ben Tuchmann, hoping he might have dug something up on the Lehmann family for me. Or possibly on Neumann in Hamburg. I didn't think there was any more chance of finding Tuchmann at the Levetzowstraße synagogue on a Sunday, though, than there had been of my finding Andy Thurston at the Military Mission. Sunday wasn't the Jewish Sabbath and I was pretty sure Tuchmann wasn't orthodox, anyway. The chances were that like the rest of us heathens Tuchmann had adopted the Christian day of rest as a convenient excuse to loosen his tie and put his New York shoes up.

If I had any sense I would do the same. But then, if I had had any sense I wouldn't have been in Berlin in the first place. So, since I had nothing better to do, instead of resting my feet I turned them north again and started back towards the river.

~

Before the war there had apparently been over thirty synagogues in Berlin. One way or another in the intervening years, most of them had been destroyed. Yet the synagogue on Levetzowstraße was still standing, having survived both the Nazis and the air raids. I had never seen the place before although, having discovered that Tuchmann was using it for interviews, I'd taken the trouble to find out what I could about the building.

The reason it had survived initially had been that from October 1941 the synagogue had been used as a collection camp for those Jews already rounded up prior to their deportation. From Levetzowstraße they went first to the Łódź ghetto and from there to the extermination camps.

My familiarity with synagogues barely extended beyond those I'd seen in London. And they hadn't been the sort of buildings that interested me until I joined the Security Service. Even then my interest was more in those who attended religious services than in the buildings themselves.

So if I was expecting the usual mixture of ornate architecture and arcane Jewish mysticism, Levetzowstraße surprised me. It had been built in sandstone and along more classical lines, which was one other possible factor in its survival.

Perhaps the Nazi thugs charged with penning their victims there had felt more comfortable with this synagogue's less alien atmosphere.

What it looked like inside I couldn't say. The doors were locked and banging my fist against them didn't change the fact.

It seemed my assumption as to how Ben Tuchmann spent his day of rest had been correct. Something which, while in some ways gratifying, still left me at a loose end. But I wasn't that far from Stromstraße so decided I might as well call in at the mill and finish the paperwork I had been avoiding. I hadn't eaten and was feeling hungry, having let the sausage and spinach I'd taken to Marthe's apartment slip through my fingers.

I knew there was tea at the mill and always a chance that Kurt had something he might be willing to share. But Kurt wasn't there and ten minutes of looking through cupboards and drawers produced nothing that looked remotely edible, with the possible exception of a box of spaghetti-like electrical wiring.

I may have been hungry but I wasn't desperate.

In the end I contented myself with a cup of tea and a cigarette while logging the most recent manifests into Schuyler's ledgers. Then, when I'd finished that and remembering it was a Sunday, I finally put my feet up.

25

Monday August 4th 1947

The weather had turned hotter again, leaving everyone sweating again and complaining about it again. The atmosphere on the U-Bahn was as foetid as it had ever been and the tramcars weren't much better. If you avoided them and chose to walk you got half-choked by the dust. The only good thing to say about the heat was that it took the edge off everyone's appetite.

In the morning I found Kurt standing at the doors that overlooked the Spree. He was ignoring the smell and smoking away his profits, gazing at the river swirling past. He stopped long enough to tell me that Bill had phoned.

'Phoned himself? He was quick. I only saw Fischer yesterday.'

'You ought to put in for overtime,' Kurt suggested. 'If they have you working Sundays. What did this Fischer want?'

'Just a talk,' I said.

'Sure, Harry. This is why Herr Harrington contacts you by telephone first thing in the morning.'

'He gave me something for Bill,' I said, seeing no harm in letting Kurt know that much. 'I sent it over through Andy Thurston at the Military Mission.'

'So, what is Fischer offering?'

'The letter was sealed,' I said.

Kurt flicked the butt of his cigarette into the river. 'We have a kettle here.'

'It's been a while since I steamed a letter open,' I said.

In fact we had employed other people to do the steaming while I was with the Security Service in London. Their job had been to copy the contents and send it over to us and since I had never learned anything worth knowing through the practice I was damned if I was going to start doing it on my own account.

'So what did Bill want?' I asked.

'The apartment at noon. That okay for you?'

'Sure,' I said. 'I've nothing on.'

First I had to get to the bank, draw out some money so I'd have tea to offer him.

'How did he sound?'

'Like Herr Harrington always sounds.'

'I better get over there then,' I said.

'And mess up the bed?'

'How do you mean?'

'You are supposed to be living there, Harry. Or have you told him you moved in with Mitzi?'

A good point. I could hear Kurt laughing as I closed the door behind me.

~

213

I let myself into the flat having made a detour to the bank and used what was left of my *Marken* to buy tea and milk and a loaf of bread. By the time Bill arrived I had the tea on the table.

He took off his raincoat and hung it on the peg by the door.

'Warm again,' he said.

'You got the letter, I take it?'

He glanced around. 'Everything all right?'

'Fine,' I said. 'We are okay to talk, aren't we?'

'Oh, I think so.'

'Good. I didn't read the contents, by the way.'

Bill sat at the table and I poured the tea.

'The letter? I was rather hoping you could explain it.'

'In what way? Fischer said you'd understand.'

Bill grunted. 'The envelope contained his schedule for the next week.'

'His schedule?'

'Yes. Where he'll be and when, that sort of thing. There weren't any names.'

He saw me smiling and raised his eyebrows. 'Something amusing?'

'When I asked him yesterday if he had brought anything for us he said nothing compromising. Nothing he couldn't easily explain away.'

'Like his schedule?'

'So it seems.'

Bill stirred in his milk. 'What else did he say?'

'That he'll bring the names with him. And when he comes he wants two senior men present. He insisted on that. He said that was non-negotiable.'

'He didn't say who?'

'No. Although I understood him to mean you as Station Chief and someone like your deputy, presumably.'

'And his schedule is to let us know when and where he'll be available.'

'So you will be able to make the arrangements.'

'To coincide with his schedule,' said Bill.

'Yes. You will know when and where he will be so as soon as you're ready, I'll let him know.'

214

'Without his first giving us anything that might indicate he's worth going to all this trouble for?'

'Actually he did say one other thing when he gave me the envelope.'

'What was that?'

'He gave me a name.'

'One of the agents?'

'I don't know. The name was Harry Dexter White. Do you know him?'

'No.'

'I asked him who White was and all he said was it wouldn't be difficult to find out.'

'Nothing else? Just the name, Harry Dexter White?'

'Yes. I don't think he expected me to know who the man was but he did say it was something to give our American allies. If we wanted.'

'If we wanted?' Bill repeated. 'Then White is an American, presumably. A suspect?'

'Your guess is as good as mine.'

'Okay, Harry. White is not a name I know but I'll pass it on to London. Perhaps they'll have something on him.'

'So you'll go ahead and bring London in now?'

'No choice,' said Bill. 'If Fischer's ready, we'll make the arrangements.'

'Without knowing his terms?'

'I imagine he'll want the usual guarantees. Safe passage ... money. A new identity.'

'And London will accept without knowing any details?'

'They'll carp,' said Bill, 'but after the Volkov fiasco I don't think there will be any serious arguments against him.'

I cut the bread. There was nothing to spread on it and when I offered Bill a slice he gave me an apologetic smile and shook his head. No doubt they could run to butter and jam out at the Reich Sporting Field. I couldn't so ate mine dry.

'What do you want me to do?' I asked.

Bill waited until my mouth was empty. I hadn't taken him for the fastidious kind but maybe it was a class thing.

'When I get a reply from London,' he said, 'I'll let you know where and when we'll be ready to meet Fischer. How will you

215

get in touch with him?'

'He showed me a dead letter drop by the *Siegessäule*. I'm to use it to contact him. Last time I had Prochnow's wife deliver the message. When I saw her she told me she was joining her husband in Moscow.'

'Voluntarily?'

'I don't think there was much of an alternative.'

'And Fischer will use the drop to contact you?'

'No, he said not. He knows how to reach me though,'

'Through this girl at the Zoo Club?'

'She's secure.'

'If you're sure, Harry.'

'What happens once Fischer comes over?' I asked. 'Won't there be repercussions?'

Bill put his cup down. 'I would think so. You'd better watch your step. I don't think it's likely they'll come after you. At least, not immediately. But the Russians have long memories about this sort of thing. If this is as big as Fischer wants us to believe, London may decide you've done your job here. If they do, they'll probably close Schuyler down and you'll get another posting.'

'And Kurt?'

'We'll take care of Kurt.'

Bill finished his tea and reached for his raincoat.

'If you need to get in touch use the Mission. I'll let you know when I hear back from London.'

After he left I drank what was left in the pot and had another piece of bread.

I considered how likely it might be for Fischer to be tracked back to the club. I assumed he had made sure he wasn't followed when he went there although, even if he was, I saw no reason anyone should be concerned by his talking with Marthe. She was just a bar girl, after all.

Despite that, I didn't care for Bill's suggestion that they might come after me once Fischer had come over. And his reassurance that if they did they wouldn't come straight away was no reassurance at all. Under those circumstances another posting would probably be for the best, even if it meant starting over again somewhere new.

If Bill was wrong, though, and they did come after me in retaliation, I wondered how they would do it. A kidnapping, or some sort of staged accident? Perhaps a suicide?

That thought brought Arthur Peston's demise back to mind, of course.

Both an accident *and* suicide had been suggested as the explanation for his death. Bill had maintained he was satisfied it hadn't been murder yet, in the light of what he had just said to me, it seemed rather odd that he had taken Peston's fall at face value.

He may have been right although nothing about it smelt right to me.

According to Bill, Peston had hinted that something big might be in the offing, although no one had suggested Peston had ever met Fischer. As far as Kurt and Bill were concerned he had been dealing solely with Prochnow. And since the information Prochnow had given us hadn't been as good as had been expected and the list of SED and KPD agents working in the Allied Zones had never materialised, I could only assume that whatever Peston had been hinting about wouldn't have been coming through Prochnow. The material Fischer was offering, a list of names of Soviet agents who had infiltrated SIS and the Foreign Office, would fit the bill as "something big" but only if it came through someone as well-placed as Albrecht Fischer. Prochnow, the SED man, hadn't been able to access anything as sensitive as that.

Which all suggested to me that even if Peston had never met Fischer, Prochnow could well have already told him about his colleague at the Air Ministry. It was something Prochnow had denied when talking to me and Peston was the only other man who would know. And Peston was dead.

But was that any reason to have him killed?

If it was, I didn't know why.

I still had plenty of questions and not many answers. I decided to let it all lay fallow for a while; to give my subconscious a chance to surprise me.

I put the bread and milk in a bag and left some of the tea in the caddy for when I was next at the flat.

Now I had given Bill Fischer's schedule and the name of

217

Harry Dexter White, it was unlikely the KPD man would want to wait too long to hear back from me. He would want to stay in touch now the ball was rolling. If that was so, I was hoping that before long he would also have something for me on the policeman, Klaus Kittel.

I would have to let Marthe know there might soon be another message.

And there was Ben Tuchmann. He had promised to look into the Lehmann family and the hard to find Herr Neumann in Hamburg.

I locked the door of Peston's flat behind me.

The ball may have started rolling but I was aware there still wasn't a lot I could do until I was contacted. By Fischer or by Tuchmann.

Until then, there was nothing for it except to go back to Halensee.

And wait.

26

Friday 8ᵗʰ August 1947

For several days nothing happened. Then, as is the way with these things, when something did it all happened at once.

The weather cooled down and the water supply became more reliable. I hadn't bathed in the lake. I'd not seen the girl for a week, had heard nothing from Ben Tuchmann, nor received any message from Albrecht Fischer. No shipments came in for Schuyler Imports and Kurt was empire building on a foundation of tobacco and nylon.

With the weekend coming round again Mitzi expected the club to be busy and had gone into the city earlier that afternoon to look for a pair of shoes with Marthe. I hung around the apartment and took a walk around the lake, as usual keeping an eye out for Shoshannah Lehmann.

As usual, I didn't find her. She found me.

With water available in the apartment to wash off the mud,

I decided to take a swim before going into town. Ever since Shoshannah Lehmann had lifted my money I had got into the habit, if I was swimming, of leaving my wallet and anything else I didn't want to lose up in the flat. So that Friday all I came down to the lakeside in was a shirt and a pair of trousers and carrying a towel. I had been splashing around for about half an hour and although the light was beginning to fade when I finally came out it wasn't so dark that I couldn't see my towel had gone. I'd left it draped over the remaining stump of the old jetty on top of my shirt and trousers. They were still there.

Naked and dripping, I stood looking around. Then I heard a giggling in the undergrowth at the back of the strand. I thought for a second it was Mitzi, come back and playing games. But Mitzi wasn't one for giggling.

I stepped a few yards to where an old rhododendron bush straddled the path then jumped in surprise when Shoshannah Lehmann leaped out at me, flapping my towel in front of her like a matador taunting a bull with his cape. She giggled again, looking at me in a way that made me conscious of the fact I had no clothes on.

'Hello,' I said, reaching for the towel. She tried to pull it back but I was too quick for her and grabbed it. She held on, though, letting me pull her closer. 'Where have you been lately?'

'Here and there,' she said, in a coquettish tone I hadn't heard before. 'Where's your friend?'

'Mitzi? She's working.'

'I want to come inside again.'

'You ran off last time,' I said.

'Because of that woman.'

I gave the towel another tug and she let go of it.

'Who, Frau Ernst?' I said, trying to towel myself off while retaining a semblance of modesty.

'She is not here today.'

'How do you know?'

'A car came for them. I saw her pushing the boy in the wheelchair.'

'Turn around,' I said. 'I want to get dressed.'

She giggled again but did as she was told.

'The boy is her son, Werner,' I said.

'Is Werner Walter Frick's son?' she asked over her shoulder.

'I don't know. Does he look like Frick?'

She shrugged. 'Perhaps.'

'What makes you think he's Frick's son?'

'Because Walter Frick and that woman lived here after mama and papa were taken away.'

I finished dressing and told her she could turn around.

'Frau Ernst lived with Frick? In your house?'

'Yes, but I never saw the boy.'

'Where were you living?'

'Anna Koch was in an apartment. She lived with a friend.' She looked at me slyly. 'They were very wicked.'

'How do you mean, wicked?'

She didn't reply.

'And you lived with them?' I asked. 'With Anna Koch?'

'Not *with* Anna Koch. It was not possible to live as Shoshanna Lehmann. I would have had to wear the *Judenstern*'.

'The star of David? So were you in hiding?'

'No. I had no need to hide. Walter Frick knew who I was.'

I didn't understand but she made no effort to explain.

'Why didn't they take you when they came for your parents?'

Again she didn't reply. She turned towards the house. I followed.

'And you say Frick was living here?' I asked again. 'You told me the last time I saw you that he was Gestapo.'

'He was policeman *and* Gestapo. He was the devil.'

'And you still came here even though Frick knew who you were?'

'Only once or twice,' she said. 'Mostly I had to see him somewhere else.'

'You *had* to see him?'

'In town or at the Alex. But I did not like going to the Alex.'

'Why did you have to see him? Did you have to report to him because you are Jewish?'

'Anna Koch was not Jewish.'

'No, I don't mean Anna Koch,' I said. 'I mean you, Shoshanna Lehmann. You are Jewish.'

'I was Anna Koch,' she said.

'You mean you were *living* as Anna Koch? You were in hiding?'

'I did not have to hide.'

I was about to ask her how, if she was Jewish, she didn't have to hide ... how she had survived. But we had reached the back door of the house and I could see she was getting nervous.

'It's all right,' I said. 'You told me Frau Ernst went out.'

I took her hand and led her up the narrow back stairs to avoid the hall. When we reached the second floor she ran ahead of me, slipping into our apartment. I closed the door behind me and turned on the light.

'They told me Walter Frick was dead,' she said, facing me. 'Is that what the woman told you?'

'Frau Ernst told me she had never heard of Walter Frick.'

Shoshannah glared at me. 'She is a liar. If she does not know Frick why is she living here?'

'You told me you saw him,' I reminded her. 'In the Schneider's old house, you said.'

'I saw him looking through the ruins.'

'Why was he doing that?'

She shrugged once more.

'Did he see you?'

'I hid. He would kill me if he saw me.'

'Why would he want to kill you?'

'You are not very clever, Harry Tennant,' she said with some irritation. 'He would kill me because I know who he is. Because I know he is not dead.'

She began walking around the room again, touching the walls and furniture as she had the last time she was there. I put the kettle on to boil and looked to see what we had to eat. There wasn't much. Mitzi rarely let food to go stale. I found an old crust of bread, already showing signs of mould, and offered it to her.

'I haven't much else here, I'm afraid.'

She took the bread, rubbed the mould off, and bit into the

crust. In the pale light she looked to me more like the ghost Mitzi had said she was than ever.

I pulled a chair out for her and sat down myself.

'Tell me about Walter Frick,' I said. 'When he was a policeman, can you remember if he worked out of the Kaiser Alle station?'

She ignored me and the chair and crossed the room to the door, opening it a crack and peeking out.

'Do you have servants upstairs?' she asked.

I laughed at the thought. 'No. An elderly couple named Bloch live there. Did you have servants when you lived here?'

'Of course.'

'Your parents were rich?'

'I suppose we were rich. We had everything we wanted. Until the Nazis took it.'

'Did Walter Frick take it?'

'I do not know where he worked when he was a policeman,' she said, finally answering my question. 'At the Alex he was Gestapo.'

'And you had to report to him there?'

She pressed her lips together like a child who does not wish to speak anymore. I made some tea. I had brought milk the previous day. We had no refrigerator, just a cupboard built over a screened window for a pantry. The milk hadn't gone off although it wasn't going to last another day.

'Would you like some tea? Or would you rather have a glass of milk?'

'Milk,' she said, looking at the bottle hungrily.

I poured a little into my tea and the rest into a glass for her. She snatched it up and drank quickly, leaving a white film across her top lip. She wiped it away with her sleeve.

'It has been a long time since I have had milk,' she said.

'Where have you been?'

'In hospital.'

'You were sick?'

'It was not that kind of hospital.'

She had left the apartment door ajar and I heard a noise downstairs.

Shoshannah Lehmann heard it too.

'She has come back!'

She swallowed the rest of the milk and slipped what was left of the crust into a pocket in her dress. She tiptoed to the door and put her ear to the crack before turning back to me.

'Do not let her see me. Please.'

'You can use the back stairs again,' I said, 'then you won't have to pass her door. Give me a minute to get my jacket and I'll go down the front stairs and distract her.'

I slipped my cigarettes into my jacket, checked I had my wallet and stepped towards her. But she was already through the door and running silently down the hall towards the back stairs.

I waited until she had reached the stairs then went down the front. Frau Ernst's door was open again and I dawdled as I passed by. She was pushing Werner and his wheelchair down the corridor, her back to me.

'You're home,' I said.

Obviously startled, she spun Werner around to face me.

'I did not hear you, Herr Tennant. You surprised me.'

'I'm sorry,' I said, nodding to Werner. 'Did I hear a car?'

'A friend kindly took us to Charlottenburg. Werner had to see his doctor and it is difficult getting his chair on and off the tram. The railway is no easier for him.'

'Of course,' I said. 'I hope there's nothing wrong?'

'He only had a routine check-up, Herr Tennant,' she replied as she always did, as if her son wasn't present.

I couldn't hear any sound from the back of the house and assumed Shoshannah had had time to leave.

'I wish I had a car,' I said. 'I'm on my way into the city now and it's not very comfortable on the trains in warm weather.'

'And Frau Meier? I have not seen her lately.'

'She is working, Frau Ernst. She will be back tonight. It is just that when she works late she sometimes stays in town with a friend.'

'She is lucky to have a friend who can give her a bed at such short notice,' Frau Ernst observed.

I peered at her, looking for an alternative meaning. But her countenance was as bland as ever.

'She is indeed,' I agreed. 'One of the girls she works with

223

lives nearby.'

'One of the girls? How fortunate.'

Since Shoshanna Lehmann would be well away I saw no reason to listen to Frau Ernst's insinuations any longer. I said goodnight, closed the door behind me and walked down the gravel road to Margaretenstraße. I caught a tram heading to the Kurfürstendamm.

Bumping along the tracks, I could smell the lake on me. Running into Shoshannah had made me forget I had intended to wash after my dip and knew the fact would irritate Mitzi. But it was too late to go back now. In the old Berlin I might have stopped at a bathhouse but those days had gone, along with much else that had made it a distinctive city.

Another entry on the debit side for Adolf Hitler and the Nazi regime, I thought. Always assuming there was still room on the debit side in that particular ledger.

I would have liked to have seen the city before the war, before so much had changed. But I could have said the same for most European cities. London, for one, and Paris. Paris may not have suffered destruction in the same way, but it had still lost something even so. That artistic and literary soul that one now could only read about in the books by those who had been there.

Then there were other cities. Warsaw, for instance. A city that no longer existed.

Bill Harrington said I would get another posting once Fischer was safely in England and I wondered where they would send me. Assuming it would be abroad, I had begun to question if that was what I really wanted. Not so much the location as the employment. Espionage and intelligence work might sound glamorous but from my standpoint it still seemed to consist of waiting for something to happen.

The previous February in London while looking into Jewish terrorism, among other things, Magdalena Marshall had suggested I had become addicted to the work. I hadn't thought she was right then and didn't now. If it was excitement and glamour I was looking for I was beginning to think I would find the stupor of an addiction to opium more stimulating.

~

If you believed the stories, Berlin back in the days of Weimar was a party that went on all night and every night. The clubs and bars heaved, the streets were packed to the gunnels... Everything anyone ever wanted was there for the taking.

Assuming one could afford the price.

Maybe everyone had more money to spend then. Or, more likely, they knew that if they didn't spend it, by the time they woke up the following morning it would have halved in value.

Things were different now. The currency was stable—or I should say currencies, for there were still several kinds in circulation—and the present problem wasn't so much inflation eating into its value as how one was to get one's hands on enough of it. And even if you could, these days the chances were that sod all was for the taking even if you did have the price in your pocket.

The party atmosphere had changed with the coming of the Nazis. Berlin, like the rest of Germany, was suffering the resultant hangover. It had imbibed too much Nazism and those who had survived the wild times were suffering the headache.

One offered cure, it seemed to me, waited squatting to the east, surrounding the city. Throbbing with maleficent intent, it sometimes felt as if it might look greedily past the capital at any moment and swallow the rest of the body as well.

~

Like most of the club and bar owners, Karl Bauer now relied on the Occupying Forces if he wanted to do anything better than a modest trade. There were still a few Germans who weren't short of cash, often the same sort who hadn't been short before the war; the sort who always managed to rise to the top and cope somehow regardless of prevailing conditions. In rather the same manner, I often thought, that scum finds its way to the surface of ponds. But it was the ordinary soldier who could get a pass for the evening or weekend who was

Karl's bread and butter.

And the occasional officer looking to slum it with the enlisted men.

By the time I got to the club the evening hadn't yet kicked off. Most of the tables were still vacant and the girls were hanging around underemployed, doubtless causing Karl to wonder what he was paying them for. The club's usual fug of cigarette smoke was almost thin enough to make out what the cardboard cut-outs of the animals fixed to the walls were supposed to be. And to see just how shabby everything else looked.

I had just sat down and was wondering why he didn't spend some money and have the place smartened up when I saw I would have the opportunity to ask him personally. He was striding across the floor towards me, a broad grin on his avaricious face and his arms stretched wide.

It was a Friday and on weekend nights Karl liked to put himself about.

He was never generally this pleased to see me, though. I wasn't exactly a big spender although I daresay he looked upon the amount I did spend as money successfully clawed back from what he paid Mitzi.

'Herr Tennant,' he said with his hand outstretched. 'It is always a pleasure.'

He clicked his fingers at one of the girls and even sat down while waiting for her to wander over. We looked at each other with fixed smiles on our faces. I don't know what he was thinking about but I was deliberating over whether the odds were shorter on my standing him a drink or him giving me one on the house. The former probably. The only drink he ever stood me was the one I'd been given after a customer of his had punched me in the face.

The girl who came to serve us was a new one on me. Pretty in a dairymaid sort of way, she looked uncomfortable when Karl circled her waist with his pudgy arm and pulled her a little closer.

'This is my latest girl, Kiersten,' he said, announcing the fact as if he had been personally responsible for her birth. 'She's from Swarbia, aren't you my dear? Bring my friend, Herr

Tennant a beer, there's a good girl. It is beer you drink is it not, Herr Tennant?'

'Swarbia is on the Polish border, isn't it?' I asked Kiersten.

She didn't answer. Karl shrugged volubly to make up for her reticence and patted her on her bottom to see her on her way.

'Who knows where the Polish border is these days?' he said. 'Now we are under Soviet occupation borders hardly matter.'

'You're still in the Allied sector here, Karl,' I reminded him.

'But for how long, Herr Tennant? Do you think the Allies will stay in Berlin? There is trouble over the police, trouble over the currency... No one is able to agree on anything. Germany needs rebuilding but all they do is argue.'

'I think the rebuilding of Germany is the one thing they do all agree on,' I said. 'None of them want it.'

'I think my friend you are what they call a cynic. But in this case you may be correct. No one would like to see a strong Germany.'

'Not till they stop voting for left-wing parties,' I suggested. 'Everyone thinks you're too sympathetic to the Russians.'

He shrugged. 'What are we supposed to do? Any party advocating a right-wing agenda in Berlin is looked upon as fascist.'

'That's because most of their membership were,' I said.

'Life wasn't easy, my friend.'

'I don't think it was meant to be.'

He brushed that off and smiled, standing up again.

'Always nice to see you, Herr Tennant. Are you expecting friends this evening?'

'I don't think so, Karl. Not tonight.'

I waited until he'd gone before I lit up so I wouldn't have to offer him one and had just exhaled my first drag when I saw Albrecht Fischer walk through the door. He was wearing his workingman's clothes again which, in the Russian sector where everyone who worked for the Party was probably required to look like one of the proletariat, was fine although here, where you were required to pay club prices for beer and cigarettes, made him stand out like Harlequin on an ice sheet.

He gazed idly around, could not have failed to see me and moved casually towards the bar. He stood with his back to me and I could see him order something. Then Marthe sidled up to him as if deciding Fischer was the mark who was going to finance her evening.

Mitzi brought my beer to the table and sat down.

'Worried I'll tip Kiersten?' I asked her.

She raised her eyebrows, giving a modicum of expression to her bored face. 'Tip Kiersten? Why should I be worried, Harry? You never tip me.'

'Who brought you the spinach and sausage last Sunday?'

'Men expect too much for their sausage,' she said.

'What have you and Marthe been doing today?'

'You know Marthe,' Mitzi said. 'She only ever wants to do one thing.'

'Are we still talking about sausage?'

She smiled a little and glanced over her shoulder.

'That one with Marthe, he is the one who leaves you messages?'

They were still in conversation. Fischer with his back to me and Marthe with hers against the bar and looking our way.

'Yes,' I said to Mitzi. 'I think I'm getting another. Do you want a drink?'

'I do not think so.'

I offered her a cigarette but she didn't want one of those either.

'Are we going home tonight, Harry?'

'I am. Are you coming with me?'

'You will not have somewhere else to go?'

'That depends on the message but I shouldn't think so.'

'You have been swimming in the lake again,' she said.

'Does it smell that bad? Karl didn't complain.'

'He would have if your pockets were empty.'

'I was going to wash after my swim but I saw the girl again. She wanted to go inside the house then Frau Ernst came home and I had to divert her while Shoshannah went down the back stairs.'

'And you forgot to wash.'

'Yes.'

She gazed at me, her face deadpan.

'When you start cheating on me, Harry, make your excuses

simpler.'

'Cheat on you?' I laughed. 'As if I dare.'

'So what did you find out about her this time?'

'Not a lot. But I think there's something odd about the business with her and her parents.'

'Do you call everything that happened to the Jews odd, Harry?'

'You know what I mean. Why wasn't she sent to the camps when her parents were?'

'Maybe she went underground. Many did.'

'So I'm told, but she maintains she didn't. She says Walter Frick always knew where she was.'

'Who was Frick?'

'Gestapo. You were there when she told me about him, weren't you? Shoshannah said she had to go and see him at the Alex. Sometimes she even saw him at the house.'

'So, maybe she was buying her freedom.'

'With sex, you mean?'

'It happened, Harry.'

I couldn't imagine from what I'd seen of Shoshannah Lehmann that she could have sold much of anything, never mind sex. But it was possible she had been different during the war. And there were men who had irregular tastes.

'Maybe that's it, then,' I said to Mitzi.

I glanced at the bar again. Fischer had gone and Marthe was now draped over a French officer I hadn't seen before. I wondered what she was doing until I saw the Frenchman was with another woman. She was tall, more handsome than pretty and looked too elegant to have suffered the privations of Berlin for long. One might have thought the woman would object to having Marthe draped over her date although, if anyone seemed to be objecting, it was the French officer. He shrugged off Marthe's arm and took his girl down the other end of the bar. Marthe watched them walk away and the girl turned, watching Marthe watching.

The little drama over she came over to where Mitzi and I were sitting. She reached two fingers into her cleavage and drew out a slip of paper.

'Your friend was just in,' she said.

'I saw him.'

Marthe gave me the note and Mitzi leaned across me to read it.

Klaus Kittel. Keibelstraße 35. Nightshift midnight-8am.

'I'll have to be up early tomorrow,' I told her.

'And will you be sleeping with me before eight or one of your other women, Harry? Which one sent you that?'

'You saw who brought it,' I said. 'Tell her, Marthe.'

'You dig your own grave,' said Marthe, which shouldn't have been a surprising retort as people digging their own graves had recently been something of a German speciality.

'Are we still going to Potsdam on Sunday,' Mitzi asked.

I put the note in my pocket. 'Of course we are. I've a couple of things to do tomorrow but Sunday is free.'

She pulled a face. 'Until you get another note?'

She stood up and took Marthe's hand. Together they looked the room over for some servicemen to part from their Reichmarks. Karl always maintained it gave the customers a thrill to see two attractive women holding hands. An idea he'd picked up in Weimar, I presumed. I couldn't speak for the customers although I imagined it gave Marthe a thrill. The only one who wasn't thrilled was me but then I knew my place.

27

Saturday 9ᵗʰ August 1947

I reached across the bed to the side table. The time by my watch was seven-fifteen. That meant I had no chance of catching Klaus Kittel at *Keibelstraße* 35 by eight, the end of his shift. I wasn't sure I'd even be able to haul myself out of bed before eight. We hadn't been in the thing much more than three hours as it was and most of that time I'd spent trying to get to sleep.

I imagined Karl Bauer had been up all night as well. Counting his money. For some reason just before midnight the place became packed. Soldiers mostly. There weren't many outfits not represented although I admit I hadn't spotted any Zouaves.

Around one o'clock a crowd of Soviet troops came in, already drunk enough to ignore the Red Army's injunction about how they should behave in the western sectors of the city. They were noisy and, once drunk, succumbed to a seemingly irresistible urge to dance. Russians, I noticed, rarely attempted to do it in any western manner. If that was through an inherent disinclination to make a spectacle of themselves or whether Stalin had prohibited it, I didn't know. Not that I'd noticed they minded making a spectacle of themselves whenever they had sunk sufficient vodka. Or anything else alcoholic they could get their hands on for that matter. And the spectacle was usually exhibited by dropping onto their haunches in the Cossack style and kicking out at the ankles of anyone not quick enough to get out of their way.

This lot remained good-humoured, though. Something that can't always be said of a drunken British Tommy. And the louder the Russians got the quicker the booze began to flow, the girls run off their feet parting them from their *ostermarks* and whatever else they might have in their tunic pockets.

By two-thirty they had moved on and the girls gave them another half-hour to wander back to their own sector and forget any lascivious designs they may have earlier entertained.

Too late for the trains and trams and without a cab in sight Mitzi and I walked home, turning down Marthe's offer of a bed which I didn't think extended to me anyway.

For once Mitzi wasn't planning to stay in bed till noon, having arranged to meet Marthe as they had heard on the grapevine that someone somewhere was selling a new miracle skin cream.

Since I had my weekly meeting with Bill at noon we pulled ourselves out of bed around midmorning and walked to one of the cafés in Halensee, open in the expectation of families coming to the lake for the day.

I say families although a German family now was likely to comprise of no more than a woman and her children. The men, if they were lucky enough to be alive and had been captured by the Allies, were still in the many POW camps that stretched from Germany to France and all the way across the channel.

Those that weren't so lucky were probably in Russian camps. According to those who knew, to all intents and purposes that meant they were as good as dead.

Mitzi and I treated ourselves by splashing out our sugar ration on two slices of *Prinzregententorte*. It may have been short on the chocolate buttercream but at least there was no meat in it to remind me of Fritz Haarmann and his boys from Hanover.

After a cup of bad coffee Mitzi got up to leave. I assumed the only place one could buy miracle cream would be on the black market so I told her to be careful. She kissed me on the cheek and said she would. I watched her walk off towards the tram stop and since I had the time ordered a Pilsner and lit another cigarette.

Bill was already waiting in the Grunwald when I reached the spot where he had taken me the first day I arrived. He had his back to me, still wearing his old mackintosh and trilby, and was staring across the river. I walked up and stood beside him.

'I'm late,' I said.'

'Trouble?'

'A late night, that's all.'

'Burning the candle both ends, Harry?'

'My problem is there's not much keeping me busy in the middle,' I said.

'It's not a game for the impatient.'

'No, I realize that now. Any news?'

He nodded and took an envelope from his inside pocket.

'For Fischer? London have given you the go-ahead?'

'We've decided to bring him in next Tuesday. He'll be ready by then, I suppose?'

I saw no reason he shouldn't be and said so.

'He told me he walks in the Tiergarten every day so he should pick that up tomorrow at the latest. That'll give him two days for whatever he has to do. What's happening

Tuesday?'

'According to his schedule, Tuesday afternoon he has a meeting with the Social Democrats.'

'The SPD?'

'The SED are still angling for a merger but since the SPD gained a majority at the last election that's not going to happen. Not for a while anyway. They still talk, though, and Fischer is part of the delegation. It seems Erich Meikle is, too.'

'Is that going to be a problem?'

'I don't think so. We've had time to look over the offices where the meeting is to take place.'

Bill tapped the envelope.

'We've laid it all out for him here. We've suggested that towards the end of the meeting Fischer excuses himself to use the lavatory. That's down the corridor by the back stairs. We'll have a car waiting for him.'

I took the envelope from him. 'Do you want me to be there?'

'I don't think so, Harry. If they have someone on the street watching, any more than the two of us that Fischer stipulated might look like a crowd. Sorry.'

'That's okay,' I said. 'There's no point taking unnecessary risks. What about that Harry Dexter White character Fischer mentioned? Anyone in London know him?'

Bill took the trilby off and wiped his sleeve across his brow.

'Yes. It turns out he was a bigwig in the U.S. Treasury in Roosevelt's administration. Truman wanted him in the IMF as White was heavily involved in setting it up. The World Bank, too.'

'And what are the IMF and the World Bank?'

'International finance and banking organizations,' Bill said. 'Structures for getting the world's economies back on their feet now the war is over.'

'Have there been any questions about his loyalty?'

'We're not sure. If there has, nothing has been said to London. What is interesting is that White suddenly resigned from the IMF in June. Left his office the same day.'

'Any reason given?'

'Not as yet.'

'So will London let the Yanks know his name has cropped

up here?'

Bill looked out across the Havel once more.

'Not immediately, no. London has decided to sit on it. You know what the Americans are like, Harry. If they get wind we have a new source they'll want a seat at the table. Then, before you know it, they've got their feet under the thing and they're taking over.'

'So we don't warn them about White at all?'

Bill pulled a face which I assumed meant no.

'As far as we're aware the man has never had access to the kind of Intelligence we deal in. His sphere is economic. He might have been in a position to leak information on strategic planning, which could conceivably be useful to the Soviets although it's all long term policy and planning. Nothing that can do immediate damage. Of course,' he added quickly, 'once Fischer's in London and we're able to debrief him properly the situation could change. At the moment, though, what Fischer's promising us is solely our concern and London want to keep it that way. At least for the time being.'

We walked along the river for a bit then Bill said:

'Get that envelope to Fischer's dead letter drop this afternoon, will you? Once he has it, unless he decides to change the plan, we'll go ahead Tuesday. We'll talk again once we've got Fischer in a safe house.'

I left Bill by the Havel, walked back to the nearest S-Bahn station and rode to the Zoo Bahnhof.

~

Being a Saturday there were more people than usual in the Tiergarten. A young couple were up on the colonnaded tier of the *Siegessäule*, holding hands and stealing the odd kiss when they thought I wasn't watching. I sauntered around, ostensibly looking at the view and smoking a cigarette, and they soon tired of me spoiling their fun. Completing my second tour of the colonnade I saw them below, crossing the road in search of somewhere more private.

It was just as well they hadn't chosen the north tunnel under the road. It wasn't anywhere I'd care to take a girl on a date, not unless she was the kind who didn't mind waiting while you wiped the shit off your shoes.

It was gloomy down there but I found Fischer's loose brick without too much trouble. After a glance fore and aft to make sure no one was about, I slipped Bill's instructions in the gap and pushed the brick back in place. Then I carried on down the tunnel, out into the sunshine and along the *Chaussee* like a tourist out seeing the sights. That there were more sights than tourists was just a sign of the times.

Most of those that were there were soldiers. Like me in '45, I supposed they were doing the rounds of what was left of the Nazi sites. There was nothing to see of the Hitler Bunker or the Chancellery now and both were in the Russian sector, anyway, and they'd probably been warned off of straying that far east.

I wondered if anyone had thought of organizing day trips out to fat Hermann's hunting lodge in Orianienburg. But that was in the Russian Zone north of the city and not too far from Sachsenhausen concentration camp. Maybe, unlike the thick-skinned and un-empathetic Goering, the sensibilities of ordinary conscripts made that a sight they wouldn't want to see.

Passing the few German families there were in the park, I got to thinking of all those families who would have done much the same before the Nazis seized power. Families who would never be able to enjoy a simple pleasure such as an innocent day out again. Many of them would have been Jewish, of course, and that train of thought led inevitably back to Shoshannah Lehmann and her family.

I hadn't learned too much that was new from her the previous day; only that her family had been wealthy enough to employ servants, that during the war she had called herself Anna Koch and had passed as Aryan, and that Walter Frick knew she was Jewish but for some reason hadn't snared her in the Gestapo's net.

She had also told me again that she had seen Frick near the house of the Schneiders, their former neighbour. I didn't suppose the Schneiders had been Jewish although that didn't automatically mean they had survived the war. Their old house was now a ruin so at some point they must have been bombed out, either before or after the Lehmanns had been sent to a camp. I wondered if the Schneiders had welcomed the removal of their Jewish neighbours or if they had lamented their deportation. It was always possible they might have sheltered Shoshannah if she had been one of those Ben Tuchmann had termed a *Taucher,* a U-Boat.

It had been at the Schneiders' house that Soshannah insisted she had seen Walter Frick. I still wasn't sure if I believed her. Anything was possible, of course, although I couldn't think of any good reason why an ex-Gestapo officer would hang around a house where he might be identified.

It was still early afternoon. I had a lot of time to play with. I was too late to find Klaus Kittel and I wouldn't have to show my face at the club much before ten that evening. Thinking about it, though, I stopped, turned and retraced my steps along the *Chaussee.*

I might have had a lot of time although it occurred to me that before I began playing with it I'd first need to put on my other shoes. My old pair were already scuffed and worn. I wasn't going to wear my best pair clambering through the rubble of a bombed house.

~

Passing through the hall, Frau Ernst materialized at her door like an apparition with extra-sensory gifts.

'*Guten tag*, Herr Tennant,' she said tonelessly, keeping her door almost closed behind her.

'Frau Ernst,' I said, feigning surprise at seeing her. 'How are you?' And before she could tell me, added, 'I don't suppose Herr Neumann has been to visit, has he?'

Now she looked surprised. 'What makes you think Herr Neumann has been to visit?'

I could have stated the obvious: it was his house and she looked after it. But stating the obvious to Frau Ernst had never got me anywhere before so instead I said:

'And he hasn't telephoned either, I suppose.'

'Yes, Herr Tennant, as a matter of fact he has. Yesterday. That is what I want to speak to you about.'

The ball of surprise was back in my court.

'Did you ask him from whom he acquired the property, Frau Ernst?'

She patted her German braid with what appeared to be some satisfaction.

'I asked him if it was a family named Lehmann, as you requested. But no, it was not and he had not heard of any family named Lehmann.'

'Then who did he buy the property from? A Walter Frick, perhaps?'

'From a lady named Müller,' said Frau Ernst.

'Müller.'

'A widow. Her husband was a Wehrmacht officer. Unfortunately he was killed in France. Frau Müller decided the house was too big for her and sold it to Herr Neumann.'

'And do you know where Frau Müller might live now?'

Her features toyed with an expression of regret.

'I believe she died from pneumonia shortly after Herr Neumann purchased the house.'

'And left no family, I suppose.'

'Unhappily not, Herr Tennant. That is why the house was too big for her.'

'A dead end,' I said.

Her expression shifted to one of smugness.

'As you say, Herr Tennant. A dead end.'

I left Frau Ernst secure in her smugness and went upstairs to change my shoes. Mitzi's torch stood on the table and I slipped it into my pocket in case I needed it. Then I went back downstairs. Frau Ernst's door was closed.

The Schneiders' house was little more than a shell. The rear and side walls remained although the front of the house, the interior and the roof had been blown apart by the explosion. The bomb, to judge from the damage, had fallen on the other side of the road where all that was visible of the building that had stood there was a water-filled crater and an encircling pile of rubble. The Lehmann's house, distant enough to avoid the worst of the blast, had been shielded by both the Schneider house and the trees separating the properties. Even so, it must have been a large explosion, big enough to damage the roof and some of the Lehmann's upper rooms despite the distance. Not that I believed the Lehmanns had been living there then. By the time the RAF and the Yanks had resumed large-scale bombing, the SS had rounded up the majority of Berlin's Jews and deported them to the camps.

If Walter Frick had assumed ownership of the house after interning the Lehmann family, though, he had ended up with damaged goods.

I supposed anything could have happened to the Schneiders. If they weren't killed in the raid they certainly no longer had a house to live in. The front had collapsed and brought the roof down with it. The whole interior lay open to the sky, even if there wasn't a lot left to see for anyone who was looking.

Except me. And I didn't quite know what it was I was looking for.

If Shoshannah Lehmann *had* seen Walter Frick coming out of the house and had not simply imagined it, I couldn't begin to guess what he had been doing there. As far as I could tell, anything salvageable had gone long ago. So, if Frick had been there what had he been looking for?

I clambered over the rubble into the house, casting a wary eye on what was left of the floor above me where a few sagging joists clung onto the belief they were still a ceiling.

In what must have been the hall a wide flight of now splintered stairs led nowhere. Beyond these was once what appeared to have been a variety of rooms.

There were no fittings left, no sign of furniture, nor any kitchen paraphernalia that I could see. Whatever personal belongings the Schneiders might once have owned had either been destroyed, gone with them, or been robbed out years ago. All that was left were piles of brick and plaster and heaps of other, less determinate detritus.

In what had been the kitchen I did find some broken crockery among the debris. And a rusting range too heavy, I assumed, to move or salvage. Even so, the doors of the ovens were missing as was the stove pipe that had once exited through the rear wall.

To one side of the kitchen was a narrow room which, to

judge by the mesh covering the single small window let high into the outside wall, had been the pantry. The ceiling here was still intact and in the gloomy light amid the other rubbish on the floor I could see broken glass and some marks on the walls where the pantry shelving had once been fixed. The wall at the far end of the pantry had not been plastered like the others but constructed of timber boarding. Another door was set in it, a rather makeshift affair hung awkwardly and looking oddly incongruous. Large gaps showed between the door itself and the frame. The door hinges were also free of rust and seemed relatively new, as if the door hadn't long been hung.

I stepped over the glass and tried the handle. The door was locked. I could see the lock's tenon bridging the gap between the door and the lining of the jamb and I tried pulling it sideways by the handle to see if there was enough play in the door to free the tenon. But it wouldn't shift.

The lining didn't look particularly robust so I went back into the kitchen in search of a lever and found a short metal bar in the rubble by the range, used I supposed for opening and closing the oven's doors.

Back in the pantry I slipped the bar between the door and the lining. It took only a small amount of pressure to ease the lock free.

It was even darker beyond the door and I took Mitzi's torch out of my pocket and switched it on. The space beyond was hardly more than four feet square and completely empty.

I was about to turn away, puzzled as to why anyone would hang a locked door into a small and empty room, when the beam of the torch arced over the floor and I saw a square of timber board with a metal ring through it lying by the far wall. No debris lay on top of the board and as I stepped closer I saw it wasn't just a sheet of timber but a trapdoor. I lifted the iron ring and pulled the trapdoor open.

The beam of Mitzi's torch showed a flight of stone steps leading down into a cellar.

I stood above them for a moment, hearing nothing except my own breathing. I took the first step down.

On the wall at the top of the steps I found an electric light switch. I flicked it up and down a couple of times but it didn't work. I continued on down, playing the torchlight in front of me.

At the foot of the stairs I found nothing more interesting than the house cellar, a dank and musty cavern with concrete walls glistening with moisture and tinged green with algae.

I supposed most houses of that age had cellars. I'd not given the matter any thought before. Now I did, I assumed that we too would have one in our house next door. I had never seen it, of course. Frau Ernst had the use of the ground floor rooms which included the original kitchen.

The Schneiders' cellar, although large, didn't hold the sort of things I might have expected. There were no wine racks or barrels, at least there weren't now. And anything made of timber must have gone for firewood when it got short during the war. What there was were two old armchairs, a table and two cots, the latter piled high with a heap of mouldering bedding. It was obvious the cellar had been used as an air raid shelter although the boarded wall and makeshift door in the pantry upstairs were later additions. If they had been constructed before Berlin had fallen, though, and designed to keep out the Red Army, someone had been deluding himself.

Disappointed, I took a last look around before retreating upstairs. That was when, in the darkness, I saw what appeared to be an alcove set in the wall beneath the steps. Ducking under the steps, however, I saw it wasn't an alcove but the entrance to a tunnel.

I shone the torch along its length but couldn't see the other end. It had been lined with brick and had a low curved roof that dripped with moisture. It was narrow and barely high enough to enable me to stand upright yet it didn't look to be anywhere near as old as the rest of the cellar. I took a few steps in, thinking that it had perhaps been constructed as an escape route during the air raids in case the house got hit and the trapdoor above blocked.

I stood at the entrance trying to work out in which direction the tunnel travelled. But I had lost my bearings in the cellar and wasn't sure which way it went. Into the garden, most probably, which like our house next door ran down to the lake. I ran a finger over the water seeping through the brickwork and, despite myself, imagined the lake on the other side of the bricks, ready to burst through into the tunnel.

But that was nonsense. The lake was yards away beyond the bottom of the garden and, anyway, the tunnel had obviously been there several years already without collapsing.

It was less liable to give way to water than I was to panic.

I took a dozen steps further in and found, after a few yards, that the bricks gave way to rock and earth, the sides and ceiling being shored up at intervals with timber props. I moved forward slowly, stooping slightly to avoid hitting my head on the roof. The tunnel didn't appear to bend.

After what must have been fifty yards, I decided it couldn't be heading towards the lake. That meant it was either going out towards the road at the front of the house or towards one of the two properties that lay to either side: the house to the left of the Schneiders' property which was in much the same condition as theirs, or the house to the right which was where I lived.

I went another twenty-five yards then began to consider whether I should turn back. The tunnel, I told myself, could be blocked by a cave-in or, if it wasn't, would end with another door, locked like the one I had forced in the Schneiders' pantry. My reasoning was so persuasive that after a few more paces I stopped, shone the torch ahead of me and took one last look.

That's when I heard the voices.

They sounded very far away and faint. I turned the torch off. Swallowed by impenetrable darkness, I strained my ears to hear. I could make out a man and a woman were having a conversation. Although their words came to me, they seemed so malformed that I couldn't decipher anything said. That they were speaking German didn't help. Although I was by now competent enough to hold up my end of a conversation, I still had to translate everything into English in my head before replying. I wasn't yet thinking in German.

I didn't move for several minutes. Indistinct as the voices were, I knew they weren't getting any closer. Neither of them were in the tunnel. The other end, I presumed, was another cellar and I was becoming convinced that it was the cellar of the Lehmann's old house.

I took a few stealthy steps closer. I was almost sure that the woman was Frau Ernst. But the man didn't sound like Werner.

I was tempted to move even closer but afraid I might trip in the dark. If I could hear them, they would be able to hear me. I would need to put the torch on again and that would risk the beam being visible in the far cellar.

The last thing I wanted was for Frau Ernst to find out I had discovered the tunnel. That went for the man with her, too.

Whoever he might be.

And I was beginning to suspect I knew who that was.

~

I was back in the apartment by the time Mitzi returned from shopping with Marthe for skin cream.

Retreating down the tunnel, I had prised the partition door in the Schneiders' pantry shut, just as I had found it, and gone back through the ruins to the Lehmann house. Despite the warm afternoon Frau Ernst's door was firmly shut. I paused to listen as I passed but could hear nothing. The flat was as still and silent as a grave. I felt tempted to knock on the door if only to see how long it took her to answer. But I was dusty from clambering around the rubble of the Schneiders' house and the tunnel and had no plausible explanation should she notice.

I went upstairs and was washing when Mitzi came back.

'Did you find what you were looking for?' I asked, fresh and not smelling of the lake for once.

'I have a jar,' she said, pulling it out of her bag. 'But it is Italian and I am not sure what it is for.'

I took a look but the label was beyond my Italian.

'Here,' I said, offering the inside of my wrist. 'Try a dab and I'll let you know if it's acidic.'

'What is acidic?'

'Something that eats you,' I told her, raising my eyebrows suggestively.

'Stop it, Harry,' she protested. 'I am too hot and tired for your games.'

242

'Fancy a swim?'

'You are clean for once. I will keep you that way.'

'Take a bath. The water's on. I thought you were going to stay at Marthe's till tonight.'

'Marthe is getting tiresome,' Mitzi complained.

'Wanted to rub the cream in, I suppose.'

'You should not joke about this. It is not funny. Besides, I wanted to change before this evening.'

'Okay,' I said, 'I'll go back in with you this evening if you want.'

'You do not have to come tonight, Harry, if you would rather not. You know what it is like on a Saturday with the weekend passes. Yesterday was bad enough.'

'I know. That's why I want to come.'

'I can take care of myself, if that is what is worrying you. I did before I met you.'

'Fine,' I said, 'but who's going to take care of me? You know what I was like before we met.'

'You are a joker, Harry, but not a funny one.'

She gave me a kiss and went into the bedroom to get a towel.

'And do not let me forget my torch tonight,' she called through the door. 'I suppose we will have to walk home again.'

'I won't,' I called back.

But of course I did.

28

Although the evening was still early the fog of cigarette smoke was thick enough to make me wish I hadn't left my old gas mask in England. Despite it, I added to the fug while marvelling at how people seemed to manage to retain the knack of enjoying themselves no matter how dire their situation.

It wasn't an observation that always held true, of course, and not everyone in Germany a bare two years after the end of the war would have concurred. What I suppose I was thinking was that most people are able to make the best of a bad job.

243

The crowd I was watching certainly were. Being a Saturday night Karl had splashed out on hiring a small band. It meant sacrificing some tables to provide a dance floor but he judged it to be a cost-effective exercise. Live music attracted the servicemen and after a drink or two no one objected to squeezing up a bit if there wasn't much room.

It wasn't easy to make out the band through the haze of cigarette smoke although I could hear them well enough. Sounding like a marching band tripping over its own feet—or musical notes, in this case—they were make a stumbling assault on Gershwin's *Fascinating Rhythm*. Not the easiest of melodies even for the musically proficient and, given the situation, I would have guessed that until fairly recently the band members had spent more time playing military marches than dance tunes. Particularly tunes written by Jewish composers.

The resulting rhythm was not quite as fascinating as Gershwin probably intended and seemed to catch the couples on the dance floor in two minds, halfway between a foxtrot and a jitterbug. In the ensuing mayhem many quit the floor.

The American servicemen were always game, though, and were making a better fist of it than most. I'd always found the Yanks were willing, and able, to dance to just about anything.

With the possible exception of someone else's tune, that is.

But that was just sour grapes on my part. I envied them, of course, having two left feet myself. And feet, moreover, which once on a dance floor behaved as if they belonged to someone else.

Mitzi had learned that lesson early which is why between being nice to the customers and being whisked away by any budding Fred Astaire, she was content to sit with me rather than suffer for my art on the dance floor.

She had just left me when I saw Ben Tuchmann pushing his way through the crowd towards me. I say "pushing" although the eagle wings on his lapels designating his colonelcy were doing most of the heavy work.

I raised a hand and he came over and sat down.

'Quite a joint, Harry,' he said looking around with a grin on his face.

It didn't know if it was his sort of place as it never attracted many officers and I'd only ever seen Tuchmann in the relatively sedate clubs of society London. But maybe back in New York boisterous barrel-houses were his natural habitat.

'It only gets like this at weekends,' I said. 'They like to dance.'

'With a girl?'

'That always helps.'

Mitzi came back to take Tuchmann's order, standing over us wearing that blank expression of hers that drove Karl crazy.

'Be nice to the customers, Mitzi,' he was always telling her. 'Be *nice*.'

'Mitzi, meet Colonel Ben Tuchmann,' I said.

He turned to her, switching on the charm I remembered so well from the previous summer. If he'd been a character in a Hollywood cartoon the rest of us would be wearing sunglasses so as not to be blinded by the glare of his teeth.

'So, this is Mitzi.' he said.

He stood up and offered her his hand. Not many of Karl Bauer's customers went to those lengths whether she was nice to them or not. I could see that she was impressed despite herself.

'Welcome to Berlin, colonel,' she said. 'You and Harry are old friends I suppose?'

'I've been in Berlin some while, Mitzi,' he told her, 'although this is my first time in your club. Harry and I know each other from London. We were both chasing the same thing, weren't we, Harry.'

'Would that have been a woman?' Mitzi asked, turning her attention to me.

Tuchmann laughed easily. 'Not this time. It was business.'

'With Harry it is always business,' she observed. 'But he does sometimes like to mix the two.'

'Now I don't believe that, Mitzi. Not with you around.'

'What'll you drink, Ben?' I interrupted, just to remind him I was still there.

'Whisky if you have it.'

'Bourbon?' Mitzi asked. 'Americans prefer bourbon, I think.'

I knew the only reason Karl had bourbon was that he got a

few bottles through Kurt from Joe Rafferty now and again. Courtesy of the American PX. I was hoping Mitzi wasn't going let Tuchmann see the label.

'Bourbon? sure. On the rocks, please Mitzi. What's yours, Harry?'

I gestured towards my beer and Mitzi headed off towards the bar.

'So that's the girl you're living with,' Tuchmann said to me as soon as she was out of earshot. 'What's her story?'

'I've never asked,' I said. 'I doubt she'd tell me if I did.'

'I know what you mean, Harry. Sometimes it's better not to know. They're not always pretty.'

'The stories or the girls?'

He grinned again. 'The stories. Mitzi's a good looking girl.'

'This place is full of them,' I said, just so he'd know there were plenty of other fish swimming around. 'Is this a social call or have you managed to dig up something on the Lehmann family for me?'

He stopped eyeing the other fish and pulled his chair closer.

'I do have a couple of things as a matter of fact. And pretty interesting they are, too.'

'Like what?'

Tuchmann took out a pack of Chesterfields, offered me one and we lit up further thickening the atmosphere.

'This Frick first. It's not an uncommon name although there was only one really important Nazi called Frick and he was a Wilhelm. It can't be him but there were several other Fricks who joined the NASPD. Only one Walter we can find who might be of interest, though.'

'Why do you assume my Frick was in the Nazi party? My Walter Frick was a policeman.'

'Because any ambitious policeman who saw which way the wind was blowing would have joined the party. And probably before Himmler's SS took over the police.'

'All right, how do you know it's not this other one, this Wilhelm? Maybe he preferred to be called Walter.'

'Wilhelm Frick is dead.'

'There's dead and there's dead,' I said, reminding him of the man he was after when we met in London who had supposedly been killed during the Normandy invasion.

'This one's a certainty. Wilhelm Frick was Reichsminister of the Interior before he took over as Protector of Bohemia and Moravia after Heydrich's assassination. We hanged him last year.'

'Not much room for doubt there, then.'

Mitzi came back with Ben's bourbon and my beer. He sipped it and told her it tasted as good as the brand the PX sold. She put my beer in front of me, her deadpan barely twitching.

'Okay,' I said when she'd gone. 'Walter Frick the policeman.'

'He joined the police in 1925. He switched to Kripo in '34 and was already a Nazi when Himmler absorbed the police in '36, which could only have helped him. He joined the Gestapo at the beginning of the war and was involved in the round-up and transportation of Jews. Then, when the special police squads were formed in the wake of the Wehrmacht's advance on the eastern front, he was given command of one of the groups in the Ukraine.'

'The special police squads? The *Einsatzgruppen*. He was a commander?'

'Yes. He was reported as killed in early '45 but the circumstances weren't entirely convincing. Walter Frick's name is still on the wanted list. If he is alive, he is someone we would very much like to get our hands on. The Soviets want him, too, for what his *Einsatzgruppen* did in southern Ukraine. Frick is one of their top targets.'

'And no one's ever had a line on him?'

'Not until now,' Tuchmann said. 'With this girl of yours.'

'Then it could be Frick living in Hamburg under the name of Neumann,' I suggested. 'He's not likely to have stayed in Berlin with the Russians advancing on the city. He must have known they'd be after him.'

'Assuming he is alive,' Tuchmann said. 'He would have got out if he could. And if Neumann is Frick then we'll get him sooner or later. The name Neumann is more common than Frick, though, and there must be quite a few people called Neumann living in Hamburg. It would help if we had a Christian name.'

'Sorry, Ben. Frau Ernst only ever refers to him as "Herr Neumann". I could ask her but I don't want her to think I'm too interested. If Neumann *is* Frick, it might frighten him off. I've probably already alerted them.'

'It's not important,' Tuchmann said. 'Hamburg is in the British Zone but I've got contacts in the Provost Marshal's office. I'll ask them to check for any possibles.'

I might have told him that I'd heard someone I suspected of being both Frick and Neumann talking to Frau Ernst that very afternoon. But I wasn't ready to explain that I'd been in a tunnel connecting her apartment to the cellar of the house next door. I decided to let him do some more of the donkey work in Hamburg first. The last thing I wanted was for him to send a platoon of MPs round to roust Frau Ernst out of bed on the strength of what I thought I'd heard. It wasn't that I was looking to do Frau Ernst any favours. If I was wrong Mitzi and I would be looking for somewhere else to live; if I was right I was going to be happier keeping a card back rather than playing my whole hand at once. In this sort of game I had learned through bitter experience that Ben Tuchmann was sharper than most when it came to expedience.

'Checking all the Neumann's in Hamburg will take a while, I suppose,' I said.

'I imagine so. Maybe it's best if you don't do anything until I hear what they come up with. If Frick is alive we don't want him slipping through the net again.'

I said I had heard there had been an escape route out of Germany set up for Nazis who were wanted for war crimes.

'Was and is,' said Tuchmann. 'It was organized when it looked as if Germany was going to lose the war. Of course, it wasn't the sort of thing Hitler would have approved of. Not that that stopped several of the more senior Nazis putting their own skins before loyalty to their Führer. He would have shot anyone he thought was planning to jump ship.'

'And the network still exists?'

'Certainly. If you know the right people and have the right sort of money there's still a way out. South America is the favoured destination. We think several of the men we're looking for got out that way. Mengle and Eichmann ... Martin

Boorman. Gestapo Müller perhaps...'

'If that's the case, why would Frick still be in Germany?

Tuchmann shrugged. 'Lack of money... Or perhaps he thinks he's safe by just changing his name to Neumann. There are a lot of former Nazi officials who never left. And many of them are still in positions of power. There's more than one in the Administration. I'm afraid that even though they have been put through the de-Nazification process, the powers that be prefer them to the alternative.'

'To the socialists you mean?'

'The Germans call it *realpolitik*.'

'They would have a name for it.'

'That's one thing about the Russians, they won't tolerate ex-Nazis. Even if their police are just as politically orientated.'

Gudrun, one of Karl's girls, swung by the table and tried to encourage Tuchmann onto the dance floor. I asked her to bring us another round of drinks.

'Still dance, do you?' I asked him.

He smiled. 'Not so much since London.'

'You should give Gudrun a whirl. She's a good dancer.'

'Maybe I will, Harry. Business first, though.'

'You've more?'

'I can confirm the house you and your friend Mitzi live in did once belonged to a Jewish family named Lehmann, Jashel and Hannah. One son, Asher, and a daughter, Shoshannah.'

I didn't know the Lehmanns had been Jashel and Hannah but if that was the extent of his detective work it didn't impress me much.

'I already gave you Shoshannah and Asher,' I said.

'Yeah, Harry, I know. But that's who they were.'

'Do you know what happened to them?'

'They were transported to Theresienstadt in '41. From there they were sent to Auschwitz.'

'Did Shoshannah go with them?'

Tuchmann shook his head. 'No. Not to Theresienstadt and she was never sent to Auschwitz. She was sent to Ravensbrück, but not until the end of '44. She was there when the Russians liberated the camp.'

'She managed to get away when her family was rounded up?

What was she, one of your u-boats? That was what you called them, wasn't it?'

'*Tauchers,* yes. And she did go underground. She had papers in the name of Anna Koch. You told me she didn't look Jewish so I guess she was able to pass. But this is the interesting part, she didn't go underground until '44. It wasn't until then that she was finally arrested and sent to Ravensbrück.'

'How did you find this out? Was she interviewed after Ravensbrück was liberated?'

'No, this was later still. About a year after Ravensbrück was liberated. She was arrested in the British sector. This came out in evidence at her trial.'

'Frau Ernst told me she had been in prison but I don't know why. What was it? Theft? Prostitution...?'

Tuchmann grimaced, the expression spoiling his usual good looks.

'No, Harry. That's not her whole story.'

'What is her whole story, Ben?'

'Anna Koch was a *Greifer.*'

I didn't know the word. Tuchmann took a deep breath as if the definition required extra oxygen.

'Originally *Greifer* was slang for a policeman. A cop. In German it also means to grab or hold something. In this context a *Greifer* means a catcher.'

29

I didn't suppose Tuchmann was talking about the man behind the plate at baseball games, the one who wears the big mitt.

I had to ask him what he meant by a catcher.

For a moment he seemed uncomfortable and unable to meet my gaze.

'*Greifers* were what the police and the Gestapo called the informants they used. Jewish informants.'

'You mean snitches? We use them back home. They're almost always petty criminals themselves.'

He looked me in the eye.

'No, Harry. I don't mean petty criminals. Not snitches. The Gestapo called them *Greifers* because they used them to catch other Jews.'

It took a second for his meaning to sink in. When it did I couldn't think of anything to say.

'It's not easy to accept that Jews would inform on their own,' Tuchmann went on. 'Not knowing what we do now. Not under those circumstances. But we're like everyone else, Harry. We're not a special people despite Moses and Isaiah and what it may say in the Tanakh. We called ourselves the "chosen people" because it made us feel better about ourselves ... all those years of slavery... Really we're just like everyone else. There are good Jews and there are bad Jews... Rich and poor, altruists and selfish bastards who don't look beyond their own wants and their own noses. It's likely that most of the catchers did what they did in an attempt to save not just themselves but their immediate family as well. Of course, there were some who did it for money. And there were others who betrayed Jews because they were trying to deny their own Jewishness and hated the rest of their kind. There were probably even some who bought into the Nazis' anti-Semitic propaganda.'

'You're telling me,' I said, finding my voice at last, 'that Shoshannah Lehmann betrayed other Jews to the Gestapo? Why would she do that?'

'She had apparently already begun calling herself Anna Koch before the war started. You have to remember she grew up amid the Nazi hysteria about Jews, constantly hearing them referred to as a sort of infrahuman species. To put it simply, she didn't want to be associated with them. At that time, even with her own family. As I say, this was before the war. She admitted as much at her trial. Later, once the deportations started, I think she must have had a change of heart. At her trial she maintained she began to cooperate with the Gestapo because they promised that if she provided them with the names and addresses of Jews who were in hiding they would not deport her family. There's no reason to disbelieve her, that she wasn't speaking the truth. Her family were not among those to be deported first.'

251

'Who did she betray?.'

'Most of them turned out to be her old school friends. Other kids she had known growing up. Some were Jews she had worked with and some were even the friends of her parents. Those who had gone into hiding. She apparently also provided the addresses of families in the Lehmann social circle who weren't Jewish themselves but who might have given shelter to Jews if they were asked. Anna Koch was familiar with the kind of place *Tauchers* would go if they could no longer go home and had to spend time on the street.'

'How many people did she give up?'

Tuchmann shook his head. 'That's not easy to say. She admitted to twenty or so. Some of the witnesses who survived and testified against her put the number a lot higher. It's only guesswork but I think it would certainly have been more than twenty. There were others, better known *Greifers* who betrayed more. People like Bruno Goldstein. Stella Goldschlag and Rolf Isaaksohn ... Ruth Danziger...'

I didn't know any of the names but there was no reason I should. Jews betraying Jews wasn't the sort of news that made the headlines. Jews were the victims, not the perpetrators.

It was common knowledge that it had been the Jewish community leaders who had drawn up the lists of the Jewish population for the SS to use, and had persuaded those on the lists to gather at the allotted detention centres prior to deportation. But it had been done under the belief that the Jews were being moved east into purpose built towns. Not to extermination camps. How many actually believed the fiction, I didn't know. Earlier in the year while in London looking into the spread of Jewish terrorism out of Palestine and into Britain, I had been given to understand that many of the terrorists were contemptuous of their fellow Jews for allowing themselves to be led like lambs to the slaughter. But that was grossly unfair and a misapprehension. Even if there were some who hadn't believed the stories about resettlement, the very idea of camps having been built specifically for the extermination of Jews would have been almost beyond imagination.

Except in the imagination of those who had conspired in

that extermination.

'But as I said,' Tuchmann went on, 'like Stella Goldschlag, Shoshannah Lehmann was pretending she wasn't a Jew even before the deportations began. She was calling herself Anna Koch and had repudiated her Jewish background. She mixed with the so-called Aryans and appeared to buy into the Nazi propaganda. From the viewpoint of the Gestapo she was ideal *Greifer* material.'

'She said to me once that she *used* to be Shoshannah Lehmann. Now I know why she put it like that.'

'Guilt?' Tuchmann asked.

'I imagine so. At attempt to distance herself from what she had done. Not that it did her any good, did it? She didn't save her family from Auschwitz.'

'For a few months she did,' he said. 'For as long as she was useful to them. In the end they were all rounded up, informants as well, like all the rest. Even after her family was taken, though, according to her testimony she was told they were safe in one of the new towns in the east. They even encouraged her to write to them. That she never received a reply must have been the first inkling she had that she had been lied to. That was when it finally sank in and she went underground.'

'With the people she'd been hunting,' I said. 'There's an irony.'

'With those who didn't know what she had been doing, yes,' said Tuchmann. 'And in the end they caught her in one of the places she had told the Gestapo Jews liked to gather. She was sent to Ravensbrück and would have ended up in Auschwitz if the Russians hadn't arrived. At least her being a camp inmate saved her from the worst of the Red Army's excesses.'

'So how was she identified as a *Greifer*?'

'By other survivors. There were enough witnesses left alive who were willing to testify against her. She was found guilty although the court accepted extenuating circumstances.'

'Because she was trying to save her family?'

'That and the fact the whole business meant she'd become mentally unbalanced. "Touched", as you put it. She was sentenced to five years hard labour. She only served about eighteen months. Once she was declared mentally unfit to remain in prison, the authorities put her out on the street.'

Tuchmann fell silent. My cigarette had burned down between my fingers unsmoked. My beer was still untouched. Only the band went on, stumbling almost unheard through the popular tunes of the day.

I was thinking that Shoshannah Lehmann really had been what she had appeared to be that first evening I had seen her. One more street waif. Another of those who had returned to where she had grown up to see what was left. Only this one had a different story, one in which she had finally become reconciled to her Jewishness.

'What was her connection to Walter Frick?'

Tuchmann tossed back the last of his bourbon.

'Frick was her handler. He had known the family while he was a policeman. Perhaps they'd had reason to complain about harassment. I don't know. I doubt it did them any good if they did, but unfortunately it brought them to Frick's attention. After he joined the Gestapo he became the man she betrayed Jews to. And the man responsible for sending her family to the gas chamber.'

Tuchmann finished and wanted to talk about other things. We spoke about London and about Julia, my wife's aunt with whom he'd had a fling the previous summer. Once the investigation into Julia's brother-in-law, my wife's father, and into a family friend had ended, he'd dropped her.

I hadn't known at the time if his interest in Julia had been a way of getting to my wife's family or whether he had genuinely cared for her. Over another drink he told me that it had been Julia who had ended things once she discovered his involvement in the investigation. I listened to what he had to say but by the time he was through I was still none the wiser.

He had another bourbon and once that was finished said he'd get back to me about Neumann and Hamburg. I told him I'd do the same should I learn anything more about Walter Frick. He wanted me to persuade Shoshannah to go to the synagogue on Levetzowstraße and talk to his people there, the ones drawing up lists of missing Berlin Jews.

I thought the odds were better of me getting Frau Ernst to tell me where Walter Frick was.

We shook hands and on his way out, I noticed, he stopped to exchange a few words with Mitzi. Then, in the early hours when Karl finally threw the last of the drunks out and the girls dropped gratefully into chairs to ease the shoes off their aching feet, Mitzi came over and told me I hadn't really needed to wait for her, that she could have stayed at Marthe's apartment.

She was right, of course, I hadn't needed to wait even if it was a bit late in the day for her to tell me so. But she wouldn't have liked it if I hadn't and I reminded her we were supposed to be going to Potsdam.

'Oh, Harry,' she complained, 'I am too tired to go to Potsdam.'

'Not *now*, sweetie,' I said cheerfully. 'Tomorrow. You'll feel better in the morning.'

Which only goes to demonstrate I can see no further into the future than the next man.

We collected her things and said goodnight to Marthe. Mitzi gave her a kiss on her proffered cheek and although I waited my turn, Marthe turned out to be insufficiently Christian to offer me her other one.

Out on the street the air smelled unusually clean. It was too late for the tram or the trains and being a Saturday the few cabs available were already taken. The walk to Halensee was a good three miles and although Mitzi generally began by complaining about it, tired as she always was, after a couple of hundred yards she usually revived, happy to leave the stench of stale beer and cigarette smoke behind.

Even so, it only took a couple of blocks for the usual smells of Berlin to return, assaulting our nostrils with the reminder that the city was still a bombsite.

'How is it you know this American colonel?' she asked out of the blue as we were walked along the Kurfürstendamm.

'He told you,' I said. 'We met in London.'

'What is his story?'

'Funny, that's exactly what he asked about you.'

'And what did you tell him?'

'Nothing. I don't know your story, do I Mitzi? You've never

told me.'

'You have never asked me, Harry.'

Which, as I have said before, was true enough.

It wasn't through a lack of interest but unless you were an interrogator with the Forces of Occupation, asking a German what they did in the war wasn't regarded as making polite conversation. If they volunteered information, all well and good, even if the sort likely to volunteer details did usually turn out to be the sort who was generally most suspect.

Otherwise the rule was: don't ask.

Mitzi had never volunteered to tell me anything much about herself and that is how I had let it lie.

Having broached the subject now made me wonder if she was not inviting me, belatedly, to ask. And I almost did. At the last moment, though, I found myself telling her how I had met Tuchmann.

'And this friend of your family was a war criminal?'

She had stopped walking. She sounded appalled.

'Friend of my *ex-wife's* family,' I corrected. 'Not mine.'

'But still you have nothing to do with your family?'

'*My* family, no. But that's an entirely different matter.'

'I think, Harry,' Mitzi said walking on, 'you are a troubled man.'

'I get along without too much trouble,' I said.

'And your friend, Ben? Does he have a family?'

'A wife, you mean? I don't know. He's never said anything to me one way or the other. But I suspect not. The war has been over two years and he hasn't gone home yet. So either she's a very understanding woman or she doesn't exist.'

'And what is it he does here?'

'He was a lawyer in New York. I'm not sure exactly what he's doing here. Something to do with the Jewish deportations. Still trying to catch war criminals, probably.'

When Mitzi didn't say anything I went on flippantly, 'If you happen to know any, I'm sure he'd be happy to talk to you.'

It was a crass remark. A bad joke in poor taste and Mitzi didn't dignify it with a reply. We walked on in silence.

I spotted a rare cab cruising by and waved my arm at it. Mitzi may have been happy to walk the rest of the way but she was tougher than I was.

She didn't say a lot in the taxi either, and when we reached the house she went up the drive while I was still settling the fare. I caught up with her at the front door.

Frau Ernst's door was firmly shut although I wouldn't have expected anything else at two-thirty in the morning. I flicked the light switch on but either Frau Ernst was saving on light bulbs or the electricity wasn't working again.

Despite her asking me to remind her, Mitzi's torch was still upstairs in the apartment so we had to feel our way up the two flights to our door.

Inside I tried the light again and, still in the dark, crossed the room to the table where I'd left the torch.

Halfway across I bumped into something that shouldn't have been there.

It moved as I blundered into it then came back and hit me again like a boxer's punch bag. It wasn't a boxer's punch bag but, whatever it was, it was suspended from the ceiling.

'Stay where you are, Mitzi,' I called. 'I'll get the torch.'

I edged towards the table and stumbled over an upended chair. Mitzi called out. I got up and felt around the table for the torch.

I suppose I already knew what I was going to see even if I didn't know who. I really should have warned Mitzi not to look. But it was too late and as I switched the torch on I heard her gasp.

My hand was shaking the beam as I trained it on the dangling body of Shoshannah Lehmann.

30

Sunday August 10th 1947

Dawn arrived before the police did. I didn't expect too much of them and I wasn't disappointed. Ex-Wehrmacht in the main, the new German police had survived the war, managed to pass de-Nazification but weren't looking to start a new career for themselves any time soon. A couple of British MPs came along for the ride and they didn't do much either, just stood around giving the impression they would have preferred to be in bed.

While Mitzi waited in the corridor I'd hammered on Frau Ernst's door until she got out of bed. She followed me up the stairs, muttering under her breath. Then she saw the body and muttered some more, although no longer under her breath as she saw who it belonged to.

'Why did the stupid girl kill herself in my house?'

She turned to me and said it would upset Werner and that I shouldn't allow him to come up. Given he had trouble getting his wheelchair over the front doorstep and was incapable of tackling the stairs, I thought her concern misplaced. But Frau Ernst only had so much sympathy to go round and it appeared that by the time it came to Shoshannah Lehmann she had run out.

Not that the girl was that easy to identify. Judging by the expression on her face she had asphyxiated rather than died of a broken neck, her face red and swollen and her tongue protruding between her lips as if she was giving the world one last insolent gesture. The chair I had tripped over was on its side beneath her but it looked as if the drop had not been sufficient to break her neck. I had detected no smell walking into the apartment nor had later so either her sphincter hadn't opened, as was usual with those hanged, or more likely it had but had nothing to relinquish. I thought the chances were she hadn't eaten anything for some while, at least not since the crust of bread I'd given her on Friday. Being so thin she weighed very little, as I found when I had first lifted her body in the hope she might still be alive. Another reason, perhaps, why her neck hadn't broken.

Mitzi had held the torch while I had tried to take the weight off the rope but only said in a monotone, 'She is dead, Harry,' as if she had seen her share of corpses and knew about these things. 'You should leave her for the police.'

I knew she was right. I had seen my share of these things as well.

Frau Ernst had a telephone so she went back downstairs to call the police. And no doubt to warn Werner not to try struggling up the stairs. Mitzi and I brewed some tasteless coffee and drank it while we waited, not caring for once what it tasted like under the circumstances.

I was taking another look at Shoshannah's body when Frau Ernst returned.

'They will come as soon as they can,' she announced.

Which didn't mean much since I assumed Frau Ernst had told them it was suicide and the police generally have enough bodies of those who hadn't cooperated in their own death to worry about first.

'I told you to tell the police about her, Herr Tennant,' Frau Ernst went on after a moment, compassion getting the better of her and apparently unable to resist the temptation of putting the blame for the girl's death on my negligence. 'They would have put her away again and she would not have killed herself here.'

'Well you won't have to worry about her anymore will you, Frau Ernst?' I said in reply and none too sympathetically.

She stared back at me pugnaciously.

'I have a reputation to think of, Herr Tennant.'

I might have asked, *a reputation for what?* if I had thought it worth asking. But she had said all she wanted to say and after a few more minutes went back downstairs to wait in the comfort of her own bed until the police arrived.

Once the door had closed behind her I went back to Shoshannah. The cord around her neck was thin and had been tied to the light fitting. Slight as she was I was surprised her weight hadn't brought the thing down when she stepped off the chair. But, as I say, she weighed very little and the fitting must have been stronger than it looked.

Mitzi had watched with distaste as I had looked over Shoshannah's body, as if she thought I was getting some sort of pleasure from the act. There wasn't much to see. I found some material under her fingernails but that could have been anything. Besides, it wasn't as if I had a lab to consult over the matter. A quick examination of the rest of her showed no obvious wounds apart from the mark the ligature made around her neck. She had nothing on her, no papers or money.

What she had done with the Reichmarks she had stolen

259

from me I didn't know. Spent them, I assumed, although it didn't look as she had squandered them on food.

'Poor girl,' said Mitzi when I finished, having said little else since telling me she was dead. 'Why would she do this?'

Knowing what I did about her after talking to Ben Tuchmann, I might have asked why she wouldn't. I hadn't told her earlier that Shoshannah had been a *Greifer* and that old prohibition about speaking ill of the dead stopped me from doing so now.

A more pertinent question, I would have thought, was why she had done it here, in our apartment? More guilt over what she had done in trying to save her parents and brother? Or was she making a point, like a finger in the eye, still convinced she had seen Walter Frick near the house?

After a while, tired of looking at Shoshannah and unable to look anywhere else, Mitzi went to lie down. When I looked in ten minutes later she was asleep.

We had all seen our share of horrors, I suppose, and while some are able to shake them off and sleep others, incapable of such insouciance, keep them fresh in their minds. So I stayed with Shoshannah, keeping her company chain smoking until first the dawn and then the police finally turned up.

They didn't stay long. Once the cursory examination of Shoshannah Lehmann's body was over they questioned me then woke Mitzi to confirm that what I had said was true. They had woken Frau Ernst on their way up and questioned her as well.

She had corroborated our story although it probably stuck in her throat to have to do so.

They told me I would have to sign a statement at the station and so I said I'd ride back with them, waiting as they carried Shoshannah downstairs then squeezing into their van alongside the body. The MPs didn't help and once we were all outside they roared off ahead in their Jeep.

We followed at a more funereal pace.

~

At the station I was escorted into the office of a yawning middle-aged *leutnant* who appeared to think he had something better to do that early on a Sunday morning.

After being briefed by his men I went through my story again and told him what I knew of the girl—at least an edited version of what I knew. I had somewhere better to be that early on a Sunday morning, too.

I described how I had met her a few days earlier outside the house and how she had told me her name was Shoshannah Lehmann and that she had lived there before the war. When we got to the bit about the house having been appropriated because the family was Jewish, the *leutnant* suddenly woke up, rubbed a hand across his stubbled jaw and said somewhat curtly that he had heard enough.

I hadn't even got to the part with Ben Tuchmann and Walter Frick, and the fact that Shoshannah had been known as Anna Koch and had been a *Greifer*. But he was a policeman so I assumed he could find that out for himself.

The *leutnant* put my statement in front of me to sign. He watched while I scratched the pen nib over the paper then adroitly swept the case under the rug. He had me out of the door quicker than any of us could say, "Heil Hitler".

I found a stall outside the police station that opened early to help those coming off-shift with a drink to chase down the miseries of their night. I bought a coffee laced with enough schnapps to chase down mine.

On top of that night's beer, no sleep, and not much more food than Shoshannah Lehmann had probably eaten in the last twenty-four hours, I should have felt faint and light-headed.

Instead I felt sharp. Almost as if, like a musical note, I'd been raised in pitch by one chromatic semitone.

I could taste the grit on the morning air ... smell the smoke still lingering from the factories in the northern suburbs... My fingertips tingled and, if I'd had a crossword to hand, I'd probably have dashed it off before I'd finished my schnapps.

But corpses will do that to you. Or, rather, they do it to me.

Some people dissolve in wretched puddles; I seem to come alive, no doubt glad it wasn't me who'd just been heaved onto the meat wagon. Perhaps it's an expression of an urge for self-preservation. But if I wanted to understand myself I'd have become a psychoanalyst.

I was more interested in Shoshannah Lehmann and her death.

She had many reasons for killing herself: grief for her murdered family, guilt for what she had done in the attempt to save them and finally, perhaps, a desire to join them as she should have years before.

But against all that, I thought of the reasons she might have for staying alive. Or of one reason in particular.

Walter Frick.

He was the one good reason I could think of why Shoshannah would not have killed herself. Whether she wanted revenge on him, or justice, or merely the chance to confront the man who had used her and had lied to her was immaterial. He was the one reason why she should stay alive.

After all, if she had wanted to die she could have walked in front of a train ... drowned in the lake at Halensee ... hanged herself anytime since being released from prison...

She hadn't. What she had done was kill herself just a day or so after telling me she had seen Walter Frick in the ruins of the Schneiders' house.

31

I lit a cigarette and fished the note Fischer had given Marthe at the club on Friday out of my pocket.

It said Klaus Kittel came off-shift at Keibelstraße 35 at 8am. I looked at my watch. It was seven-thirty and that gave me half-an-hour to get there.

According to Heinie Möser the man's predilection for breaking heads had earned him his nickname, "killer". At any normal time that would have been enough to make even the least imaginative of men apprehensive about approaching Kittel. After the night I'd spent my imagination was working overtime.

Möser had given me a description and Kittel wasn't hard to

spot. As Möser said, Kittel had no neck. Not one that I could see anywhere between his shoulders and the heavy jowls that formed the base of his head. The rest of the man seemed in much the same proportion. Broad and bulky, Kittel was the sort of obstacle anyone with any sense went around. Only an idiot was going to try to go through him.

He must have been fifty but he looked fit. I could only guess how he managed to maintain the size he was on the meagre rations the Berlin Administration provided. I assumed he would have been entitled to the Russian sector *pajoks*, the perk given to all Party employees and which must have included Paul Markgraf's People's Police. And maybe, given the job he was in, other opportunities to get his hands on extra rations would present themselves.

When I spotted him he was just coming out of the Soviet sector polizeipräsidium building, the one the Russians had moved to after their difference of opinion with the Allies over how Berlin was to be policed. Having objected to the new HQ on Friesenstraße in the American sector, the Russians had built one of their own.

I fell into step as he headed towards the tram stop. He glanced down at me momentarily—he topped me by a good couple of inches—but didn't slow his pace.

'You want something, friend?' he asked out of the corner of his wide mouth.

I cleared my throat. 'You are Klaus Kittel, aren't you?'

He looked at me again. 'Do I know you, friend?'

'No.'

'You're not German.'

'English,' I said.

His nose wrinkled the way Mitzi's did after I'd been swimming in the lake.

'My name is Harry Tennant.'

'Is that supposed to mean something to me?'

'No,' I said, 'but Heinie Möser told me you used to work Wilmersdorf, out of the Kaiseralle station.'

'Möser?'

'A thin guy. Sharp nose. He was a housebreaker when you knew him.'

'Möser is still alive?'

'He was a couple of days ago,' I said.

Kittel grunted. 'Last I heard he was in a detention camp. I'm surprised having to work for his bread didn't kill him.'

'By the look of him he never got much even if he did work. They put him in a factory when he came out.'

'So,' Kittel said, 'what's Heinie Möser to you?'

'Nothing. I'm interested in someone else. I'm looking for anyone who knew Walter Frick.'

We reached the tram stop. The queue rearranged itself to accommodate Kittel's bulk and must have taken me as his accessory, something like one of those birds that sit on the back of African buffalo and peck their parasites.

Kittel peered down the street at an approaching tram.

'Do you remember Frick?' I asked.

'What was he, another housebreaker?'

'No, he was a bull like you.'

'And Möser says I knew him?'

'No. Just that you both worked out of the same station.'

The tram stopped and Kittel climbed aboard. He walked past the driver apparently having no need of a ticket. I bought one that would take me a few stops down the road. Kittel found an empty bench and spread his bulk across the two seats. I squeezed in beside him, half hanging in the aisle.

'How far are you going, friend?' Kittel asked.

'A couple of stops,' I said. 'Unless you can help me with Frick.'

'What's your interest?'

'There's a girl who used to live by the lake in Halensee. She says Frick stole her house.'

'Oh? What would her name be?'

'Shoshannah Lehmann. The house belonged to her parents, Jashel and Hannah Lehmann.'

'Jewish?'

'That's right.'

'What's she after, some sort of restitution?'

'Not now,' I said. 'She died last night. But a couple of days ago she told me she saw Frick.'

'She's dead?' Something rumbled in Kittel's throat. 'So is

Frick. Died on the eastern front.'

'How was he killed?'

I thought he shrugged although it wasn't easy to tell as his shoulders hardly moved.

'I just heard he was dead,' he said.

He heaved himself up. I slid off the bench out of his way. Kittel paused in the aisle until I sat down again.

'There's a bar round the corner if you want to know about Frick,' he said.

He lumbered towards the tram's exit with me following in his wake.

The bar was on Heinrich-Roller-Straße, off Prenzlauer Allee and near the cemetery. The upper floors had been gutted and the bar hollowed out of a ground floor room. In the cemetery across the road gravestones tilted this way and that like crooked teeth. A decapitated angel with half a wing perched on a monument over the dead, probably wishing she could fly somewhere else.

I bought Kittel a beer and a schnapps and we sat a table near the door.

'My wife's in there,' he said, jerking his chin towards the cemetery. 'She was killed in an air raid.'

'I'm sorry,' I said.

'American raid. '44.'

'Were you in Berlin?'

'Yeah. I'd been on shift. When I got out of the shelter and came home I found the whole block had gone. I dug her out myself.'

Two or three sympathetic comments came to mind but I didn't think any of them would be of any use to Kittel so I kept my mouth shut.

'Where were you in '44?' he asked, as if he thought I might have been in a Lancaster bomber somewhere overhead at the time.

'Italy,' I said.

'First war?'

'Too young.'

'I wasn't. Just old enough and stupid enough to join up. I was in that mess on the eastern front until the Russians quit.

Then we were sent to France. For a while it looked like we were going to win. I should have known better.'

It was obvious Kittel wanted someone to listen and wasn't fussy who. I might have prompted him about Frick but I thought if I let him run he'd get there sooner or later. Big as he was there had been no need for apprehension. I sensed that the heart had gone out of him. It was buried across the road under one of those crooked gravestones.

'It seemed to me the Russians had been the smart ones,' he said. 'Got rid of the tsar and all their rotten upper-classes. It looked like we might do the same when I got back but they soon snuffed that idea out. *Freikorps* ... right-wingers... As far as I could see things weren't that bad under Weimar but it wasn't enough for some. I never bought into all that bullshit about being stabbed in the back by the Jews and the Industrialists. People always have to have someone to blame. That's what Hitler understood. Times were tough, sure, but only for those people whose times are always tough. Of course, once he'd got a bit of power he didn't waste any time in getting in bed with the same industrialists he'd been saying stabbed us in the back. Some of them may even have been Jews, I don't know, but he was going to clear out the reds and that was good enough for them. They always thought they could get rid of Hitler when the time came.'

He finished his beer and his speech and I signalled the barman for two more. Kittel pulled out a pack of crumpled Russian cigarettes. I kept my American Luckies in my pocket.

'You wanted to know about Walter Frick?' he asked when the beers came.

'Was he a friend of yours?'

'I wouldn't have called him a friend exactly. You know how it is when you work with people. You get friendly even if you don't particularly like them. That's how it was with Frick. We got on but I can't say I liked him.'

'What happened when the SS took over the police?'

'Nothing much changed,' Kittel said. 'Not to start with. There were still burglars and pickpockets to chase. And Hitler got rid of the SA scum by then which was all right by me. Until we realized that most of them had just switched to the SS and were carrying on as normal. Instead of turning a blind eye to the SA we were now supposed to ignore the SS thugs roaming the streets, harassing Jews and anyone else the Nazis didn't care for.'

'And Frick didn't mind that?'

'No. He swallowed everything Hitler fed him. Not that Frick had ever been in the trenches to get stabbed in the back. Too young like you. When the war began he got the chance to join the Gestapo so he switched. I didn't see much of him after that. Not until they started forming the special police squads for the new territories in the east. They were supposed to mop up behind the army. Frick was given a squad and he wanted me to join him. I'd heard the stories about what was happening from some of the bulls who'd come back. I told Frick the SS could do their own fucking killing. I said I wasn't going to do it for them. My Frieda wouldn't have wanted me to do something like that.'

'What did Frick think of that?'

'Nothing. They could have forced me to join, of course, but Frick didn't want anyone with him whose heart wasn't in it. Not the way his was. He'd rather avoid the trouble.'

'So you stayed in the police?'

'Yeah. I thought they'd come for me sooner or later and, to be honest, after Frieda was killed, I didn't much give a damn if they did. By then, though, the writing was on the wall. I heard Frick had been killed somewhere in Belarus. Anyway, I never saw him again.'

'What did he look like?' I asked.

'I can give you a description. Not that it'll do you much good. He was the kind that was sort of nondescript. You know, medium height ... medium build. He was blond with a pale complexion. Face like a door-to-door salesman, if you know what I mean.'

'No distinguishing marks?'

'Like scars? Not when I knew him. He might have picked some up later. Why do you want to know?'

'Curiosity, mainly,' I said. 'This Lehmann girl maintained she saw Frick and if she's right there must be people who'd be interested.'

'Like the Russians?'

'I suppose so. After what the police squads did in the east I'd have thought they'd be looking for him.'

'Yeah,' Kittel said, 'I reckon they would if he was still alive.' He looked down into what was left of his beer then up at me again. 'How'd you find me, anyway? Not Heinie Möser.'

'No, not Möser. I happen to know someone who works in records in the SED office on Liepzigerstraße. I asked him to see if you were still on the payroll.'

'Oh? Who would that be?'

'Not a friend,' I said. 'Just someone I know casually,'

'Just a casual friend?' Kittel repeated caustically. 'Yeah, we've all got those.'

He finished his beer and stood up.

'Thanks for the drink, friend. But I think you're barking up the wrong tree. If you do find Frick is still alive, though, I'd be interested to know. Bringing in someone like him would be a feather in my cap.'

I sat and finished my beer after he had gone wondering what I would do if I found that Walter Frick was still alive.

I supposed that Shoshannah Lehmann would have wanted to kill him although how she would have managed it I couldn't guess. I might have done the job for her if my heart had really been in it. I had done something similar before and in cold blood even though, like a dormant volcano, the hot lava hadn't been that far beneath the surface. As far as Frick went, I'd never laid eyes on him. I was out of the war crimes business now. Frick was nothing to me even if natural justice did dictate he should be brought to book for the crimes he committed. I could always let Tuchmann know if I found him, although the Americans didn't have the best of track records when it came to bringing all the Nazis they found to trial. If the person in question had something to offer they wanted they were just as likely to take him back home with them and give him a job and a warm pair of slippers to come home to at night. There was a story that the man who had masterminded the V1 and V2 rocket program for Hitler had been spirited away to the USA in just such a fashion so he wouldn't fall into Russian hands.

Just more *realpolitik*. I don't know that Frick had anything to offer the Yanks and Tuchmann being a Jew himself would, I'd have thought, want to ensure Frick got what he deserved. Even so, I could never be certain of that. If I did find Frick was in Halensee, though, he'd be in the British sector and easy enough for us to pick up. And, despite all I'd learned to the contrary this past winter, I still continued to believe that we British had a better sense of justice than everyone else.

As for going back to Klaus Kittel and handing Frick over to the Russians... That was another matter.

I don't know why I should think it was. But I did.

~

Everything looked much as it always did when I got back to Halensee. It was a Sunday morning and all was still. The sound of what little traffic ran along Koenigsallee didn't reach the house. There was no indication that anything had happened there.

Suicide, the police would say. Motive unexplained. Like the death of Arthur Peston.

Mitzi was still asleep and she didn't wake as I slipped in the bed beside her. Tired as I was, I couldn't sleep. Mitzi's breathing was deep and regular and I took that as a sign of a clear conscience. That was some consolation.

My conscience was clear as well. At least reasonably so. There were one or two murky areas I tried not to visit too often. But even skirting them I still couldn't sleep. I lay beside Mitzi, listening to her but thinking of Shoshannah Lehmann.

I wanted to know why she had chosen last night of all nights to kill herself, the night I had learned what she had been. She wouldn't have known that of course but I did. Why it had happened in her old family house in the room that had once been her brother's was easier to understand. Guilt and remorse would have brought her back here.

Or was I crediting her with feelings and an impulse to penitence she may not have felt herself? Surely, if it had been guilt and remorse that drove her to kill herself, would she have had the determination to survive the camp at Ravensbrück?

I wished I had examined her body more closely. Not easy

with Mitzi there and Frau Ernst complaining about her reputation, but I should have done it nevertheless. My cursory look had revealed some material under her fingernails but that could have been nothing more than ordinary dirt. I had seen no scratches or bruising on her arms, overt signs that might have indicated a struggle, that she had been held while the thin noose was slipped over her head. I'd noticed no marks on her wrists to suggest she had been tied before she died. But a closer examination might have shown some. There had been so very little of her that any resistance she might have put up could not have lasted long. It might very well have taken two people first to subdue and then hang her, but it wouldn't have been a difficult task. Leaving her in our apartment—her old home—might have been designed to look as another element in obvious suicide. But was there more to it that that? Was it also meant as a message for me?

A warning, perhaps.

I got out of bed again, crossed the room softly and closed the bedroom door behind me. I scrutinized the area around the table where she had been hanging and examined the chair she had supposedly stood upon. But everything looked much as it always did. No less dirty, which might indicate someone had cleaned up after hanging the girl; no more dirty to suggest there had been some sort of struggle.

I pulled the chair in question out, sat in it and smoked another cigarette, waiting for some thunderbolt of comprehension to hit me in the way it struck detectives in crime fiction. But I was either too dumb to recognize a thunderbolt or real life had decided not to imitate art.

I was still sitting there when Mitzi appeared at the bedroom door in her thin cotton shift.

'Did you come to bed or have you been up all night?' she asked.

'I was in with you for an hour or two,' I said.

'What did the police say?'

'Not much. As soon as I told them she was Jewish and this used to be her family home, they rushed me out.'

'No one likes to speak of it.'

'The dead certainly can't.'

'Harry...'

'Sorry,' I said. 'We were going to Potsdam today.'

'Do you still want to?'

I didn't but Mitzi always liked to do something on her days off besides sleep. And the thought of staying in the apartment for the rest of the day was not an attractive one.

Not for any of us: me, Mitzi and Shoshannah Lehmann's ghost.

'Aren't you too tired?' she asked.

'I can catch up tonight.'

'What is the time?'

'Not twelve yet,' I said. 'Is there still water?'

She turned the sink tap on. The pressure was down but it did run. She began brewing a pot of Karl Bauer's good coffee.

'Let me wash and shave while you dress and we'll get going,' I said.

I went down the corridor to the bathroom, stripped off and splashed around a bit before shaving. Looking at the face that stared back out of the cracked mirror, I had the sensation of having become less familiar with it. Mitzi came in behind me, still wearing the shift. She reached into the cabinet for a jar of her cream.

'Do you want me to put that on for you?'

'You had better put something on yourself,' she said, pointedly looking to where the thought of rubbing in her cream had begun to stir me.

'We could catch a later train,' I suggested.

The fact that Mitzi never needed much persuasion to make love was one of the things I particularly liked about her. So we went back to the bedroom, careless of anyone who might be coming down the stairs from above and spent a sticky half-hour adding life and enjoyment to the rooms that had so recently lost both.

32

We took the StadtBahn for Potsdam from Charlottenburg. Like much of Germany's infrastructure the inter-city train network had suffered badly although it had been one of the first services back up and running after the surrender. Rumour had it that was mainly because Stalin had wanted to use the train to reach the Potsdam conference. Maybe the Hero of the Soviet Union was a nervous flyer.

Like the rest of Berlin's rolling stock the carriages were dirty and in disrepair, cracked windows replaced with cheap opaque glass where they had bothered to replace it at all. We sat and rattled along then stopped at the checkpoint as we crossed into the Russian Zone. The guards gave Mitzi's papers and my passport a cursory glance and, to my surprise, she had a brief conversation in Russian with them. Then they returned our documents and we rolled on down the line into Potsdam.

The centre of the town had taken a hammering in much the same way as Berlin had although most of the damage had been done less than a month before the surrender. Potsdam was only fifteen miles from Berlin yet it retained a character of its own. Planned and built during the eighteenth century, it was a city of open parkland, of rivers and lakes purpose built for Prussian kings and princes. Its destruction had an altogether different air to the destruction in Berlin. It was as if the bombs falling on Potsdam's urban centre had removed the thin veneer the twentieth century had applied to the town, revealing once more the glory of its aristocratic nineteenth-century splendour.

Albeit ruined splendour. In the manner of Greece and Rome, perhaps.

The Allies still kept a Military Mission in Potsdam despite the town being in the Soviet Zone. The Stars and Stripes flew over the building, a note of defiance in the face of the conference held there after the war and during which the division of Germany had been agreed.

Just what the Russians thought about that I didn't know.

An RAF raid in April of 1945 had flattened the main train station and the City Palace and, given communist ideology, one might have expected the Soviets to have levelled all other evidence of a German patrician class that had ruled so oppressively; levelled it, that is, to some mutual common denominator where everyone was equally oppressed.

But, to the east, Russia apparently still had its own palaces and citadels. They remained pointing to a nobler, if unequal, past and I doubted that anywhere had a broader titled class than pre-revolutionary Russia. Or a greater gulf between privileged and poor, come to that. They hadn't demolished the tsars' and the princes' palaces in their rush to make their new society. Some churches had been knocked down, I believe, but that had been meant as a demonstration against religion and against those who still nurtured faith rather than against the buildings themselves. And in much the same way, I suppose, while the palaces remained, the Bolsheviks had made a point of shooting anyone they could lay hands on who once had claim to a title.

Despite what I had said to Mitzi about Potsdam, I had been there once before during my first time in Berlin. Getting off the train now, in the centre of the town amid the devastation of the old station and the City Palace, it seemed much as I remembered it. If with less rubble underfoot.

I suggested we should find someone to guide us through the historic buildings that had avoided the worst of the bombing and the subsequent Russian advance.

But apparently that wasn't necessary.

'I know where to go,' she said. 'I used to live in Potsdam.'

'Before the war?' I asked, wrong-footed by her admission of actually having a life before we met.

She took my hand. 'Yes. Come we catch the tram.'

Our late start precluded seeing much beyond a couple of the palaces. The town of Babelsberg to the south-east of the town would have been interesting as it had been the centre of the German film industry before the coming of sound. It was at the Babelsberg studios that German Expressionism had been born. Not to Nazi taste, though, and any avant-garde filmmaker with any sense—even those lacking Jewish blood—had hot-footed it to Hollywood before their films and perhaps they themselves ended up on Nazi bonfires alongside modernist paintings and books.

Perhaps lack of sleep was taking my mind down obscure paths but in some ways it seemed to me you could still find traces of German Expressionism in the ruins: in the facades

273

that rose at crazy angles out of the rubble of what was left; the monochrome tones of the devastation, all colour leached out along with its humanity; the alienation left behind by a missing population, made obvious only by its absence.

Trying to shake off my metaphysical speculations, I followed Mitzi as she led me through the palaces of Sanssouci and Cecilienhof, where the Potsdam Conference had been held.

It had been the last big conference of the war and the harbinger of the world to come.

By then Roosevelt was dead and Harry S. Truman had taken over the presidency. Churchill had already lost the 1945 general election and, although still representing what remained of the British Empire, he had the new Prime Minister, Clement Atlee, in tow to learn the ropes on handling those who really wielded the power.

The one constant had been Stalin. He must have looked like the great survivor and could only have been pleased, I imagine, to have in Truman at last a leader who was actually smaller than he was.

They had carved up Europe and parts of Asia between them, leaving the rest of us—that is those they no longer needed to do the fighting for them—to pick up the pieces.

And muddle on through.

At least, walking through the grounds of the Cecilienhof, that's what it felt like we were doing: muddling through without control.

I daresay there were still a few immaterial decisions that could be left to the individual. But mostly it seemed we were all drifting with the tide and lucky if we found a piece of wreckage to cling to.

It was later, sitting with Mitzi on a restaurant terrace after dinner that some sort of realization came. We had both drunk too much and spent too much and were aware that in the following days we would suffer the consequences, both physical and financial. And I saw then that we were clinging to each other, Mitzi and I, two pieces of wreckage adrift in the post-war world and finding some solace in the fact.

But even in reflective mood I wouldn't have been me if I hadn't wondered to whom it had been that Mitzi had clung before I came along.

'Were you born here?' I asked, lighting up one more cigarette.

'In Potsdam? No, Harry. In Berlin. I was a student here and very young.'

'What did you study?'

'Languages.'

'That is why your English is so good?'

'It is one of the reasons,' she said.

'And the Russian?'

'They did not teach us Russian at the university. No one thought we would have a need of it.'

'Maybe we should all start learning it,' I suggested.

'I have only a few words. Most I have picked up at the club from the soldiers.'

'I know *niet*,' I said.

'That is a very useful word with the Russians, Harry.'

'You said you lived here. Why was that? It is only fifteen miles to the centre of Berlin. Didn't you commute to your lectures?'

She made a small gesture accepting the possibility and looked off across the terrace.

'Yes. Until I married.'

'You were married?' I said, trying to keep the intense curiosity I was feeling out of my voice.

Although I had always supposed she had been, until now she had never admitted as much.

She turned back to me, regarding me closely across the table.

'Did you think you were the first man I slept with, Harry?'

'No, of course not. It's just you've never mentioned it before.'

'You never asked.'

She was echoing the accusation she had made as we had walked from the Zoo Club the previous evening. Before we had found Shoshannah Lehmann's body.

'Was your husband a student of languages, too?'

'No, he taught philosophy at the university.' She smiled faintly. 'He was older than me. I was interested in philosophy. Or perhaps I was interested in him.'

'What was his name?'

'Rolf.'

'And you lived here in Potsdam?'

'Until Rolf lost his job.'

'Why did that happen?'

'The Nazis,' she replied simply.

'Because of his politics? Was he a communist?'

'No, Harry. Rolf was a Jew.'

I was aware my mouth was open. Even if no sound came out if it.

'The Nazis removed Jews from all the professions,' she explained. 'Teachers and scientists ... doctors and academics... It made no difference what they were if they were Jewish.'

'Your husband was a *Jew*?' I finally managed to say.

'His name was Mendelsohn. Rolf Mendelsohn. Do you find it so surprising that I married a Jew?'

I shouldn't have. But I did.

Along with most of those who had fought their way into Germany, I suppose I had looked upon the German race as a people who all held the same opinions and prejudices ... *Ein Reich, ein Volk*, as Hitler had put it.

There were all sorts of reasons I shouldn't have and had made some small adjustments on the way to suit the circumstances. Mostly, though, whenever meeting a German I still dressed him in my head in a uniform of one sort or another. And when talking to a German I was always aware that there were topics one avoided. If only because I didn't care to find out what I didn't want to know.

I don't know quite what I had thought Mitzi had done during the war. Not wanting to know was one of the reasons I had made so little effort to find out. I was afraid I wouldn't like what I discovered. Even so, of all the pasts I might have given her, being married to a Jew would not have been among them.

'What happened?'

She took the cigarette from between my fingers. 'Jews were only allowed to work in menial occupations. That was yet another way of rubbing their noses in the dirt. There was nothing in Potsdam Rolf could do so we moved to Berlin. He found work as a janitor in an apartment block. I did the cleaning. We talked about leaving Germany but Rolf had family here and they convinced him it would all blow over. That people would come to see what sort of man Hitler really was and that we should wait. But we waited too long and the war started. Hitler had got rid of any opposition and the only people left who could have removed him was the army. With the success they were having at the beginning, they would do nothing, of course.

'Even then we might still have been able to buy our way out. But on a janitor's wage we could afford very little. Then the lists of Jews who were to present themselves at the detention centres were published and Rolf and the rest of his family were on them. I was not on the lists but I wanted to go with him. I think Rolf knew what was going to happen, even though everyone said the government had decided to settle the Jews in the east. He said I must stay until he sent for me. He told me to change my name back to what it had been before we were married. They held him in one of the detention camps for several weeks. The conditions they were kept in were awful and I used to visit him and take him some decent food and clean clothes.

'Then one day I arrived and they told me Rolf had gone. They would not tell me where and when I applied to the Reichsoffice in charge they only laughed at me. They said if I wanted to join my little Jew it could be arranged. Then they threw me out.'

'Did you find out where they sent him?'

'No. I waited, hoping I would hear from Rolf or his family. I never did.'

Mitzi fell silent. There was nothing I could say. Her story was just one among millions. Yet that didn't decrease the potency of the pain.

'So much for teaching philosophy,' Mitzi said eventually. 'You cannot teach people to be human.'

'You can,' I said, 'but only if they choose to learn.'

'Then what is the good of free will if they do not use it?'

'So other people may oppose and not acquiesce.'

That didn't rate a response and perhaps didn't deserve one. We sat in a longer silence. It was beginning to get dark although the terrace was still crowded. People were coming and people were going.

'If you want to try to find out what happened to Rolf,' I suggested after a while, 'why don't you ask Ben Tuchmann? The American colonel I was talking to last night? He's involved with an organization collecting the names of Berlin Jews who were transported to the camps. Do you know the synagogue on Levetzowstraße?'

'That was the detention camp where Rolf was held,' Mitzi said.

'Tuchmann is there quite often. I can ask him, if you like. Or you can leave a message for him there. He will get it.'

Mitzi reached a hand across the table and laid it on mine.

'You are a decent man, Harry. What do you think now you have heard my story?'

'I think it's a God-awful world we're living in, Mitzi, and that we're going to have to make the best of it.'

She smiled at me then suddenly asked if I'd seen my friend lately.

I assumed at first she meant Ben Tuchmann since we had just been talking about him. But as she had been there with me in the club when he arrived, I didn't understand what she meant. It wasn't that there was anyone else in Berlin I could call a friend that she knew. Certainly not Bill. There was Kurt Becker, although I didn't suppose she meant Kurt.

'Not Kurt,' she said when I asked. 'You know the one with the brown curls. What is her name?'

'Gretchen Prochnow?'

I assumed she was being mischievous although given what we had been talking about I was surprised she felt in that sort of mood.

'I would hardly call her a friend,' I said.

'Oh? Has Gretchen lost interest in you now she has her husband back again?'

'What are you talking about, Mitzi? I told you, her husband is in Russia. Gretchen has gone to join him.'

'Is that not her husband?'

She pointed across the crowded terrace to a table by the balustrade.

'I only saw him once,' she said, 'but that is him, is it not?'

I looked in the direction she indicated.

Gerhard Prochnow was sitting at a table on the other side of the terrace alongside two other men. They didn't look like the usual Russian thugs and Prochnow himself wasn't acting like a man who had recently been released from some NKVD cellar. They all appeared relaxed and must have been sharing a joke because all three were laughing.

Then they turned and stood up and for a moment I thought they had spotted me. But they were looking in another direction, at a woman who was making her way between the tables towards them. It was Gretchen, wearing what looked like a new dress and a stylish new hairdo. The curls were still brown but now under tighter control, shorter and moulded to her head.

'Do you want to go over and say hello?' Mitzi asked.

I started up. 'No, Mitzi, I most certainly do not. We're getting out of here.'

I grabbed her hand and pulled her back into the restaurant. I paid our bill at the cashier's desk and bundled her out onto the street, hoping Prochnow hadn't seen us.

'What is the matter, Harry?' Mitzi complained. 'You have gone pale. You do not look well.'

I didn't feel well. Seeing Gerhard and Gretchen Prochnow had shaken me.

We walked quickly to the railway station. I stopped at the bar for a glass of schnapps.

'Prochnow is supposed to be in Russia,' I explained to Mitzi when she kept asking what the matter was. 'Gretchen told me she was joining him there.'

'You told me that, Harry. So they have come back. What is the mystery?'

'When people go to Russia under those circumstances, Mitzi, they do *not* come back. Not after two or three weeks, anyway.'

'What circumstances? What do you mean?'

I could hardly tell her that Prochnow had been selling me secrets. Or that because the secrets had not turned out to be secret enough, he had put me on to Albrecht Fischer. And that Fischer was supposed to be coming over to our side in two days time.

'I think I have done something very stupid,' I said. 'I need to get back to Berlin.'

Mitzi was frowning and, I think, for the first time realizing that I wasn't quite the person I purported to be.

'You are a spy, Harry? Is that what you mean? Is that what are telling me?'

'If I am,' I said, 'I'm a lousy one.'

'What does *lousy* mean? I do not know this word.'

I might have told her that I felt like a lousy everything else, too. She had been telling me about her husband and how he had been deported to a Nazi concentration camp along with the rest of his family. Now all I could think of was my failings as an espionage agent.

'It's not the kind of English word you would have been taught at a German university,' I told her.

'Have you involved me in your spying, Harry? And Marthe, too?'

'No, Mitzi, not you. And not Marthe either really. She only took a message or two for me.'

She glared at me. 'A message or two? It is very well for you, Harry. You can go home to England if things go badly. Will you disappear now, like everyone else I have known? Marthe and I still have to live here! The Russians are all around us. Do you know how that feels? It feels as if we have the Nazis here all over again.'

I didn't say anything. There was nothing I could say.

When the train arrived we rode back to Berlin in silence.

Das Ergebnis

33

Monday 11th August 1947

It was dark when I slipped out of bed and dressed silently, not wanting to wake Mitzi. She had still been upset with me when we had gone to bed and I hadn't told her I would have to leave early. I didn't want to leave it like that so I wrote her a note and left it by the bedside. Not knowing what to say as usual, I merely said I needed to go into the city and that if I wasn't back before she left for work I'd see her at the club.

Then I wrote a note to Bill. Had the previous day not been a Sunday I might have stopped at the railway station and risked using a telephone to call the Military Mission at Hohenstaufenstraße. But I didn't suppose Andy Thurston would have been on duty and foresaw I'd have all sorts of problems getting past the clerk.

Relaying a message to Bill at HQ would probably involve passwords. All the boys there would have adopted esoteric names for identification, the way the military usually did whenever playing cloak and dagger. I wasn't in the club so didn't know the secret codes and handshakes and all the other paraphernalia.

That meant I had had no option but to wait until morning. Now I just wrote a brief note to Bill to say I needed to see him urgently and that I'd be waiting for him at Peston's apartment. I put the note in an envelope, sealed it and left the house. I would ask Thurston to courier it out to the Reich Sporting Field as he had done with Fischer's agenda then I'd go to the apartment to wait.

My first reaction on seeing Prochnow in Potsdam, rather than rotting in some NKVD cell in the Moscow Lubyanka as we had been led to believe, was that he had been planted on us. Planted, not only to feed us misinformation but to feed us

Fischer as well. And that could only mean that Fischer was, in turn, there to feed us something else.

Although it was a possibility that Bill and I had discussed, now, and with time to think it through, another layer of deception occurred to me.

In Istanbul Konstantin Volkov had offered us the names of Soviet agents who had infiltrated our Foreign Office and Secret Intelligence Service. If they had been genuine, as Bill had believed, it now had to follow that the names Fischer was offering us were not.

Among the names Volkov had offered was one of a Soviet agent who had worked his way into the upper ranks of SIS itself. The chances were that London had managed to convince themselves that Volkov's list was fake although, ever since the operation to extricate Volkov from Istanbul had gone sour, I imagined there must be some still looking over their shoulders wondering if perhaps Volkov was not a fake and just who that man might be. Now, two years down the road, we were being offered a similar list of names by Fischer.

The parallels were obvious. Having missed our chance with Volkov we were being given a second bite. Only this time it would be with names of agents the Russians wanted us to have.

It was an operation designed to confuse and I was becoming convinced that the reason was that Volkov had been genuine. Now, someone in SIS was getting close to the infiltrated agent named on Volkov's list and the man needed protection.

I was too early to catch Thurston. When I asked what time he would be in, a bleary-eyed clerk ran a finger down the duty roster while making a half-hearted attempt to stop himself yawning and said:

'0845 hours. That's quarter to nine.'

'Yes,' I said, 'I remember.' I put my envelope on the counter in front of him. 'Perhaps you can have this couriered over the HQ then.'

The clerk blinked at Bill's name on the envelope.

'Sergeant Thurston deals with anything for Mr Harrington,' he said. 'Like I told you, he's not on duty. If you want to wait—'

I pushed the envelope closer. 'This is urgent. Can't *you* have it couriered over?'

'Sorry, sir, but I'm not allowed to touch it. Sergeant Thurston deals with—'

'—anything for Mr Harrington,' I finished for him. 'Yes, so you've just said. It is very important he gets this as soon as possible.'

He glanced at the clock on the wall.

'Sergeant Thurston will be here in an hour. I'll make sure he sees it as soon as he arrives. Beyond that, all I can suggest is that you ride out to HQ yourself. Deliver it by hand.'

'I would,' I said, 'if I was sure Mr Harrington would be there. I could waste half the day trying to chase him down. Thurston knows how to contact him immediately if he needs to.'

'Pity Mr Harrington didn't tell you as well, then, isn't it?'

I left him yawning over my note and decided to stop by the mill to see Kurt before going on to Peston's apartment. Bill rang him there on occasion and although Kurt had never said as much I thought there might be a chance he knew where Bill lived or perhaps even have a telephone number for him.

The mill door was locked and I assumed Kurt was still in bed. I used my key, went up to his room on the upper floor and banged on the door. There was no answer so I tried the handle. That was locked too. I considered leaving him a note as well, but between writing to Mitzi and then to Bill I had just about exhausted my literary stock for one day. Kurt would have to wait until after I'd seen Bill.

I was on my way out when I collided with him on the doorstep.

'Harry,' he said, hugging a bottle of milk and loaf of bread to his chest, 'you're early.'

'Yes. I'm trying to reach Bill Harrington but Thurston's not at the Mission yet.'

He edged past me and put his shopping in the kitchen beside the sink.

'A problem?' he asked over his shoulder.

'Yes.'

'Coffee?'

'We got any tea?'

He put the kettle on and stood looking at me.

'So, what is it, Harry?'

I told him about seeing Prochnow and Gretchen in Potsdam.

'Potsdam? Are you sure it was them? He is supposed to be in Moscow. Maybe it was only someone who looked like him.'

'And Gretchen, too?'

'So, you have let Herr Harrington know?'

'Not yet. I told you, I've been trying to reach him. I've left a note for Thurston to courier over but I don't know how long it will be before he gets it. I don't suppose you've got a number for him?'

Kurt shrugged apologetically. 'No, Harry, sorry. He calls here sometimes but he is always very ... what is the English word ... circum...?

'Circumspect,' I said.

'Yes. He is always careful of what he says. You know how he does not trust the telephones. That is why he has never given me a number. Did you tell him in your note you saw Prochnow?'

'No, just that I needed to see him urgently and to meet me at the apartment as soon as he could.'

'You are going there now? Do you want me to come?'

'No. It's possible he might ring here first when he gets my message.'

The kettle boiled and Kurt made his coffee. He put some tea in the pot for me and poured water on top.

'What does it mean that Prochnow is not in Russia? And what about this colleague of his, this Albrecht Fischer?'

'I think,' I said, 'it means we can't trust him.'

'And so any information he was giving you?'

'Particularly what he was giving us. I think we we're being set up.'

Kurt sampled his coffee and managed not to grimace.

'Was it important, what Fischer promised?'

'Bill thought it was. Although I'm beginning to think that Bill already suspected Fischer wasn't genuine.'

'Herr Harrington knows? How is this?'

'It's only an idea,' I said. 'But it does explain certain things.'

'What things, Harry?'

'Like what happened to Arthur Peston.'

I stirred the teapot and poured myself a cup.

Kurt looked down at the evil-smelling liquid in his own cup. 'I do not understand.'

'Nor me,' I said. 'Not yet, anyway.'

'So what happens now, Harry?'

'Bill made an arrangement with Fischer for tomorrow. He might still want to go through with it, I don't know. That'll be up to him. I just need to put him in the picture first.'

'Okay,' said Kurt as I drank down my tea. 'If Herr Harrington telephones here I will say you are waiting for him at Herr Peston's apartment. If you need me to do more, Harry, just tell me.'

~

The weather had turned hot again. The air in Peston's flat tasted stale. I walked through the rooms opening windows and poking my head into the cupboards and drawers as I had done the evening I arrived. I wasn't looking for anything in particular and found no evidence that anyone else had been doing the same.

In the kitchen there was a dusting of tealeaves in the bottom of the caddy. Enough for a weak brew while I considered the situation so I lit the stove and got out the pot.

I thought I should perhaps have added a coda to my note to Bill, telling him to bring some alcohol with him. Something fortifying to swallow along with my bad news.

I had bought the morning papers on my way to the flat and sat at the table smoking Kurt's cigarettes while I read through them. I couldn't concentrate on anything, though, and as I read I found my mind going back to Prochnow in Potsdam and then, inevitably, to everything that had gone before.

Seeing him was like throwing a pebble into still water. The emanating ripples had disturbed the reflection and changed the picture. I tried to inversely follow the ripples as they radiated out, thinking back to the moment it had begun.

Inevitably, there were involutions and ramifications of which I knew nothing. I could do no more than ride the swell as I followed the ripples, event by event, until they eventually bore me back to that room above the hardware shop on South Parade in Acton.

I checked my watch and tried to work out how long it would take Bill to arrive. It had been two hours since I had left the note at the Military Mission. Thurston would have it sent on as soon as he came on duty and I didn't doubt Bill would come to the flat as soon as he received it. Especially, as I had said to Kurt, I was beginning to suspect Bill already believed Fischer to be a plant.

It had been a series of small things that had alerted me to the idea: firstly Bill's apparent readiness to have me handle Prochnow in Peston's stead in spite of my lack of experience; secondly his willingness to accept Peston's death as an accident. Then there were the undeniable similarities between what Volkov had offered us in Istanbul and what Fischer was offering us now, coupled with the fact that Bill was present at both operations.

His caution to me not to mention Fischer to anyone else had, on the face of it, been understandable. But not because of what had happened to Volkov as I had thought initially but, as I now believed, because he regarded Fischer with suspicion. He wanted to play the man along without any outside interference.

None of it added up to any degree of certainty, I had to admit. But for someone like me who remains congenitally unable to take what I see at face value, it was all pointing in the same direction.

Time was dragging. Impatient for Bill to arrive, I put the kettle on to boil and began pacing through the apartment and going back mentally to Acton again. I was trying to think through everything that had happened since the interview, taking each event stage by stage until Potsdam. Deep in thought I didn't hear the kettle start to boil until it began to whistle. As I went back to the kitchen and lifted it off the stove, I heard a soft knock on the door. I dropped the kettle back on the hob, glancing at my watch as I turned towards the door.

It was almost half-past twelve. Almost four hours had passed since I imagined Andy Thurston would have sent a courier off to the HQ with my note. It seemed to me that even allowing for the fact the courier may not have been able to find him immediately, surely Bill couldn't have been far from his office first thing on a Monday morning. Perhaps I was too impatient but it seemed to me a slow a response to an urgent summons.

I was unlocking the door when it struck me that it might be *too* slow.

But the thought came too late. The door flew open, knocking me back into the room.

Two men stepped in, closing the door behind them. I didn't know either of them but I recognized the pistol one had trained on me.

It was a Tokarev, the Soviet military forces standard issue semiautomatic. The man holding it waved me back into the flat with the muzzle. I didn't wave back.

His colleague shouldered past him. Neither were wearing uniform, not unless badly made Russian serge suits count, but both wore hats and, beneath the brims, the standard issue features of NKVD thugs.

But that was only a guess on my part. I didn't expect asking for identification to confirm it would have got me far.

In the kitchen the kettle was still whistling like a demented railway guard and I stood by the table with my eyes on the Tokarev while the second man stepped through and took it off the stove. He passed quickly into each room of the apartment looking around. When he came back he placed his own gun on the table. That was a Nagant, the Tokarev's older brother and a relic of tsarist days.

I knew a Nagant when I saw one because I had used one myself only a few months earlier. That had been in London and hopefully that weapon was still lying where I had thrown it, somewhere on the bed of the Thames. Disposing of it in that fashion had troubled me for a while, but only on the odd chance someone might dredge it up. If they ever did, I was thinking it wouldn't look half as dangerous as the one I was looking at on the table.

The man with the Takarov glanced past me to where the kettle was giving one last steamy gasp, then shifted his gaze to the pot waiting on the table. I made a move towards the kettle, a half-formed notion rattling through my head of what a desperate man could do with a pot of boiling water. But that idea died as the barrel of the Takarov motioned me down into a chair.

I sat.

The Tokarev's companion fetched the kettle and poured the boiling water into the pot.

'*Chaj*,' he said in Russian.

They each took a chair across the table from me and exchanged a few more Russian words I didn't understand. The Nagant's owner picked up a teaspoon and stirred the pot. He pulled the two cups I'd readied for Bill and myself towards him.

I thought of offering to be mother and pour, but I didn't want to cause any confusion. Judging by their appearance, I had my doubts as to whether either of them had anything as natural as a mother. At least, not one who might be willing to own to the fact.

We sat in silence and looked at each other. My brain was still tripping over itself trying to think of what I could do. Their dead eyes suggested theirs had vacated the premises long ago. I didn't know what to expect. Questions, if I was lucky. Or just a bullet if I wasn't.

I have had people try to kill me before although never over tea. Yet, if it was to be, I was hoping it would be the Tokarev. Being shot by a Nagant would have been too much of an irony to bear under the circumstances.

As it was I got neither. After a minute or so the Nagant's owner gave the teapot another stir before filling the two cups. They drank it hot, no sugar, no milk. They didn't offer me a cup.

We sat around the table, exchanging nothing more than glances. I could hear a clock ticking somewhere although it may have been my imagination. I opened my mouth to speak at one point then shut it again. They were the ones who had turned up uninvited, so if anyone had anything to say I decided it should be them. I was content to wait.

As nothing much else was happening I went back to what I had been thinking about just before they arrived; about the room above the hardware store in Acton with Bill Harrington and Kim Philby, and me climbing the stairs.

Some sort of fog of understanding was lying in those hard-to-reach hollows of my brain. It had been there some while only I wasn't sure when it had begun to form. Overnight, was it? Or while I had been riding into the city? Perhaps between Hohenstaufenstraße and the mill...

I think the first embryonic mist of comprehension had started to coalesce the moment Mitzi pointed Prochnow out across the restaurant terrace; the moment I had looked up and had seen him with the other two men and Gretchen walking towards them.

Now that embryo of understanding had grown, I was starting to wonder if it wasn't becoming all too elaborate. If, in reality, everything wasn't all much simpler. If I was over-thinking it, applying a veneer of my own habitual suspicion to events that really weren't that labyrinthine...

It was always possible. But I didn't think so.

If I *was* right, then they had known everything about me even before I arrived in Berlin. And if I admitted that fact, I was allowing all sorts of other extraneous possibilities to crowd in on me as well.

Maybe they were pertinent, maybe they were not. Like the jumble of electrical components Kurt was perpetually sorting through at the mill, the pertinent and those of value had to be fitted into the scheme where they could: the chaff could be discarded.

Kurt himself was one of those extraneous possibilities. As was Mitzi. And the fact she spoke Russian.

Knowing next to nothing of Russian myself, I couldn't be sure when she had spoken with the guards in Potsdam whether she knew only a few words of the language as she had claimed, or whether her facility was more extensive.

I couldn't help remembering what she had said as we left the restaurant in Potsdam. She had asked me if I was going to disappear too, after having involved her and Marthe in my espionage. At the time I thought she had meant my going back to England and leaving them in Berlin to face the consequences. Now I wasn't so sure.

Given what I was expecting to happen next, wasn't it going to seem, from her perspective and everyone else's, that I *had* disappeared?

What had it been, a coincidentally prophetic remark on Mitzi's part, or some sort of prior knowledge?

Yet it had been Mitzi herself who had pointed Prochnow out to me. Why would she do that unless she was innocently surprised to see him?

Suspicion casts a wide net and one that ensnares the innocent as well as the guilty. How was I supposed to tell the one from the other?

Yet, if what I suspected was correct, even Bill Harrington fell into the net. In fact it only worked if I regarded Bill as the key. And the lock that key fitted was the fact that Bill Harrington had been in Istanbul when Konstantin Volkov had tried to defect. It was the only fact that made sense of it all. Everything hinged upon it. Even my being cast as the incompetent dupe sent to Berlin to bring two and two together.

Although now it seemed as if I might have come up with a different answer. Not the one expected of me.

Having a suspicious nature wasn't listed among the dubious talents on my CV and whoever had chosen me for this particular rôle had taken me at face value.

But then they weren't the first to have made that mistake.

Even so, spotting Prochnow in Potsdam had been sheer chance. It wasn't the sort of thing one could ever count on. All the same, one does have to take luck where one finds it.

Sitting across the table from the two uninvited guests drinking my tea though, I had to wonder just what sort of luck seeing Prochnow in Potsdam had been. It was looking like the sort one should leave where one finds it and I began to speculate as to whether something of the same nature had not happened to Peston. If that had been the reason he'd been thrown off the top of the Zoo Tower.

It was a sobering thought and one that brought my

predicament back into sharp focus.

Someone knew I'd be at the apartment and sent these goons over to pick me up. If they knew that then presumably they also knew I was waiting for Bill.

Then what were they waiting for?

If it was Bill, wouldn't that defeat the object of the whole exercise? Yet if they just meant to kidnap me, wouldn't we have left already?

I didn't suppose murdering me would make too many waves. But killing Bill would be another matter entirely.

I might rate a short piece in the papers back home, something along the lines of "British businessman shot in Berlin", then again, I might not. I had no idea how many British businessmen got themselves shot in Berlin. It hadn't been the sort of information they had disseminated at my interview in Acton.

Being an illegal meant SIS would be able to extricate themselves from any association with me without too much trouble. Since I was working with Kurt they could suggest I was mixed up in some black market racket or other. After all, they could point to the fact I had worked for Jack Hibbert back in London and had form for that sort of thing.

But kiilling Bill Harrington would be a different kettle of fish. One that would raise the sort of stink that was in no one's interest. Bill was an accredited diplomat. The newspapers would get hold of the story and questions would be asked ... ambassadors would be summoned ... maybe even the odd trade attaché expelled.

But the handguns were clouding my thinking. Of course they wouldn't kill Bill. He was the one who was supposed to welcome Fischer into the western fold. My theory only held water if Bill was there to aid his defection and make up for the mistakes made in the Volkov affair.

Then it occurred to me that the two across the table probably didn't understand that. I doubted they would be privy to the finer points of the arrangement. They were merely following orders. I'd served in the army and in intelligence long enough to know that unless orders are spelled out in black and white—or in this case in Cyrillic—there would always be room for someone to screw up.

That idea left me with something of a dilemma.

Keeping one eye on the pistols, I glanced at my watch. It was still only twelve-forty-five. A whole history had passed through my head yet only fifteen minutes since the two goons had turned up.

The goon with the Tokarev followed my glance. I raised my head but his eyes stayed on the wristwatch.

Hoping their orders had been black and white, I decided to play white. For an opening gambit I said in German as casually as I could:

'Are we waiting for something?'

They both turned their dead eyes on me in unison.

'I am expecting someone,' I said. 'A British diplomat. He will have the military police with him.'

This piece of egregious nonsense at least prompted them look at each other rather than at me. They exchanged another word or two then the one with the Tokarev reached across the table and hit me across the face with the butt.

I must have passed out. When I opened my eyes they had finished the tea and were licking their lips. All I could taste was blood. It was dripping from my mouth. I was still in the chair, slumped untidily at the table and aware that not only my mouth hurt but that my wrist did, too. I looked down at a bloody graze where my watch had been yanked off.

Still dazed, I had the disjointed idea of writing Bill a message in blood. But I wasn't so confused that I didn't realize this wasn't a detective story and let that idea go the same way as the one about the boiling water. It wasn't that they'd be prepared to wait while I composed one. Anyway, as suddenly as the idea came to me they got to their feet. The Tokarev motioned me upright as well.

I felt blood running down my chin. I wiped a hand over it then smeared it on the table as I stood up.

Bill wouldn't need a note to be able to read that message.

The goon with the Nagant pulled a tea towel off the cooker and pushed it into my face. I held it against my mouth as they pushed me towards the door.

We walked down the corridor in single file, me in the

middle. I wondered if I could jump the one in front, grab his pistol and shoot them both in turn. I'd seen that sort of thing work in detective films. I assumed the actors would generally have time to rehearse the scene although with the Tokarev jammed in my back I didn't think I was even going to get a read through. There would be only one take and, if it didn't play the way I hoped, the chances were I'd be edited out on the corridor floor.

But I was back with the detective stories again.

Perhaps I'd been hit harder than I realized. Having always heard that discretion is the better part of valour, and since I was sitting in the stalls and not up on the screen, it seemed to me that discretion dictated I'd do better to wait.

Or perhaps the truth is that fear is the better part of valour and is an even better reason to wait.

Down on the street we walked north to the junction with Melanchthon Straße and turned left. Somewhere since I'd been in Peston's apartment I'd picked up the trivial gem that Melanchthon had been the successor to Luther as leader of the German Reformation. It made me wonder for a moment if a prayer might be in order. But as I remembered it, Luther and those other fellows believed in Predestination and as far as they would have been concerned any fix I was in was an ordained fix. That meant there was nothing I could do about it so any appeals to grim-faced Lutherans and their grim-faced God would be falling on deaf ears.

With the Tokarev behind, the Nagant at my side and prayer out the window, I began to reconsider the blood sacrifice.

If I could jump the Nagant and swing him round to catch the Tokarev's bullet...

But the Nagant had reached a parked car and I had already wasted too much time mulling over theology and playing hard-boiled detective in my head. The Nagant opened the back door of the car, pushed me in and slid along the seat beside me. Tokarev got behind the wheel.

We turned left and drove down Paul Straße, crossing the Spree by the Luther Bridge. Destroyed in the war, the bridge had been patched together again although still didn't look as if it would take the weight of a woodlouse never mind a car. But we rumbled across regardless, on to Bellevue Alle to where it joined *Chaussee*.

We drove along the wide boulevard through the Tiergarten, the east-west axis of Hitler's grandiose new capital, Germania. It wasn't looking grandiose now but the best laid plans, as the saying goes...

Then we were back in real Berlin, driving east down Unter den Linden, even if the linden trees had gone the same way as Germania.

I knew now where I was going now. I had been there only the previous morning, hanging around outside waiting for Klaus Kittel to come off shift. This time I supposed I was going to get to see what the new polizeipräsidium on Keibelstraße looked like from the inside.

~

Ordinarily, if one is abducted by two unknown heavies at gunpoint, one might expect a policeman to be the very man you'd hope to run into. Walking through the main entrance of Keibelstraße 35, along a corridor and down a flight of steps, we must have passed dozens of them. They came in all shapes and sizes: tall, short, old and young, uniformed, plain-clothed, and any other combination that came to mind... Some were even beribboned in the fashion popular with Russians who liked to flaunt their military service.

But whatever kind we passed, none paid us any heed. They were all part of Paul Markgraff's *Volkspolizei* and as such—as Bill had pointed out to me when I first arrived—had no jurisdiction when it came to Russians. A few did give me a surreptitious glance as they passed; most simply averted their gaze.

I was still holding Arthur Peston's tea towel to my swelling cheek but I had stopped bleeding by the time we descended one more flight of stairs into a sub-basement. The corridor this deep was dim and malodorous and although my two captors had ceased training their guns on me, any of those opportunities to make a break for it that I had been imagining might come along had long since disappeared.

Towards the end of the corridor the Nagant stopped and barked at a warder who was sitting at a desk. He jumped to his feet and opened one of the cells. The three of us filed in.

I decided it was time to ask why I had been brought there. Not in any great expectation of getting an answer but because it was what would have been expected of an innocent man. What I didn't expect was the fist that caught me on the chin.

I went down, head spinning again, took a couple of deep breaths, rolled onto my hands and knees then heaved myself upright. I was just straightening up when he caught me under the ribs with his next punch. That one knocked the wind out of me. I doubled over once more expecting a third blow to the temple. When it didn't come I turned my head and squinted up. He was still standing in front of me, relaxed and wearing no expression on his face at all.

I could have hit him then. In the balls, the stomach, or the head. I had the time and any variety of targets. He was so open that it was almost more than I could do to resist the temptation. Then a semblance of coherent thought wormed through my brain telling me that that was he was waiting for.

I was in for a beating one way or the other. The only question left was how bad was it going to be?

I had always believed a man will hit harder in hot blood than cold, so I decided not to provoke him. After a moment or two he tired of waiting and punched me again. Then the Tokarev joined in and they took it in turns to keep me upright while the other worked out life's little frustrations on me.

Maybe they didn't have many and were happy with their lot because it didn't last long. Just a minute or two longer than I did. They let me sag to the floor, gave me a kick in the ribs for good measure, then left me to repent the error of my ways.

I'd have been happy to oblige but the concrete floor was cool and soothing on my cheek and I lay there for some minutes thinking of very little until I decided I'd better start taking stock. I began with my head then worked my way down, detailing each part of my anatomy that was in pain.

I concluded that from the knees down I was in pretty good shape. After a while I determined to move, got myself onto my hands and knees and hauled myself onto a thoughtfully provided bunk by the wall. Stretching out with my eyes closed, I would have appreciated a glass of water. A couple of aspirin would have been a nice touch, too, although I doubted the staff at Keibelstraße 35 provided room service.

The main thing, I told myself, was not to be awkward. Don't provoke them. No wisecracks and no hitting back. If I didn't make trouble there might be a chance of remission.

But it wasn't long before I discovered there would be no remission. Only an intermission.

34

Before the war, when I was a police cadet at the Peel College in Westminster, one of my tutors obsessively stressed the importance of routine. Not only in policing but in life. A routine, he always insisted, gave existence a frame of reference.

I hadn't noticed anyone from the NKVD sitting in on the class at the time, yet my two new acquaintances must have picked up the lesson about routine from somewhere. If they hadn't stolen my wristwatch I could have set the time by them.

My cell door opened again after what couldn't have been more than an hour. I'd fallen asleep, obviously in contravention of the rules, as they seem to take exception to the fact. I don't know what they had been doing in the interim, but given the interest they began taking in my kidneys they may well have been boning up on a book on anatomy.

They dragged me off the bunk and repeated the first lesson they'd given me in brutality, adding a couple of embellishments for the sake of variety. I think I might have tried asking what they wanted once more because one paused mid-punch to look at the other. Neither seemed to know the answer or probably didn't care to share it because a moment later they went back to work.

Until I passed out for the second time.

Perhaps another hour went by. I couldn't tell. This time I was awake and cataloguing which parts of my anatomy hurt most. The door opened and through swollen eyes I watched as they approached and helped me upright.

We followed the same routine all night. I lost count of the times. If the plan was to soften me up for interrogation they missed the point. I was as soft as an overripe fruit shortly after they began.

The cell had no window. Light was provided by a single electric bulb. The bunk lacked a mattress. A bucket stood in one corner to act as a latrine and although they didn't give me anything to eat I did use it from time to time to piss a little blood.

But that, too, passed. At some point I began to feel that no serious damage had been done. The two men who had abducted me and were administering the beatings were professional. Had they wanted to cause me permanent injury or kill me they could have done so quite easily.

That they hadn't was one more small cause for hope.

Sometime around what might have been dawn I heard the door open again. The world opened up like a sinkhole. I thought I knew what was coming next, only this time I was wrong.

What came next was the frame of reference that gave the routine its purpose.

A man I'd not seen before walked into the cell. Tall and spare with his head shaved, his grey skin lent him the look of an ambulatory statue. There was nothing of the usual thug about him and he was obviously a rung or two higher up the NKVD ladder than my other acquaintances. This fact was reinforced by the warder following him in with a chair for him to sit on.

The warder placed the chair beside my bunk and withdrew. The man sat down. Thrown for a minute by the change of routine, I stayed where I was on the bunk, like a patient in a cut-price psychiatrist's office.

'Your name is Harold Tennant,' the man began without preamble, 'and you are a spy in the pay of British Intelligence.'

The voice was distinctive, his tone sharp yet the delivery a level monotone which suggested that his facts were correct and did not require emphasis or rebuttal.

I tried focusing on his face although my swollen eyes cut out most of the light coming from the weak ceiling bulb, leaving his features little more than a blur.

Had I been more receptive at the time to the irony of the situation, I might have appreciated the fact that this man, like Bill, was letting me know I didn't figure in the front rank of spies. To Bill I was an illegal; to this man I was merely "in the pay" of British Intelligence.

I did what I did for money. He wasn't even letting me hide behind the fig leaf of patriotism.

A response did start to form in my befuddled brain, something along the lines of not being *that* intelligent since I was where I was. But I was too slow, having trouble arranging the words in the right order and I remembered that I'd decided to cut out the wisecracks.

I didn't reply.

'Do you deny it?'

He required some sort of answer apparently so I muttered something about Schuyler Imports and electronic components. I even added, in case he had overlooked the fact, that I held a British passport.

'We are fully aware of this company. It is a front for intelligence gathering. We have not been fooled by British Intelligence's puerile effort to cover your operation. We also know you approached the SED employee Gerhard Prochnow. You offered him money in exchange for information. Do you deny this?'

'I met the man.'

'In the company of your associate Kurt Becker?'

'Socially, one evening,' I admitted. 'I didn't give him any money. I didn't even pay for the drinks.'

'Becker paid.'

I wondered if that meant they had picked Kurt up as well. I was about to tell him that Becker was not involved when he went on:

'You admit you approached Gerhard Prochnow?'

'I met him,' I said again.

'Who is your handler in Berlin?'

'I'm not a monkey.'

'It is William Harrington of the British diplomatic staff. Is that correct?'

'You seem to know all the answers,' I said. 'What is it you need me for?'

'Albrecht Fischer. Tell me what you know about Albrecht Fischer.'

'I don't know the name.'

At that he abruptly stood and called to the warder. The warder came in and removed the chair. They both left and my two muscle-bound friends returned.

I'm not sure how long I remained conscious after they began beating me again. Long enough to regret there had been too many wisecracks. I must have passed out, though, because the next thing I remember was finding myself lying on the bunk and alone once more.

This time I didn't bother with the mental stocktaking.

There didn't seem much point in cataloguing injuries if the treatment was still ongoing.

Pain does focus the mind.

Mostly on pain, admittedly, but it does allow room for a few other considerations. One is how to avoid any more of it.

I was mulling this over when I became aware of a voice. It seemed very far off, as though someone in the next valley was calling. The sound was so indistinct and distant that the words didn't form anything I found intelligible. I tried to concentrate, to catch what was being said, but the pain kept getting in the way. It was like being swaddled in cotton wool. But cotton wool with spikes.

The voice was persistent, though, and getting closer.

Eventually it was so close I was able to make out what was being said.

The same two words, over and over.

'Albrecht Fischer ... Albrecht Fischer.'

The walking statue was back. He was sitting in his chair. I was on the bunk. We were playing psychiatrist and patient again.

Of the two of us, I probably looked the most convincing.

'Albrecht Fischer.'

I knew I needed to keep him in his chair.

It was an uncomplicated idea and one I had arrived at while working out how to avoid more pain.

It was a simple equation: the man was in the chair, no pain; the man left the chair, pain. It was a routine that dictated that when the man left the other two returned.

The solution was just as simple. All I had to do was tell him everything he wanted to know.

'Albrecht Fischer...'

'What about him?' I mumbled through my swollen lips.

'He has defected to the British.'

'What did you say?'

'Albrecht Fischer has defected to the British.'

I slowly absorbed the fact that Bill had got him.

'Albrecht Fischer?' I repeated. 'He was still on your side the last time I saw him.'

Which was the truth and contained no wisecracks and pleased me for thinking of it.

'He disappeared last Tuesday.'

Bill must have got my letter. But all I had said was that I needed to see him urgently at the apartment. I didn't mention Prochnow. He wouldn't know that Fischer was a plant. Not unless he already knew.

'Tuesday. That would be the day after I disappeared.'

The man shifted slightly. I wondered if I had gone too far. But he didn't get up. He stayed in his chair.

'Albrecht Fischer left a political meeting on Tuesday and has not been seen since. But you know this, Herr Tennant. You helped to arrange it.'

'They arrange their own meetings,' I said.

He cleared his throat, obviously dissatisfied. I told myself to just answer the questions.

'You arranged Fischer's defection with William Harrington. We know this. It is pointless for you to deny it.'

'I haven't denied it,' I said, which was the truth even if it did contradict him. 'I want to answer your questions in a correct manner, Herr ... Herr... You have not told me your name.'

'My name is of no consequence to you.'

'I do not wish to offend you.'

'You mean you do not wish for me to leave,' he countered.

300

Well, I did say it was a *simple* equation.

All the same, if I was going to answer his questions I didn't want to rush it. I wanted him to stay in the chair for as long as possible. If I was going to talk, I wanted to talk for as long as possible. The routine dictated that when he left, they returned. And I was in no hurry to find out what would happen when, eventually, he left for good.

'What we want you to tell us is exactly what Albrecht Fischer brought you and what you offered him in return.'

'Promises,' I said. 'Safe passage ... a new identity, that sort of thing. I didn't know the details. Bill ... William Harrington took care of that. It is no more than what you probably promise when the circumstances are reversed. You must know this better than I do.'

His tone turned cold.

'When circumstances are reversed, as you put it, the people who work for us do so for the ultimate victory of the Socialist cause. They do so because it is the right thing to do. It is the only true course of action because history dictates it is to be the destiny of humankind.'

He was just like the goon, I thought, leaving himself open to the counterpunch. This time I couldn't resist it.

'Then,' I said, 'why you don't just sit back and wait for our destiny to arrive? You are going to an awful lot of trouble for what you say is destined to happen anyway.'

The cloud had cleared sufficiently from my eyes for his face to sharpen in focus. Not that I saw it was the kind of face anyone would care to dwell upon for long. Too hard. Like stone it looked inflexible. Yet he was in no way brutish like the other two. Where one might have been easily convinced that his goons belonged on some lower branch of the evolutionary tree, this man was altogether more austere, unearthly almost. He seemed so assured in his revolutionary zeal, so certain in its truth, I could easily have been persuaded to believe that he inhabited an evolutionary tree all of his own, one quite apart from that of the rest of us.

'Even providence needs guidance,' he declared while I was mulling this over. 'The sooner we weed out those who oppose its arrival, the sooner we shall all enjoy the fruits of human destiny.'

'Not all,' I suggested, deciding I might as well be hung for a sheep as a lamb. 'Not those you have weeded out. I don't suppose they enjoyed being picked before the time was ripe.'

'They are of no importance. They will have served their purpose.'

'What's that, to hasten the Marxist paradise?'

He opened his mouth, then closed it and smiled.

'We did not bring you here to discuss political ideology, Herr Tennant. And you have not answered my question. I asked you what Albrecht Fischer promised in return for his defection?'

No, I hadn't. But I'd managed to keep him in his chair for another ten minutes. Whoever he was, he was not beyond being provoked into a digression along Party lines. Something I was aware he had realized himself, which was going to make it all the more difficult to stall him the next time.

'A list,' I said. 'I was told he was bringing a list.'

'Good. A list of what?'

'Names.'

'Whose names?'

'I never saw the list.'

'But you know what was on the list.'

'Names,' I said again.

'Whose names?'

'I can't say.'

'Cannot or will not?'

'Cannot.'

'Why?'

'Because I never saw the names.'

'Whose names?'

'What?'

'*Who*? Whose names?'

'I don't know whose names. I never saw the list.'

A silence fell.

I thought that if they were taping my interrogation it was going to sound like an old Abbott and Costello routine.

The silence grew heavier. The seconds passed, one adding to the next. Second upon second, each sat on my chest like those stones torturers used in the Middle-Age to press prisoners to death.

'I don't understand,' finally I said.

But it was too late. He was already standing up. He called the warder.

I wasn't sure if their hearts were no longer in it or if they were just tired. After all, it had been a long night for them as well as me. Perhaps they were looking forward to their beds and the thought crossed my mind as to whether they were paid extra for night work. I might even have asked if I hadn't been on the floor trying to catch enough oxygen just to breathe.

The routine went on as it had before. Only this time they seem to become bored that much sooner. Perhaps they were tiring of having to pick me up. Each time they did they slapped me around as if trying to knock life back into a body that was, itself, losing interest.

Finally they gave me one of their signature parting kicks and left me in my customary heap on the cell floor.

By now I knew the routine as well as they did. I lay where I was until I was eventually able to haul myself back onto the bunk to wait for the warder, the chair, and my stone psychiatrist to return.

And, rules or not, while I was waiting I was going to sleep.

How long it was before the warder brought the chair again I didn't know. I had no frame of reference despite having thought about frames and references before.

Frames and references... How long ago? The pain was telling me and it said:

Not long.

~

'I want to cooperate,' I told him as soon as he was seated beside me again.

'Good,' he said. 'We want you to cooperate.'

'Please tell me how I can cooperate.'

'By telling us, of course.'

'Telling you what?'

303

'Everything,' he said. 'Tell me everything.'

'Everything...? Where shall I start?'

'At the beginning, Herr Tennant. Start at the beginning.'

That was all very well. Except the beginning was so long ago that I didn't want to risk boring him going back that far.

There would be all sorts of details which couldn't possibly be of interest to him, surely. He might lose interest. He might stand up and leave again.

'You'll tell me if I bore you,' I said.

'I will tell you, Herr Tennant. Do not worry.'

But I did worry.

'Where at the beginning do you want me to start?'

'Your recruitment,' he said. 'Tell me about your recruitment.'

'Acton.'

'Who is Acton?'

'No, not who. What.'

I heard the chair shift.

It was Abbott and Costello again. He didn't like that.

'Acton is a borough of London,' I explained. 'That is where I was recruited.'

'That is good. Who recruited you?'

'Bill Harrington.'

'In Acton.'

'Yes, in Acton.'

The beginning began in Acton. Wasn't that something I had once told myself?

'It began in Acton,' I repeated, and started at the beginning.

35

The man had gone. His chair was gone. I was finished.

Lying on my bunk waiting for the other two to come in I tried to go back over what I had said. Only now it was over it seemed to be more of a capitulation than a recapitulation.

Once I had started talking I'd found it difficult to stop. I was a tap I couldn't turn off. Slow to begin, once open it all came gushing out in a flow impossible to staunch. I wasn't sure I'd had enough wits left to keep back what I'd decided I needed to keep back. We were playing by his rules now and I said what he expected me to say.

I had wanted to play down Kurt's part. Yet I wondered who was fooling whom. It seemed they already knew everything about me. If that was the case they would know just as much about Kurt.

As much as I did. More probably.

I managed to keep Kim Philby's name to myself. I wasn't sure why. According to Bill, he was in Washington, out of their reach. Besides, if they had a man on the inside they would know Philby, anyway.

When I was asked who was present at my interview in Acton I said just myself and Bill Harington. They already knew about Bill. My psychiatrist statue listened to everything I said without query, seeming to accept it, although it wasn't easy to tell lying as I was on my couch.

I told him how Bill had recruited me, giving him the explanation Bill had given me, which was that they had wanted someone unknown in Berlin to take Arthur Peston's place. Since he was already dead, I dredged up all the details I could remember about Peston, dwelling upon that death and my initial suspicions about the manner in which he had died. Perhaps I was hoping to learn something more. If so, I was disappointed. No information was volunteered and when I summoned the temerity to ask I was told I was expected to answer *his* questions, not pose any of my own.

He moved me on to my arrival, demanding details of the paperwork involved with my residence. What permits were issued for Schyller Imports and which offices I had dealt with at the British HQ at the Olympic stadium.

Once he had wrung everything I could remember about that out of me he turned to the conversations I had had with Bill.

How had he and I communicated?

Where did we meet?

Describe the precise locations of the dead-letter drops I had scouted.

Then he wanted all the details and finer points of the mechanism London used to pay us. And how, in turn, I had paid Prochnow.

I told him everything. I felt impelled to keep talking. If I didn't, he would leave and the other two would come back.

Yet even as I spoke, none of it seemed to be adding up to anything. There was nothing of sufficient substance in what I was telling him to keep him in his chair. So, if there was a question to which I did not have an answer, I filled the gap from my imagination. And the deeper into the story I burrowed and the more confident I became of his acceptance of it, the more embellishments I added. I told him how I had made money on the black market, substituting myself for Kurt and telling him that a USAF sergeant supplied me with cigarettes and other goods pilfered from the American PX.

I imagined he would like that touch: a practical demonstration of the level of corruption in the American military machine. He seemed to take this in his stride, however, and listened without comment as if corruption was all anyone could expect from Americans.

We moved on to my first meeting with Prochnow and his wife at the Zoo Club. I described how I used the place as the centre of my operation and disclosed that I had initiated an affair with one of the bar girls as a cover, even to the extent of moving in with her.

When he wanted more details I saw an opportunity to spin my story out still further. I related how one evening I had found an emaciated girl hanging around the house in Halensee. She had survived the death camps, I said, and had told me her name was Shoshannah Lehmann and that she had lived in the house by the lake until her mother and father and brother had been deported.

I felt him growing impatient so I brought in the Americans. I described how I had been in touch with the group gathering information on the deported Berlin Jews. He wanted names so I gave him Tuchmann's, telling myself that neither Tuchmann nor his organization were secret. With the opportunity to digress further, I told him that Tuchmann had learned that Shoshannah Lehmann had been a Greifer who had called herself Anna Koch and that she had betrayed other Jews to a man named Walter Frick of the Berlin Gestapo.

But none of it diverted him for long. He suspected I was stalling and although he asked a few more questions he soon tired of the tale.

He dragged me back to Prochnow.

Where did I meet him?

Who had first mentioned the name of Albrecht Fischer?

I could have asked why he didn't talk to Prochnow himself.

The man was in Potsdam, after all, so why was he asking questions of me to which he already knew the answers?

It was a charade, played out on both sides, but one that was keeping the other two from returning. I was grateful to remain complicit in the pretence.

But we were back to the nub of the matter. Fischer and his names. There was no more room for stalling. And by then, even if I had wanted, I could not have stopped myself telling him everything *he* wanted.

'So, Herr Tennant,' he said returning once more to Fischer, 'he promised you names.'

'Yes.'

'Whose names?'

'The names of Soviet agents presently working in the British Foreign Office. The name of a man you have inside SIS in London.'

'He told you this?'

'Yes.'

'So you know these names?'

'No,' I said. 'He wouldn't tell me. He said he would only reveal the names once he had defected.'

'And did he?'

I managed to raise myself off the bunk and turn to him.

'You tell me,' I said. 'I've been here in this cell. All I know is what you told me. That he disappeared. So, did he defect or did you catch him?'

He didn't answer me.

He stood up. It must have been late afternoon and the game was apparently over. I was finished, empty while still trying to come up with something else that might keep him in his chair.

I asked if there was anything else he wanted to know.

He hadn't mentioned Potsdam or that I had seen Prochnow

there. I didn't know if he knew. If I should volunteer the information.

If I did I knew the pretence would finally be over. He would know that I knew Fischer was a plant and while there remained the possibility he didn't know, it was the one advantage I had over him.

But he had lost interest in me. He called the warder. The chair was taken away and he left.

The sound of the cell door slamming behind him rang through my head as I waited for the other two to return. When it opened ten minutes later, I heard myself begin to whimper.

But it wasn't them. It was the warder. This time he brought me a meal.

The hours dragged by. Was it evening? Night? Time crawled with the slow stillness of a glacier. I fell asleep only to wake at every sound. Any movement beyond the door would stop my heart as I caught my breath to listen.

An age passed and the warder appeared again with another meal. I squinted up at him through my puffy eyes, pinned to the bunk as if I were paralysed. The warder left a plate, grunted but said nothing.

The day passed, one interminable minute following upon the next, and still my tormentors did not return.

Sometime later, as I hovered between sleep and wakefulness, a diminutive spark of optimism flickered deep within my brain. A small worm of hope began to burrow through my head.

~

Days passed. It wasn't easy to tell how many. I saw no one except the warder who brought my meals and slowly that small worm of hope grew into a coil of conviction.

I began to believe that they were satisfied I had told them all I knew. I could lay on my bunk undisturbed, optimistic in the belief the beatings had ceased while my dark bruises faded brown and my cuts began to heal. What they would do with me next I didn't know. It was a subject I didn't dwell upon.

As long as things stayed the way they were I found some

contentment.

Yet nothing lasts. While the body busies itself with the process of healing, the mind remains untouched. Eventually I became bored.

Time in prison passes more slowly than it does on the outside. Ask anyone who has served a sentence.

In more fanciful moments I saw it as confirmation of Einstein's theory, that part which states time passes faster the quicker one is moving.

In a prison cell one goes nowhere and as a consequence time ceases to flow almost completely. Those on the outside and living their normal lives find time passing at a rate commensurate with their activity; the prisoner, having no activity, spends eons measuring the minutes as they pass by.

I wasn't provided with much in my cell beyond the time to think. When first locked in I had little time and less inclination to examine my surrounds. Now I had little else to do.

The building on Keibelstraße must have been more fortunate than the rest of Berlin as it never seemed to suffer a power cut. The single light suspended from the ceiling never went out. It became a constant aggravation. An ever-seeing eye that never blinked, silently and forever denying me the balm of darkness.

One consequence of having a permanent day was, of course, that I had no way of measuring the passage of time. Hunger maybe a natural timepiece, one which ordinarily measures the passing hours, although in Berlin almost everyone was hungry almost all the time. I was no different. I was fed, but sparsely. Although the food I was given wasn't much worse than anything I could have bought outside with my ration *Marken*, it became an event I looked forward to. Once I had finished eating, though, I was at a loose end again, still frustrated at any attempt to use appetite as a monitor.

Besides, as I was only too aware, my meals could have been delivered to me at any time of the day or night. I would have been none the wiser.

So time passed at an indeterminate rate. Like looking at a watch with a broken spring seeking change, it only reminded one that nothing had.

Once I was able to move without too much pain, I took the trouble to examine the cell, going over the floor and the walls for anything that might capture my attention. But it was a cell, six paces by six and much the same, I supposed, as a hundred thousand others. Once examined there was nothing else to do except lie on the bunk and think.

Left to my own devices I went back over the recent past, searching for an answer as to why things had worked out the way they had. Yet the only conclusion I reached was that the blame for my incarceration lay somewhere in limbo, hanging between those who had sent me to Berlin and myself for agreeing to come. If there was an answer, I didn't know the right question to ask.

The only question I could think of, the one that kept coming back to me, was: did they know that I knew Fischer was a plant?

~

It would be a truism to say that the day before they picked me up they either knew or they didn't know I had been in Potsdam.

A truism, but a starting point.

I had already concluded they had targeted Bill Harrington because of his knowledge of Volkov. And knowing that led me to believe I had been sent to Berlin to take over from Arthur Peston not in spite of the fact that I lacked experience in espionage, but precisely *because* I did.

Someone was getting close to the Soviet agent in London and needed to be thrown off the scent. Berlin was waiting for someone to take over from Peston and Fischer was waiting to effect his spurious defection.

All the Soviet agent in London needed following Peston's death was a naïve, inexperienced man to step in.

A dupe to pick up the pieces and put them back in place.

Right from the beginning I had questioned why I, an amateur in their world, had been sent to fill Peston's shoes.

When asked, they had told me they wanted a fresh face not

an insider.

What whoever set me up really wanted was someone who wouldn't question what was happening too closely, a neophyte who would be out of his depth.

I was a man with a chequered history, eager to get it right for once. I suppose I must have looked the ideal candidate.

According to Bill Harrington it had been Kim Philby who had originally suggested my name. That seemed odd to me as I didn't know Philby. Then Bill told me Philby had claimed a third party had passed my name to him. Who that might be I could only guess. To my knowledge I had not met anyone in SIS prior to my interview, certainly not anyone who might know enough about me and my record in the Intelligence Service to believe I might be an ideal patsy.

I thought long and hard about it even though I had been down that road before. The way was littered with discarded names, none of which had the sort of influence that could have got me posted to Berlin, and I had to accept that I wasn't going to learn any more about it while I remained sitting in my cell.

So since I saw no point chasing a dead end, I shifted my focus.

It seemed reasonable to me to assume that someone else would have been put in place before my arrival who knew about the operation and would stay close enough to ensure I did not stray off my scripted path. Given that I had only met a handful of people since my arrival, I didn't think narrowing down the field was beyond my ability.

Both Bill and Kurt knew why I was in Berlin and were the most obvious suspects.

But there were other characters and each traipsed through my head, stepping into view as I called their names. One by one they took a bow and passed across the stage:

Mitzi and Marthe ... Andy Thurston ... Joe Rafferty at Templehof ... Dai Edwards out at the Reich Sporting Field...

But I couldn't see any of them making much sense as a Soviet agent.

Frau Ernst?

But I would never have met her if not for Mitzi, and if Frau Ernst was the one then so too was Mitzi. Besides, Frau Ernst had been one of Hitler's devoted following. I couldn't picture her switching allegiance to Stalin. It was true there might be little to choose between the two under the skin, but at least with Hitler you got the colourful parades and the fancy uniforms to mask the brutality. With Uncle Joe all you got was Leninist cant and grey serge.

It didn't seem to me to be a vision of the future designed to sweep Frau Ernst off her feet.

Thinking about Frau Ernst brought Shoshannah Lehmann and her devil, Walter Frick, back to mind. My interest there had me wandering off-script, yet I couldn't remember anyone shepherding me back onto the straight and narrow. Unless one counted Mitzi's initial disapproval.

I had already considered Mitzi. She had been there when I got punched in the Zoo Club, had invited me to move into the Halensee apartment on very short acquaintance, and had a possible facility with the Russian language...

But I was only too aware that I made a habit of this sort of thing—imagining conspiracies where in reality nothing but happenstance actually existed. It hadn't got me anywhere in the past and was getting me nowhere now.

Did I really suspect Mitzi?

Wouldn't it be more likely that she was worried by my disappearance?

She would have talked to Kurt and perhaps gone to the police. For all the good that would do her. Kurt would have spoken with Bill, no doubt, and maybe some effort had been made to find out what had happened to me.

Bill would have gone to Peston's apartment as arranged. I had left a bloody handprint on the table. Surely that would have added up to something?

But perhaps my arithmetic was wrong. Why Hadn't Bill arrived before the two goons had taken me away? Perhaps my whole hypothesis was based on a false premise. If that was the case, any conclusion I did manage to reach could well provide me with nothing more than a false solution.

In the end I gave up attempting to think it through. It was easier to turn on my bunk and try to sleep, imagining what sort of hole, if any, my absence had made in the outside world.

36

Meals and a jug of water for washing appeared regularly, giving me a gauge with which to count the passing days. After what I calculated to be a week, I was escorted out of the cell and along a corridor to a room with a shower. They did not provided me with a razor and my beard and lengthening hair became another yardstick by which I was able to measure time.

By this reckoning I had been in the cell a month when one morning the door was unlocked and, instead of the expected jug of water and breakfast, a man I had not seen before entered. The warder followed him with the now familiar chair.

As the man sat down, he offered me a cigarette and introduced himself.

In my experience—recently acquired and limited as admittedly it was—a man who is planning to beat you to a pulp rarely offers you a cigarette or gives you his name.

This one did. The cigarette was Russian; the name was Leonid Globa.

He was slight of build with a narrow chin and domed forehead that put me in mind of a light bulb. He didn't have the physique or look the type of man who would hit anyone out of hand and I didn't see any chafe marks on his knuckles either, the kind that would indicate he sometimes resorted to the brass variety. That didn't mean he wasn't NKVD, of course, nor above getting some else to do his beating for him. But that was his prerogative. After all, it was his cell. One way or another I was just passing through.

As far as his name went, I was willing to take that on trust. What he might tell the man in the next cell I couldn't say.

He was clean shaven and of medium height and what was left of his neatly cut hair had already turned grey. His German was good and his English better, even if it did come with a heavy accent. While I can recognize Scots and Irish readily enough, when it comes to placing the origins of an Englishman I am no Henry Higgins; a European, as far as I am concerned, is just a foreigner. Anywhere east of the Danube is an alien landscape to me, probably peopled by werewolves and vampires.

Even so, I was pretty sure that Globa was no fairy. That was as far as I was prepared to go.

'So,' he began once seated, clipping the word short as if he were taking a parade ground drill, 'will we speak in German or English?'

'English,' I said. 'I wouldn't want any misunderstandings because of my German.'

'It is as well if you are more comfortable with your mother tongue.'

The weeks that had passed since my last beating had had a restorative effect on my spirit and I considered telling him that I had never been comfortable with my mother's tongue. That, though, was a personal matter that she and I had never been able to resolve. And despite the information they had collected on me I doubted Russian Intelligence had delved that deeply into my past.

'If we are to talk,' I told him, 'I doubt I'll be able to tell you anything more than I already told the other man.'

'The other man?'

'The one who interrogated me between beatings. He didn't trouble to give me his name.'

'That was Comrade Gornov. Do you have a complaint to register concerning your treatment?'

'Gornov, was it? No, no complaint,' I said. 'I wouldn't want to get anyone in trouble. As a matter of interest, though, who were the other two?'

'You needn't concern yourself with them, Herr Tennant.'

That was easier said from where he was sitting than done from where I was. But I wasn't inclined to argue.

'So what do you want? I've told you everything I know.'

'You haven't told *me* anything,' he replied equably. 'I am interested in something you told Comrade Gornov though.'

'What was that?'

'You told Gornov you moved into a house in Halensee after you met a girl in the Zoo Club. Is that correct?'

'She hasn't got anything to do with this.'

'Just answer the question.'

'Yes, I did move into a house in Halensee,' I said. 'But the girl knows nothing of why I came to Berlin. I only told Comrade Gornov about her and the house because he seemed to want to know everything and he was very persuasive.'

'Direct methods often are,' Globa agreed. 'The girl's name is Mitzi Meier and she works at the Zoo Club, yes?'

'Yes. That is where I met Gerhard Prochnow, as I told Gornov. But, you must understand, the girl had no involvement. She just happens to work there.'

'And she has rooms in a house in Halensee. You moved in with her after the American she was living with moved out. Is that correct?'

I always suspected the man before me had been an American. I had never heard the fact put into words before. Now it was, I didn't much care for the sound of them.

'I didn't know who he was,' I said as equably as I could manage, 'although I did assume as much.'

'He was a cipher clerk at the Mission Berlin.'

'On Clayallee in Zehlendorf?

'Yes. You knew him?'

'I never met the man,' I said. 'I just know that's where the US keeps its embassy.'

'It is not an embassy,' Globa replied, picking some nits out of his political dogma. 'The U.S. Mission Berlin a diplomatic presence, no more.'

Which was true enough. Like us, the Americans no longer had a proper embassy in Berlin. They kept what they called "Mission Berlin" in Zehlendorf. That was a suburb south of Halensee which had once been fashionable and well-to-do. The place had received its fair share of bombs but being near the Grunwald it was still a pleasanter spot than downtown Berlin.

Handy for Mitzi's friend, I couldn't help thinking. No more than a short train ride to the office in the mornings.

'You maintain you did not know him?' Globa persisted.

'Never met him,' I said again. 'I don't know what happened but he was gone by the time I moved in.'

'He returned to his wife in Baltimore.'

'You seem to know a lot about him.'

315

'Describe the house,'

That threw me a little. I would have liked to know what he knew about Mitzi's American, but talking about the house seemed harmless enough. I sketched the place out for him, saying it was near the lake and that I liked to swim since the water supply couldn't be relied upon.

That didn't appear to interest him much, though.

'Tell me about the *portiersfrau*,' he asked, fixing his gaze on me.

'Frau Ernst? Why—'

But *why* hardly mattered. I was beginning to pick up a thread in his questioning. So I told him about Frau Ernst, about Werner and about the absent Herr Neumann. I said an elderly couple lived on the top floor although I didn't know much about them.

'And it was at the house in Halensee you met a Jewish girl named Shoshannah Lehmann. Is that correct?'

'Is that what this is about? Shoshannah Lehmann?'

'Tell me how you met,' Globa said.

'Well, to start with, it wasn't at the house. The first time I saw her was on the road outside.'

'She spoke to you on that occasion?'

'No. She ran off when she saw me. Then she stole some money from my wallet.'

'From your apartment?'

'No. I went for a swim in the lake. She took it while I was in the water.'

'You made a complaint to the police?'

I smiled. I hadn't done much of it lately but all the muscles seemed in working order.

'No,' I repeated once more, 'I'm not the kind who makes complaints.'

'What did you do?'

'Nothing.'

'Did you tell Frau Meier about the girl?'

'That I had seen her, yes. Not about the money she stole.'

'Why not?'

'Because she would have thought me a fool for leaving my wallet where it could be stolen.'

'Was it stolen?'

'No. The girl took some Reichmarks, that's all. I was also carrying American dollars but she didn't take them.'

'Did you not think that odd?'

'Certainly I did. Wouldn't you?'

'Did she take anything else?'

'No. She looked at my papers. They were in my pocket along with my wallet.'

'What did Frau Meier say when you told her about the girl?'

'That she had seen her hanging around the house before. She called her one of Berlin's ghosts.'

'Ghosts?'

'I think she meant someone who has come back to Berlin looking for their former life.'

'And she thought this girl was "looking for her former life"?'

'That was just Mitzi's way of saying everything had changed because of the war.'

Globa stood abruptly. He paced around the cell for a minute then returned to his chair.

'Did this Jewish girl, Shoshannah Lehmann, tell you what it was she was looking for?'

'Not directly. At first, anyway. I think she was looking for a man named Walter Frick. She said she had seen him near the house next door. A property that had been owned by a couple called Schneider.'

'Did Shoshannah Lehmann tell you why she was looking for Walter Frick?'

'No. I learned later, though, that she had been a *Greifer* during the war and that Frick had been her Gestapo handler.'

'How did you find this out?'

'You're interested in Walter Frick, aren't you?' I said. 'That's who you want, isn't it?'

Globa ignored my question. 'How did you find out Shoshananah Lehmann had been a *Greifer*?'

'Through an American Air Force colonel I know. He's helping trace Berlin Jews who went missing in the war.'

'What is his name?'

'Benjamin Tuchmann.'

'And he is a Jew, of course.'

'Of course.'

Globa remained silent for a moment, then asked:

'Did you confront Shoshannah Lehmann with what you knew about her?'

'No. Colonel Tuchmann told me she had been put on trial after the war and given a prison sentence. She was—'

'Yes, we know the girl's history,' Globa interrupted. 'I am more interested in why, if you are telling the truth, you did not say anything to her about what she had done. Did you not think her betrayal of her fellow Jews a crime?'

What I thought was none of his business and I wasn't going to help him pin her death at my door if that was his game.

'By the time Tuchmann told me about her,' I said, 'she was already dead. She died that same evening. I got home and found her hanging in our apartment.'

'Hanging? A suicide?'

'That was what it was supposed to look like.'

'You are suggesting it wasn't suicide? Do you have any evidence to the contrary?'

'There was a lot more bruising around her neck and shoulders than she would have got from the ligature. That suggested to me there had been a struggle. I think she had been strangled before they strung her up.'

I hadn't actually seen much evidence of it during my brief examination of her body and I suppose I was taking what one might have called pathological licence. But if Globa wanted to pin her death on someone I knew who I'd like that to be.

'They?'

'Walter Frick and Frau Ernst.'

'But Walter Frick is dead,' he said.

'That is what everyone is supposed to believe.'

'And you do not?'

'No.'

'Do you have evidence he is still alive? Or is this merely a belief as well?'

'None that isn't circumstantial,' I admitted.

'Why would Frick want to kill the girl?'

'Several reasons. He is supposed to be dead but she was convinced she had seen him. Alive and near the house. Frick had illegally appropriated her family's house...'

'Illegally?'

'Above and beyond the laws the Nazis passed on their own behalf to service their own greed,' I said. 'I assume you know such things were not uncommon. The main reason Frick had for killing her, though, was that she could identify him.'

'You think Frick murdered Shoshannah Lehmann because she knew he was alive and could identify him. Surely there must be other people in Berlin who could do that?'

'Certainly. But as you said, the story is that Frick is dead. You must know what it's like, Comrade Globa. Frick isn't the only ex-Nazi walking around Germany who hasn't been brought to book for his crimes. I hear there are even I some presently working in the Berlin Administration.'

'Not in the Soviet Zone,' Globa said.

'No. I have heard that you are more particular about the people who work for you.'

'I am glad you acknowledge the fact, Herr Tennant.'

I gave him a nod and was happy to do it. What I would have liked to add was that while they insisted they drew the line at using ex-Nazis, the Russians didn't seem to mind using men of the same ilk and the same methods.

I say, I would have liked to but I didn't.

'So you think,' Globa went on, 'that Walter Frick believes himself safe now the girl is dead? He has friends in the American and British sectors of Berlin who can protect him, no doubt.'

'I wouldn't go that far,' I said. 'The more money a man has the more friends he acquires and I suspect Frick doesn't have a great deal of money. Why else rent out rooms and risk being seen? If he had money he would have bought his way out of Berlin by now. Probably out of Germany. A lot of Nazis managed to feather their own nests while they were running things. It may be that Frick let whatever he acquired slip through his fingers.'

'An interesting theory, Herr Tennant,' said Globa.

'Just one that fits the facts,' I said. 'Like why Frick is still hiding. Ben Tuchmann told me he would like to get hold of him and charge him with war crimes. If he could find him.'

'Do you believe him?'

'Yes. As you said, Tuchmann is Jewish.'

'You have heard of Werner Von Braun, perhaps?'

'Von Braun? Wasn't he the fellow in charge of Hitler's rocket programme? The V2s?'

'Do you know where he is now?'

'I haven't a clue,' I said.

'Von Braun is in the United States of America continuing the work he was doing for the Nazis.'

'That doesn't surprise me,' I said. 'It might if you told me he wouldn't be in Russia doing the same if you had managed to get to him first.'

Globa leaned towards me. 'Careful, Herr Tennant,' he warned softly. 'Remember where you are.'

I wasn't likely to forget. But that didn't mean Globa was wrong. Now my mouth was coordinating properly with my brain again, I ought to watch what was coming out of it.

'I can see that Von Braun might be useful,' I allowed. 'But I don't know what good Walter Frick would be to anyone.'

'The Soviet justice system could find a use for him,' Globa replied, getting as close to cracking a joke as I suspected he ever did.

'You'd have to find him first,' I said.

'The Lehmann girl told you she had seen him in Halensee.'

'Yes, but she didn't have all her wits.'

'Enough left for Frick to worry about and to want her dead,' he said. 'Assuming you are right and he killed her.'

'I've got a suspicious mind.'

'But if you are right, he is still in the British sector.'

'If he is, it can only be because he would have to pass through the Soviet Zone of control to leave.'

'And to do that,' Globa said, 'he would need British or American assistance?'

'I suppose so. Some sort of diplomatic protection. Obviously, if we are assuming he is still alive and still here, he hasn't got it.'

'Yet,' said Globa.

'And you aren't prepared to risk waiting until the Americans and the British leave Berlin. Is that what you're saying? You want him now. That's why you're here, why I'm still alive, and why we've been dancing all around the subject.'

'I cannot comment on why you might be alive or dead, Herr Tennant, but as to the rest you are perfectly correct. We would like to arrest Walter Frick. To put him on trial for the crimes he committed as an *Einsatzgruppen* commander in the Ukraine.'

'And you think I know where he is?'

'I think you suspect you know where he is.'

'Well, it doesn't take a mind reader to guess that's Halensee,' I said. 'But perhaps that's not enough for you?'

'Of course not, Herr Tennant. We are as bound by the law as you British claim to be. If Frick is in Halensee, he is in the British sector. We could make a request for his extradition although I suspect he would disappear once more before the request was granted. That is assuming the British or the Americans did not arrest him first. Frick committed his crimes on Soviet soil and that is where he should be tried.'

'I agree,' I said.

'Then you are willing to cooperate with us in bringing this fugitive to trial?'

He was making it sound as if he wanted to deputise me, like the sheriff did in all the good westerns. A flattering thought, but I was going to want some assurances before I pinned on the star.

'What do you need me for?' I asked. 'If you don't think the British authorities will give him to you, why not just go in and take him? You didn't have any scruples when it came to kidnapping me.'

'Kidnapping?' Globa sounded genuinely astonished by the word. 'You are guilty of espionage.'

'Guilty? I must have missed the trial,' I said. 'Perhaps you held it during one of my periods of unconsciousness. Come to that,' I added, 'if I've been arrested I don't recall having been advised of the fact.'

'Still playing the policeman, Herr Tennant?'

I wondered if maybe I should reassess how much they knew of my past. Perhaps even which stretch of the Thames to dredge to pull out that old Nagant.

'It is true,' Globa went on, 'we could arrest Walter Frick if we knew precisely where was and when and were able to make a positive identification. But we would have to be certain we had the right man. Taking him from the British sector without authorisation could have repercussions at this delicate time.'

Repercussions my kidnapping hadn't caused, I assumed he meant. But then I'd never seen myself as a *cause célèbre*.

'I still don't see why you need my help.'

'Because you know the house and who lives there. We are also hoping you can identify Frick.'

'I've never seen him,' I said. 'Shoshannah Lehmann said she did but I haven't.'

'You will not help us?'

'I didn't say that.'

Having just ventured into French, I was wondering if Globa might be open to a little Latin. As it was he beat me to it.

'Are you suggesting a *quid pro quo*?'

'I'm merely saying that there is a way what you want could be accomplished.'

'With a positive identification, Herr Tennant? How could that be achieved?'

~

Later, in the dark and some while after I had persuaded Globa to have my light turned out, I was lying on the bunk balanced precariously in that odd world between wakefulness and sleep.

Random thoughts were tripping through my head and from somewhere out of this mental kaleidoscope a picture from ancient Egypt unexpectedly materialised. It was something I had seen before although I couldn't remember where. In a book, possibly, or in the Cairo museum.

I had spent some time in Cairo during the war and while I had managed a trip out to the Pyramids at Giza, I hadn't seen the ruined temples or where the pharaohs' tombs lay although I had visited the Cairo museum. I only mention it now as it might give a clue as to the direction these random thoughts were leading.

Subconsciously, of course. But it was an indication that the decision I had made was playing on my mind.

The particular picture I recalled depicted some of those strange Egyptian gods, the ones that have animal heads placed upon human bodies.

Which gods, I can't remember. Whether it was those with the jackal's head or falcon's head ... or even that peculiar crocodile-headed god... As far as my story goes, that doesn't matter.

The picture in question was one where the gods were overseeing a ritual in which they were using a large set of scales. In one pan, a human heart was being weighed against a feather lying in the other pan. The crux of the matter was, that if the weight of the heart proved heavier than the feather, the owner of the heart would not be allowed to pass into the afterlife.

The implication of the metaphor, of course, was that only those with a heart pure and unburdened by sin may enjoy eternal life.

I daresay the Egyptian afterlife was a decent and comfortable place given all the gold and jewels they were in the habit of sending off with their dead. Well-decorated, at least, to judge from what I had heard of the tombs.

I didn't suppose our Christian afterlife would be half as gaudy. Since I had never believed in it anyway, I don't suppose it much mattered.

I have always believed in living the life we've got. And, by the time I found myself in that cell, I had come around to the opinion that given the sort of life millions of desperate people had recently been forced to live, living one single life would be quite enough.

But even for a non-believer it is difficult to escape some feeling of trepidation. In the society into which I was born Christian concepts are hammered into you from the first moment you draw breath and are capable of listening; right up until the moment the priest reads the service over your coffin.

A moment, one hopes, when one can no longer hear him doing it.

And while none of this adds up to any kind of afterlife I would ever care to contemplate, an atheist like me still finds it hard to ignore the concept of judgement.

Lying in that cell, I knew that if my heart was ever weighed against that feather, it would be found too heavy.

Again, lying in that cell, it might be fair to conclude that past sins had already decided the outcome on my behalf. Yet I always believed that everything I had ever done, at any rate in any arena that concerned the weighing of hearts, I had done with justification.

Whether I believed or not, it could be argued that I had once trespassed on God's territory and not only arrogated unto myself *His* prerogative for retribution but also compounded the sin afterwards by forgiving my own. And as to whether the particular god on whose toes I had trodden had been one in bearded human guise or one possessed of a crocodile's head: does it really matter?

My justification was that any sins I committed, I committed for the sake of someone else.

But perhaps that too is a matter for the eternal scales.

I don't know.

What I did know was, that this time, what I was prepared to do was not for the sake of someone else. Those for whom I might have claimed to be acting were all dead. They were beyond anything now other than vengeance.

Or perhaps retribution is a better word.

Semantics apart, at base what I was about to do was for my sake only. Consciously, I had decided to give the Russians something they wanted more than they wanted me. In an attempt to save my own skin.

Judged against the vastness of crimes recently committed I thought it was but a very small thing. It could be argued there was a natural justice in it. Even so, I suspected that as far as I was concerned it would still be heavy enough to bar my passage to any afterlife on offer.

Far better, I imagine, I should shoot the man myself than hand him over to jackals in human form. The secular kind, that is, those who merely assume the prerogatives of gods.

Unfortunately, though, no one was going to put a gun in my hand.

It was a sobering thought and yet not one that was going to

stop me. After all, I could argue that I had already committed sufficient crimes to have the gate of heaven bolted and barred in my face.

Then again, I was sure I remembered something in all that Christian preaching to which I had been subjected, that it is the sinner who repents and sins no more who is more welcome in God's house than a devout man.

It was my misfortunate though, that try as I might, I couldn't see that either description might be said to suit me.

37

The car turned off Koenigsallee onto Margaretenstraße and slowed to a stop where the gravel road began. The driver dimmed the lights.

'Turn it around,' Globa told him.

The lights went on again. The driver turned to look out the rear window as he reversed, reaching his arm across the back of the seat. As he did his eyes made brief contact with mine.

Klaus Kittel's gaze remained vacant.

It was a tight squeeze in the car, Globa and Kittel up front and Gornov's two goons jammed either side of me in the rear. There wasn't going to be room for a sixth.

Driving through the darkened streets of the British sector towards Halensee, I was relying on the fact.

That was my deal with Globa. Once we had Frick, I was the one to be left behind.

Once the vehicle was pointing in the right direction, Globa opened his door and climbed out. He switched on a flashlight. We followed, one of the NKVD goons grasping my bicep in his meaty paw as we stood by the car. Globa said something in Russian to him and he let go of me and loped off towards the house. I waited on the gravel between Globa and the other goon. Kittel was still in the car.

I had no idea if they already knew Kittel's history or not. Either way it must have come as a nasty surprise to him when the NKVD came to call. I had told Golba that the policeman had worked alongside Frick at the Kaiseralle station before the war and that he would be able to identify him.

I supposed Kittel might still get a feather in his cap if we caught Frick. If we did I wasn't expecting any thanks from him. If we didn't, I doubted there would be many plaudits on offer for any of us, feathers or whatever.

The gravel road in front of us was black. It was gone midnight and no lights showed in any of the houses left on Margaretenstraße. As Globa motioned Kittel out of the car, I had a vague sense of how Judas Iscariot must have felt. A bad analogy, perhaps. I had no silver in my pocket and no stretch of anyone's imagination would have ascribed anything of the divine to Walter Frick.

But I had certainly betrayed him. And, as far as I was concerned, for something infinitely more valuable than silver.

Globa jerked his chin at me to lead the way and we started down the road, our shoes crunching on the gravel. The goon beside me had his own flashlight and he played the beam on the ground ahead as we walked. I took them as far as the drive leading to the Schneiders' house and stopped.

'This one,' I said.

Globa stood next to me and shone his light in my face.

'Show us the tunnel.'

I had told him about the tunnel connecting the two houses once he had agreed to my terms. I suggested it would be the best way of surprising Frick, providing Globa had a man waiting by the front of the house in case Frick managed to elude us.

He might just as easily run out the back but I couldn't be expected to think of everything. If Globa wanted an expert in tactics he should have kidnapped Montgomery.

We walked up the Schneiders' drive and I heard Globa say something in Russian to the goon beside me. The man turned his light on the rubble of the house, lighting my way as I stepped ahead of him.

Picking my way towards the ruin, I saw a light shining across the lake through a gap in the trees, its reflection shimmering on the water as the breeze drifted over the lake's surface.

Earlier in the evening while waiting in my cell before

leaving, I had mulled over the odds of making a run for it and taking my chances once we reached the house. I knew the lake shore better than Globa would and reckoned I could pick my way through the ruins quicker than he could follow. I counted on the fact he wouldn't want to make a lot of noise chasing me and that there were plenty of places I could hide until they either gave up looking or went after Frick without me.

But even if I was lucky and I got away, Globa still knew where I lived and there would be nothing to stop him snatching me off the street again some other day. Not unless I got out of Berlin altogether and that meant getting through the Soviet Zone, something I'd only be able to do with Bill Harrington's help. It meant I'd have to get to Bill before Globa got to me.

The alternative was to hope we would get Frick and to trust that Globa would keep his end of the bargain. So far, trusting to fortune hadn't paid me much in the way of a dividend although I knew it was the easiest option to take.

I wondered if that made me lazy or merely a fool.

The flashlight suddenly shifted and left me in the dark as the goon behind me became more concerned with his own footing than mine. I stopped and told Globa I'd need one of the flashlights if I was to find my way through the house to the tunnel. He barked something guttural at the goon and the man stepped forward and pushed his light towards me, almost knocking me over. I squandered one of the few Russian words I knew on him, shone the light ahead of me and left him in the dark.

A narrow path where rubble had been pushed aside led through the house. I followed it with Globa and his goon behind and Kittel bringing up the rear. It was difficult to be sure by flashlight but nothing appeared to have changed in the weeks since I'd last been there. The ruined kitchen lay undisturbed and the door to the pantry was still shut.

'Through there,' I said over my shoulder and played the torch over the door.

'You first,' Globa said as if he didn't trust me.

I opened it and shone the flashlight inside, steadying the beam on the makeshift door at the far end. I stepped inside.

The iron bar still lay where I had left it and in the torchlight I could see the tenon of the lock still spanned the gap between the door and the frame. As I picked up the iron bar, the goon grabbed my arm.

'I used this to pry the door open,' I said to Globa, wrenching myself free. 'There's a trapdoor on the other side and steps leading down to the cellar and tunnel. It's only wide enough for one man at a time so we'll need go in single file.'

Globa came up beside me. 'Any other way out?'

'No.'

'All right, give him the bar.'

I pushed the iron bar into the goon's stomach the same way he'd given me the flashlight. But it would have taken a Tiger tank to knock him over and he barely flinched. Globa gave him an order and the goon shouldered past me. I'd barely got the light back on the door before he jammed the bar into the gap by the lock, heaved on the bar and splintered the doorframe.

I shone the light inside onto the cellar trapdoor.

I turned to Globa. 'That's the basement,' I said. 'You'd better hope Frick's down there because if he's not and he sees that frame, you won't see him.'

Globa moved closer and I felt his breath on my face.

'You are the one who had better hope he is down there, Herr Tennant.'

The goon lifted the trapdoor, snatched the flashlight out of my hand and started down the steps. He was still gripping the iron bar as though his next target was someone's head.

Globa squeezed past me. He handed Kittel his flashlight and told him to watch me then followed the goon into the cellar. That left me and Kittel to bring up the rear, his light casting my shadow on the wall in front of us like an outsize silhouette of Nosferatu.

Globa and the goon were waiting at the foot of the steps and I steered them around to the tunnel entrance.

The goon moved in front of us, making enough noise to wake everyone in the next house. I thought of Mitzi, wondering if she was home yet and in bed and hoping that, if she was, that was where she'd stay.

I reached out to Globa.

'Tell that oaf of yours to be quiet. If Frick is in the other cellar he'll hear us coming. Is the other one waiting out the front?'

'He knows what to do,' Globa whispered.

'I just want you to know that if we lose Frick it won't be my fault.'

Globa grunted and pushed the goon ahead of him into the tunnel.

'Do not worry, Herr Tenannt,' he said over his shoulder as he followed, 'I will know who to blame if we do not find Frick.'

Hardly reassured, I would have stayed where I was until it was over except Kittel gave me a shove in the back and I had no option but trail after Globa down the tunnel.

We moved in single file slowly along the tunnel until we reached the point where I had stopped the last time I'd been there.

I laid a hand on Globa's shoulder in front of me, pleased when I felt him start in surprise.

'This is as far as I have been,' I whispered. 'I don't know what's ahead. A door to the other cellar, probably. Don't make any noise. If anyone is down there they will be able to hear you.'

Globa hissed at the goon ahead of him and stopped to listen.

None of us moved.

I could hear nothing except the sound our own breathing.

After a moment Globa gave the man in front a gentle push and we moved on another twenty paces. Then the goon in front stopped abruptly. His torch beam was centred on a door a few yards ahead.

Globa squeezed past, stepped up to the door and gently tried the handle. It didn't move. He turned, came back a step or two and whispered to the goon. He went to the door, pushed the iron bar between the door and the frame and slowly leaned on it until the frame cracked under the pressure. The door still didn't move.

Globa barked an order and the goon rammed his shoulder into door. The lock shattered and the door flew open. We piled into the other cellar, flashlight beams skittering this way and that over the walls like a magic lantern. I saw a chair and a table and an empty bed in one corner. Globa's beam settled on another flight of steps that led up to the ground floor. He shouted at Kittel and the policeman and the goon took the steps two at a time, falling over each other before crashing through a door at the top.

I hung back in the shadows. Globa turned to me, the flashlight in his left hand and now with a gun in his right.

He waved the barrel towards the steps.

'Up.'

I edged past him and began climbing. Somewhere above I heard Frau Ernst scream. Then a gunshot rang out followed by two more, each echoing through the cellar.

I looked down from the steps at Globa behind me.

'I thought you wanted him alive.'

He jabbed the gun in my back. 'I do.'

I climbed to the top.

Frau Ernst wasn't screaming anymore.

Someone was shouting in Russian and a second later I heard a cry of pain. Globa pushed past me into the apartment.

I followed and found myself in Frau Ernst's kitchen. In the middle of the room the goon and Kittel were forcing a man's head down onto the table. Globa's goon was holding him by the back of the neck and blood was dripping from a wound in the man's arm. It had begun to pool on the tabletop. Beyond the kitchen I heard the sound of splintering wood and a second later the goon Globa had sent round to the front of the house came in nursing his shoulder.

Globa found the kitchen light, switched it on and bent over the table. He peered into the man's face then glanced at Kittel.

Kittel nodded.

'Up!' Globa barked.

The man was hauled upright.

I had my first sight of Walter Frick.

He must have looked more imposing in uniform. Now, despite what Shoshannah Lehmann had said, I didn't sense I was looking at the face of the devil. The former *Einsatzgruppen* commander was wearing pyjamas, the top soaked in blood and hanging open where the buttons had been torn off.

Frick wasn't looking at me. He was staring at Globa. His thin grey hair was dishevelled and there was fear in his eyes. His mouth hung open and the only distinguishing feature he possessed that I could see was the sharp angle his nose made as it protruded from his face.

Globa turned to Kittel again. 'You are sure?'

Frick frowned at Kittel as if trying to place him.

Kittel gave him another look. 'Yes. That's Walter Frick.'

Globa didn't seem to want to waste time on reunions. He jerked his chin at the two goons.

'Take him to the car. Go out the front. It's quicker.'

Frick began screaming as they dragged him out the kitchen into the corridor. Globa followed. The apartment door to the hall stood open, the way Frau Ernst liked to keep it. But she wasn't there now. Nor was Werner and his wheelchair. I thought of Mitzi upstairs and the old couple beyond, cowering probably somewhere at the top of the house.

'Who did they shoot?' I shouted at Globa, following him into the hall.

Frick had stopped one in his arm but I had counted three shots.

Globa was almost at the front door. He turned towards me.

'Thank you, Herr Tennant. We have Frick. We don't need you now.'

For the briefest of seconds I thought he meant to keep our bargain. Then a sledgehammer hit me in the chest and a gunshot filled my ears.

I felt myself floating in limbo. Then I hit the floor hard and was staring up at the ceiling, trying to catch my breath.

A voice a million miles away said:

'He is still alive ... finish him...'

A moment later Kittel's face appeared between me and the ceiling, his head looking enormous without its neck. It hung there like a huge artillery shell, filling the room as it whispered in my ear.

'Like I told you before, friend. They can do their own fucking killing.'

The universe exploded. Light and sound and pain seared

through my head and then darkness fell.

38

I first became aware that I wasn't dead when it occurred to me that the voices I could hear were not speaking in English.

This isn't to suppose I've always regarded heaven to be filled exclusively with Englishmen. Or, more to the point, that I had expected to find myself inducted one day into the cool and airy arbours of paradise.

What brought on this awareness was the understanding I was experiencing curiosity. After all, what use is an inquiring mind in an environment where all has finally been revealed?

Accepting the fact I wasn't dead and still on earth, I realized that most of the voices I could hear were German. Whenever someone did speak English, it was with an American accent.

As far as I could tell I was lying in a white room. I was unable to move my head, or much else, and it seemed an eon passed before I found myself able to formulate and voice a question. At first I couldn't comprehend any answer I was given. When at last the fog in my brain cleared sufficiently for me to grasp what was being said, I was given to understand I was in a military hospital at Templehof.

That was more than sufficient information to assimilate at one go and so it was a while before I attempted to ask anything further. The fact I was in a hospital was puzzling enough; that I was at Templehof seemed quite bizarre.

How long I puzzled over it I can't say. Fragments of memory, which could just as easily have been dreams, threw up all manner of half-forgotten names and unlikely explanations. One in particular that lingered was that a master-sergeant by the name of Rafferty had organized everything for me. Exactly who he was, I wasn't sure, but the memory stuck in my head and became quite immovable, rather like an irritating tune that proves impossible to shake.

When, over the following days answers did come, they fitted together so slowly that it was some time before a picture emerged.

And one none the less likely for all that.

By then, between long periods spent sleeping, I was able to hold short conversations with whoever came within my orbit. Mostly that was a German nurse named Heike, small, dark and attractive, and who when necessary and despite her size was able to move me around in bed with ease.

Trying to ask questions of Heike, though, while being told to swallow this pill or have that response checked, filling a bedpan or having those parts of my anatomy I generally dealt with myself wiped and washed, was a trick it took me some while to master.

Once I did, the biggest shock I received was discovering the date.

It revealed there was a hole in my life several months large. Far larger than the hole Globa had made in my chest and considerably longer than the groove Kittel had made in my head.

Once I was sufficiently receptive to assimilate what I was being told, they explained how with some difficulty the bullet had been extracted from my chest and how the shot to my head had scoured a groove across my skull.

One of my lungs had been pierced, apparently, and to add insult to an already painful injury I had subsequently come down with pneumonia. Most of those concerned had expected me to shuffle off Shakespeare's mortal coil and I was assured in no uncertain terms that, had it not been for the surgeon's skill and the care of the hospital staff, I unquestionably would have.

It seemed I had had nothing to do with it at all.

There had been talk of flying me back to England although the consensus, Heike informed me, was that I would not survive the journey.

Interesting as all this was, it was somehow peripheral to the life I now found myself living. I had always been the kind of person who expected their body to work, one way or another, and if it didn't went to the nearest medical engineer to get it fixed.

Cerebral work, I was assured, is another matter and that it was possible the confusion I felt might prove to be a permanent condition.

Since Freud and his disciples had never impressed me much, by the time I was finally alert enough to appreciate the gap in my head—my retentivity, that is, not the physical gap I was given courtesy of Klaus Kittel—I knew it was a concern I needed to address myself.

It did come back over the following weeks, but only very slowly. Everything before the knock on Peston's door came first, even if it took some time sewing the pieces back together in the proper order. My incarceration in the cell beneath Keibelstraße 35 was less clear. I knew I must have been there for over a month although the lack of any memorable events on which to hang time left most of it like a reel of underdeveloped film.

Some scenes were clear enough. I knew I had told Gornov everything concerning Prochnow and Fischer, and given him quite a lot of unconnected information besides. I had tried to downplay Kurt's part, mention Mitzi only in passing, and Philby and Marthe not at all. Not being asked about Potsdam, I had said nothing, having convinced myself I had outwitted Gornov by holding some things back, or—not so flatteringly— had been doubled-bluffed by someone smarter than I was.

Upon reflection, I suspected the second possibility was the most likely.

I did remember that while being interrogated by Comrade Gornov my main concern had been to keep him in his chair and so forestall another beating. To that end I had rambled along any unrelated tangent I hoped I might get away with while still ensuring his attention. The house in Hallensee, Shoshannah Lehmann, Herr Neumann and Walter Frick had merely been one I had wandered.

I didn't know why they were keeping me or what their eventual plans for me were. My first assumption was that they were holding me until Fischer had been taken to London. If London accepted him as genuine I supposed I was a wild card to be kept in the hand in case I later proved useful. As soon as it was seen I wasn't, I would be discarded.

The truth, though, remained one of those unanswered

questions. Like why I had been beaten but not tortured. The theory behind softening me up I could understand, yet there are quicker ways of procuring answers and far less athletic ones.

But given how things had worked out, I wasn't complaining. The alternative, I supposed, would have been either being left to rot in their dungeon or taken out into a courtyard one nameless dawn and shot.

It seemed it had been the story of a *Greifer* which had supplied one of those serendipitous twists of fate and which, in the end, had saved my life.

~

One morning in the spring with the sun throwing a shaft of sunlight through the window of my room and I was able to stay awake for an hour or two at a stretch, Heike came in and began fussing with the bed. She pulled the pillows out from behind my head, plumped them then began straightening my sheets and blankets.

'You have a visitor,' she announced. 'We must make sure you are looking your best, Harry.'

I told her if that was what she wanted she should have caught me before the war. She smiled automatically but it seemed that particular joke of mine was beginning to wear a little thin, most evidently when the recipient was a German.

So I didn't throw any good quips after bad and did as I was told, lying back on the plumped pillows to await the visitor.

I was hoping it would be Mitzi.

I had asked about her as soon as I was able to speak, afraid that something had happened to her the night I'd been shot. Shortly after Globa's goon and Kittel had broken into Frau Ernst's kitchen, I had heard three shots. Frick had been hit by one which left two unaccounted for. Since the next two had accounted for me, I had no idea what had happened at the house.

My questions about Mitzi, though, seemed to meet with evasions. First they didn't know who I was talking about. Then, once they did, they would make enquiries ... no doubt someone would be along to tell me shortly...

But no one ever came.

Once presentable on my plumped pillows, though, I tentatively asked Heike if my visitor was Mitzi.

'No,' she said. 'It is Colonel Tuchmann.'

And so it was. Breezing in and looking much the same as he always did, he made a good job of not appearing shocked when he saw me.

'Harry,' he said, laying a hand lightly on my shoulder and giving it a brief squeeze, 'you're looking better.'

Heike found a chair for him. He favoured her with one of his dazzling smiles as he sat in it.

'Better?' I croaked. 'You've been before?'

'I've been dropping by from time to time, keeping my eye on you. Mostly they have only let me see you through the glass.'

'Are you why I'm here? At Templehof, I mean?'

He had reached for a cigarette and got it almost as far as his mouth before thinking better of it.

'It was quicker than going through your people.' He gave me the cut-price version of the smile he'd given Heike. 'I can make them jump in our sector. Yours always want chapter and verse first.'

'Thanks,' I said. And meant it.

'No problem, Harry. They were talking of moving you to a British hospital once they got the slug out but you were still pretty bad for a while. The doctors here thought it wouldn't be a good idea.'

'They told me,' I said. 'I asked them about Mitzi...'

Tuchmann nodded sagely. 'She's fine, Harry. No need to worry about her. I'll let her know you can have visitors now. She can come to see you herself.'

'Thanks, Ben,' I mumbled again

'No problem. It's Mitzi you've got to thank. She's the one who found it was you when the shooting stopped. She telephoned me and I got you here.'

'She phoned you?'

'Lucky she did,' he said. 'Any longer and you'd have drowned in your own blood.'

That picture kept me occupied for a moment or two while

Tuchmann went on:

'The first shot shaved your head, Harry. The other caught you in the lung.'

I tried to shake the head in question but found that wasn't a good idea.

'Other way around,' I said. 'He shot me in the chest first. He told the other one to finish me off.'

'You sure? They told me there were powder burns so I don't see how he missed if he was that close and you were already down.'

I was sure. I'd had a lot of time to think about it.

'He didn't mean to kill me. Just before he pulled the trigger he told me they could do their own killing.'

'Well,' Tuchmann said, eyes widening, 'if he didn't mean it, he did a first-rate job of making it look good. It was touch and go, apparently. The slug in your lung was the worst but the head shot didn't do you any favours. You'll carry a nasty scar.'

As far as I was concerned Klaus Kittel had done me the greatest favour he could. If I'd had the strength I would have shaken his hand. Except I'd have to go back into the Russian sector to do it and there was no way I was ever going to go there again.

'Did you know him?' Tuchmann asked.

'We'd met before,' I said. 'He was there to identify Frick. The one who shot me was named Leonid Globa. I didn't know who his two goons were.'

'They got Frick, of course. We don't know what they did with him. There's been no word of a trial. Shot the bastard out of hand, probably.'

I vaguely remembered Globa intimating Frick would get some sort of trial. If not, why not shoot him then and there? Not that the verdict was ever going to be in doubt.

Or that anyone would care one way or the other.

With the possible exception of Frau Ernst.

I asked Tuchmann if they had shot her, too.

'No. They found Frick in bed with her as far as your people can make out. He must have had a gun and taken a shot at them. They fired back and hit him, judging by the blood. They knocked his wife cold. Werner heard the commotion and got as far as his door. They shot him. Maybe they assumed he had a gun.'

Three shots.

'Dead?' I asked.

'Yes. Werner was Frick's son according to the mother. But I guess you'd already worked that one out, Harry. Your Frau Ernst wasn't badly injured but that's as much as she's prepared to say.'

I watched his fingers play with the unlit cigarette. I hadn't had a smoke in months.

'One other point you might be interested in,' he went on. 'You were right in thinking there isn't any Neumann in Hamburg who owns that house. There used to be an Otto Neumann in Hamburg who'd been a member of Frick's *Einsatzgruppen* squad. He was killed on the Russian front. Frick appears to have taken his name but he was never in Hamburg. Had he got that far there's not much chance he'd have come back to Berlin. Neumann was just a convenient fiction to explain the owner's absence.

'I've spoke to Neumann's family,' Tuchmann said. 'They refuse to believe what Otto did under Frick's command. Or if they do believe it, won't talk about it. What they didn't want was for their son's name to be connected to Frick's in the press. To keep his name out they agreed to let me go through the letters he wrote home from the front. There's nothing in them about what the group did. Censorship would have cut that out anyway. But he does mention some names of men he was serving with. It's enough to give us a few new leads in tracking down some of the lesser criminals.' He nodded at me encouragingly. 'That's down to you, Harry.'

Heike returned and Tuchmann stood up.

'I'm told I'm not to tire you out so I'll be off. I'll drop by again. And I'll let Mitzi know I've talked to you. She'll want to come and see you herself, I'm sure.'

After Tuchmann left I lay back and thought over what he had said. I was thinking it was too late for Shoshannah Lehmann to receive justice and, after what she had done herself, perhaps she no longer deserved any. But one way or another Walter Frick had been brought to book at last, even if those who were doing the judging weren't too concerned about justice themselves.

Despite what I had told Globa I had no evidence that Frick had murdered Shoshannah Lehmann, or if his wife had helped him. I was convinced they had although by then it hardly mattered.

I was sorry to hear about Werner. He had had a short life and not a very good one. He had no say in who his father was and I suppose wouldn't have been human if he hadn't looked sympathetically towards the man who had given him life. It was just a shame that in the end it was that which had cost him his.

As for Frau Ernst, or whatever her name really was, I felt nothing at all. She had probably been responsible for Werner's attitudes and had made her own choices. Now she was going to have to live with them.

At least she still had a life with which to do it. And the time to regret those choices she had made.

39

A couple of days after Tuchmann came to see me Heike announced I must be a popular man because I had another visitor.

Assuming once again that it must be Mitzi, and feeling better now Ben Tuchmann had told me what had happened at Halensee, I asked Heike to put another pillow at my back to prop me up so I could watch her as she walked through the door.

I was watching although I wasn't watching Mitzi.

Between bouts of sleeping I had been struggling to read a book, a western novel being all Heike could lay her hands on. The man she showed in was grey and middle-aged with hair so thin the pale pate of his head showed through and the first thing that struck me was that any Indian worth his salt wouldn't have bothered with this fellow's scalp.

He was wearing a creased suit and carrying a suitcase. I

didn't know the man although the case looked vaguely familiar.

With or without a scalp he looked to me like a life insurance agent. It made me wonder if he wasn't the insurance version of an ambulance-chasing lawyer and spent his time hanging around hospitals in the hope of a sale to anyone who'd had a near-death experience.

He didn't have much in the way of patter, though. Putting the case down by the cupboard, he stood over the bed and gazed down at me through a pair of rheumy eyes.

'My name is Ronald Passmore.'

He offered his hand. That was pale, too, with elongated fingers that were probably just the thing for picking fruit. If they were, he hadn't brought me any.

'Harry Tennant,' I replied.

'Yes, I know. I've come to see you.'

Both of us having stated the obvious, he looked around for a chair. The one Tuchmann had used stood beneath the window but he had to fetch it himself, Heike not obliging as Passmore didn't seem capable of raising the sort of winning smile that had women falling over Ben.

'London sent me,' he said as soon as Heike left and he was seated. 'I've come to debrief you. They thought they'd kill two birds with one stone, so to speak.'

'What's the other bird?' I asked.

'I'm Harrington's replacement.'

Perhaps I looked surprised because he added, 'Temporarily,' as if I might be thinking he didn't look like anyone's idea of a spymaster.

He didn't, but that wasn't what had surprised me.

'So Bill's gone home?'

I had been wondering why I had heard nothing from him. It seemed to me, in my more delirious moments, that his silence was taking the fact I was an illegal to unnecessary extremes.

When I started thinking more clearly I assumed I had been wrong about his suspecting Fischer and had accompanied the man back to London. My being wrong was what had surprised me.

'You won't have heard, of course,' Passmore explained. Or,

340

to be more accurate, didn't. 'But we'll get to that later. First things first. The debriefing.'

'Do I need debriefing?'

'It's how we do things.'

'Fine,' I said.

He nodded. 'Right. How are you finding the food?'

'Better than I'm used to,' I admitted, finding it odd that if he had come with a list of questions provisions were at the top of the agenda.

'Yes,' he said, 'the Yanks don't do bad for themselves, do they?' He leaned towards the bed slightly. 'There are one or two points we'd like to get out of the way at the outset, if that is all right with you?'

Since I didn't know which points he had in mind I wasn't able to say if they would be all right with me or not. I fell back on, 'Fine,' once again.

He took some papers out of his pocket and smoothed them on his knee.

'Accounting matters, I'm afraid. A nuisance but there you are. This business of your getting shot... I have to ask how it related to the company.'

'What company?'

'The company that sent you to Berlin.'

'You mean SIS?'

Passmore frowned. 'I think we had better call them the company, don't you? Or Schuyler Imports if you prefer.'

'Sorry,' I said.

'I am told it is Colonel Tuchmann's belief that your being shot had something to do with a Jewish family and a Nazi war criminal. Is that correct?'

'You've spoken to Tuchmann?'

'He is a friend of yours?'

Not wanting to go that far, I said, 'I've known him for a couple of years.'

'Given his belief, would you say the colonel is unaware of all the ramifications?'

'Which ramifications?'

'The precise circumstances of your being here in Berlin.'

'Oh, I see. In that case no. He knows nothing of that.'

341

As it happens, I was far from convinced that Tuchmann knew nothing about it. With Ben Tuchmann one could never be sure of exactly what he did and what he didn't know.

'Good,' said Passmore. 'So the fact you were shot and particularly *where* you were shot can be demonstrated as having no relation to the commission of any Schuyler Import business. We can be sure of being on firm ground if we say that it was purely a private matter, correct?'

'Well I suppose it was,' I agreed. 'Whether we want to say so or not. Why do you ask?'

'As I said, Accounts need to know.'

'Accounts?'

'I'm afraid there will be a sizable sum in medical fees due for your treatment, Mr Tennant. The advice of our legal department is that if the circumstances of your being injured were not directly related to your work for us, the company have no liability for those expenses.'

'I'm sorry?' I said. 'You're telling me that SIS ... that *Schuyler* won't pay my hospital bill?'

Passmore cleared his throat, going on quickly, 'I am also advised that I should inform you that you will find a clause to this effect in the contract you signed before leaving England.'

I hadn't read the bloody contract. Who does?

'So I am expected to foot the bill for my hospital care myself?'

'Had you been injured on company business,' Passmore explained, even smiling as if the irony might offer me some enjoyment, 'it would be a different matter of course.'

'But I was abducted while on company business,' I said. 'And I was shot by the people who abducted me. I would still be rotting in their cell if it wasn't for this other business. Rotting, I might add, *because* of Schuyler business. So where does that leave me?'

'If you wish to dispute the decision,' Passmore replied patiently, 'I have been instructed to inform you that it will be taken under advisement. All relevant facts will need to be disclosed, naturally, and while that presents no problem as far as the company's legal department is concerned, it does mean that you yourself cannot disclose to any solicitor you may engage on your behalf any information connected with Schuyler Imports that might contravene the official secrets act.'

I felt pain in my chest again. It had nothing to do with the bullet they had taken out but was a result of the kicking I was getting.

'Am I still on the payroll?' I asked.

'Certainly,' Passmore said. 'Up until the conclusion of this debriefing.'

'What, then you're *sacking* me?'

'Again, Mr Tennant, I must point out that under the conditions of your contract, your employment may be considered terminated if you are unable to undertake the terms of that employment. For whatever reason.'

He shuffled the papers and ran an eye over the page.

'As far as Schuyler Imports are concerned you disappeared on August 11th of last year, is that correct?'

'As best I remember,' I replied stonily.

'And were recovered on October 3rd.'

'Yes. At least, I have been told it was October.'

'And naturally you remain on the company's payroll until dismissed.'

'Only if you're sure,' I replied sarcastically.

'On sick pay,' Passmore said, ignoring the remark. 'Which is calculated at one-half normal remuneration.'

At this point he favoured me with a slight rise of his eyebrows. A demonstration, I assumed, to show he was open to any comment I wished to make.

The first one that came to mind wasn't going to advance the argument so I kept it to myself.

'And it has been decided, purely as a matter of gratuity and you must understand not one to be regarded as indicating any admission of liability, that this will be the case while you remain in hospital.'

He paused, waiting for a response. When I made none he continued:

'It has also been decided to regard your employment from August 11th until October 3rd 1947 as sick pay, on the grounds that you were unable to fulfill the requirements of your contract from the former date until the latter. What you *are* authorized to receive, though, in addition to sick pay is a seat on a flight to London. Once you are fit enough to travel, naturally. The flight will be out of Gatow.'

'You wouldn't want me to stay here,' I said.

Passmore ignored that, too, and offered me a card.

'Should you wish a written summary of this decision you may contact the company's legal department at this address.'

I took the card and without looking at it placed it on the bedside table.

Passmore folded away his papers and sat back in his chair.

'Now that's over,' he said briskly, 'we can get down to business.'

'Is there anything left to discuss?'

'Quite a bit, Mr Tennant. Quite a bit.'

He was right although as far as a discussion went it was something of one-way street.

What Passmore wanted, as Tuchmann had said of us British, was chapter and verse.

As there didn't seem to be any mileage in falling into a sulk, I answered his questions and described exactly how I had been taken from Arthur Peston's flat and, as best I could remember, what had subsequently happened in the intervening weeks until Mitzi found me at the house in Halensee.

When prompted, I supplied the names I knew of those with whom I had come into contact, and descriptions of those I remembered merely as faces.

The one name I didn't give him was Klaus Kittel's.

One good turn deserved another, I thought, although I couldn't help running my fingers over the scar he had left on my skull as I thought it.

When we had finished Passmore went back to the beginning.

'So, you were waiting at the flat for Harrington? Correct?'

'Yes. I left a message for him at the Military Mission. Sergeant Thurston hadn't come on duty so I left it with the clerk on the understanding the matter was urgent.'

'You didn't use the telephone?'

344

'No. Bill didn't believe they could be trusted to be secure.'

'And the message you left for Harrington concerned Albrecht Fischer, is that correct?'

I didn't answer immediately.

'How much do you know, Mr Passmore?'

'Concerning?'

'Albrecht Fischer.'

'If you mean about the circumstances of Fischer's defection,' he replied evenly, 'I know everything there is to know, Mr Tennant. Excepting those answers I am expecting you to supply.'

He seemed a little too self-satisfied for my liking but I could only assume he knew his business.

'Then you'll know who Gerhard Prochnow is,' I said.

'The man you were sent to Berlin to contact. It was through Gerhard Prochnow, or more exactly through his wife, Gretchen Prochnow, that you made contact with Albrecht Fischer.'

'That's right. Then you'll also know we believed Prochnow had been shipped to Moscow in a crate from the Russian airfield at Johannisthal.'

'Yes.'

'Then you'll be surprised to learn that I saw Gerhard Prochnow in Potsdam the day before I was abducted.'

'You're right, Mr Tennant, I am surprised,' Passmore replied, not looking in the least surprised. 'And that is why you wanted to see Bill Harrington?'

'Yes. I didn't say as much in my note to him, but I was beginning to suspect that Fischer was a Soviet plant. I wanted to let him know this before the arrangements made for Fischer's defection went ahead.'

'Because you believed you had seen Gerhard Prochnow in Potsdam.'

'Yes. If Prochnow wasn't in Moscow as we thought, and as Fischer *said* he was, then the whole operation was a set-up.'

'What were you doing in Potsdam, Mr Tennant?'

'What?'

'Why were you there? Potsdam is in the Soviet Zone of Occupation.'

'To get away for a few hours,' I said, wondering why it

mattered.

'Exactly when was this?'

'I went there the day before I was abducted. Last August.'

'You said you wanted to get away. Away from what?'

'Halensee. The house... Tuchmann told you what happened there, I suppose?'

'Are you referring to the kidnapping of Walter Frick?'

'No. I'm talking about last *August*. How I found the girl, Shoshannah Lehmann, hanging in my apartment.'

'The suicide of the Jewish girl?'

'It was murder, not suicide.'

'Very well, murder,' Passmore said. 'But, as you said yourself, that had no bearing on Albrecht Fischer. Or does it?'

'No, none at all. But after finding the girl that night I thought it would do me and Mitzi some good to get away from that house. That's why I was in Potsdam.'

'This is Mitzi Meier, the woman you were living with.'

'Yes.'

'Why Potsdam?'

'No particular reason,' I said. 'Because I wanted to get out of Berlin, I suppose. Mitzi was a student there.'

'In Potsdam?'

'Yes. Although I didn't know that at the time.'

'Whose idea was it? To go to Potsdam?'

'Mine.'

'Not Miss Meier's?'

'No. Look,' I said. 'That's irrelevant. It was sheer chance I saw Prochnow. In fact I didn't see him first. It was Mitzi who pointed him out. We were having a drink on the terrace of a restaurant. Prochnow and Grechen were there with a couple of other men. This while, as far as we were aware, they were supposed to be in Moscow. Gretchen told me herself a day or two earlier that she had been told to join her husband there.'

'You couldn't have been mistaken? You saw a couple that resembled Prochnow and his wife, perhaps?'

'No.'

Passmore rubbed one of his long fingers across his chin just below the lips.

'And this is why you decided Fischer must be a plant? You

had no other evidence.'

'Not then.'

'You found some later?'

'Yes, naturally. Why else would the NKVD kidnap me? The only reason could be because I knew Fischer was bringing us false information about the names of their agents in SIS and our diplomatic service. It only makes sense if Fischer was a plant.'

'And they admitted this to you during your interrogation?'

'No, of course not. I wouldn't have expected them to. But they did want to know everything I knew.'

'Surely they would have wanted to know that regardless of what you suspected about Albrecht Fischer,' Passmore said.

'Yes, naturally,' I agreed.'

'Let us go back to Miss Meier for a moment. You say she was the one who pointed Prochnow out to you? She knew him, then?'

'She didn't *know* him. She had seen him at the Zoo Club.'

'This is the establishment where she worked and where you first met Prochnow and his wife.'

'Yes.'

'How often had Miss Meier seen Prochnow at this club?'

'Just the once.'

'So she might have been mistaken in Potsdam.'

'Well, *she* might have been. I wasn't.'

'You're positive it was Prochnow and not someone who may have looked like him?'

'Yes, I'm positive. Besides, as I said, his wife was there, too.'

'Gretchen Prochnow.'

'Yes. It's possible to mistake one person but hardly two. A couple. It was them.'

'What did you do when you saw them?'

'We left.'

'Did they see you?'

'I didn't think so. Not then.'

'Later, perhaps?'

'Yes. I thought at first that was why I was abducted. Because I saw Prochnow and would realize Fischer was plant. It was obvious they couldn't risk me warning Bill, so they kidnapped me.'

'But you *had* warned him, hadn't you? In the note you left at the Military Mission.'

'I didn't go into details. I just said I needed to see him. I didn't say why. Bill hadn't wanted me to let anyone else know about Fischer so I didn't use his name or mention Prochnow in the note.'

'You had taken this communication you received stating Prochnow had been sent to Moscow on trust, I assume?' Passmore asked, changing tack again.

'Not just on trust,' I said. 'Prochnow had disappeared. No one had seen him, not even his wife. Then a Cargo manifest was sent to us showing a crate had been shipped to Moscow from Johannisthal airfield. It was Kurt Becker who said it must be Prochnow. Later that morning Bill told me he had also received information from some man of his at the airfield that corroborated the story. A day or two after this, Gretchen Prochnow told me Fischer suspected that her husband had been arrested. In fact Fischer said as much to me.'

'Do you think it was Fischer who sent you this cargo manifest?

'I didn't know. I still don't.'

'So, despite all the circumstantial evidence to the contrary, you couldn't actually be certain that Prochnow *had* been arrested and sent to Moscow.'

'No, of course not. Not one hundred percent certain. How could you be? Everything pointed towards it, though. He had missed a meeting with me and Bill said it was too much like the Volkov affair not to credible.'

'Volkov? This is the Russian diplomat who wanted to defect in Istanbul two years ago?'

'That's right. And if you know about him, you must also know Volkov wasn't a diplomat but a member of the NKVD.'

'Go on.'

'Konstantin Volkov was the whole point, you see.'

'In what way?'

'They were targeting Bill. Because he had been in Istanbul at the time Volkov tried to defect and knew all about it. They knew if he got a second chance at getting the names of the

Soviet agents Volkov had been offering, he'd jump at it. What he wanted in particular was the name of the man who had infiltrated SIS.'

This time Passmore didn't baulk at my mentioning the Service. He regarded me in silence for several seconds. Then said:

'So your suspicion of Albrecht Fischer is founded solely upon what you now say is an erroneous assumption. That Gerhard Prochnow had been taken to Moscow.'

'If you want to put it that way, yes. And because Fischer corroborated the story.'

'So when you saw Prochnow in Potsdam, you assumed Fischer was a Soviet plant.'

'*Yes!* Because he had lied to me.'

'Then it might surprise *you* to learn that Albrecht Fischer denies any knowledge of Prochnow's supposed abduction. Or telling Gretchen Prochnow or you that her husband had been arrested.'

'Not particularly,' I said. 'What else would he do but deny it? What does surprise me is that Bill Harrington accepted Fischer at face value. I was beginning to suspect that Bill knew there was something wrong about Fischer from the beginning, even before I sent him the message. He *did* get it, I suppose? He couldn't have missed the blood on the table in Peston's flat. Either way he must have known something was up.'

'Why do you say that? Did Bill Harrington tell you he suspected Fischer before you thought you saw Prochnow in Potsdam?'

'I did see him,' I said. 'But no, Bill never said anything outright to me about suspecting Fischer. It was small things ... things that started adding up. Mostly Bill's willingness to accept Arthur Peston's death was an accident. Even though it was plainly more than that.'

'The police accepted it was an accident,' Passmore countered.

'The police? They took Shoshannah Lehmann's death at face value too.'

'What else was there that made you think Harrington suspected Fischer?'

'He told me not to mention Fischer to anyone else. Not until he cleared it with London. You'd expect as much, I suppose, but I think he was remembering what had happened to Volkov. What I think he really wanted was to see the names Fischer was promising before London took over. I think he already suspected they would be bogus.'

'That's a great deal of supposition, Mr Tennant,' said Passmore.

'I agree. What does Bill say?'

'Bill Harrington isn't saying anything.'

'What do you mean, he isn't saying anything? Why not? Where is he?'

'We don't know.'

'I don't understand.'

Passmore regarded me steadily.

'Bill Harrington appears to have defected,'

'*What*? Are you joking? You're not serious.' I started to laugh.

'I am serious, Mr Tennant. Sergeant Thurston at the Military Mission confirms he sent your message on to Harrington as you requested. We believe that when Harrington received it he contacted his Soviet handler and made arrangements to have you picked up at the apartment. After that, as far as we can tell, he went to the premises of Schuyler Imports to meet Kurt Becker.'

I still didn't think Passmore was serious.

'You're saying Bill's a Soviet spy? I don't believe it.'

Passmore appeared unperturbed. 'All the evidence points to it.'

'What evidence? And why would Bill go the mill to see Kurt Becker? He had told me to keep Fischer between ourselves. He didn't know Kurt knew anything about him.'

'He told you not to tell Becker anything about Fischer?'

'Yes. I told you, not to tell Kurt or anyone else.'

'Didn't you think that strange? After all, Becker was working for us. He brought you Prochnow in the first place.'

'It was because of what happened to Volkov in Istanbul. Bill didn't want to risk the same thing happening to Fischer. His defection getting back to their agent in London.'

'Because Fischer was bringing us a list of Soviet agents who had infiltrated us and this man's name would be on it.'

'Exactly.'

'But you thought Fischer was a plant. The name of this supposed spy in our midst wouldn't be on Fischer's list, would it? This agent you say is in London would have nothing to worry about, would he?'

'I didn't know Fischer was a plant then,' I said. 'The agent in London would only be worried if Fischer was genuine. And I'm sure that is what Bill wanted to verify first.'

'But let's look at it another way for a moment,' Passmore suggested. 'Suppose one of the names on Fischer's list was Bill Harrington's?'

'I've already said. I don't believe it. But, just for the sake of argument, if Bill's name was on Fischer's list he wouldn't want the man to defect, would he?'

'Certainly not,' said Passmore. 'He would do anything he could to stop it.'

'Then wouldn't he have tried to persuade me to ignore what Fischer was promising?'

'Wouldn't you have thought that odd if he had?'

I said that under the circumstances I supposed I would.

'But it makes more sense if Fischer's list is fake,' I insisted. 'That in giving us Bill's name, Fischer was not only protecting the man in London but also disrupting our operation here in Berlin.'

'If that was the case wouldn't Harrington want to confront Fischer?'

'Certainly,' I said. 'How do you know he didn't?'

'Because Harrington disappeared the same day you did.'

'What? But the arrangement was that Fischer was to defect the following day. While attending a meeting between the SED and the SPD. Are you saying that didn't happen?'

'No. We believe Harrington planned to stop Fischer coming over to us, one way or another. But Fischer didn't attend the meeting. We think he heard you had been kidnapped and went to ground. Luckily neither Harrington nor the Russians could find him. We assume Volkov was arrested in Istanbul following a tip-off from Harrington but this time Harrington couldn't tip his handler off because no one knew where Fischer was. We think Harrington went to see Kurt Becker hoping he might know but when Becker couldn't tell him Harrington must have decided his cover was about to be blown and so defected himself.'

'Look,' I said. 'That doesn't make any sense. If Fischer was genuine and had Bill's name why not simply tip off the Russians beforehand that Fischer is about to defect? Problem solved.'

'As happened with Volkov?' Passmore asked.

'Exactly.'

'Except that, while something like that happening under Harrington's watch once might be taken as chance, it happening a second time might look too suspicious.'

'According to Bill,' I said, unimpressed with his reasoning, 'Volkov was betrayed because too many people knew. The agent in London, in particular. That's why Bill didn't want anyone else to know about Fischer until we had him.'

'Or until he had time to work out another way of handling the situation?' Passmore suggested. 'Did he tell you that London had agreed to go ahead with Fischer?'

'Yes.'

'London knew nothing about him. Harrington lied to you.'

I didn't say anything. London would hardly deny it if Bill had told them about Fischer. There had to be a reason Bill had said what he did to me, apart from the one Passmore was offering. But if there was I couldn't think of it.

'He dropped off our radar after you did,' Passmore went on. 'We initially thought he had been kidnapped, risky though that would have been for the Russians. We heard about you in due course but there has been nothing concerning Harrington. Our suspicions that he might have defected were confirmed when Fischer finally came over and told us that one of the names he was bringing was Harrington's.

'The belief now is that he will resurface in Moscow at some point. But not until the Soviet's are satisfied they have made as much out of our confusion as they believe they can.'

'Unless he's dead,' I said. 'The two goons who picked me up knew I was waiting for someone. Perhaps they had already sent another pair round after we left to deal with Bill.'

'I hardly think that is likely,' Passmore said. 'Why not simply continue to wait and deal with Harrington when he arrived?'

'Perhaps they wanted to get me out first.'

'Is that how it seemed to you at the time?'

I had to admit it didn't. The pair had seemed in no hurry to leave, despite the fact I'd told them I was waiting for a British diplomat They had even stayed long enough to drink my pot of tea.

'I know it is hard for you to believe that Harrington fooled you,' Passmore said, 'but there is more evidence to back up these suspicions than Fischer's names.'

It seemed to me that if there had been any fooling going on, I wasn't the only one who had been taken in. Nor was I convinced the fooling had finished.

'Such as?' I asked.

'As I have told you, we believe Harrington was the man who informed the Soviets in Istanbul that Volkov wished to defect. We also think he killed Arthur Peston because Peston had learned from Fischer that Harrington was a double agent. He recruited you because he believed he would be able to manipulate you when it came to handling Prochnow and Fischer.'

'Manipulate me? It wasn't Bill who recruited me. It was Kim Philby.'

'Who told you that?'

'Bill did,' I said.

'There you are,' said Passmore. 'I'm afraid Kim was under the impression your recruitment was Harrington's idea. He says he never met you until your interview in Acton. As a matter of fact, when you first went missing there was some suspicion that you may have defected yourself. But it was pointed out that you had no access to any sensitive material or that you knew enough to be of any use to the other side. Even when you were with MI5 you weren't privy to anything important. By the time we learned you were being held, of course, Harrington had gone over.'

I didn't know what to say. If Passmore was right, I had been played for a dupe. I had already more or less come to the same conclusion, that I had been recruited to be the patsy. What Passmore was suggesting was that the operation had been even more successful than I had imagined.

'Tell me,' said Passmore, 'if, as you believe, Fischer was being planted on us, why do you think they would go through this charade of pretending to have Prochnow arrested? After all, the man was bringing Fischer to you. Why over-complicate things?'

I had thought about that myself.

'To inject some urgency into the business,' I said. 'After Peston died everything stalled. I don't think their man in London wanted to wait any longer and risk being exposed. So they made it look as if Fischer needed to get out before he was implicated in what Prochnow had been doing.'

'If that is the case and what you say is true, aren't you concerned that they will try to kill you again? Before you can tell us that Fischer isn't genuine?'

'I already have,' I said, 'but it seems you don't believe me. Will London believe it, assuming I even get a chance to tell them? They almost killed me once but now London has swallowed Fischer's story, wouldn't trying again give some credence to what I am saying?'

'It's an interesting theory,' Passmore said but I could see he wasn't convinced.

'What about Kurt?' I asked. 'What does he have to say about it all?'

Passmore shook his head.

'Kurt Becker was pulled out of the Spree two days after you disappeared. He'd been shot.'

There had been more. Passmore told me they had changed their mind about my possible defection when they discovered I wasn't being treated like a Soviet Hero of the People. They had lodged a protest with the Soviet authorities but, my being an illegal and as I had already surmised, as far as the rest of the world knew I was a British businessman being held on suspicion of spying.

And the rest of the world would only have learned that

much if it happened to stumble over the small paragraph to that effect put in the British press.

I don't know if the protest and the publicity, such as it was, did me any good. It might possibly have persuaded Comrade Gornov not to have me shot out of hand. Whatever it was that had stopped him, I had been lucky to languish in his cell long enough to come to Globa's attention.

After Passmore left Heike came back to fuss with my pillows and sheets again, as if my visitor had interfered with my bedding.

'Herr Passmore brought your case and some clothes with him, Harry.'

She was leaning across me in what in my more carnal moments I would have taken to be a provocative manner. Just at that moment, though, carnality was the last thing on my mind.

'The clothes you came in,' she went on conversationally while tucking in the sheets, 'were all bloody. They had to be cut away. We still have your shoes and a hat, I think.'

I didn't suppose I was going to need either any time soon although it was reassuring to learn that I wasn't going to be released to the world barefoot.

'I will put the case in your cupboard,' Heike said. 'Herr Passmore brought good news, I hope?'

I considered how *Herr* Passmore had informed me that I was out of work again and that I would be expected to foot my medical bills myself; that Bill Harrington was a spy and had defected to the Russians; and that Kurt Becker had been murdered.

I gave Heike a smile.

'Not altogether good news,' I said.

40

It was several days after Passmore's visit that Mitzi finally came to see me. Walking in, I sensed something different about her and I might have taken her for a hospital charity visitor rather than the girl I had lived with for two months.

Until she opened her mouth.

'You look like shit, Harry.'

She bent over and gave me a brief peck on my forehead. Had I not been paying attention I might have missed it altogether.

'You look good,' I said.

And she did. She wasn't wearing her usual clothes. There was a new dress and a new hat. Nylons, too, if I wasn't mistaken. I had never seen her in nylons although how long it would be before she snagged the mesh on those calloused hands of hers I couldn't guess. I told her I appreciated her taking the trouble to dress up just to see me.

'Oh, Harry,' she said.

Whatever that meant.

I said that Ben Tuchmann had told me she found me that night.

'I must look better than I did then.'

She sat down, putting her new handbag on the floor beside the chair.

'The shooting woke me. But I did not come down until everything went quiet.'

'If it was me I would have stayed in bed with the covers over my head.'

'Of course you would, Harry,' she replied sarcastically. 'You have never been interested in other people's business.'

It had been several months since I'd last seen her but she still had the measure of me.

'Well, I might have taken a peek,' I admitted. 'It was lucky you had Ben Tuchmann's telephone number.'

'He had been worried about you. I did not know who else to call. Our hospitals take so long to send an ambulance. I thought you would die.'

'So I would. You saved my life.'

'What was I to do?'

'I was told they shot Werner, too.'

'That boy,' said Mitzi. 'What had he ever done?'

Berlin was a difficult place to find out what anyone had ever done, but I understood the sentiment.

'Not that I care,' I said, 'but how is Frau Ernst taking it?'

'I do not know, Harry. I could not stay in that house after what happened.'

'You've moved out?'

'I stayed with Marthe for a while.'

'I was lucky you were there when it happened.'

'I thought you must have left Berlin or were dead.'

'I left a note,' I said.

'That you would see me at the club. But you did not.'

'You didn't think I defected, did you?'

'Defected? Do not be ridiculous, Harry. Why would you defect?'

'A man I talked to last week thought I had. He told me about Kurt, too. Did you know he had been shot?'

'Yes. When you did not come home for two days I went to see if Kurt knew where you were. But I find he was missing, too. Then Karl tells me Kurt has been found dead. He was most upset by this.'

'I imagine he was. He'd have to find a new cigarette supply.'

'That is unfair, Harry. Karl was not so bad.'

'He's bearing up then, is he?'

She turned her head and looked out of the window.

'I do not know. I no longer work at the club.'

'No? What about Marthe? Or have you both left?'

'I no longer live with Marthe,' Mitzi said.

'Where are you now?'

'I am living in Steglitz.'

'That's in the American sector, isn't it? It's a long way out of the centre. What are you doing there?'

'I have no work yet. But I have been thinking I might teach again. There are opportunities here for teaching with American families. Did I tell you I used to teach?'

'No. You told me your husband taught philosophy.'

'In Potsdam, yes. I used to teach a little as well. After we were first married.'

'Well, that sounds wonderful,' I said, trying to sound as if I meant it. 'It certainly beats being *Trümmerfrau* or working in a club.'

'I think you are right.'

'So, what do you have in Steglitz? An apartment?'

I suppose the unspoken question was, was there still room for me? But if it was unspoken it also remained unanswered.

'An apartment, no,' Mitzi said. 'I am living in a house. It is by the Teltowkanal and very nice.'

'A house? Isn't that expensive?'

'I share,' she said.

'With other teachers?'

'No,' Mitzi said, lifting her chin a little and looking at me directly. 'I live with Ben Tuchmann.'

For once I didn't have a reply to hand. We stared at each other for a while as if the first to look away would be the loser. But I was conscious that that decision had already been made.

'You were gone so long,' she said eventually. 'It is really because of you, Harry.'

'Someone has to take the blame.'

'Do not be like that, Harry. What I meant was I met Ben because of you.'

'At the club,' I said.

'No, after. After you went missing.'

'You thought he could help?'

For the first time she looked embarrassed.

'No. Because of Rolf.'

'Your husband, Rolf Mendelsohn?'

'Do you remember that day in Potsdam you said Ben was collecting information on Berlin Jews who had been deported to the camps? That he might be able to find out what happened to Rolf?'

I remembered that day in Potsdam very well. Chiefly because it was there I saw Prochnow and realized he wasn't rotting in an NKVD prison in Moscow. In my cell I'd had all the time in the world to think of Potsdam. What else had happened hadn't figured too brightly although now she brought it up I did recall telling her what Tuchmann was doing. I had suggested he might be able to help in finding out what happened to her husband and his family.

'After I heard about Kurt I thought you must be dead, too. So I went to see Ben. You told me he was sometimes at the synagogue on Levetzowstraße.'

'I remember.'

'He did not know you were missing.'

'There was no reason he should,' I said. 'Was he able to find out anything about Rolf?'

'Not immediately, no. But he came to the club a few days later to tell me you were not dead as I thought but still in Berlin. That you were being held by the Russians.'

'How did he know that?'

'He said he had friends in the British sector.'

'Ben has friends everywhere,' I said.

'It was good of him to find this out for me, Harry. He thought he could help you but there was nothing to be done.'

She dabbed an eye with a handkerchief although it might have been dust in the room.

'Ben is a good friend to you, Harry,' she said.

'One of the best,' I agreed.

'Afterwards he would come to see me if he had news of you or if there was something about Rolf he had discovered.'

'I shouldn't think there was much news of me,' I said.

'No. But he did find out that Rolf had been gassed at Auschwitz. I was very upset even though I already knew. Ben was a comfort to me.'

I bit back my initial response and said instead:

'So you decided to move in with him?'

'No, not straight away. Of course not. I am not like this, Harry. You know how I am.'

'I didn't mean to imply anything.'

'It is more than security, Harry. You have to understand.'

'You mean love?'

'He is a good man. And he is Jewish, like Rolf.'

I could have told her about my ex-wife's aunt Julia who had a fling with Tuchmann in London until he had got the information he wanted about my wife's family. I had wondered at the time if he didn't have a wife and kids back in New York or wherever he called home. I was still wondering but knew only too well that if I said anything Mitzi would put it down to jealousy.

'And when he goes back to America,' I asked, 'like the other one?'

'What other one?'

'The American you were living in Halensee. Before me. The cipher clerk at the Mission Berlin?'

She stared at me stonily. 'How do you know this?'

'From one of the Russians who interrogated me. They seemed to know all about him. They never told me his name, though.'

Her lips were pressed tight and I didn't think she was going to admit it. Then she relaxed.

'His name was Frank,' she said. 'Frank Grüber.'

'German?'

'His grandparents were German. What did they tell you?'

'The Russians? Just that you lived with him and that he went back to Baltimore.'

'Cincinnati,' Mitzi said.

'Oh? His wife lived in Baltimore.'

'Wife?'

'He didn't tell you about her?'

'No.'

'I suppose the Russians approached you.'

'They wanted me to find out about his work at the Mission Berlin.'

'Did you?'

'No! Of course not, Harry. I am not a spy.'

'Did you tell Frank?'

'Yes, and he told his superiors.'

'Did they come to see you?'

'Yes. They wanted me to pass information to the Russians and pretend it came from Frank. When I refused they sent Frank home.'

'Out of temptation's way?'

Mitzi didn't say anything for a moment. Then she leaned towards me.

'I have not told this to Ben. Will you tell him?'

'Me? I've no reason to tell him. He's a big boy, Mitzi. He can take care of himself.

'Ben wants to take me back to America with him.'

The conversation didn't really have anywhere to go after

that. We talked a little longer even though there wasn't much left to say. In the end she stood up, leaned over and kissed me goodbye. On the lips this time.

I watched her as she walked out of the room. There were no backward glances.

41

The Berlin airlift began on June 25$^{th.}$

Once able to concentrate on what I was reading, *Der Tagesspiegel,* the American sector daily newspaper, kept me abreast of the worsening political situation. Following a currency dispute and some acrimonious exchanges, the Russians closed land access to all Allied traffic through the Soviet Zone of Occupation. This left the air corridor to the Allied sectors as the only way in to Berlin from the west.

Unlike the ground routes, air access had been agreed between the occupying powers in writing in 1945. It was an error on the Soviets' part that left them a stark option: either allow the airlift through or renege on their agreement and shoot down unarmed civilian planes.

According to *Der Tagesspiegel,* there were several attempts to harass aircraft in the corridors. One had to suppose that a mushroom cloud like the ones that had hung over Hiroshima and Nagasaki influenced their thinking. In the event the Soviets let the planes through and so there was no cloud over Moscow.

Lying in bed, listening the C-47s droning overhead, I couldn't help reflecting on the irony of it all. During the war Germany had attempted to starve Britain into submission by sinking our Atlantic convoys. Now, a scant six years later, here we were helping to fly in food to feed hungry Berliners.

I suppose, if nothing else, that at least demonstrated where the moral ascendance lay.

~

Sometime mid-summer I received a letter from England.

Dear Harry,

You will be surprised to hear from me after all this time. I am writing now because several months ago a girl at work brought me a cutting from a newspaper saying a man in Berlin named Harold Tennant was being held by the Russians on spying charges. We immediately suspected it might be you and so I asked my friend Jane, whom I am sure you remember, if she could find out anything from her previous employers. They were unwilling to tell her much, as you might imagine, but did confirm that the Harold Tennant being held was indeed you. However, they maintained that it was nothing to do with spying and you were being held over illegal currency and black market dealings. Knowing both you and Jane's former employers, I suspected there was probably more to it than this.

Jane heard nothing further until last March when she was informed—in the strictest confidence they stressed— that you had been freed but were seriously ill in a military hospital in the American sector. I wanted to write to you then but Jane advised against it as she had been told that you were not expected to live.

Now I hear you have recovered and might soon be returning to England. If you do, I would very much like to see you. Providing you are well enough and feel you would also like to see me, would you please contact me? I am still at the old address in Archery Close.

With fondest regards,
MM

~

As I had been able to get out of bed for some while and walk through the wards, a week or two after the airlift began and growing tired of wearing a dressing gown, I decided to get dressed. The suitcase Passmore had brought with him was still in the cupboard and I hauled it out onto the bed.

As soon as I opened it I discovered why the thing had looked so familiar.

Inside, neatly folded, I found Arthur Peston's clothes.

Passmore had obviously found them at the flat, taken them to be mine and packed them into the suitcase Peston had left at the foot of his wardrobe.

I looked at them, reliving the irritation I had felt at Passmore's visit. Then I pulled a shirt and a pair of trousers out of the suitcase and tried them on. Until then I had never given Arthur Peston, the man, much thought beyond the manner of his death and what he had been doing in Berlin. Now I discovered he must have been a fairly small man. Turning to the mirror, my reflection reminded me of a character in a music hall act with my arms and legs protruding several inches beyond my shirt and trouser cuffs.

I pulled the clothes off again and pushed them back into the suitcase. When Heike came in I told her to give them to some charity.

Without clothes or money I thought myself doomed to be trapped in the hospital like a modern Tantalus, with everything I desired just out of my reach. I wasn't sure what to do next.

Until I thought of Tuchmann.

That nonpareil, who appeared able to solve all problems, really did owe me one this time.

I sent him a note through one of the nurses and by the following morning received a bundle of clothing in return. Not an outfit as new as the one Mitzi had sported but at least the shirts and underwear were new. Courtesy of the PX, I assumed. The suit, being of good quality and well cut, was second-hand and probably one of Tuchmann's cast-offs. It made me wonder if a metaphor wasn't hidden somewhere within its folds and he was making a point.

Something along the lines of exchange is no robbery ... or one cast-off for another.

The fault with that reasoning, of course, was that I hadn't been the one to cast Mitzi off.

~

A couple of weeks later and conscious of my mounting bill, I explained in an interview with the hospital administrator that I needed to visit my bank in order to transfer funds to meet their bill. Then I persuaded the doctors to discharge me altogether.

Since I had been admitted under the auspices of Colonel Tuchmann, they seemed happy to trust me to leave unescorted in the expectation I would return to settle my account. I did briefly consider doing a moonlight flit and letting Tuchmann pick up the bill. But they had saved my life and, after all, having persuaded myself at the start of the airlift that the Allies were occupying the moral high ground in Berlin, I supposed the least I could do was take up that small portion of the territory that it was my ethical duty to share.

And without both Mitzi's and Tuchmann's swift response I would have bled to death on the floor of Frau Ernst's apartment.

So a day or two later I thanked all and sundry for my care, kissed Heike goodbye and, dressed in Tuchmann's suit but my own hat and shoes, I rode the S-Bahn into the city.

It was summer again and warm and once back on the streets, no matter how ruinous, I felt the way any man newly freed from incarceration and master of his own fate once more would.

Looking around, although I found much appeared still the same, there had been changes. At the Tiergarten I found the Zoo Tower had gone.

I was told the British had finally demolished it at the third attempt, leaving a pile of rubble to mark the spot like X on a map. Beyond it, the remnants of the small L-Tower still canted over on its side like a squat drunken soldier abandoned by his feckless comrade.

Inordinately pleased for some reason to find that the scrub of bramble and buddleia still continued to reclaim the old park, I sat amid the remains of the zoo for a while before taking the U-Bahn north towards the mill on Stromstraße.

The Russians had taken everything from me at the

polizeipräsidium on Keibelstraße. My passport, papers, keys, wallet and money ... all had been inventoried and none of it returned. The night we had driven to Halensee I had been so pleased to be finally out of the cell that it didn't occur to me to ask for my belongings back.

Globa, of course, knew I wasn't going to need any of it.

Passmore had had the locks changed at both the mill and Peston's apartment and given me a new set of keys in case I needed to pick up any belongings I had left behind. Or if I needed a bed for a night or two before I took the flight home. Once at the mill I slipped Passmore's key into the lock and pushed the door open.

The place smelled musty with that underlying odour of flour that I remembered from the first time I had been there. And it all looked much the same as it always had. The packing crates were still stacked against the wall and various electrical components remained scattered over the tables. Some scraps of our paperwork littered the floor, as if someone had looked through all those Schuyler invoices and bills of lading so assiduously kept to maintain the fiction it was an import company. And I saw my desk was in a muddle. But that was a muddle of my own making and hadn't needed the intervention of a third hand to leave it in disorder.

All in all, little had changed. If Passmore had wound up Schuyler Imports he had done little more than shut and lock the door on the enterprise. Electrical components still stood boxed where Kurt had left them and a confused tangle of wiring waited on a table as if he had just stepped outside and would be back any moment.

It may all have looked the same but that wasn't how it felt. Now the place exuded an aura of emptiness, abandoned as was the claim that Schuyler had once been a bona fide business.

I walked through the rooms feeling unexpectedly affected by Kurt's absence. After all that had happened to him during the last decade, it seemed to me grossly unfair that having survived the invasion of the Netherlands, forced labour and the air raids, Kurt had died a pawn in a game over which he had no control.

I climbed the two flights up the worm-eaten mill steps to his room. Curiously, the door was locked. None of Passmore's keys seem to fit so I kicked it in.

There was no indication of anyone having been through his belongings, which suggested to me that the investigation into his death had been as rigorous as the one into Peston's. Once they had pulled his body from the Spree and discovered how he died, I suppose the police had been instructed not to investigate.

Which side had done the instructing was still a matter of conjecture. Whether Allied or Russian, though, they had closed the case and had left the door to his room in the same fashion.

Passmore had surmised that Bill had come to the mill to find out from Kurt how much I had known beyond what I had put in my note to him. I hadn't told Passmore I had mentioned Fischer's name to Kurt but even so, Bill would have gone to Peston's flat before he went anywhere else. Once he had seen the blood I'd smeared on the table he might well have come back to the mill and Kurt. It was a small difference although it might be a pertinent one.

Kurt's bed was still unmade. Then he had never been the most fastidious of housekeepers. Piled in one corner, and the most obvious indication that no one had been there, was a small stack of cigarette cartons. There were various brands: Lucky Strikes, Camels, Chesterfield, and one or two others. That there weren't more suggested Kurt had probably been planning to visit Joe Rafferty for a fresh consignment. In the event, he had got himself shot before he had the chance.

I looked around at the few personal belongings in the room. On a shelf by the bed stood a photograph of a couple in their thirties who I took to be his mother and father. Beside it were two or three German novels. Some clothes hung in the cupboard and, tucked away in a drawer beneath, I found his socks, underwear and, oddly, a tyre lever.

Next to that lay a gun.

It had been wrapped in oilcloth, was loaded and clean. As far as I could tell it showed no sign of having been fired recently and certainly wouldn't have been the gun that killed Kurt.

On the floor next to the bed I saw the old holdall he had used to carry his contraband cigarettes, so I wrapped the gun back in its cloth and put it in the bag. I piled half a dozen cartons of cigarettes on top. There were a few packs of German and Russian smokes among them but I left those where they lay.

Spotting a carton of filter Viceroys—the healthy option—I lit one and tossed the rest into the holdall.

Beneath the bed was a suitcase that looked battered enough to have followed Kurt through his years of forced labour. That was locked, too. I prised it open although there was little inside except a decent suit of clothes I assumed he kept for best and some papers in his appalling handwriting that looked to be an accounting of the cigarettes and other items he sold.

I stood in the doorway of the room. There didn't appear anything else to see. Not in plain sight, anyway.

No obvious hiding places offered themselves to me although anything hidden, of course, wasn't going to be left anywhere obvious. A threadbare rug covered the floorboards and I kicked it aside and examined them. They were nailed down and didn't appear to have been disturbed for years. I ran my hands over the walls and then around the frame of the bed. I shifted the chest of drawers and even examined the ceiling.

Finally I heaved the bed itself aside. It squeaked and groaned like a pig loath to move. It wasn't any sound I recognized. Kurt could only have moved it when I wasn't there.

At first glance the floorboards seemed no different from the rest but a closer examination showed that two of the boards had been sawn since the floor was laid and a groove chiselled in one of them.

I went back to the drawer where I'd found the gun and took out the tyre lever. Pushing it between the cut boards, the end of the lever fit the chiselled groove like a finger in a glove. I prised the lever against the boards and they came up without resistance.

I had always known Kurt must keep his money somewhere. He wasn't a man to trust a bank, particularly a German bank given that as a child he would have lived through the years of hyper-inflation. He might have kept a safety deposit box, of course, although I doubted he would have been comfortable with inquisitive eyes watching his comings and goings. Curious, perhaps, as to what it was he was squirreling away.

He might have hidden it anywhere in the city, of course, but even years after the bombing ceased scavengers still scoured every ruined building in the hope of finding something of value others had missed and Kurt wouldn't have risked that.

It all added up to the probability that he would not have felt comfortable unless his money was close at hand. And that meant with him at the mill. And where was closer than beneath the bed in which he slept?

A calico bag lay beneath the boards in the gap between the joists. Inside I found bundles of US Dollars and German Reichmarks.

There was no Sterling. Perhaps Kurt had had no faith in the British post-war economy.

Housekeeping apart, he had been a methodical man. It was a virtue I had noticed in the way he sorted and arranged, prior to resale, all the electrical components that arrived for Schuyler Imports. That same predilection for order was evident in the way he had packaged his banknotes: by currency and denomination and each wrapped in paper on which he had scribbled the amount.

It made it so much easier to count.

By my reckoning, Kurt's stash amounted to over twenty thousand dollars. I sat on his bed, lit another of his cigarettes and stared at it.

It was an impressive sum and I couldn't help wondering how long he would have been prepared to go on adding to it before he quit. I supposed the chances were I would have turned up at the mill one day and found him gone, Kurt having concluded that the amount he had was greater than the risk he was prepared to take on getting caught.

Quit while you're ahead is the adage. Or maybe I hadn't known him well enough and the temptation to keep adding to his pile would have outweighed both the risk of his getting caught and the amount he already had.

Whichever way Kurt had looked at it, in the end it seemed he had stayed a little too long.

He had had no family I was aware of. Both his mother and his father were dead and there had been no siblings. There might be a surviving uncle or aunt somewhere, or cousins in Germany or Holland. But if there were, Kurt had never spoken to me about them. And I wouldn't have known where to begin looking even if he had. Besides, would their claim on the money be any better than anyone else's?

I could have handed the cash into the Berlin authorities although, if I did, I suspected I wouldn't have reached the exit of whichever building I'd left it in before it was being divvied up between those in the know.

Then there were my ex-employers. They had some sort of claim to at least a portion of the loot since Kurt had made money from the electrical bits and pieces they had supplied. But given what Passmore had told me, as far as money went, I regarded my former masters as standing on as morally thin ice as everyone else.

Rather than hand it to them, I would just as soon have kept it until the weather turned cold, made a bonfire of the notes and warmed my hands over it.

There was always charity, of course, although from where I was standing—or sitting on Kurt's bed to be more exact—I felt I was as deserving a case as any other.

In fact, the longer I thought about it, the more I managed to convince myself that Kurt would have wanted me to keep it.

Out at the Reich Sporting Field the roar of the planes overhead filled the air. They were coming in and out of Gatow as regularly as they had at Templehof. Tegel in the French sector was apparently the same. Only at Johannisthal in the Soviet sector would things be relatively quiet. The Russians didn't believe the Allies could sustain an airlift for long and eventually they would have to seek terms. But it wasn't just the Occupying Forces who were involved. The Australians and New Zealanders and the South Africans were lending their weight, too.

And, crucially, the Americans had a new president.

Harry Truman was a pugnacious little fellow who, so it was said, wouldn't swallow Stalin's blandishments as readily as

Roosevelt apparently had.

I stood watching the planes come and go for a while then went to find Dai Edwards.

As perky as a bantam, the corporal was bustling around his office as though the relief of Berlin rested on his shoulders alone.

'Hello Harry,' he chirped. 'Long time no see. I thought you must have gone home.'

'I've been unavoidably detained, Dai. I was in hospital for a spell after that.'

'I heard a rumour,' he said. 'You're not looking great, either.'

'That's what Mitzi told me. Only she wasn't as polite as you.'

'How is she?'

'Moved on to fresher pastures.'

'Sorry to hear that, Harry,' he said sympathetically. 'She was a tidy piece.'

He leaned towards me, looking over his shoulder like a London spiv.

'So, what can I do for you?'

I heaved Kurt's holdall onto his desk and pulled out a carton of Luckies.

'You can smoke these,' I said, 'and maybe put me in the way of someone who can change currency. Without asking questions, that is.'

'What are you after, U.S.?'

'Reichmarks into Sterling.'

I was planning on handling the dollars myself.

'As a matter of fact,' he said, 'I do know a bloke over in the paymaster's office. He can do that for you although he always wants one and a half percent for dollars. Plus the rate, of course. I don't know what he charges for Sterling. Much the same probably. How much you got?'

He whistled when I told him.

'That could take two or three days, Harry. You in hurry?'

'Not particularly. Give him what he wants, Dai, and one percent is yours in case you need to grease any other palms. That okay?'

'More than generous, Harry. You got a number I can call, or

do you want to come back?'

I wasn't sure yet if I would be staying in Peston's flat or at the mill. Despite what I had said to Passmore at the hospital about their killing me reinforcing my story, that wasn't to factor in human vindictiveness. And changing the locks at Peston's apartment and the mill wouldn't be enough to stop Globa sending someone round to finish the job of killing me if he had a mind to. I didn't think it likely but I wasn't going to take any chances.

'I'll come back,' I told Dai.

There was no one around so I hauled the wads of Reichmarks out of the bag and placed them on his desk so he could count them for himself. Taking off the paper wrapping Kurt had used to keep track of the amounts, my eye was caught by some writing in English on the reverse side of one.

'You all right, Harry?' Dai asked. 'You've gone white.'

I stuffed the paper into my pocket.

'Yeah,' I said. 'I'm fine.'

Dai finished counting the notes and dropped the bundles into his desk drawer.

'I'm going to need a seat on a flight home, too, Dai, if you can arrange it. In a week or two if you can. Ronald Passmore, the new passport officer has authorized it.'

Dai cocked his head as another plane droned overhead.

'No shortage of empty planes going west at the minute, Harry.' He leaned towards me again and lowered his voice. 'There's been another rumour. About the old one.'

'Old what?'

'Passport Officer. You know, Bill Harrington. You heard anything?'

'Me? No, I've been out of circulation. Sorry.'

His eyebrows went up, suggesting he thought otherwise but he let it lay. And I should have asked what the rumour was of course. Not showing curiosity was another slip, but then I was out of practice.

'Well,' he said, grinning, 'I suppose it'll all come out in the wash.'

It was true that I didn't know much. But I did doubt that Bill would ever come out in the wash.

371

~

I let myself into Arthur Peston's apartment with the key Passmore had given me. That same musty smell pervaded the rooms, suggesting no one had spent any time there recently or that Passmore had wasted any time picking up the wrong clothes for me. There were still a few shirts and a couple of suits hanging in the wardrobe, empty shrouds no one was going to fill any time soon.

Out of habit I went through the rest of the place but nothing had changed. Even the teapot and two cups were still on the kitchen table where Gornov's goons had left them, the pot's contents now nothing more than a small heap of dried tealeaves and a brown stain on the china.

I put the pot and the cups in the kitchen sink to wash, lit another cigarette and sat at the table.

I took out the piece of paper Kurt had used to tally his ill-gotten gains.

Bill. Zoo Tower 9th 7pm.— Arthur

June 9th had been the day Peston's body had been found at the foot of the Zoo Tower.

The note was handwritten. I couldn't remember seeing any examples of Peston's handwriting although I didn't doubt it was his. It certainly wasn't Kurt's. With those missing fingers he couldn't produce anything more than a scrawl.

As I've already said, I'd had a long time to think while rotting in Gornov's cell beneath Keibelstraße 35.

It was true that Ronald Passmore telling me Bill had been a Russian agent had given me pause. But not for long. Now Arthur Peston's note arranging a meeting at the Zoo Tower—a note it looked as if Bill had never received—had cleared up the question altogether.

In the message I'd left for Bill at the Military Mission, I hadn't said anything about seeing Prochnow in Potsdam. That meant, unless Prochnow had seen me which I doubted, only two people knew about it. The first was Mitzi who had pointed Prochnow out across the crowded terrace. If she hadn't done so, there was a good chance I wouldn't have seen him at all.

The second person was Kurt. I had told him at the mill before going on to Peston's flat to meet Bill.

When I had suggested to Passmore that Gornov might have sent another pair of goons to the apartment to pick up Bill after they took me, he had scoffed at the idea. He was probably right. But only because it happened the other way around.

What I now thought had happened was that the goons who had picked me up had first waited outside for Bill to arrive, snatched him off the street and driven him to some pre-arranged rendezvous in the Russian sector. Then they had come back for me. The reason they had been in no hurry was with Bill already in their hands, my line of communication had been broken. They knew I'd still be waiting at the flat and I was, thinking it odd that Bill was taking so long to answer an urgent summons.

It hadn't worried Gornov's men when I said I was waiting for a British diplomat. They already knew.

I went through any other possible permutations, hoping that the sum of my calculation would add up to a different figure. But it never did. The figure I always ended up with was Kurt.

I imagined he must have telephoned his handler that morning the moment I left the mill. After all, if as Bill suspected the line was tapped, Kurt wouldn't even have needed to dial a number.

Perhaps I'd always suspected the truth and finding the note from Peston meant for Bill, which Kurt had used to bundle up his Reichmarks was just final confirmation.

Kurt had told me he didn't know why Peston had been at the Zoo Tower but that had been a lie. He told me he didn't know how to contact Bill if I needed him, although Peston's note suggested otherwise. And he'd also said he didn't know who Fischer was. I had let the name slip but that hadn't worried me as I had taken Kurt at his word when he said Arthur Peston hadn't taken him into his confidence.

It now seemed obvious that, like me, Peston had come to the conclusion that Fischer wasn't genuine; that his defection was a Russian operation. He must have told Kurt and Kurt was to have passed on the note to arrange the meeting with Bill.

If Bill was getting close to the spy the Soviets had infiltrated into SIS in London, Fischer's names were designed to throw him off the scent. Perhaps they would have done if Peston hadn't smelt a rat. Once they realized, probably through Kurt, that Peston was suspicious, they had no choice but to eliminate him before he could tell Bill. That done, their man in London could then arrange to have Peston replaced with a someone else, someone new to the game who could be manipulated.

Enter Harry Tennant, novice espionage agent.

Passmore had been right in saying I was a dupe. My history in Intelligence must have suggested I was just the kind of incompetent they required. Someone to be led by the nose and, in turn, lead Fischer and his disinformation over to our side.

But they had underestimated my capacity for suspicion. My habit of never taking anything at face value.

Admittedly more often wrong than right, I had made a career out of sticking my nose into places it didn't belong. And, true to form, it hadn't been long before I smelt the same rat Peston had. Like him, they thought I was about to warn Bill that Fischer's defection was a put-up job, so like a chess piece they took me off the board just as they had done with Peston.

I may have been nothing more than a small cog in the larger machine but I think Bill was different.

Had he already alerted London to his doubts about Fischer? It would have been a risky strategy given what had happened to Volkov, unless he knew the Soviet agent in London was in no position to find out.

I couldn't be sure but I suspected the Russians had been forced to rethink their operation. Instead of Fischer defecting as arranged from his meeting with the SPD, he gone to ground until a new plan was decided.

It was only supposition on my part but it could well have been then they had decided to add Bill Harington's name to Fischer's list of Soviet agents.

As it turned out it had worked well. If Bill had become suspicious of their man in London, pointing the finger at Bill himself was the icing on their poisonous cake. After Bill disappears, Fischer comes over with his list including Bill's name and making it look like he has defected.

It was still possible, as Passmore had surmised, that Bill *had* shot Kurt. If he had discovered Kurt had betrayed not only me, but Peston and himself, he might have decided it was time to take the Dutchman out. Just when he had done it was another matter.

It seemed to me more likely that the Russians had done it themselves.

Having Arthur Peston employ Kurt in the first place to bring us likely informants must have been more than they could have hoped for. It meant they could turn a blind eye to his black market dealings and keep both him and us jumping to their tune like marionettes on a string.

Whether, though, they decided to kill Kurt to implicate Bill further I could only guess. It might have been that they were finished with him anyway and nervous what he might tell us if our side interrogated him.

As Passmore had said to me at the hospital, that was a lot of supposition. I had no proof and I doubted I would get any.

Not until Bill surfaced in Russia as Passmore predicted.

Although I didn't think he'd surface the way Passmore meant. And I didn't think he'd surface at all until the ice on the Moscow River melted.

They kept me alive, I supposed, just long enough to satisfy themselves Bill hadn't passed any suspicions back about their man in SIS; until London had swallowed Albrecht Fischer whole. Then, unlike Prochnow, I really would have been *Warenübershuss zu den Anforderungen:* goods surplus to requirements.

It had been my good fortunate while being interrogated by Gornov to have mentioned Walter Frick's name. Maybe they had made transcripts of what I said. One way or another Globa had picked up on the name and decided I was of more use to them alive than dead.

For the time being, at least.

That he meant to kill me in the end anyway became obvious in Frau Ernst's apartment. But he shouldn't have used "Killer"

Kittel to finish the job. The man had become too soft-hearted. He wasn't prepared to do anything of which his dead wife Freida would not have approved.

In a way I owed my life to Shoshannah Lehmann. If she had stolen all my money that night by the lake instead of the few Reichmarks she did take, I might never have become interested in her. That she only took part of what I was carrying made her an object of curiosity.

Perhaps I am wrong in believing fate is random, that nothing is ordained. I usually take some persuading of the fact, but at times it is hard to accept that I am not always right.

If one cares to believe that at some point we are all eventually assessed in some grand scheme akin to those Egyptian scales I had been reflecting upon while in Gornov's cell, it might be argued that my life was weighed against the betrayal of those whom Shoshannah Lehmann denounced to the Gestapo while she was Anna Koch.

If that is so then I cannot help but think that their souls helped tip the scales in my favour.

Das Ende

42

At the end of the week I went out to the Reich Sporting Field. Dai Edwards looked slightly apologetic as he passed the exchanged currency back across his desk to me.

'I'm afraid he couldn't give you much of a rate, Harry. Better before the war. You want to count it?'

'If you listen to the people here,' I said, 'everything was better before the war. And no, no need to count it, Dai. Thanks.'

'I can get you on a flight tomorrow if that's not too soon.'

I thought about it, but I didn't think for long.

'Why not?' I said.

'Be here for eight tomorrow morning and I'll have the paperwork ready.'

I picked up the cash, added it to what I was already carrying in Kurt's old bag and took the S-Bahn back into the city.

Having Kurt's dollars, I had already settled my bill at the hospital at Templehof, phoning ahead to let them know to expect me.

On arrival I had been shown an office where a sergeant with a mid-western accent and who was probably more comfortable handling a pen than a rifle sat me down and pulled my file from the cabinet. He checked through the itemised bill and twisted it around on the desktop so I could see the bottom line.

The total was big but perhaps not as big as I had expected. And given the bottom line added up to my life I wasn't about to argue.

It had been calculated in dollars but the equivalent in Reichmarks had been included as well.

'I'll pay in dollars,' I said. 'Cash okay?'

He raised an eyebrow. 'Like it says on the dollar,' he replied laconically, 'In God we trust. Everybody else pays cash.'

So we counted out the bills and, taking his wishes for good

health, I left.

~

I wondered if I would not have been better off leaving Berlin as soon as the hospital bill was settled rather than mooch around Peston's flat as I had. I even went back to the Zoo Club and bought the morose Marthe a drink. She managed against type to be civil, at least as long as it took her to drink it, but even so she still blamed me for Mitzi's defection.

I suppose it would have been better from Marthe's point of view if it had been Mitzi who had betrayed me to the Russians and not Kurt. Then if Mitzi had gone over to them, Marthe could have followed her.

But the glum half-hour I spent with Marthe wasn't the main reason for my regret at not leaving Berlin as early I as I might have. The real consequence of my delay was that it gave time for my conscience to kick in.

So, on the way back from picking up Kurt's money at the Sporting Field, I called in at the office on Bayreuther Straße where I'd spoken to the American girl who worked for Ben Tuchmann. I had taken the trouble of phoning ahead but Tuchmann wasn't there. It didn't matter. In fact it was preferable.

She was still working, as neat and vivacious in her civilian clothes as the last time I'd seen her. I put Kurt's holdall on her desk and asked to make sure Tuchmann got it.

'He'll know what to do with it,' I told her. 'I've left a note inside.'

'Is he expecting it?' she asked.

'No. It'll be a surprise.'

'The colonel will be in this afternoon,' she said. 'I'll make sure he gets it.'

I thanked her and watched as she put the holdall in his office. My note was short:

> *Dear Ben,*
> *I'm sure you can find some good cause that will be able to use this. It's clean—relatively speaking—in that no one*

*is now the worse for it being with you. Hopefully some
people will be the better for it.*
    Give my love to Mitzi and take care of yourself.
    Your friend,
    Harry.

As I had discovered, the worst thing about having time on my hands was that I spent it deciding there really were more deserving cases in Berlin than myself. In fact I imagined if there had been a list I would have figured a pretty long way down it, somewhere near the bottom. So, what was left over after paying my hospital bill—something I think I did deserve—I decided to leave the rest with Tuchmann. It was still a sizable sum, although a shame I had taken the trouble to change a lot of it into sterling, and consisted not just of whatever Kurt had managed to earn through selling cigarettes and other black market goods but also the proceeds of the electrical components SIS had sent him. I imagined, too, that some of it had come to him from the Russians for services rendered.

That little irony gave me a great deal of satisfaction. The fact that money from both our and their Intelligence organizations went, courtesy of Ben Tuchmann, to those survivors who had managed to live through the past horrors was, by itself, almost worth giving it all away.

And they could make better use of it than I could.

I left the girl and the office, having no qualms about trusting Ben with the cash in the same way I had no qualms about trusting him with my life.

It was just women I could never trust the man with.

~

At my bank I closed my account and transferred the balance to London. Even on sick pay, I discovered that with no withdrawals for several months there would be enough to keep me afloat for a few weeks once back home.

The following morning, with Magdalena's letter in my pocket, I climbed aboard the Dakota at Gatow. We rattled down the runway and took off and the plane turned in a circle over the ruined city in much the same way as had the plane I arrived on that day in June 1947.

I gazed out of the window as the city's gutted buildings passed slowly beneath our wings. We turned west and, looking back, I kept them in view as long as I could. When I couldn't see them any longer I looked forward again, having said goodbye to Berlin.

Made in the USA
Middletown, DE
02 June 2023